BOOKS BY FRANK SLAUGHTER

THE SINS OF HEROD

DOCTORS' WIVES

GOD'S WARRIOR

SURGEON, U.S.A.

CONSTANTINE

THE PURPLE QUEST

A SAVAGE PLACE

UPON THIS ROCK

DEVIL'S HARVEST

TOMORROW'S MIRACLE

DAVID: WARRIOR AND KING

THE CURSE OF JEZEBEL

EPIDEMIC!

PILGRIMS IN PARADISE

THE LAND AND THE PROMISE

LORENA

THE CROWN AND THE CROSS

THE THORN OF ARIMATHEA

DAYBREAK

THE MAPMAKER

SWORD AND SCALPEL

THE WARRIOR

THE SCARLET CORD

FLIGHT FROM NATCHEZ

THE HEALER

APALACHEE GOLD

THE SONG OF RUTH

STORM HAVEN

THE GALILEANS

EAST SIDE GENERAL

FORT EVERGLADES

THE ROAD TO BITHYNIA

THE STUBBORN HEART

IMMORTAL MAGYAR

DIVINE MISTRESS

SANGAREE

MEDICINE FOR MODERNS

THE GOLDEN ISLE

THE NEW SCIENCE OF SURGERY

IN A DARK GARDEN

A TOUCH OF GLORY

BATTLE SURGEON

AIR SURGEON

SPENCER BRADE, M.D.

THAT NONE SHOULD DIE

Under pen name C. V. TERRY

BUCCANEER SURGEON

THE DEADLY LADY OF MADAGASCAR

DARIEN VENTURE

THE GOLDEN ONES

THE SINS OF HEROD

THE
SINS OF HEROD

*A Novel of Rome and
the Early Church*

FRANK G. SLAUGHTER

Garden City, New York
DOUBLEDAY & COMPANY, INC.
1968

Library of Congress Catalog Card Number 68–14208
Copyright © 1968 by Frank G. Slaughter
All Rights Reserved
Printed in the United States of America
First Edition

This book is affectionately dedicated
to my daughter-in-law,
TAYLOR BARNETT SLAUGHTER

CONTENTS

CONTENTS

AUTHOR'S NOTE

Except for a few passages from the Authorized or King James Version of the Bible, easily recognizable as such, all quoted biblical passages in the text are taken from the Jerusalem Bible, published by Doubleday & Company, Inc., in the United States and by Darton, Longman & Todd, Ltd., in England. I am indebted to these, the copyright holders, for their kind permission to quote from the translation without crediting individual passages, which would, of course, be impossible in a work of fiction.

In re-creating an authentic picture of an ancient period and its people through the medium of the novel, I have, as always, relied on hundreds of references, far too numerous to be acknowledged individually. However, I should like to note my indebtedness particularly to: *The Later Herods* and *The Life and Times of Herod the Great* by Stewart Perowne, Abingdon Press; *The World of Josephus* by G. A. Williamson, Little, Brown & Company; *It Began on the Cross* by Guy Schofield, Hawthorn Books, Inc.; *Vanished Cities* by Hermann and Georg Schreiber, Alfred A. Knopf, Inc.; and *The Life and Works of Flavius Josephus*, translated by William Whiston, The John C. Winston Company.

In my stories of the ancient world, I have been amazed again and again by the remarkable frequency with which fact is indeed stranger than fiction, but never more than in the history of Agrippa I, last of the kings of Israel. The closing events of my novel, dramatic though they are, were first described in detail by Josephus, the great Jewish historian, almost nineteen hundred years ago; they may be read in the Whiston translation referred to above, as may the remarkable edict of religious freedom given to Philo Judaeus by the Emperor Claudius. A slightly different version of Agrippa's death from that of Josephus is given by St. Luke in the Acts of the Apostles.

FRANK G. SLAUGHTER, M.D.

Jacksonville, Florida
September 6, 1967

"Herod was furious when he realised that he had been outwitted by the wise men, and in Bethlehem and its surrounding district he had all the male children killed who were two years old or under, reckoning by the date he had been careful to ask the wise men. It was then that words spoken through the prophet Jeremiah were fulfilled:

> 'A voice was heard in Ramah,
> sobbing and loudly lamenting:
> It was Rachel weeping for her children,
> refusing to be comforted
> because they were no more.' "

MATTHEW 2:16–18

"For I, Yahweh your God, am a jealous God and I punish the father's fault in the sons, the grandsons, and the great-grandsons of those who hate me."

EXODUS 20:5

Book One

TIBERIAS

Between Magdala and the magnificent new capital Herod Antipas was building on the heights overlooking the Sea of Galilee—renamed the Lake of Tiberias in honor of Rome's Emperor—the range of hills forming the western side of the deep cup in which the harp-shaped body of water lay rose sharply with almost no shore for a distance of about three miles. Antipas had chosen this area of jagged basalt cliffs for two reasons: its commanding position as the location of a palace-fortress, and its inaccessibility to an invading army.

Two roads converged back of Magdala, where the shore line began to descend to the lovely Plain of Gennesaret, an area so fertile that the melons grown there were not allowed to be sold in Jerusalem during the religious festivals, lest the enjoyment of them keep worshipers from a proper devotion to the Most High God. One road led by way of the old provincial capital of Sepphoris, where Upper and Lower Galilee met, to the seacoast at Ptolemais, the old Mediterranean port of Akka just north of Mount Carmel. The other followed the west side of the lake southward from Capernaum, the brawling fishing center that was also a way point on the ancient caravan route called the Way of the Sea, oldest road in the world. Behind Tiberias the road wound near the crest of the range of hills through a forbidding area of jagged boulders, crags and caves, the latter infested with brigands who preyed upon caravans and attacked small parties of Roman troops traveling from one military post to another.

Galilee was the most important part of the tetrarchy allotted to Antipas under the will of his father, Herod the Great; the rest consisted of Peraea on the east bank of the Jordan south of the lovely blue lake. Roman troops were garrisoned in several sensitive spots in the tetrarchy, however, lest the always volatile Galileans rebel again, as they had done shortly after the death of the elder Herod.

The western third of what had been Herod the Great's kingdom, lying for the most part south of Antipas' domain, included both Judaea—the Jewish heartland where the Holy City of Jerusalem was located—and Samaria, a hated name to all Jews. Since shortly after the death of Herod the Great, the province had been ruled from the seaport city of Caesarea by Roman governors, or procurators, the latest being Pontius Pilate. But though heavily garrisoned with Roman troops, Judaea was even less stable than Galilee. Like a seething volcano, it was always ready to explode into rebellion, and the only really peaceful part of the old kingdom was a patchwork of districts dominated by the towering height of Mount Hermon lying generally northeast of the lake. Known usually simply as Ituraea, but including also Auranitis, Trachonitis and Batanaea— with some others—it was governed by Philip, the most capable and the quietest of Herod's sons and grandsons.

More than once the hills and valleys of beautiful Galilee had been drenched with blood, beginning nearly two thousand years earlier when Abraham, patriarch of the Jews, had led his followers in a swift strike northward as far as Damascus to defeat a group of Syrian kings who had raided deep into ancient Canaan. The most recent conflict had occurred twenty-odd years earlier, when the youngest surviving son of Herod the Great, Archelaus, had been unable to control turbulent Judaea, assigned to him under his father's will.

A rebellion led by a self-styled Messiah named Judas the Gaulonite had touched flame then to the ever smoldering tinderbox of revolt in Judaea, resulting in what had been called the War of Judas. The fighting had quickly spread to Galilee, when Judas was forced to retreat, and there the conflict had ended with the Romans crucifying the false Messiah and two thousand Jews before Sepphoris. But the hatreds which had caused it still burned throughout the land.

All was calm one spring afternoon during the latter years of rule by the Emperor Tiberius, however. The tall youth walking along the road from Tiberias to Magdala felt no need to hurry, when he came to the crest of the ridge not far from the junction of the main road from Sepphoris to the new capital. For although this particular area was known to be the lair of bandits, they rarely troubled the Galileans of the lake cities, and the road was deserted. Pausing beside a very large boulder near the road, he climbed to its top, but even from the same perch it was hard to believe that just a week ago he had watched this very thoroughfare filled with happy Galileans on the way to Jerusalem for the Passover, most holy of the religious festivals.

More than just idle curiosity had made Prochorus, son of Chuza, take an early leave that afternoon from his studies in the scriptorium and university established by Herod Antipas; his mother, Joanna, was accompanying a group who were following Jesus of Nazareth to Jerusalem. The preaching and startling miracles of the inspired young teacher had convinced thousands—when he had first come down to the populous lake region from the hills to the west—that he was the Messiah who would free them from bondage to Rome. And although after Jesus had refused to name himself king in Galilee much of his following had dwindled away in the nearly four years since his first appearance on the religious and political scene, many still believed him to be the Expected One promised by the prophets as the answer to all of Israel's miseries.

Prochorus had hoped that afternoon for a glimpse of the Nazarene himself and his hope had been realized, though not fulfilled. Seen from atop the boulder, the teacher had seemed almost frail compared with Simon Peter, the brawny fisherman who walked close beside him as a protection from the crowd that sought to touch him because of the healing power he was reputed to possess—even in the folds of his robe.

On the other side of the Nazarene were John ben Zebedee and his brother James, old friends of Prochorus' family from the days when they, too, had lived in Capernaum. And as he wiped sweat from his forehead now with the sleeve of his robe, Prochorus recalled another day long ago, when he had skipped classes in the synagogue school to prowl the waterfront and watch the fishermen preparing their nets and boats for the night's work. . . .

John had been mending a sail, the needle in his hand threaded with the tough goat's-hair cord called *cilicium* flashing in and out

of the fabric so swiftly that it had almost made the boy dizzy to
watch.

"Why aren't you in school?" John asked when he saw Prochorus
standing on the pier.

"I—I want to be a fisherman—like you."

"And not have to go to school?"

"Y-yes. Besides, I already know everything Rabbi Eloichim can
teach me."

"Not everything he can teach you. But all he takes the trouble
to teach you." John's smile had enveloped the boy like a warm
cloak in winter.

"It's the same thing."

"Perhaps you're right. But only one who is as much Greek as
Jew would know that."

"Do you know me?" Prochorus asked in surprise.

"Your father is my friend. He sometimes buys fish from us for
the Tetrarch's household." John's face was sober. "And since he is
my friend I must urge you not to give up your schooling. We
need Jews who can read and write, not just our own tongue but
Greek and Latin as well. Do you write Latin?"

"No. But I can write Greek. Father taught me."

"Chuza is a wise man, else Antipas would never have made
him steward over his plantations. You might even go higher, young
Prochorus, if you study hard and earn the respect of the Romans."

Somewhat conscience-stricken now at having skipped school,
Prochorus was turning dejectedly away, but John called him back.
"But since you've already missed part of a day's schooling, let's
not waste the rest of it," he said with a grin. "Do you know how
to tie a fisherman's knot?"

"No—no. Will you teach me?"

John picked up a length of cord as Prochorus took a seat beside
him on the pier. "No matter what you decide to do, it will do
you no harm to know how to tie a good knot."

For the next hour, the boy had fumbled with it, trying to tie
the intricate knot with fingers that seemed to be all thumbs. Only
much later did he realize that his new friend had deliberately
set him a task he was not likely to master without many hours

of practice in order to teach him to apply himself fully to whatever he tried to do. Once, as he worked, John's hands had become still and the look in the dark eyes that could be so warm with friendship and understanding for a clumsy boy had been far away for a moment and a little sad. "I wanted to be a rabbi," he confessed. "But Father has spent his life developing the fishery and my older brother James is too impetuous to handle people well."

"The people call both you and James Boanerges—Sons of Thunder."

"That's mainly because of James. I would still prefer scrolls and the exercise of the mind to pulling nets." John reached over to punch the boy affectionately on the shoulder. "But you are too intelligent to be merely a fisherman, Prochorus ben Chuza. Your Greek heritage from your father"—Chuza was from the Decapolis, the confederation of ten cities east of the lake and the Jordan whose inhabitants were largely Greek—"is fused with the Jewish heritage from your mother, so I suspect you have the intelligence and the ability to acquire most of what is best in both worlds."

"But—"

"Say no more, if you would be the friend of John ben Zebedee." Then the fisherman's eyelids crinkled again in a smile. "Will you make a bargain with me?"

"What is it?"

"I shall fish while you study and after school you can tell me what you have learned. In return, every day I shall give you a fish to sell in the market and buy with it whatever you wish."

That summer had been a period of warm companionship and, before it was over, a strong bond of something more than friendship had grown between the man and the boy. John was in every sense a Jew, the heritage of two thousand years of pride in having been chosen by God for His own particular people written in the sharp planes of his cheekbones, the proud thrust of his nose, the slightly olive hue of his skin. In Prochorus, on the other hand, the Jewish heritage from his mother's side had been softened and molded by the Greek strain from his father. What was more, in the boy the fierce pride and burning ambition of the Jew were tempered by the Greek capacity for rational thought and a love of beauty, both seen in the world about him and unseen in the mind.

With the money gained from the sale of the fish John faithfully gave him each day, usually the largest of the night's catch, Prochorus had been able to buy scrolls written in Greek and filled with things that were not even mentioned in the synagogue school. In them he discovered a world of the mind fully as exciting as the feel of the steering oar in one's hand, the tug of the sail, or the silver gleam of fish schooling in great leaping masses at the northern end of the lake, where the Jordan, ice cold from the snow melting on the ever white summit of Mount Hermon, struck the waters of the lake, heated daily in their protected cup by the rays of the sun.

Chuza and his family had moved from Capernaum the next year when Herod Antipas decided to develop his own fisheries at Magdala. John and James ben Zebedee, Prochorus heard, had become part-time disciples of another John, called "the Baptizer," because of his penchant for immersing in water after the Essene custom those who responded to his forthright doctrine of sin and the need for repentance. Later still Prochorus learned that the two had left off fishing entirely to become full-time disciples of the Nazarene teacher called Jesus, whose family was related to them through their mother, Salome.

Of his next contact with John ben Zebedee, Prochorus knew only what his father and mother told him later. Sometime after they moved to Magdala, he had been delirious for many days with one of the raging fevers that so often attacked people in the lake region with the coming of warmer weather. Death had seemed only hours away when John ben Zebedee appeared at Magdala and told Chuza to go to Jesus of Nazareth at Cana where, a short time before, the teacher had startled guests at the wedding feast of a kinsman by turning water into wine. The Nazarene had refused to come back to Capernaum with Chuza, but as he was riding home sadly, certain that he would find Prochorus dead, a servant met him with the news that the boy had been healed miraculously—or so it seemed—at the very moment when he had been talking to Jesus at Cana.

Later, Prochorus had tried to find John and also Jesus, to thank them for his cure. But by then the teacher was being followed by such crowds that he had not been able to come near—until the day just a week ago when he had stood on this very boulder and watched the procession pass on the way to Jerusalem. Seeing him there, John had dropped out of the procession and reached up to help the youth down from the boulder.

"Prochorus!" he cried, embracing him warmly. "Come with us to Jerusalem."

"My classes at the scriptorium are almost finished and the teachers would never give me a certificate of competency as a scribe, if I left now," said Prochorus, then added with a grin, "Besides, don't forget that you started me on this course, one day when I had decided to leave school and become a fisherman like you."

"I remember very well. Have you ever regretted it?"

"Oh no! I hope to go to Alexandria next year and study philosophy—"

"Once I dreamed the same dream," said John. "But that was long before I was chosen to serve the Messiah. When do you expect to leave for Alexandria?"

"My studies will be finished by the end of the summer. Father says I can go then."

"Leave as soon as you can." There had been a curious urgency in John's voice. "Jerusalem is always a bubbling pot during the religious celebrations, no one can be sure just what will happen."

"You're worried about the Nazarene, aren't you?"

John nodded soberly. "The chief priests have tried to arrest him before but we always managed to outwit them by leaving the city. This time he has vowed to stay until the Passover ends."

"If Jesus really is the Son of God as some claim, Yahweh himself will look after him," said Prochorus. "Nothing you can do will be of any avail."

John had given him a startled look, then threw his arm across the young man's shoulders—by now the two were almost the same height—in the old gesture of affection.

"It has been truly said, 'Out of the mouth of babes and sucklings'—No, that is an insult; you are far wiser than I already. In fact you have restored a faith and a strength I almost lost because I was afraid."

"When will I see you again?" Prochorus asked.

"God twined our lives together that day when I taught you to tie a fisherman's knot in Capernaum," John assured him. "You can be sure our paths will cross again."

Prochorus looked down the road again toward Taricheae at the south end of the lake, half expecting to see John still there, so vivid was the memory of his friend's parting words. Instead, his eyes fell upon a stocky man who was leaning on the shaft of his spear a dozen paces away. And when he saw hanging from the other's belt the curved dagger called a *sicarius* that was almost a badge of the brigands in the hills, he recognized danger.

ii

"Those who fall into a trance in these hills often never leave them." The tone was sarcastic and the tongue Aramaic, the universal language of the area. But the accent was rough even for the Galileans, who were said to be distinguishable by their speech no matter where they were.

"I—I was just thinking." Prochorus climbed gingerly down from the boulder, quite conscious of the man's weapon although as yet there had been no physical threat.

"What is your name?"

"Prochorus."

"The son of Chuza, Herod's steward?"

"Yes."

"Aren't you a friend of John ben Zebedee?"

"Yes—but I have seen him only once lately."

"At this very spot—a week ago?"

"How did you know that?"

"More than eagles have nests among the rocks up there." The other man's craggy features were creased momentarily by a smile as he nodded toward the heights above the road. "I watched you talking to John last week but the crowd was too great for me to show myself. What did he tell you?"

"He thinks there may be trouble in Jerusalem."

"The son of Zebedee thinks—and talks—too much," said the brigand. "Do you know who I am?"

"Manahem—the son of Judas the Gaulonite?"

"What have you been told about me?"

"That you are a leader of those who would wrest our land from control by the Romans." Prochorus chose to repeat the best of the many things he had heard about the brigand leader.

"As my father almost succeeded in doing nearly thirty years ago, when I was but a babe in my mother's arms," said Manahem proudly.

It was somewhat difficult for Prochorus to envision this hard-bitten man with the craggy face and burning eyes as ever having been a babe in anyone's arms but not at all hard to believe he had inherited the mantle of the rebel Judas. For many years the acknowledged leader of the largest and fiercest of the roving robber bands infesting the hills west of the lake, Manahem had become the leader of all who had sworn defiance of Rome following the capture of another brigand called Barabbas by the Romans a few months earlier, during an abortive attempt to stir up a revolt in the Temple at Jerusalem.

"Where are you going?" Manahem asked.

"To Magdala—for the Passover."

"What were you doing in Tiberias?"

"I am studying at the scriptorium and the university there."

"Training yourself to take your father's place as Herod's steward?"

"No." Prochorus was losing his fear of the brigand. "I hope to go to Alexandria to study with Philo—and perhaps even to Rome."

"Where you will become a lackey of those who hold our people in bondage?" Manahem's voice was heavy with sarcasm now.

"I am of priestly lineage through my mother and also in the line of David," Prochorus said proudly, but the bandit was not impressed.

"Even the High Priest Caiaphas works with the Romans so he can keep the Temple treasures for himself," he said, then changed the subject abruptly: "How many Galileans were in the train of the Nazarene last week?"

"You saw them—a few hundred."

"Others were supposed to come from surrounding towns; they could have joined the party at Scythopolis." The only one of the Decapolis cities located west of the Jordan, the latter was a major road junction a little south of the lake.

"Father says not. He was in Scythopolis a few days ago."

"What does Chuza think of the Nazarene?"

"My mother believes he is the Messiah. But Father says that if he really is the Son of God he wouldn't have let John the Baptizer die."

"Whether the Nazarene is the Expected One or not makes little difference—as long as people think he is," Manahem said with a shrug. "Those with him in Jerusalem will seize control tomorrow and free Barabbas from prison. Once that is accomplished, we will arouse the people of Galilee and seize fat Antipas' province, before he gets back from Jerusalem. When will you be returning to Tiberias?"

"Four days from now."

"Would you help those who wish to free our people from bondage?"

"H-how?"

"Until word comes that Jerusalem is in our hands, I cannot launch an attack here in Galilee to prevent the Romans from reinforcing the Jerusalem garrison. Besides, Antipas has much armor and weapons hidden at Machaerus east of the Salt Sea. We will need to seize that as soon as war begins."

"How will you know? It takes almost a week to get to Jerusalem."

"We have arranged for a courier on a swift camel to bring us word as soon as Jerusalem is in our hands. But the Romans have been watching the highland roads closely since Barabbas was captured and, if the courier doesn't get through, I need to know what is happening. Many Galileans leave Jerusalem as soon as the Passover feast is eaten and return home. You can be my eyes and ears in Magdala and Tiberias and bring me news of anything you hear."

"Why doesn't Jesus simply proclaim himself king and Messiah, as the prophets foretold?" Prochorus asked. "Then he could strike down our enemies with the power of God."

"Judas of Kerioth has been given the task of betraying the Nazarene to the High Priest and forcing him to declare himself," Manahem explained. "But even if he isn't the Messiah, we can still seize Jerusalem while the crowds are around him there."

The plan sounded risky to Prochorus but he didn't argue.

"Bring me word four days hence of all you hear," Manahem continued, "and when we control the kingdom, I will see that you realize your ambition to study with the great Philo in Egypt. Who knows?" he added. "You may one day be a leader of our people yourself."

Only when he was entering his father's house at Magdala, a half hour later, did Prochorus remember that John ben Zebedee had said much the same thing years before.

iii

From Magdala to Tiberias was less than a two-hour walk along the rough road that scaled the heights overlooking the lake. Usually Prochorus remained at home until the last minute, leaving just enough time before dark to reach Tiberias and the rather spartan quarters of the university students. Even if darkness should catch him on the way, he had no real reason to be concerned—on any other day but this—for with the setting of the sun torches blazed everywhere on the ramparts of the palace-fortress Antipas had built at the highest point in Tiberias. With good reason, too, for some years earlier Antipas had put away his first wife, the daughter of King Aretas of the Nabateans—the large and aggressive Arab nation west of the Jordan and the Salt Sea with its capital at Petra—in order to marry Herodias, former wife of his brother Herod Philip. Aretas had reacted predictably to what he considered the insult to his daughter and a state bordering upon war had existed between him and Antipas, with the Tetrarch of Galilee now living in constant fear of attack or assassination.

Today, however, Prochorus left home earlier than was his custom, troubled by fragmentary reports reaching Magdala about a strange sequence of events in Jerusalem. These had been brought by some Galileans who had fled from the Holy City, remembering very well the occasion barely six months earlier when Pontius Pilate had cut down a group of Galilean rebels led by Barabbas inside the Temple itself. The leader had been put into prison to await execution upon a suitably important occasion, but the blood of the others had stained the floor of the Temple, an act of desecration that would have brought down upon the Procurator the hatred of all Jews, had they not feared even more the holocaust that would follow seizure of the Temple and the adjoining Roman fortress of Antonia by the rebels.

Remembering the boasting of the rebel leader about the drama to be acted out in Jerusalem, Prochorus had no desire to be the bringer of bad tidings. But he had no way of knowing that the expected rebel courier from Jerusalem had failed to arrive by way of the shorter route through Samaria and the Judaean highlands, leaving Manahem with no knowledge of events there. And even though he was purposely early, he had barely reached the crest of the rocky hillside when he saw Manahem and several others, all heavily armed and grim of countenance, waiting beside the road, obviously for him.

"What have you heard from Jerusalem?" the rebel leader demanded at once.

"A few pilgrims left as soon as the Passover feast was eaten but they knew little of what happened," said Prochorus, hoping to avoid telling everything he had learned.

"Speak the truth!" The dark skin and hawklike profile of the speaker betrayed his part-Nabatean ancestry. "Or you will be vulture bait before nightfall."

"Hold your tongue, Harith!" Manahem said sharply and turned to Prochorus once again. "Did you hear anything about how Jesus was received in Jerusalem?"

"The travelers told of a great body of people entering the city with him, shouting Hosanna and naming him the Messiah. It was also reported that one of his own disciples betrayed him to the authorities."

"Who was it?" Harith demanded.

"They named Judas of Kerioth, and said Jesus was seized on the orders of the High Priest and condemned to death by the Sanhedrin that very night."

"The Sanhedrin must meet twice before it can condemn a person to death," said Manahem.

"Apparently the law wasn't observed," said Prochorus. "Another man left the afternoon following the Passover and came on horseback by way of Samaria. He claims to have seen the Nazarene hanging from the cross, crucified by the Romans."

"And his followers?"

"They were scattered abroad. No one knows where they are."

"What about my brother Judas?" Harith asked.

"He is said to have hanged himself beside the Jericho road."

"Liar!" Harith jerked his *sicarius* from its scabbard, but when he would have attacked Prochorus, Manahem put out a hand and thrust him back.

"The boy would have no reason to lie," he snapped. "Did you say the Nazarene made no resistance?" he asked Prochorus.

"I heard of none. Pontius Pilate himself sentenced Jesus to death."

"Stoning would have been our way," Manahem said thoughtfully. "Crucifixion is a Roman form of execution so it must have been the Romans who killed him."

"The sons of Zebedee claimed the Nazarene was the Messiah, and Judas believed them," said Harith bitterly. "Now the Romans have killed him too."

"The traveler said Judas of Kerioth hanged—" Prochorus broke off at another scowl from Harith.

"Did you hear anything about Barabbas?" Manahem asked.

"It is customary at the Passover to free a criminal. Jesus of Nazareth was executed in Barabbas' stead."

Manahem's craggy features brightened a little at this news. "Then the scheme wasn't entirely a failure—"

"Failure?" Harith exploded. "My brother is dead because he was selected to force the Nazarene to declare himself the Messiah. If we had gone to Jerusalem and seized the Temple the way I wanted us to do, none of this would have happened. But John and James were so sure the Nazarene could stop the Romans only by raising his hand." He turned savagely to Prochorus. "Where are the sons of Zebedee?"

"No one knows. The followers of Jesus are scattered abroad."

"They listened too much to the mouthings of the Nazarene about peace on earth and good will toward men, so we're better off without them," said Harith. "From now on this blade shall be our doctrine. Whoever refuses to follow it shall die."

"Can—can I go now?" Prochorus asked.

"And let the Fox know what you have learned here?" Harith demanded, but again Manahem came to Prochorus' aid.

"The boy can tell Antipas nothing about us he doesn't know already," said the brigand leader. "Have you forgotten the monthly tribute I pay Herod for letting us rob travelers this close to his capital? Besides, I promised the boy he would not be harmed."

"So many mistakes have been made already in this matter," said Harith with a shrug, "another one can't make much difference."

"From time to time in Tiberias you will be accosted by a one-eyed beggar named Phinehas," Manahem told Prochorus. "Tell him anything you think I should know. And if you see James ben Zebedee, tell him I wish to know everything that happened in Jerusalem."

"Don't forget that the blade of a *sicarius* can find your ribs as easily in Tiberias as it could here." Harith's harsh voice followed Prochorus along the road southward, but betrayal was the last thing in the youth's thoughts.

iv

All that week the cities around the lake where Jesus of Nazareth had spent most of the past three years—since making a dramatic appearance one sabbath in the great synagogue at Capernaum and healing a man seized of evil spirits for many years—buzzed with accounts of what had happened in Jerusalem during the Passover.

Listening to them at school and in the market place of Tiberias, Prochorus found that they all followed the same general pattern and therefore probably represented a reasonably accurate account of the real events.

Jesus of Nazareth, it appeared, had been acclaimed in the Holy City, not only by the company of Galileans who had been with him but also by a great multitude already living there or pouring in for the Passover, the most important of the Jewish religious festivals. There seemed to be no doubt about the genuine warmth of his welcome by the people. Just as there had been no doubt for more than a year that the priests and the party supporting them intended to destroy the Nazarene because of his appeal to the Amhaaretz, the common people who, should they decide not to render the annual tribute of half a Tyrian shekel to the Temple as well as the tithe and other levies, could sharply curtail the wealth of the luxury-loving priesthood.

The pattern of events on the night of the Passover and the following day would have been much more difficult to understand if Prochorus had not already learned from Manahem and Harith about the elaborate scheme of rebellion in which they had been waiting to play their own assigned roles in Galilee. Taking advantage of the fact that Jerusalem would be crowded with people who might be easily aroused, the rebels had planned to attack the Temple from the inside. The Temple police who guarded the sanctuary itself could no doubt have been overcome quickly by the stealthy wielders of the *sicarius*. And once the Temple was secured, the attackers could have moved through the passageways devised by the Romans to allow the garrison of the adjacent fortress of Antonia quick access to the Temple courts in time of trouble, overcoming the relatively small Roman detail quickly and seizing the city. Moreover, the capture of Jerusalem would then have been the signal for an uprising throughout the land, with Manahem and his followers leaving their hiding places in the hills of Lower Galilee and the Judaean highlands to attack the small garrisons of Roman troops in the major cities throughout the former kingdom of Herod the Great.

Looked at from the viewpoint of pure logic, the plot seemed more foolish than even the attempted uprising led by Barabbas in Jerusalem, which had resulted in his capture and sentence of death. But the rebels had obviously counted heavily upon one element which had not been present in that previous attempt at insurrection —the presence of Jesus of Nazareth and the opportunity to proclaim him the expected Messiah at a time when the city would be packed with people who could easily be swayed by him. Moving swiftly according to their plan then, Manahem and his followers had expected to gather much of the countryside to their standards, seizing the entire area quickly and facing the Romans with an already accomplished fact.

The trigger that would set the whole scheme in motion had obviously been the announcement of the Messiah and in preparation for it a rather elaborate test had been devised to which the Nazarene teacher would be put. Judas of Kerioth had been selected to betray him to the High Priest Caiaphas on the night of the Passover, forcing Jesus at last to use divine power to save himself and his followers, an act that was certain to convince the multitudes that he was indeed the Messiah and bring them flocking to his standard. Nor did the rebels have anything to lose by betraying the Nazarene to the authorities for, if he were indeed the Messiah, his power would place them in immediate control. And if he were not, seizure of the Holy City would enable them to launch a new war to drive the Roman conquerors from their homeland.

Obviously, however, the wily High Priest, Joseph Caiaphas, had caught the rebels by surprise and, seizing the Nazarene in the dead of night, had him sentenced to death by a portion of the Sanhedrin sitting as a rump court. Transferring Jesus to the Roman authority of the Procurator Pontius Pilate for the death sentence before the city itself was awake, Caiaphas had further made certain that Pilate would approve the execution of the Nazarene, by rousing the Temple rabble—beggars, thieves, sellers of all kinds of wares, and others who held licenses for their activities at the will of the High Priest and paid a considerable amount into the Temple coffers for their privilege—to demand the crucifixion of the gentle Galilean.

Thus still another of the many plans with which rebels had sought to wrest control of the Judaean heartland and the city of

Jerusalem from Rome had gone awry. But this time the victim had been one who taught the very antithesis of violence and greed, the simple doctrine that every man should love his neighbor as himself.

v

The annual journey of Herod Antipas to Jerusalem for the Passover was part of the solemn farce that he was a Jew, though actually he was the son of an Idumean father and a Samaritan woman named Malthake. His return to Tiberias from Jerusalem brought a new spate of details concerning the recent dramatic occurrences there. The most startling of these, which Prochorus discounted immediately because it seemed much too fanciful to believe, was the claim that Jesus of Nazareth had risen from a rocky tomb on the third day following his crucifixion and had appeared to some of his followers in a resurrected form.

About a week after Prochorus' encounter with Manahem and Harith on the road above Tiberias, he was called from his classes one morning by his tutor in Greek and Latin, an old scholar named Nestor.

"The Tetrarch's chief scribe became ill on the way back from Jerusalem," Nestor told him. "Antipas needs a capable scribe to write a report to the Legate in Antioch. Get your pens and ink board and go to the palace at once."

In his quarters, Prochorus filled a small bottle with lampblack and quickly washed the polished board with the hollowed-out cups in which it was mixed with water and gum to form ink. Putting these into a small goatskin bag, along with a sheaf of freshly sharpened quills, he left the school and started for the palace. He couldn't help feeling a little apprehension at being suddenly pressed into service as a scribe for Galilee's ruler when he had not yet finished his courses. On the other hand, he knew Nestor had selected him because he was by far the best student in the school and, besides, most of his studies during this last year of schooling had been concerned with the detailed documents required by the Romans from provincial authorities.

It was a lovely day and Prochorus would much rather have been setting out for a sail in one of the pleasure boats moored to the stone quays at the foot of the long stairway leading down from the palaces of the rich members of Antipas' court to the water. Or, better still, being rowed around by slaves while reclining upon the cushions of one of the pleasure barges with their colorful awnings arranged to protect passengers from the sun. Such an eventuality was so remote, however, that he put it from his mind as he hurried toward the magnificent building crowning the elevation on which Tiberias was built.

At the palace he was shown by a servant into an anteroom where he was left alone. Through a door leading into an enclosed garden or court, he could see a fountain fed by a tiny artificial waterfall, so constructed that the small stream broke up into a mist as it fell, letting the sun paint it with the colors of the rainbow. Old Nestor had told him the colors were only the many components of sunlight, broken up by water in the same way that they could be separated by a triangular-shaped bit of glass. But it had still been hard to believe so many beautiful hues could be bound up in a single beam of sunlight that had no visible substance.

Busy arranging his pens and scrolls on a table and preparing a supply of ink in one of the small wooden cups, Prochorus was startled to see a girl cross the garden to the waterfall, where she stood looking down at the pool. She was a little younger, he judged, than he and her pale gold hair shone in the sunlight. When she turned her head to look into the room he saw that she had the delicately lovely features of a Jewish aristocrat, tempered with something of the same beauty he'd seen in a Greek statue at Hippos across the lake, when he'd gone there once with his father to buy grain.

Her robe of white silk was more Grecian than Jewish, too. Cut in a style called a stola, it was belted at the waist with a golden cord. When she stepped upon the rocks at the edge of the pool he saw that her sandals, too, were of a golden color, as was the small circlet she wore over her hair.

Watching the girl, Prochorus barely heard the door behind him open in time to turn quickly, almost knocking over the stool upon which he had placed the board for mixing the ink. Herod Antipas came into the room, followed by the armed guard who went with him everywhere, because of his constant fear of assassination, and the slave who tasted all his food and wine, lest he be poisoned. The Tetrarch of Galilee and Peraea was a corpulent man of middle age, with pouches of dissipation showing beneath heavy-lidded eyes.

"I asked for a skilled scribe," he said sharply. "Not a mere boy."

Prochorus flushed. "I have finished the prescribed courses of studies in your School for Scribes, noble Antipas," he said a little stiffly.

"So?" Antipas seated himself in a chair pushed under him by the slave. "What is your name?"

"Prochorus ben Chuza, sir."

"The son of my steward?"

"Yes, sir."

"I saw you last when you were but a babe in your mother's arms, long before—" The Tetrarch put his hands to his eyes for a moment as if suddenly weary. "So you wish to follow in your father's footsteps?"

"I hope to study later in Alexandria—and perhaps in Rome."

"When you are very young, your world has no limit. But when you are old—" Antipas shook his head like a sleepy lion. "Once I dreamed such dreams but now it is all I can do to keep my scheming brother-in-law Agrippa from stealing what little I have by lying about me to Tiberius." His eyes went to the door leading to the garden and warmed at the sight of the girl outside.

"Did you notice my ward out there in the garden, Prochorus?" he asked, then his laugh boomed out. "But that's a foolish question, isn't it? She is my great-niece—an orphan." Antipas rose and lumbered to the door. "Mariamne," he called to the girl in the garden. "Come here a moment."

"Yes, Uncle Antipas." Her voice was as lovely as she was and, when she moved across the garden to the open doors, Prochorus thought he had never seen anything so graceful—unless it was a fawn he had startled beside the road one day on the way back from Magdala.

"I want you to meet a fine young man, Mariamne," said Antipas. "His name is Prochorus." The girl started to smile, then her eyes fell upon the tools of a scribe spread out on the end of the table before Prochorus.

"A scribe?"

"He is the son of my steward," said Antipas, "and very ambitious, too. He tells me he plans to go to Alexandria to study—perhaps even to Rome."

"I like it better here than in Rome, Uncle Antipas." The girl seemed to have lost interest in Prochorus, who was blushing painfully. "May I sail one of the boats moored down at the quay?"

"In good time, my dear; the lake can be very treacherous. Come to think of it, Prochorus grew up in Capernaum where there are many boats. Perhaps he can spare time from his studies one day to sail with you."

"I shall be happy to obey the orders of the Tetrarch." Prochorus couldn't resist the chance to sting the girl in return for her summary dismissal of him because he was only a scribe. When he saw Antipas smile, he knew the Tetrarch was enjoying pitting the two young people against each other.

"Don't trouble yourself," said Mariamne tartly. "Your studies must take most of your time."

"Let us to work then," said Antipas. "I shall see that you go sailing, Mariamne—if I have to take you myself."

The girl went out into the garden again and Antipas began to dictate a report to the Legate in Antioch. Writing in Greek, which was as much his native tongue as the Aramaic of the lake country, Prochorus transcribed it swiftly and skillfully with ink and quill on a small papyrus roll. The letter was an account of the arrest of Jesus of Nazareth in Jerusalem, of Pontius Pilate's attempt to shift the burden of ordering his execution to Antipas, and the subsequent scourging and crucifixion of the prisoner.

"Unquestionably the man was part of a well-organized plot to seize control of the Temple and put the Jerusalem garrison to death," Antipas dictated in closing. "Had the Procurator of Judaea and Samaria acted swiftly while the followers of the Nazarene were still in Jerusalem, the entire plot could have been revealed and its leaders put to death. But so much time was wasted by the Procurator in seeking to escape responsibility that the man's disciples were allowed to flee. Pilate even released the brigand Barabbas, who is known to be in league with the followers of Manahem, the son of Judas the Gaulonite who led the rebellion here in Galilee over twenty years ago. Now I must begin to hunt down the rebels, since the Procurator seems reluctant to do so."

Remembering from his conversation with Manahem that the rebel leader had hinted at some sort of an arrangement between himself and the Tetrarch of Galilee, Prochorus doubted that Antipas' sentiments in the letter were entirely true—but had the good sense to keep his reservations to himself.

"Is it true that the Nazarene rose from the dead, sir?" he asked when the letter was finished.

"What did you say?" Obviously the question had both startled and shocked the Tetrarch.

"It is rumored that the Nazarene rose from the dead."

"When is this said to have happened?"

"On the third day after the Passover was eaten."

"We left early and stopped at Jericho." Antipas seemed to be speaking to himself but the sickly light of fear was still in his eyes. "Tell me what you know about this."

"They are saying in the market place that the Nazarene was put into a tomb belonging to the merchant Joseph of Arimathea—"

"That much is correct. Pilate would have let him hang on the cross but the man's followers could have claimed that he was desecrating the holy feast day, so I urged him to let Joseph remove the body. But it was sealed in Joseph's tomb with a large stone and Pilate put guards at the tomb, lest the Nazarene's disciples steal the body and use it to arouse the people."

"The rumor is that on the morning of the third day, some of Jesus' followers came to the tomb and found the stone rolled away and the body gone."

"Then they must have stolen it!" Antipas' face brightened a little.

"Joseph of Arimathea was known to be a follower of the Nazarene. He could have bribed the guards to look another way."

"Jesus is also said to have appeared to some of his followers and instructed them to return to Galilee, where he would meet them."

Antipas looked as if he were going to faint and put out a hand to the table to steady himself. The slave who followed him everywhere scurried out, returning almost immediately with a flagon and a silver cup. Slopping wine into the cup, the Tetrarch drank deeply; by the time he put down the cup and wiped his mouth with the sleeve of his robe, some of the color was beginning to creep back into his cheeks.

"Has—has the Nazarene been seen here in Galilee?"

"No, sir."

"Pontius Pilate must be behind all this. He would like nothing better than to make me responsible for the man's death and cause trouble for me with the Emperor. Can you write in Latin?"

"Yes, sir."

"Make a Latin copy of that report to the Legate; I will send it directly to Rome." Antipas drank deeply again while Prochorus collected his pens and his scrolls.

"You have done well," he said as Prochorus was leaving. "Until my scribe is well again, you can serve in his place."

"Thank you, sir."

"On your way back to the university, stop in the market place and listen to what they are saying," Antipas added. "You can bring me word of it, when you come tomorrow."

vi

The morning was gone by the time Prochorus finished making a copy in Latin of Antipas' report to the Legate of Syria, to whom the Tetrarch of Galilee was directly responsible. Obviously Antipas was hoping to bring his complaints against Pontius Pilate to the Emperor's attention over the head—as it were—of the Legate. It was a risky procedure, but the stakes were high—control of Jerusalem and the wealth that poured into it from Jews all over the world.

When he left the palace, Prochorus did not return immediately to the school but crossed from the palace to the market place. Workmen were everywhere. The tapping of hammers; the clink of stonemason's tools shaping stone quarried in the hills; the creak of rope and windlass as massive blocks were hoisted into place; the ebb and flow of human voices—all coalesced together into a familiar melody.

People of all kinds thronged the city, too: dark-skinned men from the desert areas to the east; fishermen whose clothing still reeked of the night's catch; Greek merchants crying jewelry and other fine wares; an Assyrian from Antioch and a Phoenician from Tyre, rubbing elbows with a giant Nubian slave from Africa; a Roman officer in his short tunic, cuirass and crested helmet followed by a legionary with the lines of a dozen campaigns carved into his face.

The magnificent forum with which Herod Antipas planned to make his new city a small counterpart of Rome was almost finished. Workmen were putting into place the gilded eagles, cast by metal-workers in Elath far to the south at the head of the Gulf of Aqabah, where furnaces in use since the time of King Solomon nearly a thousand years ago were still fired by the howling winds that blew through the gorges at the extreme southern end of the Arabah.

To really pious Jews, the combination of the hated eagles of Rome—graven images in their minds—and the desecration of the cemeteries which had occupied this very site before Antipas decided to build a new capital there put the city of Tiberias beyond the pale religiously. But though fiercely patriotic and passionately devoted to the worship of the One True God, most Galileans were troubled but little by the strict interpretations of Mosaic law given by the teachers of Jerusalem known facetiously as the "Rabbis of the Porch" because they uttered their pronouncements interpreting the law from the Porch of Solomon in the Temple. Moreover, except for the very pious, the opportunity of a day's work building Tiberias at the pay of a copper denarius far outstripped any question of ritual contamination.

It was the first time Prochorus had ever been inside the still unfinished forum and he was forced to dodge between scaffolds, ladders and an occasional falling timber or brick, in order to reach the great audience chamber. The dais at one end where the Tetrarch would dispense justice or harangue his subjects was still unfinished and so was the huge room, or scriptorium, where scribes would work, setting down the complaints of those who demanded justice before the courts which would be held in the smaller rooms around the forum.

The Great Sanhedrin—or even the lesser sanhedrins which dispensed justice in smaller towns—would never sit here; being essentially religious courts—Jewish civil law and religious law were too bound up with each other to be really separated—they could not be held in a place considered unclean by the Jewish faith.

In a secluded part of the forum Prochorus turned quickly when he felt a tug at his sleeve, half expecting to see Harith with a naked blade by his side. Instead he found himself looking into the gleaming single eye of a ragged beggar.

"I have no money—"

"My name is Phinehas." There was none of the whine of a beggar in this one's voice. "What were you doing in the palace this morning?"

"The Tetrarch's scribe is sick. I was writing a letter for him."

"To whom?"

"The Legate in Antioch." Prochorus looked around to make sure no one could overhear. "About the crucifixion of the Nazarene in Jerusalem."

"The Fox"—it was a name freely used for Herod Antipas in the area—"is losing no time in placing the blame for whatever happens on Pontius Pilate."

"Is something going to happen?"

"What doesn't go into your ears cannot come out of your mouth," Phinehas said briskly. "When are you going to Magdala again?"

"Tomorrow—after the noonday meal."

"When you are ready to leave Tiberias, go to the waterfront and ask for the boat of Mahol. He will take you to Capernaum."

"But my family lives in Magdala—"

"At Capernaum seek out the fishing establishment of Zebedee and look for his son James."

"Has he returned from Jerusalem?"

"Swift horses were stabled at Bethany for him and John, so they should be back by now. Tell James to come to the Horns of Hattin before noon day after tomorrow."

The area mentioned was a sort of natural amphitheater—some said it had once been the site of a city—located between two sharp peaks which, seen from the shore as one looked up to the hills of the west, gave the outline of a pair of horns. It lay not far from the main road leading from Magdala through Upper Galilee to the Great Sea.

"It's a long way from Capernaum back to Magdala," Prochorus said pointedly.

"Mahol will also sail you home. If James ben Zebedee has not returned to Capernaum, he will bring me word." The beggar handed him a coin. "I will follow you from the forum begging alms. Give this to me outside so no one will suspect we have been talking here."

Prochorus took the coin and left the forum, followed by the whining voice of Phinehas—quite different from the tone he had used inside the structure. In the street outside, he tossed the coin to the beggar and turned his steps toward the school, where it would now be time for the noonday meal.

As Prochorus was leaving the palace shortly before noon the next day, he saw Princess Mariamne standing just inside the main entrance. Suspecting that she might be waiting for him and having no desire for another encounter with her tart tongue, he looked for another gate, but she saw him before he could make his escape.

"You there, scribe," she called and, since he was carrying the leather bag with the tools of his trade in his hand at the time, he could hardly pretend that she wasn't speaking to him.

"Yes, Princess."

"I've decided to let you take me for a sail on the lake."

"I'm sorry, Princess. But I must leave for Capernaum at once."

"On a mission for my uncle? Then you can take me with you."

"I'm on the way to spend the sabbath with my parents," he explained.

"But you live in Magdala."

At another time he might have been flattered by the knowledge that she had talked to someone about him. At the moment, however, he was too concerned lest Antipas learn of his connection with the brigands to think of anything else. Phinehas had left little doubt of the danger to him if he failed to carry out the orders of Manahem, yet he knew Antipas would look with even less approval upon one familiar with his correspondence having anything to do with the rebel leader—even as a messenger boy.

"I must sail to Capernaum first to carry out an errand for my father," he told her. "Then I shall come back to Magdala."

"Go on then." She drew herself up haughtily, but he heard the note of disappointment in her voice and suspected that she might be lonely in the palace with no one else of her own age around.

"I could take you next week," he offered.

"Don't trouble yourself. I shall find someone else."

He stood watching her until she disappeared along a path leading through the palace grounds. Being young himself, he knew how disappointment could hurt the very young and was sorry he had been forced to refuse her request.

vii

At the foot of one of the stairways leading down to the quay built of stones quarried from the mountainside behind Tiberias, Prochorus saw a fisherman working at his boat. The man glanced up momentarily at his approach but went on mending his net without speaking.

"My name is Prochorus," the youth said. "Are you Mahol?"

"You look too young to be the scribe of the Tetrarch."

Having just come from the palace, Prochorus was in no mood to be badgered by a fisherman; besides, he was still a little angry because he'd been forced to refuse Princess Mariamne's request.

"Phinehas told me you would take me to Capernaum in your boat," he said. "But if you have no wish to—"

"Hold on, young cockerel." The leathery countenance of the fisherman cracked in a smile. "I didn't say I wouldn't take you. Help me put this net in the tub and we will leave at once."

The type of net used by the fishermen of Galilee was a long affair with wooden floats spaced along the upper edge and leaden weights on the lower. Carefully stowed in a large wooden tub that occupied the front part of the boat before the mast, the net was kept ready for instant use as soon as a school of fish was spotted.

The boats were handled by two men: one to row after the sail that carried them to the fishing grounds was lowered, the other to pay out the net over the side. Once in the water, the weights along the lower edge of the net held it perpendicular to the surface. With the ropes attached to each end secured to the boat, both men then rowed, gradually drawing the two ends of the net together in a giant elongated purse string that trapped the fish inside. Once the net was closed, both men could then drag it in with its catch, transferring the trapped fish to the bottom of the boat and stowing the net once again in the large wooden tub.

It was a beautiful afternoon, with no hint in the sky of one of the sudden storms that could turn the lake surface into a maelstrom of surging waves before the fishermen were able to pull in their nets, facing them with the choice of risking drowning to save their means of livelihood, or cutting loose a net which might cost the year's profit to replace. Fortunately a brisk wind was setting northward, as usually happened at this time of day, and the oars, except the steering sweep at the stern, were not needed.

Once they were clear of the quay and well out into the lake, Prochorus took the steering oar while Mahol finished patching his net. John ben Zebedee had taught him well and, with the water rushing beneath the prow, the sturdy boat drove northward on a steady course. Magdala came into view while Tiberias was still visible behind them, magnificent in its elevation against the western sky with the citadel upon its highest point a reminder of the might of Rome, at whose command the district was ruled by Herod Antipas. Older than the capital, its elevation less precipitous, Magdala seemed almost to squat at the edge of the water like a mother hen, her brood the fishing fleet moored to the quays and piers that lined the shore with the multicolored sails of the boats making a brilliant pattern against the darker blue of the water near the shore.

After nearly an hour's sail the large white mass of Capernaum began to be visible along a section of the shore to the north. It was midafternoon and already the water was changing hue as the waning sun beat down upon it with lessened intensity. By the time they touched the long dock of Capernaum's largest fishing establishment, that of Zebedee and his sons, the boats were already being prepared for the evening venture to the fishing grounds at the northern end of the lake.

At the landward end of the pier Prochorus entered a long shed where a large group of women were cleaning the last of the night's catch. Much of this was already in place on the drying racks outside of the building, the rest being salted down in casks for shipment to markets in other cities or smoked in long sheds from which came the acrid smell of slowly burning wood.

"I seek James ben Zebedee," the youth told the foreman in charge of the sheds. "Can you tell me whether he has returned from Jerusalem?"

"Why do you wish to see him?"

"I am Prochorus, son of Chuza."

"Herod's steward?"

"Yes. The message I bring is for the ears of James alone—or his brother John."

"You will find the sons of Zebedee at the large house there." The foreman nodded to where a considerable dwelling was located not far from the landward end of the pier. "But call out your name as you approach."

Prochorus was shocked by his first sight of James and John. Only a few weeks ago they had been eager young men, remarkable for their fierce energy and enthusiasm. Now the fire which had earned for them the nickname Sons of Thunder seemed to have gone out, leaving them old men with little interest in life.

"You are ill," Prochorus said impulsively. "Let me go for a physician."

"The physician who could heal us is dead," said John. "The Romans crucified him and all is lost."

"Then he didn't rise from the dead as we heard in Tiberias?"

"The tomb was empty when we went to it the third morning and at the time I thought I saw the Master himself. But now—"

"You must believe, not think." James's voice was harsh and, looking at the two brothers now, Prochorus couldn't help being struck by the differences between them.

John was slender, his features delicate like those of a poet or a singer. Today, however, his eyes bleak with suffering and despair, though Prochorus knew how they could glow with sympathy or dance brightly with humor and joy. James, much shorter and the older of the two, reminded Prochorus a little of Manahem: there was the same toughness in his face, the same strength of purpose, the same strong set to his shoulders, bowed down though they were now by weariness and despair.

James, the youth remembered, had always been the leader of the two. But it was to John that Prochorus himself had felt an instant attachment the first time he had seen him years ago, an affinity of spirit and an instinctive understanding and feeling of kinship— none of which he had ever felt for James.

"I bring you a message given me by a beggar in Tiberias named Phinehas," Prochorus told the older brother. "You are to be at the Horns of Hattin by noon tomorrow."

"Why were you chosen to bring it?" John asked.

"I met a man on the heights above Magdala last week, as I was going home from Tiberias for the sabbath. He asked me to bring him news of the Nazarene and yesterday he sent the beggar with the message for James."

"Does your father know of this?" John asked quickly.

"No."

"And have you spoken of it to no one else?"

"No."

"The boy need not be involved any further," John said to his brother. "Chuza is our friend and Joanna one of the women who served the Master. We must not let any harm come to them."

"I still don't see why Mana—the man you met on the road— chose you as a messenger," James said to Prochorus.

"It may be because I am now serving as chief scribe for the Tetrarch," said Prochorus.

"Do you handle official correspondence?" James demanded.

"Yes."

"What did Antipas report to the Legate?"

"That the affair in Jerusalem is ended because Pontius Pilate delayed arresting all of you while he tried to escape sentencing Jesus of Nazareth."

"I still say the boy should not be involved," John protested but James cut him off.

"Don't you see how valuable he can be to us?" the older brother demanded sharply.

"It's enough that one who selected us as his first disciples was hanged from a tree like a common criminal," said John. "Now you are involving others."

"My brother is too easily discouraged," James told Prochorus. "Thank you for bringing me the message."

"Your task is finished." John took Prochorus by the arm and guided him toward the door. "I will send you back in one of our boats."

"Mahol brought me here from Tiberias. He is supposed to take me back to Magdala."

"Then I will walk out on the quay with you."

"Is the Nazarene really the Messiah?" Prochorus asked when they were out of earshot of James. "It is rumored in Tiberias that he rose from the dead."

"I saw the empty tomb myself," said John. "So did Peter and some of the others."

"Where is he now?"

"I don't know." Once again all the animation had gone out of John. "I try to believe he rose from the dead but I cannot remove the memory of his body hanging on the cross from my mind."

"What are you going to do now?"

"Go back to fishing, I suppose—as soon as Peter and Andrew get here. James and a few more still—" He broke off without finishing the sentence.

"Did Judas and the others really try to seize control of the Temple and Jerusalem during the Passover?"

"Where did you hear that?"

"Manahem boasted about it when I first saw him on the road between Magdala and Tiberias."

"There was a plot," John admitted. "Judas was the leader—and James, with some others. They thought if Judas betrayed the Master so he would be arrested, Jesus would be forced to name himself the Messiah in order to save himself and the rest of us."

"What went wrong?"

"Perhaps too many people talked too much. It was obvious from the way the High Priest Caiaphas acted that he knew what was going to happen and was waiting for us."

"But if Jesus was the Messiah, why didn't he use the power of God to save himself and take control away from the High Priest and the Romans?"

"I don't know. I don't know." John's voice was torn with agony. "While he was alive, Jesus tried several times to tell us something about himself, something that set him apart from all other men. But we were convinced that he would soon rule in Israel as David did long ago. And we were all so greedy to have a high place in his kingdom that we couldn't understand what he really meant."

"Do you understand now?"

"Not quite. A prophecy of Isaiah keeps coming into my mind, though, the passage that pictures the Messiah as:

"a thing despised and rejected by men,
a man of sorrows and familiar with suffering,
a man to make people screen their faces;
he was despised and we took no account of him."

"But the meaning lies just beyond me." John shook his head in a gesture of sadness—and frustration. "Like something that will not be recalled."

"I had to learn the whole passage in the synagogue school," said Prochorus. "The rest of it goes:

> "And yet ours were the sufferings he bore,
> ours the sorrows he carried.
> But we, we thought of him as someone punished,
> struck by God, and brought low.
> Yet he was pierced through for our faults—"

"'Pierced through for our faults'!" John cried. "What else could that be but the crucifixion?" His voice took on a tone of awe. "I can recall the next part of it now:

> "crushed for our sins.
> On him lies a punishment that brings us peace,
> and through his wounds we are healed.
> We had all gone astray like sheep,
> each taking his own way,
> and Yahweh burdened him
> with the sins of all of us."

"Jesus was telling us he had to die according to the prophecy," John cried. "I remember that he said to Nicodemus one night in Jerusalem: 'God loved the world so much that he gave his only Son, so that everyone who believes in him may not be lost but may have eternal life.'"

viii

When he returned from Magdala after the sabbath, Prochorus was informed that the scribe whose place he had been filling was not expected to live and for the moment, at least, he would continue to take the dying man's place. Quarters were assigned to him in the palace, a small cubbyhole set back against the side of the hill, but, since he took his meals with the servants, he was actually only one step higher than the slaves who performed the menial tasks of the household. Nevertheless, he was excited at the prospect of being closely related to the activities of the Tetrarch's palace.

The detail of Roman troops attached to the palace guard as a reminder to Herod Antipas of his allegiance to the Legate of Syria, and through him to Rome itself, was commanded by a decurion named Cassius Longinus. An intelligent and capable young officer in his early twenties, whose family was quite prominent in Rome, he and Prochorus quickly became friends. And, since the young scribe was large for his age, they exercised together daily in wrestling, spear throwing and even in the use of weapons where Prochorus needed a great deal of instruction, for he had only used a bow and arrow occasionally while hunting in the hills and almost never a spear. He was an apt pupil, however, and quickly learned the rudiments of using military weapons even though he had little enthusiasm for them.

Also resident in the palace was a distant relative of Antipas' named Manaen. An intelligent and energetic man, he was the keeper of the treasury and, since Prochorus was assigned to help keep the accounts when not needed by Antipas for correspondence, the two soon became good friends. Only after he had known Manaen for several weeks did Prochorus learn that, like many other Galileans, the older man had been a follower of the crucified Nazarene. Manaen had come to know Jesus through a taxgatherer named Matthew, who had been in charge of the customs post where the Way of the Sea crossed over from Galilee to the territory of the Tetrarch Philip, not far from where the Bridge of Jacob's Daughters spanned the upper Jordan.

During the first week of his residence in the palace Prochorus didn't see Princess Mariamne face to face. But more than once, while wrestling with Longinus, he noticed a flash of white from behind one of the columns supporting the balcony around the palace court and suspected that she was watching. Then one day, just as the Tetrarch was finishing his dictation to Prochorus, Mariamne came into the room.

"May I borrow your scribe for a few moments, Uncle Antipas?" she asked, paying no attention to Prochorus, who had risen to his feet immediately when she came in.

"Whom are you writing to?" the Tetrarch asked. "A sweetheart in Rome?"

"Oh no. I'm much too young for that."

"If you are, the young men of Rome are greater dolts than I

remember their being," said Antipas. "I've noticed the way Prochorus here watches you and I'm sure he will be glad to write your letters."

Prochorus busied himself sharpening a quill until the Tetrarch, his guard and his slave left the room. When he and Mariamne were alone he took a parchment sheet and dipped the point of a quill in ink. "What do you wish to write, Princess?" he asked, deliberately emphasizing the title to remind her of the difference in their station.

"A letter to Uncle Agrippa."

"Agrippa?" he asked, startled by the name.

"Why shouldn't I write him?" she demanded.

"You may write to anyone you wish, of course."

"But you don't approve of my writing to Uncle Agrippa. Why?"

"Surely you know the Tetrarch suspects Prince Agrippa of plotting to gain the throne of his grandfather."

"And who has a better right? After all, we are descended from the Jewish royal family."

"No one questions that Hasmonean blood flows in the veins of Herod Agrippa, and in yourself, Princess," he said. "But you may recall that your great-grandfather Herod murdered his own son, when he thought Antipater was plotting to seize the throne."

The reminder of the bloody history of Herod the Great brought her up short and she turned away from him toward the door to the inner court, where he had first seen her. He wished he could do something to soften the truth that, as a descendant of Herod the Great through a line that included the most recent of purely Jewish rulers, the Hasmoneans, she might one day find herself in serious danger as a pawn in the tense game being played for the high stakes of controlling the riches of the Jewish heartland, but there was no altering the facts of history now.

When the girl seemed lost in thought, Prochorus asked, "Where is your uncle Agrippa now?"

"At Malatha near Beersheba." She turned back into the room and he saw that her eyes were bright with unshed tears. "Aunt Kypros interceded with Aunt Herodias for him and Uncle Antipas has promised him a position here in Tiberias as *agoranomus*, inspector of markets. Queen Herodias and my mother were sisters."

"Was your father a Jew?"

She shook her head. "He was a Roman official. After my parents died, Uncle Agrippa and Aunt Kypros took me as their ward, and when the Emperor forced him to leave Rome I came with them to Idumea." She shivered. "It's cold and windy there; I didn't like it at all."

"Do you like Tiberias?"

"Oh yes. Aunt Herodias has been very good to me and so has Uncle Antipas. I don't think I'll write that letter after all," she added. "You promised the other day to take me sailing; can you go this afternoon?"

"If that is your wish. I will finish the letters the Tetrarch dictated to me by the noonday meal. We can leave soon afterwards."

"Good!" Her face brightened. "I will meet you at the quay where Uncle Antipas' barge is moored."

She seemed happy once again but as he watched her leave the room Prochorus found himself wondering just what place Mariamne had in the schemes which, he had learned during his week of residence in the royal household, the Tetrarch of Galilee and his ambitious wife were constantly plotting to gain control of the entire former kingdom of Herod the Great.

ix

When he returned to the small room in the palace where he lived and carried on his studies, Prochorus found his father waiting for him. Chuza's duties were mainly confined to overseeing the fisheries and the plantations belonging to Herod Antipas in that area, so he spent little time in Tiberias. The strictly financial affairs of the Tetrarch were handled by Manaen, whose duty it was to supervise the building of the new city, and the collection and disbursement of revenues and taxes, while the markets were supervised by an official called the *agoranomus*.

"Has Mother returned from Jerusalem?" Prochorus asked.

"She and Salome, Mary Cleopas, Mary of Magdala, and the mother of Jesus came back two days ago," said Chuza.

"Does she know what really happened there?"

"Jesus was the victim of a plot—that much seems clear. But I'm sure he was innocent of any wish to rebel against Rome."

"What about John and James? And Peter and Andrew?"

"They've gone back to fishing. The trouble seems to be over— unless others continue it."

"Then you think there may still be a rebellion?"

"With Barabbas free and Manahem determined to succeed where his father failed twenty-odd years ago, I'm afraid trouble is as inevitable as the rising and the setting of the sun. I only pray that when the fires break out again the whole land will not be consumed as it almost was in the days of Judas the Gaulonite."

"Why is Prince Agrippa at Malatha, Father?"

"Why do you ask that?"

"His niece, Princess Mariamne, is here in the palace. This morning she asked me to write a letter for her to Prince Agrippa."

"Did you?" Chuza asked quickly.

"No. When I discouraged her, she decided against it."

"You were wise," said Chuza. "If you had written the letter and there should be trouble, some could claim you were a conspirator too."

"What trouble could there be?"

Chuza stepped to the door, opened it and looked out into the hall, then came back inside and shut it carefully. "The Tetrarch Philip is ill with what his physicians say is a mortal sickness. When he dies, his tetrarchate may go to Antipas."

"Why?"

"Emperor Tiberius likes Antipas and he has been careful to stay in favor with the Romans, all of which is in the Tetrarch's favor. But Tiberius is in poor health, and when Agrippa was in Rome he was careful to court Gaius—the one they call Caligula. In fact he was banished from Rome because the Emperor heard about it."

"It's like a game of dice, isn't it?"

"With very high stakes," Chuza agreed soberly. "Antipas has no children and Agrippa is well liked in Rome. If Antipas were to die—

and it wouldn't be the first time a descendant of Herod the Great suffered violent death—Agrippa would almost certainly be next in line. The area around Beersheba where Agrippa has been living is in Pontius Pilate's territory and I suspect both Pilate and Antipas are happy to have him where they can watch him closely rather than in Rome, where he could be plotting to gain the favor of the Emperor and rule here himself."

"But he is coming to Tiberias."

"When did you learn that?"

"Today—from Princess Mariamne. She says Queen Herodias interceded with the Tetrarch in Agrippa's favor and he is to be appointed *agoranomus*."

"He couldn't cause much trouble in that job—it's largely an honorary position," said Chuza. "Agrippa is Queen Herodias' brother, but if I know the Queen she is bringing him here so she can watch him. In Rome he has the reputation of being very clever." The steward smiled. "Now that you know something of palace intrigue, what do you think of it?"

"It's exciting."

"And dangerous—see that you don't get mixed up in it yourself."

"I have no intention of doing that," Prochorus assured him. "By the way, Father, did you happen to come to Magdala in our small boat?"

"Yes. Why?"

"I might be able to get home more often, if you would leave it here. Couldn't you use one belonging to the Tetrarch?"

"Of course. I should have thought of that before. The boat is tied at the quay. Come home for the next sabbath if you can—your mother and I will be happy to have you."

x

Mariamne was waiting when Prochorus descended the long stairway to the boat landing in front of the palace. For the afternoon she had changed from the Greek-style chiton she usually wore in the palace and was dressed in a colorful robe of fine cloth woven on the looms of Byblos by Phoenicians who had been clothmakers for more than a thousand years.

"You're late," she said with a hint of the same imperious tone she'd used when he first saw her only a little more than a week ago.

"My father stopped by to tell me my mother had returned safely from Jerusalem," he explained. "He left us his boat." He gestured toward a trim little craft moored to the quay and her eyes lit up with pleasure.

"I like this better than the big ones out there at the end of the quay," she said. "Come on."

Running out along the quay, she jumped down into the small craft, rocking it so dangerously that she was forced to seize the mast to keep from falling into the lake. Moving more cautiously, Prochorus stepped down into the boat and steadied it against the quay.

"I hope you know how to swim," he said.

"Probably better than you." She wrinkled her nose at him. "We used to go to Baiae with the Emperor's household in the summer, when the fever is bad in Rome. I went swimming every day there."

"You can sit at the stern," he told her and went forward to raise the sail. When it filled, the small craft began to move through the water like a spirited colt, heeling over as he steered eastward to clear the end of the quay.

"Who taught you to sail?" she asked.

"John ben Zebedee, a friend in Capernaum. We lived there for a while before we moved to Magdala."

They were out in the lake now and he changed course, steering northward about a half mile offshore. Driven by the same afternoon breeze the fishermen used to take them to the fishing grounds at the northern end of the lake with the coming of night, the spirited little boat fairly skipped over the water.

"What is that city there at the northeast end of the lake?" Mariamne asked, pointing toward a white shape upon the shore line.

"Bethsaida Julias."

"Oh, that's where Uncle Philip lives. If Uncle Agrippa hadn't taken me when my parents died, I would have been sent to him."

"What is Rome like?" he asked.

"It's crowded—and exciting." Her eyes grew bright and her cheeks pink. "There's always something going on—not like that terrible Malatha where Uncle Agrippa is." She leaned over the gunwale of the boat and trailed her fingers in the water rushing past, setting up a spray that dampened the sleeve of her robe.

"Emperor Tiberius was furious when my mother married my father. He was a tribune in the Roman Army, highborn and very handsome. Mother once said the Romans like to move the descendants of my great-grandfather Herod about like pieces on a game board. She and my father were married before the Emperor realized they were even in love; that's why my father was sent to Egypt."

"Wasn't that rather cruel?"

"Mother said those who rule often have to be cruel. They must always think of the welfare of the empire first."

"Some put ambition before that."

"I know. Aunt Herodias is always pushing Uncle Antipas, trying to make him ruler over most of the territory my great-grandfather once ruled. Uncle Agrippa wants the same thing too, and Aunt Kypros says there's bound to be a clash between them one day."

A sudden gust of wind required all of Prochorus' attention at the moment but he found himself hoping that, when the clash did come, the lovely young girl sitting there beside him on the boat wouldn't end up as simply a pawn in the dangerous game the emperors of Rome had played so many times with those who served them as client kings in the far-off reaches of the empire.

"What a lovely house!" Mariamne's cry of pleasure brought Prochorus back to the present. They were opposite Magdala now and he saw that she had spotted a beautiful home nestled against the side of the rather precipitous slope, at the foot of which was a large fishing pier with the usual shed for the preparation of fish for drying and salting.

"That's the home of Mary of Magdala," he said.

"Do you know her?"

"Very well. Her family and mine have been friends for a long time."

"Could we go ashore and visit her?"

"Of course. Father told me this morning she had returned from Jerusalem." He turned the boat in toward the shore.

"The house looks different from others along here," Mariamne observed as the boat nudged the long pier where several fishing boats were moored, their crews busy preparing the nets for the night's work. "More like a villa at Baiae."

"Mary grew up in Magdala but later went to Alexandria, where she was a famous actress and dancer," he explained. "After she was seized with the falling sickness, she had to come back to Magdala to live."

"Perhaps we shouldn't go in if she's ill."

"Jesus of Nazareth cured her. She was the leader among the women who followed him."

Dropping the sail, Prochorus went forward to secure the boat to the quay, then reached down to help Mariamne step up to the level of the pier. As they were climbing the stairway leading up from the water, a tall lovely woman with red hair appeared around the side of the house, a basket filled with flowers hanging from her arm. At the sight of the visitors she set it upon the low wall bordering the path leading down to the water and came to the head of the stairway.

"Prochorus!" she cried. "I heard you were in Tiberias with the Tetrarch."

"This is Princess Mariamne, Mary."

"How lovely you are, my dear." Mary of Magdala took the girl's hands and stood back to look at her. "I remember my mother telling me about your great-grandmother Mariamne long ago. From what she said, you must look very much like her."

"I've been told that I do." Mariamne flushed with pleasure at the compliment.

"My garden has been growing wild; I've had so little time for it lately," Mary said as they approached the house. "It will take weeks to get it back to what it was like before."

"Then you are going to stay in Magdala?" Prochorus asked.

"Until Jesus calls me for another task," said Mary. "Come inside, it's cooler there."

The house was built after the Roman style around a court where a fountain played, fed by a nearby spring. The water, like most of that bursting from the steep rocky slopes along this side of the lake, had a faintly sulphurous smell but was not at all unpleasant. The rooms were bright and airy, the furnishings mainly Greek and Roman. In every way the house showed wealth and good taste and Mariamne's eyes sparkled as Mary took them on a tour of it. Finally they came back to the small court and were served wine and sweet cakes by a serving-woman.

"You haven't told me what you are doing in Tiberias," Mary reminded Prochorus as they were eating.

"The Tetrarch's chief scribe is ill. I'm taking his place—at least for the time being."

"That is an honor!"

"If living in the servants' quarters and eating with them is high position, I have it," Prochorus said with a grin. "But I'm learning a lot and I hope to go to Alexandria soon to continue my studies."

"With Philo Judaeus?"

"If he will accept me."

"I know him well and will give you a letter of introduction to him." Mary turned to Mariamne. "Prochorus was very ill about four years ago with one of the fevers that trouble people so much in this region. The physicians at Capernaum had given him up until a friend of ours named John ben Zebedee told his father to consult Jesus of Nazareth—"

"The one who was crucified?" Mariamne asked.

"Yes. Jesus healed Prochorus without even leaving Cana. When Chuza got back from Capernaum, he found him well."

"What about the rumor that the Nazarene rose from the dead?" Prochorus asked.

"I saw him myself at the tomb on the morning of the third day," said Mary. "So did John and Peter and some of the others."

"Where is he now?" Mariamne asked.

"None of us know," Mary admitted. "We were told by an angel to return to Galilee and that he would meet us here."

Prochorus glanced quickly at Mariamne to see whether or not she realized the political significance of what Mary had said. In Jerusalem, the Tetrarch of Galilee had been able to disclaim any responsibility for Jesus of Nazareth on the grounds that the crime with which he was charged—that of blasphemy against the Temple itself—had been committed within the jurisdiction of Pontius Pilate. But if Jesus now returned to Galilee as the Messiah, claiming to have survived the crucifixion through divine intervention, even though it had been by a trick, the cry of rebellion against Rome would no doubt be raised here where the memory of Judas the Gaulonite, Manahem's father, was still warm.

Actually, a group of Galileans had tried to name the Nazarene king, after he had fed five thousand with only a handful of fish and bread. Jesus himself had forbidden them to do so then but, if he were to appear from the grave now, and summon all who would see Jews free from Rome to follow him, hardly a man in Galilee, Peraea, Judaea or even Ituraea would hesitate to take up arms.

Mariamne seemed not to realize the potentialities of what Mary had said, however. Nor indeed did the woman of Magdala herself unless she were keeping quiet about it. Nevertheless, Prochorus changed the subject.

"We should be leaving," he told Mariamne. "The evening breeze is against us and I may have to row all the way back to Tiberias."

"Will you come again?" Mary asked Mariamne. "Prochorus and I are old friends but I would like to know you better."

"Will you tell me about your life in Alexandria as an actress?" the girl asked.

"All that is behind me." For only a moment did a spasm of pain show in the older woman's lovely dark eyes, then she smiled. "But perhaps I can remember a few things that might interest you."

"She's very lovely," Mariamne said as they were going down the path to the boat landing. "I particularly like what she said about my great-grandmother. You've read a lot, Prochorus." It was the first time he remembered her using his given name and the sound of it upon her lips was very pleasant. "Did you ever read much about her?"

"That was over sixty years ago. When Herod the Great was made King of the Jews by Mark Antony."

"I know the story of Antony and Cleopatra; my teacher in Rome told us about that. But he didn't mention Great-grandfather Herod —or his Queen Mariamne."

"She was the granddaughter of Hyrcanus, who had been both High Priest and King in the line derived from the Maccabeans, or Hasmoneans, as they were called," Prochorus explained. "Mark Antony had already made Herod the Great King of the Jews and, since she was in the Hasmonean line of descent, his marriage to Mariamne strengthened his claim to the kingdom. The story is that he loved her very much but, as he grew older, he became moody and suspicious."

"Uncle Antipas is like that already."

"That's because he's never been able to get the death of John the Baptizer off his mind. Herod the Great finally became suspicious that Queen Mariamne was plotting to overthrow him and make one of her sons king, so he had her killed."

Mariamne shivered although the day was still warm. "Sometimes I almost wish I wasn't of royal birth," she said. And looking at her, so lovely, fresh and desirable, Prochorus found himself echoing her wish.

xi

Prochorus saw Agrippa for the first time a few days later, when he was sent by Antipas with a scroll of instructions for the new inspector of markets. Agrippa was a corpulent man of about forty, with bitter brooding eyes and a rather abrupt manner.

"Aren't you rather young to be the Tetrarch's scribe?" he asked as Prochorus was about to leave.

"I was studying at the university here when the royal scribe became ill," Prochorus explained. "My teacher sent me to serve in his place."

"What did you say your name was?"

"Prochorus, sir."

"That isn't an ordinary Jewish name. Are you a Jew?"

"My mother is descended from King David, sir. My father is a Greek—the steward of the Tetrarch's fisheries and plantations."

"Chuza?"

"Yes, sir."

"I know him from the markets. Do you live in the Tetrarch's palace?"

"In the servants' quarters—yes, sir."

"And you write all his letters?"

"Yes, sir." Prochorus was beginning to understand the import of the older man's questioning and was troubled by it.

"Are you ambitious?" Agrippa's eyes had lost much of their brooding look now and were filled with interest.

"I hope I am a good scribe, sir."

"Why not a lawyer? Or a Roman government official?"

"I hadn't thought much about it." If that was being less than truthful, Prochorus judged it to be the better course at the moment.

"I have friends in high places in Rome," said Agrippa. "A word from me could get you into the royal school where provincial civil servants are trained and you might even go higher than your father has gone."

"It—it's an interesting thought, sir."

"Think about it some more and come to see me again. I like to see young people who are ambitious get ahead."

Prochorus left as quickly as he could but, instead of going directly back to the palace, detoured by way of the quay at the lake level, hoping his father would be inspecting the boats which would put out at the approach of darkness for the fishing grounds. He found Chuza in the long building on the quay where the women were working on the catch of the night before.

"What do you think he meant?" Chuza asked, when he finished an account of his talk with Agrippa.

"That I should be his spy in the Tetrarch's household. What else?"

"That at the very least," Chuza agreed, "though one can never tell exactly what someone as clever as Agrippa has in mind."

"What could he do, Father? They say in the palace that the

Tetrarch only gave him the post of *agoranomus* because Lady Kypros asked Queen Herodias to find a place for him before he went mad in Malatha."

"My guess is that Antipas brought Agrippa here because he would rather have him in Tiberias under his heel than free in Idumea, where he had access to the ear of Pontius Pilate," said Chuza. "Agrippa is one quarter Jew—which is more than Herod Antipas is. Besides, he knows the ways of Rome far better than Antipas and it's rumored that the Emperor is half mad, so Agrippa could be recalled to Rome at any time."

"Are you saying I should do as he suggests, Father?"

"I think you must decide soon which way you wish to go, son. One way lies the route of the scholar and I can understand your being attracted to it. But if you believe our people and yourself are best served by the rule of Rome, much can be said for being a civil servant, as Agrippa suggested."

"Which would you choose?"

"Neither, I think now."

"Why?"

"I chose Rome when I became steward for the Tetrarch. But lately I can see merit in another course."

"What is that, Father?"

"Your mother is convinced that Jesus of Nazareth is really the Messiah and that he actually did rise from the dead. I may give up everything else and follow him."

"But surely the Messiah wouldn't have let himself be crucified."

"That troubles me too," Chuza admitted. "But if the Nazarene did rise from the dead, then he will be stronger when he appears again than he was before."

"That would mean joining the rebels?"

"Perhaps not," said Chuza. "Since I wasn't born a Jew, I don't have the same feeling about the Messiah that Jews do. It may be that what happened in Jerusalem during Passover has another meaning, though I can't say exactly what it is. The best course may be for all of us to wait—until the truth about Jesus of Nazareth is finally revealed."

xii

Prochorus was writing a letter to the Legate of Syria the next morning when the Tetrarch paused in his dictation.

"Does your mother believe this foolish rumor about Jesus of Nazareth being alive?" he asked.

"I haven't talked with her since she came back from Jerusalem, sir." It was only part of the truth, but it seemed to satisfy Antipas. Picking up a small scroll from a packet that had arrived the evening before by an imperial courier, he unrolled it and studied it for a moment, then rolled it up again.

"Pontius Pilate assures me in this letter that the rumors are without foundation," he said. "Is it true that the sons of Zebedee have gone back to fishing?"

"I believe so, sir."

"What about Simon—the one the Nazarenes called Peter?"

"I heard that he was fishing again too."

"What did Prince Agrippa offer you to spy on me?"

Antipas laughed when Prochorus gave an involuntary start. "So he rose to the bait?"

"I—I don't understand."

"Why else would I send you to him with instructions that just as well could have been given to your father, since he actually runs the markets?"

"I only obeyed your orders, sir."

"You are an unusually skilled scribe for one so young, Prochorus, but that isn't the main reason why I selected you. A ruler must have honest people to serve him, else he will be betrayed. Knowing your father as I do, I was sure you would be the same."

"Thank you, sir."

"I imagine Agrippa offered you the use of his influence in Rome and the promise of helping you get an appointment there. No, don't answer; I can see it in your face. You see, I know what he wants."

"He told me nothing, sir."

"Agrippa was quite content to stay in Rome and live in the imperial household as long as he was in favor with Tiberius. But the Emperor has retired to Capri now and sees no one from Rome, so the imperial sun no longer shines on my brother-in-law. In his case I should be hoping to be named governor of some district." Antipas grinned wolfishly. "Preferably Galilee and Peraea; or the territory of my half brother Philip when he dies."

Prochorus chose to be silent and, when Antipas spoke again, it was on a different subject.

"I sometimes wonder whether I did wrong in refusing to let Pilate shift the responsibility for sentencing the Nazarene to me." He seemed to be talking to himself as if he had forgotten he was not alone in the room. "The man was already half dead and he couldn't have been of much further use to Manahem and the fools who were using him as a tool, thinking they could overthrow Roman rule because the people would follow the Nazarene if he claimed publicly to be the Messiah. I killed one harmless prophet but I might have been able to save this one.

"Why can't the Jews content themselves with Roman rule?" Antipas continued. "They're more prosperous under it than they've ever been before. Even under David there were wars with the Philistines and rebellion and bloodshed. Solomon burdened them so heavily with taxes they were always complaining, but Rome brings peace and prosperity and the right to worship God as we choose. It is no more than right that the people should pay for peace and prosperity, yet men like Manahem and Barabbas are stirring up the rabble they lead to drench the country in blood once again."

"I never heard the Nazarene speak, sir," said Prochorus. "They say he taught only love for another."

"When Jesus was teaching in Galilee, I sent spies to listen to him because I knew some of his disciples were allied with the brigands," said Antipas. "But they discovered nothing that had not been taught by prophets before—men like Micah and Isaiah—or even Rabbi Hillel. I knew the Nazarene was innocent of any desire to rebel, so I could have saved him in Jerusalem and shut him up somewhere like Machaerus, where his followers couldn't use him to stir up trouble." He sighed. "But it's too late now."

"Not if he's still alive, sir."

"As well believe the lake out there will one day run dry. Or that my citadel will topple into the water. Pilate says in his letter that the man was unquestionably dead; one of the soldiers even had compassion upon him and thrust a spear into his side while he was still on the cross, so he wouldn't have to suffer. The Nazarene's disciples overcame the guards at the tomb by night and stole his body away so they could claim he had risen; that is the only explanation anyone with sense can believe."

Antipas suddenly thrust aside the pile of scrolls and the letter from Pontius Pilate with so sharp a gesture that some of them fell to the floor.

"We will go on with our letter," he said, and Prochorus picked up his quill once more. But he knew now what was disturbing the Tetrarch of Galilee. And he could understand—even sympathize —with Antipas who, by failing to save the Nazarene, had not only neglected an opportunity to expiate his crime in executing John the Baptizer but, if Jesus were actually the Messiah, was himself guilty of the even worse—and wholly unpardonable—crime of having helped to execute the Son of God.

xiii

The next few weeks were busy ones for Prochorus. Having been away from his new capital of Tiberias for several weeks in connection with the celebration of the Passover at Jerusalem, Antipas had received considerable correspondence which needed to be answered. Besides, Prochorus had to help Manaen with the task of keeping the treasury records, separating the tax monies, part of which must be passed on to Rome through the Procurator Fiscal of Syria, from the income earned by the Tetrarch's own vast holdings throughout Galilee and the fertile area along the Jordan south of the lake known as Peraea.

Busy in the palace most of the day, Prochorus missed many of his classes at the university and was able to keep up with his reading only by burning a candle at night long after most of the servants had gone to bed. He was well liked in the palace, however, and Manaen had placed a small room at his disposal, so he had a certain amount of privacy and a place where he could keep his scrolls and other possessions. Besides, he liked Manaen and through working with him was gaining a valuable insight into the innermost details of Roman provincial government.

He was pleased that Antipas had not sent him again to Agrippa who, Chuza said, was sulking in his small house and paying little attention to his duties as inspector of markets. The increasing amount of responsibility Antipas placed upon Prochorus required him to move about teeming Galilee frequently on confidential missions and on a journey to Capernaum he took time to meet his old friends again. He found James and John mending nets with other fishermen at the pier of the House of Zebedee, but their spirits were even more depressed than following their return from Jerusalem, for as the days passed the furor over the apparent resurrection of Jesus of Nazareth had begun to subside and the number of those who still believed him to have been the Messiah grew smaller daily.

"How can you serve the Fox," James asked Prochorus brusquely, "when he could have saved the Lord but let him die instead?"

"Would you have him hunted down for disobeying the Tetrarch?" John came to Prochorus' defense.

James shrugged and went on with his work, but John put down the ball of cord with which he had been mending the net. He was thinner than when Prochorus had seen him over a month earlier, and the normal warm light in his dark eyes was dulled by a look of sadness and grief.

"Your father says Antipas has great confidence in you," he said. "Are you happy with your work?"

"Yes—except that I have so little time for studies."

"I should have kept on with mine. Perhaps then I could understand the Master's purpose for us."

"If you would listen to me, you would know," James snapped.

"When Jesus returns, we will go on with our plans and he will rule over Jews everywhere in glory."

"I'm not at all sure that is what he meant," said John.

"You are not sure of anything any more," James said in disgust and turned to Prochorus. "Has Antipas talked to Pilate about what happened at the Passover?"

"Only by letter. The Procurator says the Nazarene's disciples stole his body from the tomb to make it seem that he had risen from the dead."

"That's a lie!" James cried. "Jesus rose on the morning of the third day."

"Where is he now?" Prochorus couldn't resist asking and for a moment it seemed that the stormy little fisherman would lash him with the length of cord he was using to repair the pursestring that drew the net shut when being used. John, however, stepped between them to protect Prochorus and James threw down the cord in digust and left the shed.

"It was a great disappointment to James and some of the others when they couldn't force the Master to declare himself King of the Jews and strike dead those who seized and persecuted him," John explained. "Besides, Manahem is continually plaguing him because he thinks we know where Jesus is and will not tell."

"Do you?"

John shook his head. "I'm not even sure it was Jesus I saw at the tomb. We were all stricken with grief and each seems to remember something different."

"Mary of Magdala is certain it was the Nazarene."

"Mary admits to having sometimes seen visions before she was cured of the falling sickness. Something like that might have happened there at the tomb."

"Are you going to continue with the teachings of the Nazarene?"

"We are as divided on that as we are on what we saw at the tomb," John admitted. "Some want to keep on with the rebellion against Rome. But if we teach publicly that Jesus is alive and will soon return to rule over us, we could be executed for treason."

"He taught other things."

"I know—and people listened because they saw him heal the sick and even give them food. But they believed he was divine, and how can we carry on his work when we don't even know whether he has been taken up into heaven? Or whether, if he did rise from the dead and will come again, it will be to rule as king?"

"Or Messiah?"

"They are the same."

"The prophet Daniel said of the Messiah or prince: '*He shall be cut off but not for himself.*'"

"I wish I were more of a scholar," John admitted. "What do you think the passage means?"

"Perhaps that he would be crucified—as the Nazarene was. The rest of it says: '*The people of the prince that shall come shall destroy the city.*'"

"Jesus foretold the destruction of Jerusalem and the Temple; that was the basis for one of the charges of blasphemy the priests brought against him. But if Daniel's prophecy is now being fulfilled, it can only mean that James and the others are right and that when he comes again, as he promised, it will be with the sword and with fire to destroy all his enemies."

"Why didn't he use that power instead of forgiving his persecutors and letting himself be crucified?"

"I have asked myself that question a dozen times each day and prayed for the truth to be revealed to me. But the Lord has turned his face away from me, even though my mother and his were sisters and we are kinsmen." John looked out across the lake and when he spoke again his voice was bitter. "Instead, Jesus chose Simon Peter to lead his disciples—even though Peter denied him thrice on the night when he was taken. What have I done to deserve such treatment from one I loved like a brother?"

Prochorus didn't answer, recognizing that nothing he said could help his friend remove the festering sore of envy and resentment whose presence had just been revealed. For as long as John ben Zebedee envied others, he was not likely to see the essential truth expressed by the Nazarene when he had said: "*You must love your neighbor as yourself.*"

xiv

In the upper section of the *ghor*—the vast rift in the earth where the Jordan pursued its winding course southward—summer was already advanced. On the hillsides of Galilee it was still spring, however, and the thorn trees planted around the vineyards to discourage both animals and men from stealing the fruit of the vines were a sea of scarlet blossoms. The daffodils that bloomed early in protected spots among the rocky areas around the lake were almost gone now, but the sea leek was in full growth, along with the lovely white blossom with its star-shaped pattern called the "flower of Sharon."

Here and there a flash of lilac color showed where the "cuckoo flowers" grew. And the carob, source of food through its pods for both animal and man, was beginning to leaf out fully, adding a touch of green to the steep slopes which had been sere and brown most of the winter.

With the advent of summer the burning heat in the deep cup where the lake lay would begin to parch most growing things. Even the fishermen would find their catches small for a season then, as the rays of sun upon the water drove the fish into the depths, from which they would reappear in great schools only with the coming of autumn and the waning of the sun.

On the Way of the Sea that circled the northern end of the lake, groups of pilgrims from Jewish communities in Babylon and elsewhere throughout the country of the Parthians began to appear, on their way to Jerusalem for the Feast of Pentecost, the second of the great religious festivals associated with the coming of warmer weather and the gathering in of the wheat harvest.

From Galilee itself, small groups of pilgrims were also preparing to start southward along the pilgrim road that led south of the lake to Scythopolis. There they would cross the river and follow the regular pilgrim route along the east bank of the Jordan through Peraea, lest they intrude into Samaria and not only become ritually unclean from contact with the hated Samaritans, but also lose their lives at the hands of those who, in their hatred for Jews, had once gone so far as to desecrate the Temple in Jerusalem.

The household of the Tetrarch Antipas was also preparing to move, its destination the magnificent summer palace at Sepphoris among the rolling hills of Upper Galilee. Prochorus was to accompany the retinue of the Tetrarch and, although there was no love between Antipas and Agrippa, the latter and his family were also to be in the party, since Antipas was not likely to leave his scheming brother-in-law alone in Tiberias where he could not be closely watched.

Mariamne, too, was going, as she told Prochorus one afternoon when, having finished the letters and records for the day, he paused in the small enclosed court with the fountain to look at the fish swimming there in the pool. He didn't realize he was not alone until he saw her reflection in the water.

"I'm surprised you even take time for something so foolish as looking in a pool." Her tone was a little tart and he remembered that he had hardly seen her at all during the weeks since they visited Mary of Magdala.

"Most of your uncle's letters these days have to be written in both Latin and Greek so a copy can be sent to Rome," he explained. "I've had little time left even for my studies, but just last night I did learn there is something to be said for looking into pools—or rather wells."

"I don't like riddles." She tossed a pebble into the pool, sending the fish scurrying and breaking up her own image into a hundred wavy fragments which quickly coalesced again into a beautiful girl as the tiny waves subsided.

"This is no riddle. Nearly three hundred years ago, someone journeying up the river Nile through the city of Syene—"

"I've been there. My father was governor of a district in Egypt when I was a little girl."

"Then you are ahead of me. I've only been as far as Jerusalem once—when I became a Son of the Commandment."

"Tell me more about Syene?"

"The traveler I was speaking of noticed that shortly after the middle of the month of Juno—according to the Roman calendar—the sun shone directly into the bottom of a well at midday."

"Showing that it was directly overhead at that time?"

"Why, yes." His surprise at her logic showed in his voice.

"Women are not so foolish as men think," she said with a sniff of disdain. "Why was that important?"

"It wasn't to most people—but to one man it did mean something. His name was Eratosthenes and he was head of the great library at Alexandria."

"I've been there too."

"The library?"

"No, Alexandria. It's hot and dirty."

"The next year Eratosthenes set up a pole in the courtyard of the library, and at noon on the same day in Juno he measured the angle cast by the shadow of the pole upon the earth. He found it to be the fiftieth part of a circle—do you know anything of the propositions of Euclid?"

"N-no."

"My father had a friend, a Greek scholar, who taught me a little about them. By using those propositions and knowing that at the same moment the sun was directly overhead at Syene, Eratosthenes was able to calculate that the angle made by the three points—Syene, Alexandria and the center of the earth—was the same as that of the shadow cast by the pole."

"The fiftieth part of a circle?"

"Yes."

"Then he had only to multiply the distance between Syene and Alexandria to know the size of the world."

"That's what he did." Prochorus was a little crestfallen that the acuteness of her mind seemed to be equal to his own. And yet he felt a warm sense of pleasure that she showed so much interest in the sort of things that interested him.

"Could I read some of the scrolls where you learned all this?" she asked.

"Of course. They're in the library of the university here at Tiberias. But most girls can't even read—except such things as how to put on powder and paint their cheeks."

"You're angry because I'm as intelligent as you are," she accused him, her eyes dancing with mischief.

"Of course not."

"But you are. I can see it." She reached out to take his hand and her voice became warm. "That's why I like you so much, Prochorus. You're not like most boys—rough and ignorant and thinking of nothing but their own pleasure."

Stunned by the sudden change in her, he was dumb. But if his tongue couldn't move, not so his heart; it was hammering away in his throat, threatening to choke him.

"That's why I picked you out for myself the first time I saw you," she confided.

"But you're a princess—"

"Really only half a princess," she corrected him. "My father wasn't of noble birth. I'd rather not be a princess either, because then the Emperor would marry me to some king in order to cement an alliance. Since I'm not, I can marry you one day."

Prochorus gulped and once again lost the power of speech.

"Say something!" she cried. "Don't you find me pretty?"

"You're the most beautiful thing I've ever seen," he said fervently.

"That's better. Of course we can't be married for a while. I'm not old enough yet and you're only a scribe, but everyone says you'll be an important man someday. Uncle Antipas already depends on you more than he does on any of the others who serve him. And Uncle Agrippa—"

She didn't go on with whatever she had intended to say, but Prochorus was too excited by what she had already said to notice the slip.

"How—" The word was little more than a squawk so he cleared his throat and tried again. "How do you know I'm worthy of you?"

"Women have an instinct for such things. Aren't you flattered that I chose you?"

"Oh yes. Very flattered."

"Now you're making fun of me." She was suddenly a little girl again. "And I don't like to be made fun of."

"I'm not. It's just that—I haven't had time to think much about such things."

"Men rarely do," she assured him. "Now that we are betrothed, don't you even want to kiss me?"

Prochorus was not so startled by what had happened that he could fail to take advantage of such an opportunity. A quick glance around told him they were unobserved, for already the shadows had begun to fall across the area where they were standing. Putting his arm about her waist, he drew her back into the shadows and was startled to feel how soft and yielding she was—and how utterly desirable.

His lips found hers and for a single instant he forgot there was anything else in the world except the two of them there—until he felt her pushing frantically against him and released her. She moved an arm's length away from him, staring at him with eyes so wide that it seemed he would drown in their depths—with no desire to escape.

"Oh!" she cried. "I didn't know it would be like this!" Turning suddenly, she ran into the house, leaving Prochorus standing by the pool and not even sure he was the same person—until he looked down and saw his own reflection in the water.

xv

Busy with preparations for moving the household of Herod Antipas to Sepphoris for the summer, Prochorus had little time in the week that followed to seek out Mariamne. When he did glimpse her occasionally in his goings and comings through the palace, he got the impression that she was avoiding him, for she quickly turned aside each time into another room though not before the sight of her made his pulse quicken with the memory of the kiss in the shadows beside the pool.

Toward the end of the week a letter came from Lucius Pomponius Flaccus, the newly appointed Legate of Syria and Antioch, requesting that Antipas meet with him and Pontius Pilate at Caesarea some three weeks hence to discuss the affairs of their several provinces. And since such a request was the equivalent of an imperial order, Antipas made plans to go on to Caesarea from Sepphoris, after leaving his family and household there.

The thought of visiting Caesarea and listening—if only in the capacity of a scribe—to the deliberations of these officials was infinitely exciting for Prochorus. But on the day before Antipas and his household were to begin the journey to Sepphoris—no more than a day's travel across the hills to the northwest in Upper Galilee— something happened that changed Prochorus' own course sharply and, indeed, was to influence his whole life.

He was busy preparing the letters he had written that morning for Herod Antipas so they would be ready for the official courier who would take them to their next point on the imperial post— the marvelously complex system of routes and stations whereby mail, both official and personal, was carried efficiently and with rather amazing rapidity throughout the empire—when a servant came to tell him that a man was asking for him at the gate of the palace.

It couldn't be his father, Prochorus was sure, for Chuza was well known in the palace and would have been admitted without question by the guards at the gate of the citadel. And he doubted that the beggar Phinehas, who served as a spy for Manahem and his brigands, would dare to seek him out in the palace. To his surprise, the visitor proved to be John ben Zebedee and Prochorus needed no second glance to realize that something dramatic indeed had happened in the period of no more than two weeks since he had last seen the slender fisherman.

At Capernaum that day, John had been depressed, his eyes dull with hopelessness and grief over the loss of one who had been almost like a brother to him. Today his shoulders were straight, his manner assured, and his eyes shone with their old light of purpose.

"You don't even look like the same person," Prochorus said. "What happened?"

"Come over here." John led the way across a space of perhaps a half dozen paces that had been left between the edge of the rocky outcrop upon which the palace stood and the wall of the building, as a protection against the natural wearing away of the cliff face by the weather. At the very edge a columned overlook had been built at a slightly lower level, with benches and a roof to protect those enjoying the magnificent view of the lake and the surrounding mountains.

"We have seen the Master again," John confided.

"When?"

"Two nights ago. Simon, Andrew, James and myself were fishing with a few others but had caught nothing. You know the spot we call the Seven Springs, don't you?"

"Yes." It was located on the shore of the lake well to the north of Tiberias between Capernaum and the fertile Plain of Gennesaret, a spot where several springs burst from the rocks.

"The cold water of the springs strikes the warm depths of the lake there," said John. "Sometimes fish will school in the shallows there, when they cannot be found anywhere else, and we hoped to catch at least enough to provide for our families. As we were approaching the shore a man was standing there. He seemed to look familiar but I couldn't see him very well and didn't even recognize his voice when he asked whether we had caught anything. But when he told us to cast our nets on the right side of the boat and we found them suddenly filled with fish that hadn't been there before, I cried out: 'It is the Lord!' "

"Was it really Jesus?"

"Yes."

"In the flesh? Or as a spirit?"

"A spirit, I think. After we had eaten and talked together he disappeared."

"Then you actually talked to him?"

"He spoke mostly to Peter, telling him to feed his sheep, but all of us realized he was telling us to go back to Jerusalem and build a congregation of our own so we may teach what we called the Way when we followed him to those who come there from all parts of the world." John's voice took on a more vibrant note, a tone of deep conviction. "After telling Peter to feed his sheep, Jesus started to walk away. Peter followed to ask more about what we should do and I was just behind him, so Peter asked, 'What about him, Lord?' "

John paused for breath. " 'If I want him to stay behind until I come,' the Master answered, speaking of me, 'what does it matter to you? You are to follow me.' "

"What did he mean by that?"

"What else except that I shall be alive to see him when he returns in glory—as he promised us before he was crucified?"

"But when will it be?"

"That doesn't matter. Jesus himself will choose the time and the place to return as the Messiah over all and I shall be there to greet him." John embraced Prochorus quickly in a gesture of parting. "The others are already on the way to Jerusalem and I must be going. The city will be filled with people for the Feast of Pentecost and we will preach to all."

"When will you come back to Galilee?"

"Who knows? Jesus told us before he was crucified to go out into the world and preach but we were afraid. Now we must begin by building a congregation in Jerusalem so we will be ready to welcome the Son of God when he returns to earth to rule there."

"Those who killed the Nazarene will oppose you," Prochorus warned.

"They crucified Jesus because they claimed he wished to become King of the Jews, but we have no political purpose. Our task is to testify that he really is the Word made flesh, the Son of God promised by the prophets and sent to bring eternal life to all who believe in him."

"The authorities may arrest you—as they did the Nazarene."

"We shall obey the law and sacrifice and pray in the Temple like everyone else does," said John. "When the chief priests and the Roman authorities see that we are not a threat to them, they will let us alone."

"What about Manahem? And the rest of the rebel elements?"

"What they do is their own concern. The Master has shown us the way to eternal life and our task now is to reveal that way to others. He has said I shall be alive to greet him when he returns so I can be sure of a high place in his kingdom."

As he stood watching the receding figure of the man who a few short weeks before had been bent and depressed with all desire to

live drained from him by the tragedy of the Passover, Prochorus
thought that, if Jesus had accomplished no more than the miracle
of giving a renewed purpose in life to John ben Zebedee, it was
all worth while. But as he turned away, the words John had told
him the Nazarene had spoken at the place of the Seven Springs
that night came once again to his mind:

*"If I want him to stay behind till I come, what does it matter to
you?"*

In his excitement over seeing the spirit of Jesus, John had taken
the words to mean that he would be alive to witness the promised
return of the man he was convinced now was the Son of God. But
to Prochorus, whose business was words, the *if* in those of the
Nazarene loomed larger. And as for John's belief that he was
assured of a high place in the coming kingdom of God on earth,
Prochorus could not put from his mind something Mary of Magdala
had once told him about a sermon in which Jesus had said: *"The
greatest among you must be your servant. Anyone who exalts himself will be humbled, and anyone who humbles himself will be
exalted."*

Book Two

ANTIOCH

John had barely disappeared from view when the slave who always followed Herod Antipas touched Prochorus on the elbow. "The Tetrarch wants you," he said.

Accustomed by now to abrupt demands, Prochorus followed the slave to Antipas' chamber. When he found his employer looking out through a window that afforded a full view of the small overlook where he and John had talked briefly just now, he understood the reason for the summons.

"Who were you talking to out there?" Antipas demanded.

"John ben Zebedee."

"From Capernaum?"

"Yes, sir."

"What did he want?"

"John is an old friend. He once arranged for me to be cured of a fever by Jesus of Nazareth."

"When was this?" Antipas asked sharply.

"Nearly four years ago, sir. John and I were friends before that but ever since then there has been a special bond between us. He came to tell me good-by."

"Where is he going?"

"To Jerusalem—for the Feast of Pentecost."

"He was just there for the Passover. What he's really going for is to stir up more trouble over the Nazarene, isn't he?"

"I'm sure John doesn't intend any such thing, sir. They are going back—"

"They?"

"The disciples of the Nazarene. Jesus appeared to them again two nights ago—"

"The man is dead!" Antipas almost shouted the words. "You read the letter from Pontius Pilate yourself."

"I think it was really his spirit they saw, sir. John said Jesus told them to go back to Jerusalem and start a congregation of their own."

"Why would they do that?"

"Many groups have their own synagogues in Jerusalem. The freed slaves call themselves the Libertines. Then there are the Alexandrians, the Cilicians and—"

"Are you telling me the followers of the Nazarene have no desire to overthrow Roman rule—or to depose me?"

"John says Jesus told them only to look after those who followed him." Prochorus thought it best not to mention that John and his fellow disciples fully expected the man, whom they now confidently believed to be the promised Messiah, to return in the flesh—and with that return to name himself king.

Antipas stroked his beard while he studied the young scribe thoughtfully. "How would you like to go to Jerusalem?" he asked at last.

"Very much, sir. But I thought I was going to accompany you to Sepphoris and Caesarea."

"You can serve me better in Jerusalem at the moment. If the followers of the Nazarene try to stir up trouble there as they intended to do at the Passover, you can learn of it and take a ship from Joppa for Caesarea. That way you can report to me before Pontius Pilate learns the details from official reports."

"Am I to spy on them, sir?"

"Call it what you will." Antipas shrugged. "If they really intend to become a peaceful congregation, you can do them a favor by making it possible for me to report to the new Legate that the connection of any Galileans with rebellion at Jerusalem is now ended."

It was a clever move and a logical one. Having newly come to Antioch as viceroy of the vast area known to the Romans as Syria— including the territory southward as far as Egypt and eastward to the always uncertain border with the Parthians—Lucius Pomponius Flaccus could hardly have much firsthand knowledge about the affairs of either Judaea under the rule of Pilate or Galilee under Antipas. And if the Tetrarch of Galilee could demonstrate a greater knowledge of events in Jerusalem and Judaea than did its own procurator, Flaccus might recommend to the Emperor Tiberius—or the freedmen who really ran the Roman Empire now through a vast and cumbersome bureaucracy—that the rule of the procurators be ended and the Holy City and its rich province be returned to the control of a descendant of Herod the Great.

"I will leave as soon as I can get some extra clothing from Magdala, sir," said Prochorus.

Antipas dismissed him then. He was descending the stairway to where the small boat his father had left at Tiberias for him was moored, intending to sail to Magdala even though one of the frequent summer storms was making up to the southeast, when he heard a familiar voice call his name. Turning, he saw Mariamne running down the steps after him.

Since the evening when she had suddenly broken from his embrace in the garden, he had been almost afraid to seek her out, being by no means certain of just what had happened to them there in the courtyard and what its portent might be. But when he saw Mariamne running down the stairway, her face flushed from the effort, he found himself filled with a sudden flooding of happiness that washed away all doubt.

"Where are you going?" she called.

"To Magdala—for more clothes."

"Are you coming back here?" She had now arrived, panting, beside him.

"Yes."

"Take me with you."

"Of course. Be careful where you step." Putting his hands around her waist, he lifted her down into the boat. It rocked a little with the weight of both of them and for an instant her eyes, warm and bright, and her lips, soft and moist, were hardly a hand's breadth from his own. Moved by an impulse stronger than his will, he leaned forward to kiss her, but she drew back.

"Not here—where everyone can see," she protested in a whisper.

"I don't care—"

She grinned impishly. "Unless you're ready to marry me and support me as a princess should be supported."

The words were like a cold douche upon his impulse and he released her, turning to loosen the lines holding the boat against the pier. "Forgive me for presuming, Princess," he said a little stiffly.

"I said don't kiss me *here*—not don't kiss me *at all*." She settled comfortably on the after thwart of the boat. "Why else do you think I ran after you?"

"You haven't been running after me much lately." He went forward to raise the sail, still a little peeved at her for emphasizing the difference in their status.

"I was too forward the other evening in the court," she admitted. "The way I felt when you kissed me scared me."

"Scared you? Why?"

"You know perfectly well why. Another moment and I would probably have behaved like a hussy."

Startled a little at her frankness—and quite entranced with the picture it conjured up—Prochorus said with a grin, "I'm sorry I let you go—since you're such a weakling."

"Weakling!" For a moment he thought she was going to smash the steering oar over his head and prepared to fend it off. Instead, she put it into the water, making the boat suddenly veer and the sail flap dangerously in the freshening breeze as it jibed, almost tumbling him into the lake.

"A woman is more than the equal of a man any day," she said and, busy scrambling to maintain his footing, he had little choice except to agree.

"Why do you need more clothing?" she asked, when he finally controlled the sail and took a seat upon the after thwart with her, putting his hand over hers on the steering oar.

"I'm going to Jerusalem."

"Why?"

"Your uncle is sending me there on a confidential mission. When it's finished, I will embark at Joppa and join him at Caesarea."

"Then I shall not see you for several weeks?"

"The conference at Caesarea is three weeks from now and I imagine the Tetrarch will return to Sepphoris immediately afterward. I will be with him."

"Why is he sending you to Jerusalem now?"

"Jesus of Nazareth appeared to his disciples a few nights ago and commanded them to return there and pick up work again. Your uncle wants to know what happens."

"Will you miss me while you're gone?"

"Of course. But the more the Tetrarch trusts me, the more important my position will be—for the future."

The answer seemed to satisfy her, for she squeezed his hand on the oar and began to chatter about other things. The boat soon nudged the pier of Antipas' fisheries project at Magdala but when they reached Prochorus' home they discovered that Joanna was away at Capernaum, helping Salome, the mother of James and John, care for Mary of Nazareth, the mother of Jesus, who had returned with the other women from Jerusalem.

It didn't take him long to gather up a few changes of clothing which he made into a bundle and slung over his shoulder. A brief period was required to claim the kiss Mariamne had promised him as they were leaving Tiberias, and when they came out of the house he saw that the storm, one of the many that often flogged the lake in summer and made fishing hazardous, had been coming up rapidly from the south. Looking at the dark mass of clouds and the way the wind was already whipping the surface of the lake into a froth, he knew he couldn't risk Mariamne's life on the lake in the little boat for the return journey.

"We'll have to walk back to Tiberias," he told her. "The storm is coming up too fast."

"What about the boat?"

"It belongs to my father. I'm not going to be here for several months, so I can leave it tied to the pier." He glanced down at the thin-soled sandals she wore. "I'm afraid those won't last long on the road, though. Maybe Mother has a pair you could wear."

The sandals they found were somewhat too large, but had strong soles of wood that could withstand the rocky road across the hills between Magdala and Tiberias, so she put them on and he stowed hers in his pack.

"I like this better anyway," Mariamne confided, as they climbed the rocky hillside back of the house to reach the main road leading along the crest of the ridge to Tiberias. At another time Prochorus would have been pleased by her obvious happiness at being with him, but a danger much worse than the roughness of the road or the nearness of the storm troubled him now—though he tried not to let Mariamne see it as they took the road across the hills.

She chattered gaily as they walked along hand in hand, skipping every now and then with happiness in spite of the size of his mother's sandals. But she gave a gasp of startled surprise when, at the crest of the rocky hill between the two cities, a man with a spear in his hands stepped out into the road from a crevice in the rocks and lowered the shaft to bar their way.

As Mariamne instinctively moved close to him, Prochorus gave her hand a reassuring squeeze. Unarmed as he was, it would be futile to oppose the brigand. But when he saw the avid look in the man's eyes as they centered upon the girl, he decided to attack with the only weapon he had.

"My name is Prochorus," he announced boldly. "I am a friend of Manahem."

Reluctantly their captor took his eyes from Mariamne but even that small change told Prochorus he had been right in assuming that this was one of Manahem's men, posted as a sentry to watch the road.

"Where are you going?" the man demanded.

"To Tiberias. I am a scribe in the service of the Tetrarch Herod Antipas."

"And the girl?"

"She is the Tetrarch's niece, Princess Mariamne."

"A princess—and a scribe?"

"I'm also a friend of James ben Zebedee. Manahem will be angry if we are not allowed to go on."

The man's reaction to the mention of James confirmed Prochorus' belief that the older of the sons of Zebedee was much more closely allied with the brigand element among the followers of the Nazarene than was his brother.

"You know so much of Manahem," said the brigand. "Tell me who is his chief spy in Tiberias?"

"A one-eyed beggar named Phinehas."

It was the right answer and the sentry stood aside for them to pass, though not in the direction of Tiberias.

"I will take you to Manahem," he said. "But make no false move or you will feel the point of my spear."

When their captor pointed to a crevice in the rocks, Prochorus stepped through it, holding Mariamne by the hand. The crevice gave access to a path that wound upward for a climb of perhaps a quarter of an hour, during which they passed two other sentries, equally as fierce-looking as their own captor. By the time the path ended at the mouth of one of the caves with which this whole area was pocked, the rain had already begun so they were glad to step inside.

The cave looked as if it had been the headquarters of the robbers for a long time, confirming the fact that Manahem had made some sort of an agreement with the Tetrarch of Galilee to let him operate here so close to the new provincial capital without fear of being hunted down. Such an arrangement could conceivably serve three purposes, as far as Antipas was concerned. It would bring in money, help to keep his own dominion relatively peaceful and, probably most important of all, cause trouble for the Procurator of Judaea and nearby Samaria, since from the base in the hills the brigands could launch raids on several important roads along which both Roman troops and merchant caravans often moved.

Manahem had apparently been somewhere nearby, for he came into the cave a few minutes later, accompanied by Harith, the brother of Judas of Kerioth.

"What were you doing on the road from Magdala in the middle of the week?" he demanded.

"The Tetrarch is sending me to Jerusalem," Prochorus explained. "I sailed home to get some clothing but the storm caught us so we decided to return by land. This is Princess Mariamne—of the Hasmonean house."

Prochorus had deliberately identified Mariamne as a descendant of the Maccabees, who had successfully defied a Greek overlord centuries before, knowing they were heroes in Jewish history almost equaling David and Solomon.

"You need have no fear of us, Princess," Manahem said courteously to Mariamne, then turned back to Prochorus. "Why are you going to Jerusalem?"

"For the Feast of Pentecost. I was hurrying to catch up with John."

"John ben Zebedee?" The brigand's look of surprise told Prochorus he had not yet heard about the return of the Galileans to the Holy City. "Why would he be going back to Jerusalem?"

"Jesus appeared to some of his disciples at the Seven Springs one night when they were fishing and told them to go back."

"The Nazarene is dead," Harith said sharply. "How could he appear to them?"

"The disciples think it was his spirit. John stopped at Tiberias this morning to tell me they were going back to Jerusalem."

"And Antipas is sending you there to spy on your friends?" Manahem asked.

"Not to spy." Prochorus flushed. "Only to report what they do."

"Why don't you admit that you were snooping among the rocks, hoping to find our hiding place and betray us to the Romans for the reward?" Harith demanded.

"Would I have brought Princess Mariamne if I had wanted to spy on you?"

"I can think of many reasons why a man would bring a beautiful young girl to a place where there are caves," Harith sneered.

Momentarily blind with anger, Prochorus lunged toward him and in an instant the shining *sicarius* was plucked from its scabbard. The brigand waited, grinning with anticipation, but Manahem reached out a brawny arm and stopped Prochorus.

"Put up your dagger, fool!" The brigand leader's voice was icy when he spoke to his lieutenant. "We know the Fox would like nothing better than to lure Pontius Pilate into mingling the blood of the Nazarene's disciples with the sacrifices in the Temple, as he did when Barabbas was captured last winter. And Princess Mariamne is too valuable a pawn in the game Antipas is playing with Aretas for him to let her be with someone he didn't trust implicitly."

Harith shrugged and slid the knife back into its scabbard, but Prochorus knew he had gained an enemy.

"What are the Nazarene's disciples planning to do in Jerusalem?" Manahem asked.

"John says they are going to establish a congregation there and wait for Jesus to return."

"When will that be?"

"He's sure it will be soon. Jesus himself told John he would still be alive when it happens."

Manahem stroked his beard thoughtfully for a moment, then turned to Mariamne. "I hope you will forgive us any discomfort we have caused you, Princess," he said with the same courtesy he had shown her ever since he had come into the cave.

"I haven't been uncomfortable at all," she told him with a smile. "You aren't nearly as fierce as I expected."

"And you are as lovely as your great-grandmother was," he assured her. "I remember my father speaking of her."

"I think the rain has already stopped," said Prochorus. "Can we go now?"

"You are free," the brigand assured him. "But it might be just as well, Princess, if you didn't mention your visit here to your uncle."

Only when they were safely down the path from the cave and again on the road to Tiberias did Prochorus dare to breathe deeply once more. At the outskirts of the city they met the beggar Phinehas, puffing up the hill toward the bandit's lair. Prochorus could guess the news Phinehas was taking his master—and what his displeasure would be at finding out that another had been before him. But he wasn't really troubled about the beggar, sensing that, where Manahem was concerned, he was amply protected—at least at the moment. What did worry him was Manahem's reference to Harith concerning the game Antipas was playing with his former father-in-law, King Aretas of Nabatea, and particularly Mariamne's role of the pawn in it.

But she seemed not to have noticed what the brigand had said, so he didn't mention this to her either.

ii

Since he was planning to leave early the next morning, Prochorus said good-by to Mariamne in the palace garden before going to his quarters in the servants' area that night. When he finished the evening meal and returned to his small room, he found Manaen, in his capacity as Antipas' treasurer, waiting with a purse to cover his expenses for the journey to Jerusalem and Caesarea.

"I was collecting taxes in Taricheae today," said Manaen. "Everyone was talking about a rumor that Jesus had been seen somewhere around the lake. But no one seemed to know where."

Prochorus told him of John's visit and of the sudden change in the future plans of the Nazarene's disciples.

"He promised to return—and he has kept his word." Manaen's voice was vibrant, just as John's had been this afternoon. "This time we must not fail him."

"What do you mean?"

"Jesus once said: '*If any man serves me, he must follow me, wherever I am.*' He has sent the others to Jerusalem, so that is where he will come when he returns. I must go there too."

"But it will mean giving up everything you have here."

"The Master also said there would be no profit for a man if he gained the whole world but lost his own soul," said Manaen. "Even though I possessed the riches of my kinsman, Antipas, I would still have to give them up and follow where Jesus leads me. What time are you leaving tomorrow?"

"At dawn."

"I will join you on the road southward," Manaen promised. "Fortunately, my accounts are already in order in preparation for the journey to Sepphoris. Only today's collection remains to be put into the treasury and I shall be ready."

True to his promise, Manaen was waiting for Prochorus when he left Tiberias at dawn. The sun was just rising above the hills to the east of the lake, revealing the tablelands of the district called Gaulonitis—from whence had come Judas, the father of Manahem, one of the many false Messiahs who had lured the Jews into rebellion. Farther south on the other side of the Jordan, the mountains of Bashan and Gilead, famed in the colorful stories of the Jewish scriptures, could be seen, still in the shadow of night because the sun had not yet topped them. To the right were Mount Tabor, the mountains of Gilboa, and the northern side of the Valley of Jezreel.

Behind them to the north as they followed the road along the shore toward Taricheae and the outlet of the lake into the lower

Jordan, the sun's rays bathed the snow-crowned peak of Mount Hermon with a pinkish hue. The roadway was a busy one for, though much of the traffic between the cities of the lake region was by water, produce from the inland farms and from the Plain of Gennesaret to the north poured into Tiberias by cart and muleback each morning, ready for the opening of the markets there.

Some two hours' walk southward brought Manaen and Prochorus to Taricheae, where they paused to buy bread and cheese from a roadside vendor. All along the shore of the lake, springs burst from the sides of the rocky cup surrounding it. And, wherever there was an area of level land, fields were ready to harvest, the wheat beginning to ear and the figs in full blossom. Other growing things were in equally bountiful profusion, with thorn and oleander forming an almost impenetrable thicket along the shore of the lake between the cities.

Prochorus had not taken this route since he was thirteen and his parents took him to Jerusalem for the Passover in celebration of his becoming a Son of the Commandment, responsible in his own right for obedience to the laws of Moses and therefore no longer a child. Now he found himself reveling in the panorama of beauty as he looked back along the lake shore and saw the water dotted with the multicolored sails of the fishing fleet returning to their home ports after the night's labor, ready to disgorge their catch upon the piers, where women had already gathered in the long sheds to begin the day's work of cleaning, salting and drying.

Soon they passed through the rift in the rocky cup where the Jordan poured southward once again, after its brief expansion as the Sea of Galilee, and the lake itself was shut from view. Now the whole character of the terrain changed with startling suddenness. Known for countless ages as "the desert," this region just south of the lake was rocky, bare and forbidding, with the Jordan tumbling between steadily deepening banks on the way to its final terminus in the Salt Sea. No city of any importance was near the stream. But on the west side, well away from the river, lay Scythopolis, the thriving Decapolis city that was the only one of the ten largely Greek centers ruled directly from Antioch by the Legate on that side of the Jordan.

Crossing the river opposite Scythopolis along the pilgrim road, the travelers ascended somewhat to follow a route that traversed the beginning of a succession of tablelands rising toward the mountain range that shut away, as if by a physical barrier, the encroaches of the great desert to the east.

Here, at the edge of the Arabian plateau between Mount Gilead and the river, the country was well adapted to the flocks and herds of the dark-skinned, fierce-looking men who were its major inhabitants. Though the territory was nominally under the rule of Herod Antipas, the people of the countryside were largely Nabateans, giving allegiance to King Aretas at his capital of Petra far to the south at the eastern edge of the Arabah, the continuation of the great rift of the *ghor* southward from the Salt Sea, rather than to the Tetrarch of Galilee and Peraea.

At Pella, a small city with a fairly large Jewish colony, the travelers spent the night at the caravansary on the outskirts of the town. Several times during the night, Prochorus awakened with a chilly feeling, although the temperature here in the depths of the *ghor* was now that of midsummer. And, in the morning when they resumed their journey, his very bones seemed to ache with a feeling he remembered experiencing once before, just before the onset of the fever of which Jesus of Nazareth had cured him.

He said nothing to Manaen, who was anxious to push on and learn the sort of reception the disciples of the Nazarene had found waiting for them in Jerusalem. But the fever grew worse as the travelers continued southward and, though Manaen hired a mule on the third day for Prochorus to ride, by the time they reached Jericho, still a hard day's journey from Jerusalem, he could go no farther. Fortunately, since Manaen was a relative of the Tetrarch and was known at Antipas' winter palace in Jericho, quarters were provided for them there. At Prochorus' insistence, Manaen went on to Jerusalem the next day, placing the now delirious patient in the care of a Greek physician who served the household of Antipas when he was in residence at Jericho. And under the Greek's treatment, mainly a noxious concoction made from the essence of several barks and herbs, Prochorus slowly threw off the fever.

Built upon an oasis in the desert country just north of the Dead Sea, Jericho was watered by a number of springs that burst from the limestone range forming the west bank of the Jordan in this area. Surrounded by green fields irrigated by the waters of a brook called Kelt issuing from the so-called Fountain of Elisha, and replete with elaborate gardens and beautiful homes of Romans like Pontius Pilate, who preferred it as a winter resort, Jericho was surpassingly beautiful even in summer.

Since he was on his first mission of importance, however, Prochorus was anxious to go on to Jerusalem and a week after the departure of Manaen undertook the long ride. By then the Feast of Pentecost was over and, even if he had not been in a hurry to complete his journey, rumors of strange events in the Holy City would have been enough to draw him there.

iii

Looking down upon Jerusalem from the tower called Phasael, part of the great citadel-palace built by Herod the Great to guard the western approaches of the city from Bethlehem, Hebron and Idumea to the south, as well as the seaport of Joppa on the coast less than a day's journey away to the west, Prochorus felt little of the sense of lofty exaltation that had gripped him the first time he saw the Holy City.

At thirteen his first glimpse of the Temple, its golden roof shining in the afternoon sunlight when he came around the shoulder of the Mount of Olives on the road from Jericho, had so filled him with emotion that he hadn't been able to speak. And when he had made his first sacrifice the next morning—even though it was only a dove purchased at the lower level of the Temple and plucked out of the dirty crate in which it had been brought to Jerusalem from the spot in Galilee called the Valley of the Doves, where thousands of the birds lived and built their nests—his heart had been almost ready to burst.

Returning to Jerusalem some five years later now, and under considerably different circumstances, he saw things today that his eyes had overlooked on that previous occasion. The narrow, dirty streets. The beggars displaying deformed limbs, rubbing sightless eyes, uncovering festering sores to create sympathy. The merchants hawking their wares, eager to cheat unsuspecting pilgrims. The rabble of thieves and pickpockets, known to be at the beck and call of the High Priest, who had shouted so loudly for the crucifixion of Jesus of Nazareth that Pontius Pilate had finally given the order. The haughty Pharisees, each seeking to outdo the other in the length of the tassels upon his robe, the size of the leather phylactery at his forehead, or his pious shouting of prayer in public places. All of these were only too evident now in the city that was a holy shrine to Jews everywhere and, for that reason alone, should have represented everything that was sacred to a people who claimed to have been selected by their God above all others.

Besides, Jerusalem was not even ruled now by a Jew but by a Roman politician bent on accumulating enough wealth through bribery and taxes during his brief stay in a foreign land to enable him to live in ease and luxury the rest of his life, so it was all very depressing to one who had not yet recovered completely from the fever that had felled him on the road to Jericho and could walk only a little distance without sitting down to rest.

The chamberlain at the Palace of Herod either knew nothing or—more likely—did not wish to tell of the strange events, rumors of which had brought Prochorus to Jerusalem against the advice of his physician. Rumors that told of strange happenings indeed, of the largely unlettered fishermen from Galilee who had made up the company of Jesus' closest disciples speaking in strange tongues, of flames darting about within the building where they were meeting but causing no damage to it, and of a great rushing wind that swept through part of the city, filling everyone with fear and terror.

The reports he'd heard in Jericho and along the way were so varied that Prochorus was inclined not to put much credence in them, knowing that in an excited crowd of people even minor events could be magnified as they went from tongue to tongue. On one account, however, all agreed: Simon Peter and John ben Zebedee had emerged as the unquestioned leaders of the little company.

From the balcony of a house in the southern part of the city,

Peter had spoken on the day of Pentecost with a fire and eloquence no one had known he possessed, denouncing the High Priest for slaying the man he named the Son of God, the Expected One of the prophets. On that day, too, more than three thousand people were reported to have followed Peter's bidding that they repent and be baptized after the fashion of the Nazarenes, making the newest of Jerusalem's more than a hundred congregations the largest in the city.

As Prochorus was starting down from the tower, a servant came to announce that two men were waiting for him below. One of them, he saw when he came across the inner court of the palace, was Manaen; the other was a slender youth of about his own age.

"This is Mark," said Manaen. "He is a scribe like yourself."

"Shalom, Mark," said Prochorus and smiled. "Right now I doubt that I could lift an ink board."

"Are you well enough for a half hour's walk?" Manaen asked. "I am anxious for you to see John and Peter."

"If we go slowly I can make it," said Prochorus.

"It's only into the Lower City," said Mark. "To my mother's house."

"The place from which Simon Peter spoke?"

"What do you know of that?" Manaen asked.

"Even in Jericho people were talking of three thousand led by Simon Peter in one day to follow the Nazarene. Is it true?"

"All you heard is true—and more," said Manaen. "You'd better take a cloak against the coolness of the evening, in case we are late returning. The weather is much different here than it was in Galilee."

At Mark's home on the lower slope of the Tyropean Valley, in the older and poorer section of Jerusalem, Prochorus found a warm welcome from John and others among the disciples of the Nazarene. The upper room of the house seemed to be their headquarters and Mark proudly identified the balcony outside as the very spot from which Peter had delivered his stirring sermon on the day of Pentecost.

"When Manaen brought word of your illness, we started praying for your recovery," John told him. "When did you reach Jerusalem?"

"Yesterday."

"Why didn't you send word to us that you were here?"

"Because I had almost decided not to seek you out at all."

"Why?"

"While I was recovering from the fever, I had a chance to think about the reasons for my coming here," Prochorus confessed. "Antipas helped destroy the Nazarene and I think he would destroy the rest of you, if he could be sure you plan a revolt. When I heard about what happened here at Pentecost, I knew I couldn't spy upon friends, so I decided not to make a report at Caesarea at all, but to try to get a ship for Alexandria from Joppa."

"But we want Antipas and Pilate and the new Legate to know that we wish no rebellion."

"What about Manahem and those who seek to overthrow Rome?"

"Some of those who dreamed of using Jesus to stir up the people for rebellion still hoped to carry out their purpose after we came back," John admitted. "My brother James was even torn by two desires for a while. But when the Holy Spirit came upon us all here in the upper room that day, everything connected with a rebellion among us was swept away."

"How?"

"Simon Peter can tell you that better than I."

"Is he really to be the leader of your congregation?"

"Peter was selected by Jesus." For an instant a spasm of pain passed over the mobile features of John ben Zebedee and Prochorus realized how deep was his friend's disappointment that Peter—and not he who had been so close to Jesus of Nazareth—had been chosen. "After all, Peter is older and stronger than I—and a natural leader of men."

When John introduced Prochorus to the man who had been known as the strongest and most successful fisherman in all of the lake region, he could find no reason to argue with the decision, for Simon Peter was tall, broad-shouldered, with an almost majestic face.

Just so, Prochorus thought, Moses must have looked striding along at the head of the Children of Israel on their epic journey out of Egypt through the perils of the wilderness. There was an air of assurance about Simon Peter, too, a quiet strength and lack of fear oddly at variance with the story he had heard that, on the night when Jesus had been taken prisoner, this same man had three times denied any connection with the Nazarene in his hour of greatest need. Looking at him now, it was hard to believe he had ever been afraid or had cowed in hiding, while Jesus was being scourged by the Romans and mocked by Antipas and his court.

"This is Prochorus ben Chuza, Peter," said John.

"The boy Jesus healed of the fever long ago?"

"Yes. He now serves as chief scribe for Herod Antipas."

"The Tetrarch sent me here to find out why you and the others returned to Jerusalem," Prochorus explained. "I was to report to him in Caesarea where he is meeting with Pontius Pilate and with Lucius Pomponius Flaccus, the new Legate of Syria."

"Was to report? Then your instructions have been changed?"

"No. I have decided to make my way to Alexandria and find employment there in a scriptorium."

"Did your conscience lead you to this decision?" Peter asked. "Or the desire to go to Alexandria?"

"My conscience," Prochorus admitted. "As long as I was convinced that you had come here mainly to organize another synagogue, I thought I might help by reporting that you and your group are no threat to either the Tetrarch or the Procurator."

"Why did you change your mind?"

"I heard about the three thousand. And I know about Manahem and Harith."

"Are you afraid you may do us harm by revealing our activities here in Jerusalem?"

"If you are planning rebellion—yes."

"Jesus sent us back only to organize a congregation and make preparations for his coming," Simon Peter assured him. "We are here to do the Master's will—nothing else."

"Do you still oppose the Temple authorities?"

"We teach that Jesus came as the Messiah, was crucified and rose from the dead. And we ask only that those who would have eternal life believe in him and be baptized as a token of that belief. Go to Caesarea, Prochorus. Go even to Alexandria, Rome, or wherever you will and tell what you have heard here—that all men who believe can be saved."

"You have seen that we live as other Jews live," said Manaen as he and Prochorus were walking back to Herod's palace together after the brief talk with Simon Peter. "We make sacrifices in the Temple and pray as others do and we pay the tribute demanded of us by the law—both to the Temple and to Rome. Who can say we are in rebellion against anyone?"

"Some will still believe it."

"Not after tomorrow."

"What is to happen then?"

"John is convinced that we must prove our right to exist on the same basis as other congregations in Jerusalem. To do that the truth that Jesus is the Son of God and that he rose from the dead must be preached from the Porch of Solomon in the Temple. He has persuaded Simon Peter to go with him there, when the gates are opened tomorrow."

"They could be walking into a trap."

"John says it must be done—and Peter agrees." They were at the gate of Herod's palace now but Manaen refused Prochorus' invitation to come inside. "Come to the Temple tomorrow morning and listen," he urged. "You will hear eloquence you never believed a mere man could possess."

iv

People were beginning to move toward the Temple from all directions early the next day, when Prochorus joined the stream of pilgrims and faithful who went every morning to pray before beginning their daily activities. Crossing a bridge that spanned the Tyropean Valley and gave access to the sanctuary area, he entered the Royal Porch through a gate near the southwest corner and moved on toward the Court of the Gentiles which occupied the lower level of the Temple itself.

He saw John and Peter almost immediately, for the latter was easily distinguishable because of his rather commanding height. They were moving through the crowd, and Prochorus quickened his pace, hoping to intercept them and perhaps persuade his old friend against what he was convinced was an unwise move so soon after the tragic events of the Passover. Before he could reach them, however, they came to what was called the Beautiful Gate.

A beggar seated by the gate was calling for alms in a whining voice and pointing to his flaccid and useless legs. When Peter stopped beside the beggar his bulk made it difficult for anyone to pass through the gate and the press of the crowd backed up rapidly behind him, as those in the rear, thinking something unusual was happening, tried to press forward.

"I have neither silver nor gold but I will give you what I have." Peter's voice with its somewhat rough Galilean accent rose above the noise of the crowd as he spoke to the beggar. "In the name of Jesus Christ, the Nazarene, walk."

A hush of expectancy had fallen over the crowd at his words; it was replaced by a murmur of excitement, when Peter reached down to give the cripple his hand and lift him to his feet. At first the man stepped fearfully, as if uncertain of just what had happened to him. But as the realization that he was actually healed finally came to him, he began shouting the news of his cure. And it did indeed seem that a miracle had occurred, for the cripple who had appeared to be completely paralyzed was now leaping about like a youth in the full possession of his strength.

Peter did not remain with the man he had healed, however. Accompanied by John, he passed through the gate and made his way toward the cool shadows of the Porch of Solomon, where the rabbis customarily taught their pupils and answered questions put to them by onlookers. Ascending one of the low platforms on which the teachers usually sat at a slight elevation above their pupils, Peter began to speak. And as his voice rolled out across the crowd now thronging the porch, drawn by the swiftly spreading news of the seemingly miraculous cure of the paralytic, Prochorus was startled once again by the compelling majesty of the man who, until only a little more than a week ago, he had known by reputation as a relatively unlettered fisherman of Galilee.

Tersely but eloquently, Simon Peter assured his listeners that only faith in Jesus of Nazareth had given him the power to perform miracles, denying any power of his own. He went on to name the Nazarene as the Son of God and testified to his death on the cross and his resurrection, urging the listeners to repent of their sins so they, too, would be ready when Jesus came again in his role of Messiah.

So strong was the power of the big Galilean's preaching that Prochorus himself felt a strong urge to join those who were surging forward, begging to be accepted into the company Peter described as awaiting the return of Jesus of Nazareth. Then a new sound, that of marching feet, shattered the spell the speaker had cast upon his audience. Turning his head in the direction of the new sound, Prochorus saw a detail of Temple guards making its way along the porch.

The guards stopped before Peter and John but neither of the men showed any sign of fear or sought to escape. In fact, the light of excitement and exaltation in John's eyes made Prochorus wonder whether he, at least, had not actually courted arrest by accompanying Peter and encouraging him to preach so boldly in a place ordinarily reserved only for the learned rabbis who made much of their high position as teachers from the Porch of Solomon. Then the detail of guards swept the prisoners away, and they were lost from Prochorus' sight.

Although only little more than a week remained before he was to report to Antipas at Caesarea, Prochorus decided not to go to Joppa at once, but to remain in Jerusalem for a few days and try to determine what promised to be the fate of the two prisoners. He knew the Great Sanhedrin met only twice a week but it was common gossip in Jerusalem that people were often held in dungeons for months without being brought before the court, so he expected no news of Peter and John when he visited the house of Mark the next afternoon. To his surprise and joy, however, he found both of them there, rejoicing with other members of the band at their deliverance from prison. With so many coming and going, Prochorus wasn't able to get any details of what had happened, until he managed to gain John's attention and the two of them went to another room.

"How did you escape?" Prochorus asked.

"We made no attempt to escape," said John. "The Priestly Council heard our case this morning."

"The same group that condemned Jesus to death?"

"Yes. When we challenged them to judge whether it was right in the sight of God to listen to them more than we did to God himself, they could not hold us."

"Do you think the Sanhedrin will leave you in peace?"

"Why shouldn't they? We teach only the words of the Son of God." Obviously a change had come over his friend since the night before, and Prochorus thought he might have the answer.

"You deliberately provoked a test of strength between you and Peter and the priestly authorities, didn't you?" he asked.

"Why would I do that?" John asked—with a grin.

"To settle once and for all whether the power of the Nazarene has been transferred to you. And to build up the courage of any who might be afraid."

"You are wiser than your years, my young friend," John told him. "I never doubted the power, after the Holy Spirit filled me here on the day of Pentecost. But there were some who still needed strengthening."

"Why didn't you heal the cripple yourself yesterday? And speak from the Porch of Solomon?"

"When I saw you on the road outside Tiberias a few weeks ago, I was elated because Jesus had promised that I would be alive to meet him when he comes again. I even yielded to the sin of being proud, but on the way to Jerusalem, I remembered the Master's teaching that he who would be first must be the servant of all— and understood at last why he chose Simon Peter to be our leader and spokesman."

"I still don't understand—especially after he denied Jesus."

"Peter is big and men naturally look up to him, while I am ordinary in every way—"

"Except in intelligence—and enthusiasm."

"They are worth something, too, but the average person doesn't appreciate them as you do. People will listen to Simon Peter, because he is big and strong."

"Someone must still write the words."

"Jesus did that. I can lay no claim to even so much as an *iota* or an *aleph*."

"You have the gift of being able to persuade others to do what you wish."

"Only if I am convinced that what I wish is best for them. And more important, for spreading the good news about the Son of God." John changed the subject. "When do you leave for Caesarea?"

"I plan to go to Joppa tomorrow and take ship there. Now that you are free, there is no need for me to stay here."

"Tell Antipas and Pilate—and the new Legate—that we Nazarenes seek to save men's souls. The only rebellion we would foment is one against sin."

"I shall pray for your continued safety—and for the success of your work," Prochorus promised. But he didn't remind John that those who did not believe Jesus of Nazareth was the promised Messiah could hardly be expected to grant his followers immunity forever because they taught in his name. That John would discover this for himself—and probably before long—he did not doubt for a moment. Yet he was sure that, when the time came, the new John ben Zebedee would face it as calmly as he had faced arrest by the same people who had brought about the death of the man he believed to be the Son of God.

v

At Joppa, ships were not able to anchor close in because the water was shallow for some distance offshore. Travelers debarking and embarking were therefore carried through the usually low surf upon the shoulders of fishermen, who extracted an exorbitant fee for the service. Since most of those coming and going were pilgrims, however, and since debarking at Joppa saved them the several days' journey involved in leaving ship at Caesarea and ap-

proaching Jerusalem from the north across brigand-infested mountain trails, they were quite willing to pay the extra fee.

Prochorus obtained passage on a coastal vessel the day after he
reached Joppa. The weather was good and, with the wind steady,
the small ship made good time, depositing him at Caesarea a little
over twenty-four hours later.

Guarding the harbor of Caesarea was another of the palace-citadels
built by Herod the Great. Constructed according to the Roman
fashion, it served as both living quarters and fortress. Behind it,
against the hills, stood a magnificent amphitheater from which, as
he debarked on the massive mole of stone blocks extending out
into the water for half a mile in a curving line, Prochorus could
hear the roar of the crowd attending one of the gladiatorial games
that were an important part of Roman life, even in the provinces.

Caesarea was a busy, prosperous and thoroughly pagan city. The
harbor was filled with shipping and the streets, he saw as he moved
through them toward the palace, were lined with shops where
everything was for sale from the delicate glassware of the Phoenicians
to the parchment sheets of Byblos—already taking the name of the
city that produced them—and tiny images of pagan gods and
goddesses fashioned by the furnaces and hammers of the silversmiths who always made up a considerable part of the artisan
population in these cities. At the palace, Prochorus identified himself as the scribe of the Tetrarch of Galilee and Peraea and was
taken immediately to a chamber where Antipas met him.

"I didn't send you to Jerusalem to gawk at the Temple like a
pilgrim," the Tetrarch said shortly. "Why did you take so long?"

Prochorus explained his having become ill, the week's stay at
Jericho and his arrival in Jerusalem to learn of the startling events
of the day of Pentecost among the followers of the Nazarene.

"How do they explain what happened?" Antipas demanded.

"John says the Holy Spirit came upon them."

Antipas frowned. "What is that?"

"I don't know, sir—unless they were seized by the power and
presence of God, like the holy prophets of old. But, whatever
happened, none of them is the same."

"In what way?"

Prochorus described the change in John and, from what he had been able to learn, in Peter also. When he came to the healing of the paralytic and the trial before the subcourt of the Sanhedrin, the Tetrarch's face grew thoughtful.

"You have done well," he said at the end of the account. "Beginning tomorrow, you shall be given the pay of my chief scribe."

"Thank you, sir."

"It is little enough, since you've been doing his work for several months. Hold yourself in readiness this evening after I have dined with the Procurator and the Legate to report to them. Tell them what you have just told me, but they may question you, so be careful what you say. It must not seem that any men of Galilee are trying to subvert Roman authority."

Prochorus didn't know Agrippa had also come to Caesarea, until he was summoned to the triclinium—as the dining chamber of Roman houses was called—and found the inspector of markets seated with Antipas and two Romans. Pontius Pilate was a rather heavy, brooding man of middle age, who had obviously been drinking heavily. The new Legate of Syria, Lucius Pomponius Flaccus, however, was a lean, clear-eyed soldier who made no attempt to hide his disdain for the other three.

"Be seated, scribe," said Flaccus, when Prochorus came in. "The Tetrarch tells me you have just visited Jerusalem."

"Obviously on a mission for Antipas," said Pontius Pilate. "Another case of interference in the affairs of my province."

"Nay, Pontius," said Antipas in a cajoling tone. "It is just that since the trouble when the Nazarene was crucified—"

"A Jewish court found the man guilty of blasphemy according to your law. I said then and I say now that I found no wrong in him according to Roman law."

"Why did you order him crucified, then?" Flaccus asked curtly.

"The people were excited and demanded a spectacle, so I gave them their choice of seeing Jesus or the brigand Barabbas executed. They chose the Nazarene."

"Releasing a man who is now leader of the rebels in this region," said Flaccus. "It would have been simpler to release the Nazarene."

"You are not yet familiar with the temper of the Jerusalem Jews, noble Flaccus." A note of heavy sarcasm was in Pontius Pilate's voice. "If I had overridden them in a decision made according to their law, the whole city would have turned against me. Besides, the man's followers numbered some of the most active rebels against Rome. There was reason to think they planned to use his arrest to stir up a rebellion that would have swept the province like a fire in midsummer."

"The man was a Galilean, so you could have taken custody of him, Tetrarch." When Flaccus addressed Antipas, Prochorus suddenly realized what he was doing. By subtly prodding each of the subsidiary rulers in turn, he sought to learn more about the inner workings of their own provinces than they would have cared to reveal, had they realized his intention.

Agrippa recognized the stratagem, Prochorus realized when he looked at the inspector of markets and was startled to see him wink. But the grandson of Herod the Great only sat and listened while Pilate and Antipas tilted verbally in a joust of insults.

"To have taken the Nazarene out of Judaean jurisdiction would have been an affront to the Sanhedrin," Antipas protested. "As a Jew I—"

"A Jew by adoption only, Antipas." Agrippa spoke for the first time since Prochorus had entered the room. "Your father was the son of an Idumean and a woman of Nabatea, while your mother was a Samaritan. Only the scribe and I are Jews here—not you."

"Let us not argue about your ancestors." Pomponius Flaccus raised his hand in a gesture of peace but Prochorus could see that he was enjoying watching the client rulers claw at each other. "It is obvious that Antipas had a chance to assume custody of the Nazarene, but chose to humiliate him for the pleasure of his court. You, Pilate, chose the easy way to placate the Sanhedrin and a man who may have been innocent of any crime died. You both erred but what is done is done. We are concerned now about what mischief the followers of this Jesus can accomplish. On that score, I think we should hear from one who has just returned from Jerusalem. You may speak, scribe."

Prochorus told his story in as few words as possible. He left out all mention of Manahem and did not reveal his knowledge that, beneath the surface of the happenings he had witnessed, there might lie a quite different intention from that which was apparent.

"You say the followers of the Nazarene claim he rose from the dead?" Flaccus asked.

"It's a lie they trumped up!" Pontius Pilate broke in before Prochorus could answer. "They stole the body from the tomb."

"I thought you placed guards there." Flaccus' tone was crisp and Pilate flushed angrily.

"We expected no trouble! The man was dead; a soldier had even thrust a spear into his side to hasten his death and save him from suffering."

"Yet you allowed the body to be taken down, though he had hung for only a few hours on the cross."

"Only because a most respected merchant named Joseph of Arimathea assured me that he was dead and begged for the body, so it wouldn't hang there during the Passover season and inflame the Jews. They make much of any defilement of the dead."

"Perhaps giving the man's followers his body allowed you to expiate some of the guilt you felt for having executed an innocent man," Flaccus suggested.

Pontius Pilate started to answer angrily, then seized a silver goblet filled with wine instead and drank from it deeply, spilling some of it over his tunic in his haste. The Procurator's hands were trembling though not, Prochorus suspected, only with anger against Pomponius Flaccus.

"Go on, scribe," said the Legate. "Tell us the rest of your story."

As he told of the thousands who had been moved by the sermon of Simon Peter to repent and join the Nazarenes, Prochorus saw Flaccus' face grow grave.

"These people could be gathering a following to join the brigands under Barabbas," he observed.

"I'm sure they are not, my Lord Governor," said Prochorus. "They wish only to worship God as a congregation, while they wait for the coming of the Nazarene."

"Coming? I thought you said he had already come—and been crucified."

"The Nazarenes teach that Jesus was crucified for the sins of the world, but that he rose from the dead and ascended into heaven, from whence he will return as the Messiah."

"Messiah?" Flaccus frowned. "I'm not familiar with the word."

"It means a great leader—or prophet—sent from God. A council of the Sanhedrin has already examined the leaders of the Nazarene congregation and could find nothing with which to charge them according to Jewish law."

"When was this?"

"Only a few days ago, sir."

"I know Simon ben Jonas and John ben Zebedee very well, my lord," Antipas said when Prochorus finished his account of the incident in the Temple, the arrest of Simon Peter and John and their subsequent release by the Priestly Council. "Zebedee owns a large fishing establishment in Capernaum and no more loyal subject exists in my tetrarchy."

"Or a larger taxpayer," said Agrippa with an ironic smile.

Flaccus ignored the interruption; of the three, it seemed to Prochorus that he came nearest to respecting Agrippa, which seemed strange, until he remembered that Agrippa had spent most of his life in Rome, in the household of the Emperor.

"I think I have a fairly clear picture of what is happening in your several provinces," said Flaccus, ending the discussion. "You seem to be governing them well except, perhaps, in the matter of the Nazarene. And we can do nothing about that now."

*

vi

Prochorus fell asleep almost immediately in the room he shared with Decurion Cassius Longinus, commander of Antipas' Roman guard. He was packing his few belongings for the journey to Sepphoris and a reunion with Mariamne the next morning, when his Roman friend came in from an early morning inspection of the legionary detail.

"I'm glad I caught you before you left, so I could say good-by." Longinus unbelted his harness and hung it on a peg in the wall.

"Aren't you going back with us?"

"General Flaccus has assigned me to his household troops in Antioch." The decurion filled a basin with water from a pitcher on a small table in the corner and began to wash his face and hands. "I don't expect to be a soldier forever and he thinks it's time I learned something of governing."

Prochorus knew that young men of noble equestrian birth, planning a career as administrators of Roman government and justice, usually served for a while—rarely more than a year—with troops in the field. In this way they became familiar with the problems arising in the military side of government, which in the border provinces could never be separated from purely civil functions.

"It's a great help to have friends in high places," Longinus added with a grin. "My father and General Flaccus have been close friends for many years."

"How soon do you expect to be emperor?"

"That may take awhile. First I must become governor of a major province, as Flaccus is of Syria. He's an experienced administrator as well as a soldier. I can learn much from him in Antioch and in the field."

"I wish you only the best," Prochorus assured him, for he was genuinely fond of the young Roman.

"How would you like to go to Antioch in the Legate's service?"

"As well hope for Rome—or the moon."

"Maybe not. Flaccus was very much impressed with the way you handled your mission for Antipas in Jerusalem and capable scribes are hard to find in this part of the world. I took the occasion to recommend you for service in the Legate's retinue."

"But I've had no experience in that sort of thing."

"You served Antipas well. What is even more important, through handling Antipas' correspondence you have had a chance to learn what goes on in the tetrarchy and also in Judaea and Samaria, as well as in the domain of Philip. I pointed out to General Flaccus that this knowledge might be of great value to him in keeping a close watch on Pontius Pilate and Herod Antipas."

"A spy again?"

"It can be a worth-while occupation—if you work for the right people. This time you would be in the service of the most powerful man east of Rome itself."

"But my father is a mere steward."

"You are a Roman citizen by birth," Longinus reminded him. "Don't forget, either, that freedmen now hold the most important posts in the government at Rome."

The prospect his friend pointed out was breath-taking; not even in his rosiest dreams had Prochorus considered the possibility of rising so fast and so high in governmental service, if he chose that field. Then he sobered, for to go with Pomponius Flaccus to Antioch now—if he were offered the position—meant putting a great distance between him and Mariamne.

"I—I don't know," he said doubtfully.

"If it's Princess Mariamne you're concerned about," said the decurion, "she's a lovely child and I can understand your being in love with her. But she is still just that—a child."

"Women mature earlier than men."

"True—and she's far more intelligent than most. But look at her position. Herod the Great was the best ruler his region ever had, from the viewpoint of Rome. He took the area the Maccabeans wrested from Antiochus Epiphanes and made it into a prosperous and stable kingdom as large as, or larger than, the empires of David or Solomon you Jews like to boast about. Mariamne is a great-granddaughter of Herod the Great, so she's a member of the most recent royal family in the whole area extending from the valley of the Orontes south to the Egyptian border and eastward as far as Parthia."

"That is true but—"

"Hear me out, please—for your own good; it may save you much heartache later. A complicated game is being played for control of the empire left by Herod the Great, with moves and countermoves being made on every side. The Tetrarch Philip is dying and Rome is already considering who will rule east of the Jordan in his stead. It could be Antipas, if he settles his quarrel with King Aretas."

"But how could he—?" Prochorus broke off as he suddenly remembered Manahem's cryptic remark about Mariamne the day they had been taken to the cave hiding place of the brigands.

"Aretas has a son named Aboud who will inherit his throne," said Longinus. "After the way Antipas treated Aretas' daughter, he's not likely to get very far by proposing a marriage between Mariamne and Aboud, but he will probably try anyway. It's another matter with Agrippa."

"Prince Agrippa is in disfavor everywhere."

"At the moment—yes. But don't forget that Agrippa grew up in Rome as a prince in the imperial household and has friends at the highest levels. Tiberius can't rule forever. When another emperor takes the throne, Agrippa may well gain his favor and with it the territory of Philip—or even more."

"He has a long way to go from being inspector of markets in Tiberias."

"Perhaps not as far as you think," said Longinus. "What Antipas and Agrippa both want is to rule in Judaea, of course. Jerusalem is the prize because whoever rules there can command the loyalty of Jews everywhere, plus an incalculable wealth in tribute and trade. Antipas might have had it once; he hasn't done a bad job with Galilee and Peraea. But with Aretas waiting to sting him whenever he can, it's not likely that Jerusalem will ever be given to him."

"Rome is far away. Surely these details aren't—"

"Believe me, these details, as you call them, are followed very closely in Rome," said Longinus. "At this moment the eastern front is the most unstable part of the empire. Germany has been conquered and Egypt and Africa are under control, but the Parthians are only waiting to take advantage of any weakness we show, military or otherwise. That's why a general of Flaccus' stature was made Legate of Syria and you can be sure he will overlook nothing. I would wager he has already heard rumors of that little arrangement Antipas has with the brigands."

"Not from me," Prochorus protested.

"Of course not," said Longinus. "Your greatest weakness may be your highly developed sense of loyalty. But in the struggle for Herod's old empire, Agrippa's hands are clean—at least for the moment. He may appear now to be only a client of Antipas, but you can be sure he is moving his own pieces carefully, waiting for something to happen either here or in Rome that will give him the advantage he needs. Besides, Aretas covets Damascus and, when Philip dies, he may persuade Tiberius to break up the tetrarchy of Ituraea into several small kingdoms like Chalcis, with him the controlling influence to serve as a buffer against the Parthians. If that should happen and Agrippa could arrange for the marriage of his niece to one of these rulers—perhaps Aretas' son—he would be in an excellent bargaining position himself."

"What you're saying is that Princess Mariamne is so valuable to both Agrippa and Antipas that neither would be likely to allow her marriage to a commoner, aren't you?"

"Do you doubt it?"

"No. I suppose not."

"You're no fool, Prochorus, just in love, so I suspect that nothing I have said is really news to you. Princess Mariamne is a lovely girl and will soon be an extremely beautiful and intelligent woman. Such women have been able to change the course of empires and, when she realizes the power that may lie in her own person—" Longinus didn't finish the sentence but the implication that Mariamne would look higher than a mere scribe in her uncle's employ was obvious.

"Are you telling me to give her up completely?"

"That might be the wiser course and certainly it would appear to be the most practicable one," said Longinus. "But I'm romantic enough to want you to win her—which is another reason why I spoke to General Flaccus about you."

"How could that possibly make any difference?"

"If freedmen can govern Rome—as they do now—a freeborn plebeian can aspire to a high place in the provinces and eventually in Rome—though being part Jew might hold you back there. With your intelligence and ability, you can reach almost any goal you set for yourself; after all, the grandfather of Herod the Great was only an Idumean chief before he made himself indispensable to the Hasmonean kings—and got to where he could destroy the last of them and take over the kingdom. Judaea should be ruled by an enlightened Jew. As a provincial governor, you could aspire to the hand of a granddaughter of Herod the Great with a good chance of having the Emperor approve the match."

vii

The summons from the Legate came before the noonday meal. Prochorus found Flaccus with a scribe who was trying to write a letter he was dictating, and doing a rather poor job of it, much to the Legate's irritation.

"You, scribe—what is your name?" Flaccus demanded when he saw Prochorus standing just inside the room, waiting for his presence to be noticed.

"Prochorus, noble sir."

"My blood is no more noble than yours," Flaccus said testily. "I am a soldier with little talent for diplomacy and deception. Can you write well?"

"Yes, sir."

"Take this scribe's place and we will go on with the letter I am trying to write."

The man who had been trying to keep up with Flaccus' rather rapid-fire dictation fled from the room and Prochorus took his seat. The salutation of the letter was all that had been written, and that rather badly.

"If you will give me a moment to rewrite this, sir," he said, as he reached for another piece of parchment, now widely used in correspondence instead of the less easily obtained papyrus, and a sharpened quill, "I will be ready."

The letter was addressed to King Aretas of Nabatea at his capital Petra. Prochorus quickly gave it the proper salutation and looked up to where Flaccus was standing by the window.

"I am ready now, sir," he said.

"Read me what has been written," Flaccus commanded.

" 'Lucius Pomponius Flaccus, General of the Army, Consul Designate, of Tribunician Power, Legatus of Syria, to his Majesty Aretas IV, King of the Nabateans, Greeting:

" 'I had hoped to visit you already, but the Parthians have chosen this time to raid our frontiers, so I must return to Antioch and launch an expedition against them.' " Prochorus paused, waiting for Flaccus to continue, but instead the Legate came around to the end of the table and stood looking over his shoulder at the portion of the letter he had already written.

"Decurion Longinus tells me you are a capable scribe, and I can believe it from the way you were able to straighten out the mess that dolt made," he said. "Tell me something of yourself."

"My father is a Greek born in the Decapolis. My mother is a Jew, of the line of David."

"Which makes you of royal lineage." Flaccus' eyebrows lifted and Prochorus flushed.

"I did not mean—"

"You should be proud of both your Greek heritage and your Jewish one," said the Legate. "You may represent the best of both if your friend Longinus is to be believed. Would you like to become my *secretarius ab epistulis*?"

"Very much, sir. If you think me worthy?"

"That you must prove. If you accept the position, your loyalty must henceforth be entirely to me and to Rome."

"I prize my Roman citizenship very highly, sir."

"It isn't something to be gained lightly. But you Roman Jews are sometimes torn by a double loyalty and long for a Jewish state. Some even plot against Rome to achieve it but I can have no divided loyalties among those who serve me. Any knowledge you may gain that concerns Rome should be at my command."

"I told you all I know last night, sir."

"Then you are convinced that these Nazarenes no longer represent a rebellious movement against Roman authority?"

"I am sure of it, sir."

"What of the one they call Barabbas? And Manahem? And Judas of Kerioth?"

"I know nothing of Barabbas except that he is said to be a leader among the brigands in the mountains of Lower Galilee and Judaea. I have seen Manahem but I am sure he isn't associated with the Nazarenes any longer. Judas of Kerioth appears to have been the link between them and a rebel band, but he hanged himself after betraying Jesus of Nazareth to the authorities."

"Imagine betraying a man you believe to be the Son of God in order to make him announce his divinity and use his power against Rome. Still, belief in divine beings who come down to earth and interfere in human affairs is nothing new; the old Greeks did it all the time." Flaccus smiled. "Though, as I remember it, they were usually interested in beautiful young girls. Nevertheless, there have been times when I would have welcomed such intervention, on my side of course, but the so-called— What is the word you use for gods in earthly forms?"

"The Jewish word is Messiah, sir. In Greek, it is Christ."

"A romantic concept. But we Romans are a practical people. We make gods of our emperors and in that way have some choice in selecting them and also removing them, if they prove too ambitious— even for a god. It's a convenient arrangement and seems to serve both sides very well. I'm not likely to be troubled by questions of whether or not to become a god, though, so let us get on with the letter to Aretas. I suspect that he's only waiting to test my mettle before sticking a dagger into Antipas' back. But if I'm firm enough with him, he may wait until I have subdued the rebellious Parthians."

The dictation went swiftly but Prochorus was able to follow, setting down the message in Greek which, fortunately because of Chuza's ancestry in the Decapolis, was fully as familiar to him as the Aramaic of the Galilean cities or the Hebrew of the Jewish synagogue school—and even more than the Latin which Chuza had also insisted that he learn. When the letter was finished, Flaccus glanced over it quickly, nodded approval, and slashed his signature across the bottom in a rough scrawl.

"We leave for Antioch just after the noonday meal," he said. "Will that give you time to get your belongings together?"

"I have only the clothing I brought from Jerusalem, sir."

Flaccus smiled. "Now you have reason to purchase a new supply at government expense, so you have already learned the first principle of becoming a successful civil servant."

One thing remained before departure and that Prochorus found most difficult of all—the writing of a letter to Mariamne to be delivered by Antipas' chamberlain. To the task of explaining to her why he could not afford to refuse Flaccus' offer of a position usually filled by a far older and more experienced man, his ordinarily fluent pen proved less than adequate. Haltingly, he wrote of the opportunities for advancement the position afforded and what they would mean to him in the future. But when it came to expressing his sadness that he would not see her again soon and his love for her, he bogged down again, ending with a stilted sort of a message that did not say at all what was really in his heart. By that time Cassius Longinus was knocking at the door, warning that if he didn't get aboard the galley at once he would be left behind, so there was no time to rewrite the letter.

Standing on the deck of the vessel as the galley slaves carefully warped it around the end of the great mole and out into the open sea beyond, Prochorus was gripped by a deep sense of depression, in spite of the future represented by the imperial shield and emblem at the prow of the swift military vessel. To the east, the hills rose in a steady progression toward the range that hid the great plain of Esdraelon and the lake country he loved. Beyond the range of hills to the northeast, almost on a line with Mount Hermon's snow-capped height, lay Sepphoris and Mariamne. And the thought that it might be years before he would see her again tore at his heart.

"Cheer up!" Cassius Longinus' voice sounded beside him. "Antipas can do nothing without the approval of the Legate. As soon as the Parthians have been chastened, Flaccus plans to travel through Galilee and visit Aretas in Petra so you will see her again soon. Meanwhile a whole new world awaits you."

"A world where I could easily get lost."

"A Roman is never lost. All roads lead to the golden milestone in the Forum. And who knows? One day you may stand there as *secretarius ab epistulis* for the empire."

viii

With regular reports to Rome on the many subject rulers under his direction required from the Legate of Syria, the job of *secretarius ab epistulis* was far from being a sinecure. As months fled swiftly into years, Prochorus found himself supervising the work of a dozen scribes.

Almost in the center of Antioch, the river Orontes split to form an island called simply the *insula*. Here were located the buildings housing the administrative center for the entire district of Syria and the palace of the Legate, second only to the Emperor himself and the visual symbol of imperial authority in the entire East. Prochorus had little time to investigate either the beauties or the pleasures of Antioch, but from the window of his somewhat spartan quarters, he could see the great colonnaded thoroughfare called the Via Caesarea that bisected the city to end in the foothills of Mount Silpius. Upon that elevation stood the imposing castle built by the Romans to guard Antioch from attack from the east or the west while serving also as a constant reminder of the power and majesty of Rome.

Like most major Roman cities, Antioch had a fairly large colony of Jews. For the most part they lived in the lower section of the city, just beyond the south bank of the Orontes, where a large commercial district was located. Here there were several synagogues and, always devout, Prochorus worshiped regularly there on the sabbath, when he was not traveling with Flaccus.

Sometimes as he walked beside the river and watched the richly canopied pleasure barges on which Romans and rich merchants alike took the air on warm evenings, he felt a wave of yearning for the Lake of Tiberias and for Mariamne. But for the most time he was so busy by day and so tired when night came that her memory soon began to blur, requiring an effort to recall.

Pomponius Flaccus had come to depend more and more upon the counsel of his young secretary in dealing with the problems that arose continually in governing the former empire of Herod the Great. One of the Legate's first actions upon coming to Antioch had been to call upon the subject rulers for auxiliary troops which he had fashioned, along with the cohorts of the regular legions under his command, into an army that could swiftly put down anything resembling an insurrection, even across the desert wastes forming a physical barrier between the *ghor* and the valley of the Tigris and Euphrates rivers, the cradle of human civilization. As a result, King Artaban of Parthia had been intimidated by the show of force and was quiet—at least for the moment.

The enmity between Antipas and the Nabatean king, Aretas—still anxious to avenge the insult to his daughter when Antipas had divorced her in order to marry Queen Herodias—continued unabated. Neither could make any move against the other as long as a strong legate ruled in Antioch, however, so the situation between them remained one of stalemate.

Equally at dagger's point, according to reports filtering into Antioch from Galilee, were Antipas and Agrippa. The latter still existed on the generosity of Antipas in the nominal position of inspector of markets at Tiberias, but he was constantly seeking ways to seize a portion of his grandfather's empire for himself, and for his family, now numbering two daughters, Berenice and Drusilla, and a boy named Agrippa—in addition to his wife Kypros.

Ituraea, a hodgepodge province that included Auranitis, Trachonitis, Batanaea and Paneas, had been ruled effectively by the Tetrarch Philip since the death of Herod the Great. With Philip's death both Antipas and Agrippa had hoped to be given his territory, but Flaccus hesitated to increase the domain of the wily Antipas and place him in a position where he might attack Aretas, whose domain bordered both tetrarchies. The Legate therefore decided to hold the province of Ituraea under his personal control and let the tax revenues accumulate there until the Emperor might make some final decision about the disposition of the territory. The presence of these funds formed a treasure which all who could lay claim to it as descendants of Herod the Great coveted, and was therefore a potential source of trouble.

Meanwhile a third factor had entered into the complex political situation, the appearance at Antioch of Agrippa's brother Aristobulus, named after their father. Poised like a scavenger, he was quite ready to accept the domain of his brother, Herod of Chalcis—a small kingdom lying just north of Upper Galilee and the valley of the Orontes—or whatever else of his grandfather's possessions the Legate and the Emperor might see fit to give him—preferably the tetrarchy of Ituraea.

With all this conniving going on and Herodias continually prodding Antipas to seize a larger portion of empire, a veritable morass of intrigue seethed constantly throughout the entire territory. Reports of this jockeying for advantage filtered into Antioch constantly from Roman tax collectors and military commanders throughout the area, along with letters of complaint from each of the participants. To add more fuel to the fire that kept the cauldron of intrigue constantly bubbling, complaints were mounting almost daily from Judaea and Samaria concerning the behavior of Pontius Pilate.

In the evaluation of these reports, which naturally came through his hands when replies to them were written to the various participants, Prochorus was of steadily increasing help to Flaccus. Not only did he know many of the participants personally, but he was familiar with their histories and with the many factions among both the Jew and gentile populations whose actions must be taken into consideration in making final decisions. Placed at the center of power and wielding no little of it himself as agent for the Legate, Prochorus matured rapidly during these busy years from the youthful student of his days at Tiberias and the university to a new place of importance as a Roman civil servant—the future Cassius Longinus had predicted for him.

Then in rather sudden fashion things began to change. At a dinner in Tyre, the ancient Phoenician capital on the coast north of Caesarea and Ptolemais, Antipas and Agrippa quarreled bitterly while drunk. When Antipas denounced Agrippa publicly as nothing more than a lackey who existed upon his generosity, the latter fled north-ward to Antioch and laid his complaint before Flaccus.

Agrippa's fortunes might have taken a favorable turn at that point because, having known him in Rome, Flaccus naturally favored him. But his ambition, prodded by his continual lack of funds, led him to engage in a deception which resulted in a considerable backset for his own fortune.

Negotiations had been going on for some time between Damascus, one of the Decapolis cities, and the Phoenician territories of Tyre and Sidon on the seacoast concerning the boundary between them in the neighborhood of the Anti-Lebanon range of mountains. When a group of rich merchants from Damascus, knowing of Agrippa's friendship with Flaccus, approached Herod's grandson with a proposal that he use his influence in their behalf, he demanded a bribe in repayment for using his influence with the Legate. Unfortunately for Agrippa, his brother Aristobulus was equally ambitious and, learning of the arrangement, immediately betrayed Agrippa to the Legate. Flaccus was naturally angered at this abuse of his hospitality and turned Agrippa out, forcing him to flee south-ward to Phoenicia, where he eventually obtained money to reach Alexandria and Rome.

There, according to reports, Agrippa's period of disfavor in the eyes of Tiberius seemed to have come to an end, for he was shortly appointed tutor to the grandson of the Emperor. More important for Agrippa's fortunes, he was able to resume his friendship with the heir to the throne, Gaius. Known by the nickname of Caligula or "Little Boot" from his habit of having worn small boots like the Roman legionnaires as a child, Gaius had been adopted by the powerful Praetorian Guard as its mascot, a fact that was to play an important part in his future course.

About this time, Lucius Pomponius Flaccus was recalled to serve in a military capacity in another part of the empire—a task considerably more to his liking than that of diplomacy and intrigue which had comprised a large part of the duties of the Legate of Syria. In his place, a new viceroy was appointed to rule in the East, a former consul and highly respected administrator from Rome named Lucius Vitellius.

ix

In the period between the departure of Flaccus and the arrival of Vitellius, the functions of government in Antioch were almost at a standstill, since no one knew exactly what would be the policies of the new governor. Left with few duties, Prochorus was walking back to the city one afternoon, having climbed to the foothills of Mount Silpius where he could look down upon the vast sprawl of Antioch on both banks of the Orontes, when he noticed a commotion in the street ahead of him. A man seemed to be the center of an altercation with some street urchins, who were pelting him with rocks and shouting epithets at him. And when Prochorus came nearer he saw that most of the attackers were Jews. This in itself was surprising, for the Jews of the Diaspora ordinarily sought to avoid any disturbance which might give rise to charges against them of causing trouble. And when he further recognized the man being attacked as Manaen, the kinsman of Herod Antipas who had been his friend in Tiberias, he waded unhesitatingly into the fray.

At the insistence of Cassius Longinus, Prochorus had continued exercising after he took up residence in the *insula*, both in wrestling and boxing and in sham battles with weapons. His presence now quickly turned the odds against the attackers and they soon scattered, still shouting the word "Christian" at Manaen.

"You arrived just in time." Manaen's face was scratched and a small cut had been opened over his left eye where a stone thrown by one of his assailants had found its mark. "Those devils would have blinded me if they could."

"Why did they attack you?"

"Their elders put them up to it; you can wager on that." Manaen wiped blood from his face with his hand. "But the damage isn't serious."

"I still don't see what they would have against you, a kinsman of the Tetrarch."

"All that is changed since I became a follower of the Christ."

"Christ—Christians." Prochorus frowned over the Greek word, then his face cleared as he translated it into the Hebrew equivalent of Messiah. "Do you mean Jesus of Nazareth?"

"Yes."

"But why here?"

"It's a long story."

"My quarters are just across the bridge in the *insula*," Prochorus suggested. "Come with me and I will have a servant clean up your wounds, while you tell me about it."

"Obviously you're a person of some importance here," Manaen said as he sank to a bench in Prochorus' comfortable room. "I had heard of your success as *secretarius* to the Legate but I hesitated to try to see you because we aren't looked on entirely with favor here in Antioch."

"I don't understand why not," said Prochorus. "Anyway, my job may be over soon. The new Legate will probably bring his own staff with him."

"But none who knows the country and the people as you do." A servant arrived just then with water in a pitcher and clean cloths. Prochorus bathed his friend's scratches and bound the cut on his forehead with a bandage.

"Now tell me all about yourself," he said as he poured a cup of wine and handed it to Manaen, who was still a little shaken from the experience of being stoned in the street.

"Do you remember what it was like in Jerusalem after the Holy Spirit came upon us at Pentecost?" Manaen asked.

"As I recall, some five thousand or more had chosen to become followers of the Nazarene before I left. But I've seen nothing about your congregation in the reports that come to us from Jerusalem."

"Things changed rather rapidly after you were there. Many of those who were closest to Jesus were scattered abroad—as I was—by the persecution."

"Why would you be persecuted? Roman law grants all Jews the right to worship God."

"The High Priest Caiaphas has things his own way now," Manaen explained. "Some say Pilate is torn by guilt because he allowed Jesus to be crucified; others think he is really mad. Whatever the reason, he spends much of his time brooding or in savage rages and lets the High Priest do as he wishes in Jerusalem."

"Why would Caiaphas want to destroy you?"

"Perhaps because of his own guilt for having sentenced the Expected One to death."

"Then you really believe the Nazarene was the Messiah?"

"*Is* the Messiah," Manaen corrected him. "Jesus still lives, Prochorus—in Heaven."

"I'm sure you believe that, but—"

"How can I doubt it—when I feel his presence constantly in my soul?"

"You spoke of persecution," Prochorus reminded him.

"It began with the murder of Stephen. You would have loved him, Prochorus. He was part Greek like yourself, a scholar and one of the most eloquent men I ever heard speak."

"I don't remember that name among the Nazarene's disciples."

"Stephen was one of the first converts in Jerusalem. After Peter and John spoke out from the Porch of Solomon and the Sanhedrin was unable to find any wrong in them, people flocked to join us and the congregation soon became so large that seven deacons had to be appointed to look after its affairs. Stephen was one of them and the most eloquent of all. In a few years our power would have been as great as that of the priests but Caiaphas sent a man named Saul of Tarsus against us and accused us of blasphemy. Stephen was seized and the Temple rabble murdered him as they did Jesus."

"Only a Roman governor can sentence one to crucifixion," Prochorus objected.

"The rabble dragged Stephen from the chamber of the Sanhedrin and stoned him to death," Manaen explained. "Afterward Saul of Tarsus went about like a raging lion, throwing people into prison and persecuting them. Some recanted to save their lives but many died for their faith. Barnabas, Lucius of Cyrene, Simeon and I were sent out of Jerusalem by Peter because we are all of the Diaspora. We were instructed to start a church here at Antioch."

"Have you had much success?"

"Almost as much as the Synagogue of the Nazarenes did when

Peter and the others were sent back from Galilee by Jesus," Manaen said proudly.

"What happened to John and James?"

"John went to Babylon. It has a large Jewish colony and seemed a good place for him to start a new Nazarene congregation. James went into the hills; he has—friends—there. The others are scattered abroad, some as far as Rome."

"I still don't understand why you were stoned today?"

"When we first came to Antioch, we spoke only in the synagogues," Manaen explained. "Many chose to follow Jesus but the elders of some of the congregations decided we might cause trouble for Jews here."

"I can understand their reasoning. After all, the Nazarene was executed by Rome for treason."

"Jesus never meant treason, Prochorus. He sought only to show men the way to God."

"I'm sure of that, but what about Judas of Kerioth? Or Barabbas and Manahem?"

"I can see why you were so valuable to the Legate; no wonder he rewarded you with all this." Manaen's gesture took in the comfortable room, the court outside and Prochorus' own robe of excellent cloth and cut. "Yes, there was a conspiracy once but the Master was never part of it. Perhaps his crucifixion and resurrection were the only way those around him could be made to realize that he had no wish to be an earthly ruler."

"I don't think all who follow him understand that yet."

"That may be," Manaen conceded. "Not until I was forced to flee for my life did a full understanding of Jesus' purpose come to me. But when people call me 'Christian' now, I consider it a badge setting me apart from those who are not so fortunate as to know Jesus.

"I must go." Manaen got to his feet. "If it is told here in the *insula* that you are a friend of one who follows a crucified Jew, those who envy your rise might use it against you with the new Legate."

"What a turn your life and mine have taken, when a kinsman of the Tetrarch of Galilee is troubled lest he bring disrepute upon one of the Amhaaretz."

"You were never one of the common people—the unwashed," Manaen protested. "Your lineage is from both priestly and royal lines through Joanna—"

"Is the persecution you spoke of likely to extend to Galilee?" Prochorus asked quickly, reminded by Manaen's words of his mother and his friends who had followed Jesus.

"No. Antipas knows better than to let a division be created there."

"But if this man Saul is so powerful, he will surely try to destroy the Christians in Galilee."

"We are not troubled any more by Saul. He has become one of us."

"But you said just now that he was responsible for the death of Stephen."

"Saul was present at the execution and even held the cloaks of those who cast the first stone, though he played no part in the actual charges against Stephen. Afterward, he did harry our people and send many of them into prison. But as he was going to Damascus on a mission for Caiaphas to arrest others of our people, he was suddenly struck blind on the road by the glory of the Lord. Jesus spoke to him there, calling him to become one of us."

"I find that story hard to believe."

"Others in the caravan Saul was with saw him stricken blind, though they didn't hear the voice that spoke to him. Later, in Damascus, some of our people were instructed by Jesus to take care of him and restore his sight."

"Where is he now?"

"Somewhere in the desert. When he preached in the synagogues at Damascus that Jesus was crucified and rose from the dead as the Messiah, there was great opposition to him and he was finally forced to flee."

"This is a strange thing—a persecutor turning sharply about and becoming one of the persecuted. I find it hard to believe."

"What happened to Paul is no more strange than that I, who grew up in the household of Antipas almost as a brother, should give it all up and be taunted for being a Christian here in Antioch. Jesus said those who follow him must take up their cross and bear it, as he bore the *patibulum* until he fell in the dust on the way to the Place of the Skull to be crucified." Manaen's voice took on a note of pride. "Wounds and scars are the signs by which people shall see Jesus in us."

Only after Manaen was gone did Prochorus realize that he had neglected to ask what, when he had first come to Antioch, would have been his first question—about Mariamne. But though he tried now to call up again from his memory the picture of her as she had been that first morning in the palace of Antipas in Tiberias, even the outline of her face was faint and far away.

Is this what happens to young love? he thought sadly. *Is it always consumed by the fires of ambition, always erased by the cares of growing from boy to man?*

Then, though he still could not see her clearly in his mind, memory came rushing back and he found himself longing for the sound of her voice, the remembered sweetness of her lips and the softness of her body in his arms.

Logic told him that even if he were with Mariamne he would be no nearer claiming her for his own than he had been that day in Caesarea, when Cassius Longinus—now with Flaccus—had persuaded him that going to Antioch was his only chance to raise himself to where he could hope one day to make her his wife. He could wish that logic would take flight, if only for a moment, leaving him at least the happiness of memory. But as he turned back to his lonely room, only a verse from the loveliest of the poetic books of his people's sacred scriptures came to his mind:

> *Set me like a seal on your heart,*
> *like a seal on your arm.*
> *For love is strong as Death,*
> *jealousy relentless as Sheol.*
> *The flash of it is a flash of fire,*
> *a flame of Yahweh himself.*
> *Love no flood can quench,*
> *no torrents drown.*

Long ago a king had written those words to his beloved, secure in the knowledge that whatever he wished would be his. But what hope was there for a scribe who aspired to the love of a princess?

x

The new Legate of Syria was tall, spare, graying and in every way the epitome of a Roman aristocrat; yet the light of intelligence in his eyes and a warm graciousness, as he acknowledged the greetings of the officials waiting at the palace, led Prochorus to hope Vitellius was not only a statesman but also the possessor of understanding and tolerance. These qualities, more than any others, were badly needed in those delegated to govern the often turbulent eastern part of Rome's empire, with its many subrulers and often warring peoples. Summoned to the presence of Vitellius on the day following his arrival, he found the Legate in the audience chamber of the palace, sitting at a table flanked by a battery of scribes who had come out with him from Rome.

"Isn't Prochorus a rather odd name for a Jew?" the Legate asked.

"My father is a Greek from the Decapolis," Prochorus explained. "My mother is a Jew."

"But you follow the Jewish faith?"

"Yes, sir."

Vitellius picked up a sheet of parchment from the table and glanced at it, before looking at Prochorus again. "Flaccus thought so highly of you that he left a letter of recommendation for me, suggesting that you be elevated from the position of *secretarius* to that of my chief adviser on Judaea, Samaria, Galilee, Peraea and Ituraea."

"I am very grateful to him, sir. He raised me from a simple scribe to a position of confidence."

"I doubt that you were ever a simple scribe." From among the scrolls lying before him, Vitellius selected two. "I find myself in need of your advice on the first day of my tenure. Read these while I finish dictating a letter to King Artaban of Parthia, assuring him of my desire for peace on the eastern frontier. Then tell me what course of action you would advise."

The first scroll, a confidential report from the military commander of the Roman forces assigned to the Procurator of Judaea and Samaria, was both startling and disturbing. At the beginning of his term as Procurator, Pontius Pilate had ridden into Jerusalem with the emblems of Rome uncovered, an insult to the sensitivities of the Jews, whose religion forbade all graven images, that had made his relations with them difficult ever since. Now, according to the letter, he had managed to accomplish the same thing with the Samaritans, who considered Mount Gerizim, lying a little to the south of their capital city of Samaria, or Sebaste, to be a holy place where sacred vessels brought by Moses out of Egypt were buried.

A magician named Simon Magus had recently assured the Samaritans that he was sent by God to raise them to their rightful place in divine favor, well above the haughty Jews to the south, whom they hated as bitterly as the Jews hated them. When Simon further promised to reveal the location of the sacred vessels of Moses on Mount Gerizim, a great crowd had gathered at the foot of the mount. Fearing that this gathering might be the beginning of a rebellion similar to the one he had averted by the arrest of Barabbas and the crucifixion of the Nazarene, Pilate had acted precipitately, setting Roman troops upon the unarmed crowd. In the ensuing slaughter, hundreds of Samaritans had been massacred and their leaders had naturally raised a cry of protest against the blood bath in a letter to the Legate charging Pontius Pilate with murder.

Vitellius had completed his letter to Artaban by the time Prochorus finished reading the scrolls containing the charges of the Samaritan leaders.

"What do you think?" he asked.

"I would not presume, sir—"

"If you are to be my adviser, you must know enough about the areas I entrust to you to form a valid opinion and defend it. Otherwise you will let me make a wrong decision because you wish to agree with me."

"I think you have no choice except to suspend Pontius Pilate as

Procurator of Judaea and Samaria until you can investigate this affair," Prochorus said firmly.

"A Roman officer as important as the governor of a province should not be removed for one mistake, particularly if he has friends in the imperial household." A wintry smile appeared on Vitellius' face. "Rome considers Pontius Pilate a good governor. Do you think differently?"

"Pilate made some early mistakes, mainly because he was unfamiliar with the special conditions that exist where Jews are concerned. In general, though, he was a good governor—until a few years ago when he crucified a Nazarene teacher just before Passover."

"I know about the case. The man was the leader of a group of rebels."

"Pilate himself stated before he condemned Jesus of Nazareth that he could find no fault in him."

"Then why was he crucified?"

"I suspect to please the High Priest, Joseph Caiaphas, and a small clique who desired the death of the Nazarene. Since then, I am told, Pilate has been increasingly moody and has practically turned over all government in Jerusalem and Judaea to Caiaphas and his group."

"These are serious charges. Are you prepared to support them?"

"I have talked to friends from Jerusalem who assure me that they are true," said Prochorus. "Rome guarantees freedom of religious worship to all people, yet the followers of the Nazarene have been persecuted and some even murdered by mobs stirred up by the High Priest and his agents."

"Go on."

"As for the affair in Samaria, I only know that the Samaritans have been restive for some time under Pilate's rule. You will find other complaints from them in the records of the province, so this affair on Mount Gerizim is not a single occurrence."

"Suppose I suspend Pilate and send him to Rome for trial—what then?"

"I think it is time for a new procurator, a new High Priest, and a visit by you to Jerusalem," Prochorus said without hesitation. "Next month is the Passover, the most important of our religious holi-

days. A few gestures of tolerance from you at that time would do
much to quiet the unrest Pontius Pilate and Caiaphas have caused."

"What kind of gestures do you recommend?"

"For one thing, a general proclamation of amnesty in Judaea and
Samaria would reassure the people about Roman justice."

"I can see that," Vitellius agreed. "What else?"

"Since the time of Herod the Great, the holy vestments worn by
the chief priests at important religious ceremonies have been kept
by the ruler of the province and only given to the priestly authorities
a few days before each ceremony. This has been a constant source
of resentment against Rome and, if you give the vestments back to
the priests, every pious Jew will applaud your action and consider
you a generous ruler."

Vitellius smiled. "I can see why Flaccus valued you so highly,
Prochorus. Have the necessary documents drawn up for my signature, proclaiming an amnesty and suspending Pilate. I will send
him to Rome for trial later, after I have investigated this affair.
Draw up another order appointing Marcellus, my military commander, Procurator of Judaea and Samaria for the time being. I shall
rely upon you to select the new High Priest and to advise Marcellus."

When he finished his work at the palace that afternoon, Prochorus
crossed over the bridge connecting the *insula* with the rest of
Antioch and sought out Manaen.

"Who shall be appointed High Priest in Caiaphas' stead?" he
asked after telling his friends about Vitellius' decision.

"A son of the old High Priest Annas named Jonathan is very
devout," said Manaen. "He has no prejudice against the followers
of Jesus and I am sure will be tolerant and fair."

"I will suggest his name to the Legate."

"Will you be going to Jerusalem for the Passover?"

"Yes. Why?"

"Herod Antipas usually spends the holidays in Jerusalem. Princess
Mariamne will probably be there too."

"I had thought of that," Prochorus admitted. "But I don't know
whether she will want to see me."

"Why not?"

"I wrote her from Caesarea before I came to Antioch, and I have written several times since—without an answer."

"There could be many reasons for her silence," said Manaen. "She's old enough to marry now. What if Vitellius asks your advice on that? Will you tell him that a marriage with the son of King Aretas could promote peace between Antipas and the Nabateans and possibly establish a strong buffer against Parthia?"

"I don't know," Prochorus admitted gravely, but it was still a sobering thought and his steps were slow as he returned to the *insula*.

xi

Jerusalem seemed to have changed not at all. But whereas on his last visit Prochorus had ridden into the city still sick from fever and disturbed about the role Herod Antipas had asked him to play as a spy upon the Nazarenes, he now rode behind the Legate Vitellius and Procurator Marcellus, an experienced soldier who could be expected to be firm but not necessarily very imaginative in his administration of the government of Judaea and Samaria.

Vitellius' action in ordering the priestly vestments freed from Roman control, carefully publicized by Prochorus through letters sent to the Temple authorities ahead of their visit, had caused great joy in Jerusalem. The removal of Caiaphas had been generally favored, for the powerful High Priest had earned many enemies for himself by his peremptory use of power. Too, Jonathan, the new prelate, was known to be more moderate in his views of the High Priest's role as religious head of the Jews, rather than as a ruling theocrat.

The streets were lined with cheering people as the Roman column, its emblems carefully covered to avoid offense to the pious, rode through the Gate of Benjamin in the north wall on the way to the Antonia, the palace-fortress at the northwest corner of the sanctuary area upon which the Temple stood. Prochorus and part of the military detail were left there, while the Legate and the Procurator, with their own guard, continued across the city to the Palace of

Herod on the western side. Antipas and his retinue, Prochorus learned at the Antonia, had yielded the Palace of Herod to Vitellius and occupied the smaller Palace of the Hasmoneans between the two citadels that dominated Jerusalem.

Continuing his efforts to gain the good will of the people of Jerusalem, Vitellius had invited many of the leading citizens of the city—along with his own entourage—to a great banquet and reception at the Palace of Herod where he and Marcellus were quartered. As confidential adviser to the Legate, Prochorus had also been invited and, just as darkness was falling, left the Antonia and crossed the city to the magnificent palace. He had been careful to put on his finest robe and, as he made his way through the teeming, joyful city, the thought of seeing Mariamne again quickened both his footsteps and his pulse.

The palace was ablaze with lights and through the colonnaded entranceway he could see pools and fountains and gardens of flowers just now coming into full bloom after the rather sharp winter that often saw snow cover the Judaean hills. In the great banqueting chamber and the anterooms, rich Pharisees in expensive robes; Sadducees of the priestly class, equally richly attired and laden with golden chains and jewels; minor Roman officials; swarthy chieftains from Idumea to the south; rich merchants from the city rivaling in the magnificence of their garments even the wealth of the priestly class, who enjoyed the sole use of the Temple revenues— all jostled together.

Since the holy season of Passover had not yet begun, there was a plentiful supply of meat and other viands, arranged on tables for the guests to refresh themselves. A constant procession of servants circulated through the crowd, too, bearing trays of silver goblets filled with wine, while around the walls rows of low couches, upon which Romans ordinarily reclined during their meals, had been arranged for those of the guests who might care to lie down—or be forced to do so from the abundance of wine.

The Tetrarch of Galilee was standing with Vitellius and Marcellus at one end of the long audience chamber. The Romans were in full military uniform while Antipas wore a robe of rich purple produced by the Phoenician dyers of the seacoast cities to the north. A

jeweled coronet was upon his head and his pudgy fingers flashed
with rings. Beside him Herodias, too, was dressed in royal robes
and equally as heavily ornamented as her husband.

Prochorus' eyes searched the crowd as he moved through it, looking for Mariamne, but Vitellius saw him and beckoned for him to
approach the royal party.

"What is the son of my steward doing here?" Antipas demanded
icily.

"Prochorus is my most valuable adviser." Vitellius cut him off in a
voice as sharp as the blade of a sword. "He handled the problem
of Pontius Pilate so well that I plan to make him my *secretarius a
petitionibus.*"

The meaning of the title was not lost on Antipas for, of the
four main secretaries ordinarily serving an emperor or his legate,
the one controlling petitions could decide who would be granted
access to the governor and thus wield a considerable power, even
over subject rulers.

"He was a good scribe—until Flaccus stole him from me," Antipas
acknowledged somewhat grudgingly.

"We in Rome know well the value of advisers whose loyalty
is beyond question." Vitellius finished putting the Tetrarch of
Galilee firmly in his place. "The real business of empire is handled
largely by freedmen and by loyal and intelligent advisers like Prochorus."

Prochorus managed to retire after that, but the attempt of Antipas
to humiliate him before the Legate and the Procurator had left
him depressed, and he decided to leave the palace. As he passed
a doorway leading out into a lovely enclosed garden, however,
he saw a young woman surrounded by a bevy of Roman officers.

It was Mariamne.

In the years since he had last seen her, she had matured from
a lovely child to a startlingly beautiful young woman. Yet the
change was not so much physical, though her body had filled out,
too, with the coming of womanhood, as it was in her manner—a
combination of beauty and pride of birthright that could hardly
be called anything except regal.

She saw him at almost the same moment and he knew she

recognized him, for a sudden flush stained her cheeks and an angry glint came into her eyes. She did not acknowledge the recognition in any way but, instead, turned her head to speak to one of the young officers, deliberately ignoring him. Swept by a sudden anger, Prochorus approached the group about her and, since the Roman officers were from Vitellius' personal guard and knew him well, they made room at his approach, leaving her no choice except to acknowledge his presence.

"I'm glad to see that the Princess Mariamne is even lovelier than when I last saw her," he said, bowing low.

For a moment he thought she was going to keep up the farce of not knowing him, but when one of the Roman decurions said, "Prochorus is one of the Legate's most trusted advisers, Princess," she had little choice.

"Oh yes, I remember now." She was the gracious lady, warming a subject with her most dazzling smile. "I believe you served my uncle Antipas once—as a scribe."

"I did have that honor—and also the privilege of delivering the princess from great danger when she was captured by brigands."

"How could I have forgotten your bravery? And without a weapon, too?"

"The mind is often a better weapon than a sword, especially when the odds are weighed against you. Have I your permission to withdraw, Princess?"

He saw her hesitate, apparently torn by the desire to humiliate him still; instead, she said, "Only after you have shown me the gardens. I believe you stayed in the Palace of Herod once before, so you must be familiar with them."

"I shall be happy to do your bidding." He held out his arm so she could place her hand upon it and the Romans around her moved away with murmurs of disappointment.

"Why did you try to humble me in there?" he demanded, when they paused at the other end of a pool which had been cleverly lit by placing reflectors of polished silver behind torches to throw the rays down upon the surface of the water where fish were darting about.

"It was no more than you deserved—after all these years with no word from you," she answered heatedly.

"I sent you a letter before I left Caesarea for Antioch, explaining everything. And I wrote you several times after that but received no answer."

"Why should I believe you?" she demanded.

"Because I'm not in the habit of lying. You should know that."

"How were your letters sent?"

"The first was by your uncle's chamberlain. The others by the imperial post."

"And you received no word from me?"

"Not once in three years since I kissed you good-by in Tiberias."

"Uncle Antipas must have ordered those letters destroyed." She sank to a bench beside the pool and reached out blindly for his hand to draw him down beside her. "When I think how hurt I was—"

"And I thought you had decided not to remember me."

"Were you no more certain of my love than that?"

"You are a princess of the Hasmonean house," he reminded her.

"What has it gained me?" she cried. "Uncle Antipas keeps me a prisoner, hoping to marry me to that horrible Aboud so he can appease the anger of King Aretas."

"Your uncle Agrippa is in Rome. Couldn't he help you?"

"He's in prison."

This was news to Prochorus, for the last thing he had heard about Agrippa was his appointment as tutor to the Emperor's grandson, a post the ambitious Agrippa would certainly consider a steppingstone toward regaining high position in Rome and, hopefully, in its eastern affairs.

"When did you learn this?" he asked.

"Uncle Antipas had word of it from a merchant who landed at Joppa yesterday."

Antipas was up to his old tricks, he thought, corresponding with members of the imperial household without notifying the Legate.

"I overheard him and Aunt Herodias talking about it last night," Mariamne confided. "They said Uncle Agrippa sought to gain the favor of Gaius—the one everybody calls Caligula—by telling him he should be ruling the country but the Emperor heard about it. He put Uncle Agrippa in chains, but even if he were free and in power, he would only try to marry me to some lesser king to help him in his schemes."

"There is a way out."

"What?"

"If you were married to me, you could no longer be moved about by Antipas or Agrippa like pieces in a game of senit—that is, if you love me still?"

"If I love you! How could you doubt?"

"You tried to humiliate me just now."

"Only because I was angry at you—for not writing."

"Will you marry me—if I can get permission from your uncle and the Legate?"

She came into his arms, giving him the answer he needed, but after a long sweet interval, she moved a little distance away from him on the bench and, when he would have followed her, put out her hand to restrain him.

"We must think now, darling," she said. "Think and plan."

"The authority of the Legate is second only to that of the Emperor himself," said Prochorus. "Antipas certainly doesn't want to earn the displeasure of Vitellius when he has just become governor of Syria, so if the Legate approves our marriage, he can hardly refuse."

"Do you have that much influence with Vitellius?"

"Probably not yet," Prochorus admitted. "I must choose the time and place to ask carefully—perhaps after we return to Antioch."

"When will that be?"

"Vitellius is going back immediately after the Passover, but I am to stay here awhile and advise Marcellus until he is familiar with Jewish customs and the various forces at work in Judaea and Samaria. It might be several months."

"We don't have much choice except to wait then," she agreed.

"In any event Antipas can't marry you off without Vitellius' permission, so I shall know about it in time to prevent it." He got to his feet. "We'd better go back inside before your uncle learns you are out here with me. He tried just now to humiliate me but Vitellius cut him off short. I don't want to give him another opportunity."

"When will I see you again?"

"I have no special duties tomorrow."

"Tomorrow morning I shall say I'm going to visit the bazaars. We will meet accidentally—but where?"

"Shall we say the Street of the Silversmiths?" It was one of the most public places in Jerusalem and therefore the safest. "At the third hour?"

"I'll be there," she promised—then, being a woman, added, "Wait for me."

"If it takes the whole day," he promised fervently. "Or the rest of my life."

xii

Prochorus left the Antonia a full hour before his appointment to meet Mariamne, welcoming the opportunity of a casual stroll through the streets of Jerusalem. They were packed now with pilgrims, not only from the rest of the province of Judaea and from Galilee and Peraea, but also from distant parts of the world, come to the wellspring of their faith to celebrate the holiest of all seasons.

In the Street of the Potters artisans were at work at their wheels, shaping small vases and other objects into which the stamp of the Jerusalem potters—a profile of the Temple—would be pressed before the clay was fired in furnaces fed by the dried branches of the burnet thorn that made a very hot fire but left little ash. Purchasers of articles bearing that stamp could thereafter display them in their homes as mementos of their pilgrimage to the holy shrine.

In another street tentmakers were busy spinning tough threads of goat's hair, which were then woven into cloth upon heavy looms. Jerusalem enjoyed an active trade not only with the cities of the coast but also with the Nabateans of the desert areas beyond the Jordan. To these nomads, a tent was a home as they moved their flocks from one oasis to another along the grassy plateaus of the upland areas east of the Jordan.

In another street Phoenician glassmakers displayed their delicate wares, shaped from soft molten glass by the force of their breath blown through long quills, expanding it into sand molds which could then be broken to free the finished product. Elsewhere sellers of cloth displayed fabrics from Hebron to the south, from Byblos to the north, and even linen from Alexandria, brought by the caravans which regularly traveled along the Way of the Sea paralleling the shore between Jerusalem and Joppa.

Even before he reached the Street of the Silversmiths, Prochorus could hear the music of their hammers, shaping silver and gold into settings for jewels, or into the thin leaf used to decorate expensive vases and dishes. Mariamne had not yet arrived and he paused to watch the artisans at their work until, conscious that someone was watching him, he looked up to see a young man whose face seemed vaguely familiar.

"Is your name Prochorus?" the youth asked.

"Yes." Prochorus' face suddenly cleared. "You are Mark, aren't you? The scribe I met in the Lower City when I was here before?"

"Yes."

"Is John ben Zebedee in Jerusalem?"

"John went to Babylon during the presecution of Saul."

"Manaen told me that in Antioch but I thought he might have returned."

"John is still there but some of the other apostles have come back," said Mark. "Is it true that we have no more to fear—now that Marcellus is Procurator and Jonathan the new High Priest?"

"You are safe as long as you obey the law and pay the required tribute."

"Peter and the others will be happy to hear that. They even considered moving the congregation from Jerusalem for a while, but James wouldn't hear of it."

"I thought James fled into the hills."

"James ben Zebedee has been hiding since the persecution was at its height," Mark explained. "Caiaphas had sworn to destroy him, believing him to be in league with the brigands led by Barabbas, so he had no choice. This James is from the family of Jesus."

"When did he come to Jerusalem?"

"After the persecution by Saul. When the apostles were driven away for a while, he became the *mebaqqer* of the Congregation of the Nazarenes." Prochorus was familiar with the title; it meant ruler or leader, the most important post in any congregation—often referred to as a synagogue.

"It must be very large now," he said. "When I was last here, you numbered nearly five thousand."

"Things have changed since then. Now we are only a few."

"But how could that be, when so many came to follow Peter and John after they were arrested in the Temple and freed?"

"They were arrested once more after that," said Mark. "Caiaphas wanted them stoned that time but Rabban Gamaliel warned the court that if the miracles Peter and John performed were from God, the Sanhedrin would be defying the Most High himself by sentencing them to prison or death, so they were freed. Right after that Caiaphas loosed Saul of Tarsus upon us."

"Surely one man couldn't destroy such a large congregation."

"Saul drove most of the apostles away and many others feared for their lives." Mark hesitated a moment and when he spoke again there was a note of resentment in his voice. "But much of the decline is because James doesn't want us to grow and call attention to ourselves in Jerusalem. He wants the Nazarenes to be just another Jewish sect—like so many others here."

"Are Peter and the others content with that?"

"John particularly wanted to continue preaching here in Jerusalem. But James ben Joseph was afraid, so John went to Babylon."

"What about Peter?"

"He spends most of his time in other cities now, but he will be here tonight—to eat the Passover supper with us."

Just then Prochorus saw Mariamne coming down the street. She had put on a dark robe and wore a kerchief over her hair to make herself less conspicuous, but tendrils still escaped from beneath the cloth and were turned into spun gold by the morning sunlight. Even the most shapeless of garments could not hide the slender loveliness of her body, however, and the tinkle of the silversmiths' hammers upon the anvils were silenced as she passed—an unconscious tribute to her beauty.

"I had to slip away," she said breathlessly, flushing a little at the attention she was getting. "I think Uncle Antipas suspects that I talked to you last night and learned that he destroyed our letters."

"This is Mark, a student in the scribes' school of the Temple," said Prochorus. "He is a friend of Mary of Magdala. You may remember her from the day we visited her home."

"I do remember," Mariamne said with a smile for the youth, who was about her own age. "I'm glad to see you, Mark."

Mark had difficulty in speaking for a moment, so stunned was he by the beauty and presence of Mariamne. But when he finally found his tongue, Prochorus envied him the fluency of his words.

"The beauty of the princess is known to all," he said. "Now that it shines upon me, I am blinded and stricken dumb."

"He's a poet, Prochorus!" Mariamne cried out with delight.

"Only a scribe, Princess," said Mark. "And no longer in the Temple school. When Caiaphas heard I was a Nazarene, he dismissed me."

"Mark lives in Jerusalem with his mother," Prochorus explained. "I met them when I was here before."

"My mother and I would be honored if you and the princess would celebrate the Passover with us," Mark dared to say.

"Could we, Prochorus?" Mariamne cried before he could object. "The Passover is just a gesture with Uncle Antipas and Aunt Herodias to make people think he's still a Jew. I've never even eaten it in the old way."

"Your uncle will be angry," he warned.

"I will send word to the palace that I am celebrating the Passover with some friends from Galilee," she said. "Uncle Antipas is always drunk by the time dinner is finished; he won't even know I'm gone."

"You have persuaded me," he told her. "But as soon as the Hallel is sung, I shall have to take you back to the palace."

They found Simon Peter at Mark's home. With him was a thin man with the pale skin and deep-set eyes of a mystic, who was introduced as James ben Joseph, the kinsman of Jesus who was now the chief elder or *mebaqqer* of the Syngogue of the Nazarenes. Everybody obviously regarded James with a great deal of respect but Prochorus could see that none of them showed toward him the affection and warmth they seemed to have for Simon Peter, bearing out what Mark had already told him about the new leader of the Nazarene congregation.

Not long after Prochorus and Mariamne arrived, James ben Joseph left for the building nearby which the Synagogue of the Nazarenes had taken over as its meeting place and where he lived, Mark said, in a room of spartan simplicity. Obviously an ascetic, James compelled respect for his piety, but there was none of the bluff heartiness and personal warmth about him that was such a marked characteristic of Simon Peter—and which Prochorus remembered so well about his friend John.

"I saw your mother and father only a few months ago in Magdala," Peter told Prochorus. "They are proud of you—and rightly so. *Secretarius ab epistulis* to the Legate Flaccus and now one of the chief advisers to Vitellius; you have come a long way, my son."

"I can remember when you were the mightiest fisherman on the lake," said Prochorus. "Every boy there wanted only to be the equal of Simon ben Jonas."

"I'm still only a fisherman; the Lord has given me the task of catching men now. And this lovely child is surely the fairest flower of Galilee." Peter turned to Mariamne. "The blood of one of Israel's noblest houses is in your veins, my dear."

"Did you know my great-grandmother?" Mariamne asked.

"I remember my mother speaking of her. She was lovely—like you. And every cubit a queen—as you are a princess."

"Careful," Prochorus warned him. "You will make her dissatisfied with the idea of marrying a commoner."

"Does Antipas know of this?" Peter's face was sober.

"I intend to ask the approval of the Legate Vitellius when the time is right," said Prochorus. "Antipas can hardly refuse after that."

"What about Prince Agrippa?"

"He's in Rome."

"But very much interested in what goes on here, even though in prison."

"How could you know that, sir?"

"When the persecution of Saul scattered our people abroad, some went to Rome," Peter explained. "I receive letters from them regularly and hope to visit them before long. Only a few days ago I learned that Prince Agrippa is in prison, but with the political situation changing as rapidly as it does, now that the Emperor is dying, he could be back in favor any day. Both Antipas and Agrippa are ambitious to rule the domain of Herod the Great so their courses are bound to collide one day."

"Are you saying I should not marry Prochorus?" Mariamne asked.

"No. After all, he is of the line of David and no purer blood can be found in all of Israel. I am only warning you both that those in power may have other plans for you, Princess."

Mark and his mother were busy preparing the Passover supper that evening, so Prochorus suggested to Mariamne that they climb the Mount of Olives outside the city walls and seek the camp of the Galileans, who usually put up their tents together when they visited Jerusalem for the religious festivals. His ostensible purpose was the hope of seeing some of his friends from the lake region but much more important was the chance to be alone for a part of the afternoon with Mariamne.

Leaving Jerusalem through the Water Gate near the southeast corner of the city, they followed the banks of the brook Kedron past the Spring of Gihon and, crossing the brawling stream on an arching stone bridge, started to climb the eastern slope of the Kedron Valley toward the lovely garden called Gethsemane. On the slope of the Mount of Olives facing Jerusalem the smoke from hundreds of campfires joined the thick plume that already hung over the Temple, for not only the pilgrims but also the inhabitants of the city prepared the flesh of the paschal lamb in the traditional way, roasting it slowly over a bed of coals in a pit. Halfway up the slope of the mount, Prochorus helped Mariamne climb the last rocky ledge that gave access to the garden and dusted off a place for her on a large flat boulder facing toward the Temple.

"I never saw it like this before!" She caught her breath at the beauty of the massive structure crowning the elevation to the west. "We always came in from the north so Uncle Antipas could impress the Samaritans with his wealth."

"I was trying to do just the opposite," said Prochorus. "Marcellus would have ridden through Judaea with the Roman standards uncovered, as Pontius Pilate did when he first came here and stirred up a near rebellion. I persuaded him to cover them and prevented another flare-up."

"Uncle Antipas knows how much you have done to ease the tension between the people of Jerusalem and the Romans," she assured him. "That's one reason why he hates you."

"And why we must go slowly with our marriage plans," he said, but she tossed her head imperiously—the same gesture he had noticed that first morning in the palace of Herod Antipas at Tiberias.

"I shall soon be of age, then I can do as I please."

"You are a princess of the Herodian house and subject to the will of the Emperor," he reminded her soberly. "So far Vitellius has taken my advice where political affairs in the province are concerned, and if I succeed in handling future crises as well as I seem to have done with the problem of Pontius Pilate and Caiaphas, he may feel sufficiently indebted to me to recommend approval of our marriage."

"Do you have any idea what these future crises—as you call them —might be?"

"This whole part of the world is like tinder, needing only a spark to set it aflame. Antipas would like to become Tetrarch of Ituraea, now that Philip is dead, but that would drive a wedge eastward from the Lake of Tiberias between the territory of the Nabateans and the city of Damascus. Aretas badly needs to control Damascus because of the caravan routes and he already hates Antipas because of the divorce. So with Antipas on both his northern and eastern flank, as he would be then, Aretas would have no choice except to make war."

"I never realized just how complicated it all is."

"Vitellius was sent to Antioch to arrange a treaty with Parthia and stop the raids on our eastern frontier. Until he can accomplish that, nothing must be allowed to disturb the balance of power that presently exists in what was your great-grandfather's kingdom. The rebels led by Manahem and Barabbas will certainly try to stir up trouble for a new Procurator in every way they can and your uncle will help them. My task is to see that they are given no excuse through any official act of the Legate or the Procurator."

She shivered and moved closer to him. And as he put his arm about her, he saw that across the Kedron Valley a change in the wind had driven the heavy pall of black smoke that hung over the Temple downward, almost obscuring the golden dome from view and partially hiding the sun as well. Remembering what Cassius Longinus had said to him in Caesarea about his chances of ever claiming Mariamne as his wife, Prochorus felt a sudden sense of forboding that made him draw her even closer. It was then that he had a sudden inspiration.

"I remember my mother telling me about an ancient betrothal ceremony she and my father went through before they were married," he told her. "Would you go through it with me—in secret?"

"Why not publicly?"

"You are not of age, for one thing. And I am not yet so important to the Legate that I can take a chance on causing his disapproval if he heard of it. This way, we could be betrothed in secret while I work to gain your uncle's consent."

"How could that be—when you know he hates you?"

"More than anything else Antipas wants to rule in Judaea and Samaria," he explained. "Except for conniving with the rebels to make Pontius Pilate look bad, he has done a good job in Galilee and Peraea. The Legate is occupied now promoting the treaty of peace with Parthia but, when that is over, I might be able to convince him that Judaea and Samaria would be more stable with Antipas as tetrarch than under a Roman procurator."

"Do you really believe that?"

"I'm beginning to think so, particularly since Pontius Pilate almost caused the Samaritans to revolt. Antipas is only part Jew but he's acceptable to the priestly authorities in Jerusalem. And his mother was a Samaritan, so they should accept him, too. Manahem and the other rebels would still be a threat but I don't think Antipas would hesitate to sacrifice them if it meant gaining control of Jerusalem. I could logically use all these arguments before the Legate after making it clear to Antipas first that the price for pleading his cause would be approval of our marriage."

"Cassius Longinus told me there was no limit to how high you can go. I'm beginning to understand why."

"Especially if I have a beautiful wife—who is also a princess."

"So that's why you claim to love me?"

"Claim? What more proof do you want than I've already given you?" She reached up to kiss him and for a long sweet moment all thought of political affairs were far from their minds.

"I shall want proof over and over again, but that's enough for today," she said at last. "Where are those Galileans of yours? I'm beginning to think you made that up about visiting them in order to lure me out here."

xiii

The camp of the Galileans on the western slope of the Mount of Olives was a busy and cheerful scene. The women worked around the cooking pits while the children played among the tents that dotted the slopes, and the men lounged in groups exchanging gossip and talking politics. Halfway through the camp, Prochorus was greeted warmly by a powerful man with features gnarled by the weather. About him hung the unmistakable odor of sheep, which no amount of washing could remove.

"Cleopas!" he cried. "Is Mary with you?"

A woman emerged from a nearby tent, leading a small boy of perhaps four. Her face broke into a smile at the sight of Prochorus and she came forward to embrace him too.

"This is Cleopas and Mary from Galilee," Prochorus told Mariamne. "They were neighbors of ours when we lived in Capernaum."

The Galileans acknowledged the introduction shyly, awed at being in the presence of a princess. But the ice was quickly broken when Mariamne reached down to the toddler and he held out his arms to be taken.

"Who is this young man?" she asked as she swung him aloft, crowing with delight.

"His name is Simeon," said Mary Cleopas, the name by which Prochorus had known her since childhood.

"Do you know whether Mother and Father came to Jerusalem this time?" Prochorus asked.

"Chuza was too busy with the fisheries," said Cleopas. "Antipas has just bought the establishment of Zebedee. With James and John no longer fishing on the lake, Zebedee wasn't able to supervise the work closely."

"I hear that John is in Babylon," said Prochorus. "Do you know anything about James?"

"Why do you ask?" There was a guarded look in Cleopas' eyes.

"Someone told me he was hiding from the wrath of Pontius Pilate. I want him to know that Pilate is being sent to Rome in disgrace and that the Legate has issued a proclamation of amnesty to all who may have been in opposition to Pilate, if they will swear allegiance to Rome."

Mariamne had gone with Mary Cleopas to look at the flesh of the paschal lamb cooking on the coals. She was still carrying the baby Simeon, who had taken a great fancy to her.

"James is here in the camp," Cleopas confided to Prochorus. "Would you have time to talk to him?"

"Of course." Calling to Mariamne that he would be back in a little while, he followed Cleopas through the Galilean camp to a tent near the edge. Unlike most of the others, its flap was closed.

"It is Cleopas, James," the shepherd called. "Prochorus is with me."

For a moment there was no answer, then the flap was opened

partly and Prochorus saw the familiar short, somewhat bandy-legged figure of James ben Zebedee standing inside.

"What brings the son of Chuza here?" he demanded suspiciously.

"I was looking for friends from Galilee and Cleopas told me you were in the camp," Prochorus explained. "Is this how the son of Zebedee greets an old friend?"

For a moment it seemed that James was going to close the flap again; then he pulled it aside and allowed Prochorus to enter. Cleopas didn't follow but turned back toward his own tent and campfire, leaving the two men alone.

"Why are you hiding?" Prochorus asked.

"Pilate issued a warrant for my arrest. Caiaphas has been trying to destroy me, too."

"Pilate is on his way to Rome in disgrace and Caiaphas has been deposed, so you need fear them no longer. I persuaded the Legate to issue a proclamation of amnesty for all who had been in opposition to them."

Seeing James's eyes light up at the word "amnesty," Prochorus was sure he had done right in seeking out his friend.

"There have been rumors of the order," said James. "But I didn't know whether to trust them."

"I wrote the proclamation myself and witnessed its signing by Vitellius." When James seemed not quite convinced, he added, "I know little of the Nazarene but you obviously cannot serve his cause by associating with brigands like Manahem and Harith—or Barabbas. They have no real interest in anything except gain for themselves, else they wouldn't conspire with Herod Antipas to keep Judaea in turmoil so he can gain control of Jerusalem and its riches for himself."

"I will think about it," said James but his tone told Prochorus he was weakening.

"Princess Mariamne and I are going to eat the Passover supper with Peter, Mark and his mother," he urged. "Why don't you come with us? I know they will be happy to see you and, if you don't want to stay in the city, you can always come back here afterward."

xiv

When Prochorus and Mariamne returned to the city, James ben Zebedee accompanied them. The sun was almost touching the hills to the west and, as they passed through the narrow streets, people were beginning to gather inside the houses while the women lit candles in preparation for the ritual of the Passover. The reunion of James with Peter and others of his former companions was heartening; afterward, while Mary was preparing to serve the Passover feast, Prochorus drew Peter aside.

"Princess Mariamne and I wish to become officially betrothed," he explained. "I remember my mother telling me of a religious ceremony where a couple repeats their vows privately before an elder of the congregation, but their betrothal remains a secret until they are ready to reveal it."

"I know of it," said Peter. "But why must yours remain secret?"

"Antipas dislikes me and might petition the Emperor to set our vows aside. We can reveal the betrothal later, when the Tetrarch comes to look with favor upon me."

"It is rumored that Antipas hopes to marry the princess to a Nabatean prince."

"I think he would like to arrange a marriage but I shall do everything I can to prevent it."

"You may not have much trouble at that," said Peter. "Some say Antipas already regrets putting away Aretas' daughter, but Queen Herodias is strong and jealous. She even persuaded Antipas to behead John the Baptizer because John named her an adulteress after her divorce from Antipas' half brother Herod Philip."

"Didn't you say you remembered the betrothal ceremony I mentioned?" Prochorus reminded him.

Peter nodded. "It's an old ritual, using words spoken by Ruth, the Moabite, to Naomi, when they returned to Israel. James ben Joseph is *mebaqqer* of the synagogue, he could hear—"

"Aren't you an elder?"

"Yes."

"We would rather speak our vows before you."

"In that case," said Peter, "I will gladly hear your vows of betrothal and keep your secret. Bring the princess outside and I will meet you there."

The simple ceremony of betrothal was carried out beneath a tree outside the home of Mark and his mother, with only the three of them present and the rising moon as a witness. First Prochorus, then Mariamne, repeated the beautiful words with which for centuries Israelite young men and women had vowed their love:

> "Wherever you go, I will go,
> wherever you live, I will live.
> Your people shall be my people,
> and your God, my God.
> Wherever you die, I will die
> and there I will be buried.
> May Yahweh do this thing to me
> and more also,
> if even death should come between us!"

Both were silent and a little awed as Peter blessed them, but Mary called to them just then that the Passover ceremony was about to begin and the solemn mood was broken. Inside the house, they all gathered around a low table while Simon Peter poured wine into a cup and blessed it. Each of them then drank from the cup in turn and, after the ritual washing of hands, Peter spoke the prayer of the Shema which Jews repeated everywhere during a worship service.

A plate of unleavened bread was passed around next and each ate a small portion, a custom which, Peter explained, had been inaugurated by Jesus on the night when he was seized by the soldiers in the Garden of Gethsemane. Afterward, too, each sipped from a glass of wine and ate from a dish of vinegar mixed with dates and raisins, symbol of the clay used when the Israelites had been slaves in Egypt long ago. The scroll of the Torah was then brought out and Mark read from it the story of how the Children of Israel had been freed from servitude in Egypt, when the Angel of Death struck down the firstborn in every household, except those of the Jews where the blood of a lamb had been smeared upon the lintels of the doorways. This passing over by the Angel of Death and sparing of the chosen people of God was the act which the lovely ritual ceremony preceding the joyful feast was intended to represent.

The experience was a deep and moving one for all of them, but especially for Prochorus. And as he felt Mariamne's hand slip into his while the candles flickered and Mark's young voice read the stirring story, he was more moved than he ever remembered being before. Only when the ritual which had become a part of Jewish worship throughout the centuries was complete was the succulent dish of roast lamb, garnished with lentils, chick-peas and other delicacies, passed around.

Now the occasion took on a more joyous hue and Prochorus was happy to see how easily Mariamne fitted into this gathering of people who had never known riches but were yet rich in the fullness of their happiness at being together. When the meal was finished, they all went outside to sing the Hallel, the traditional hymn ending with the words:

> *"O give thanks to the Lord, for he is good;*
> *For his steadfast love endures forever."*

"I must take Mariamne home," Prochorus said as they listened to the sound of hymns floating across the city from the thousands in Jerusalem or camped upon the Mount of Olives across from it. When Simon Peter offered to go with them, he was glad to have the broad shoulders of the powerful fisherman to guard them, having been troubled all evening by the thought of possible danger to Mariamne while they crossed the darkened city.

Nothing disturbed them as they made their way up the western slope of the Tyropean Valley to the Palace of the Hasmoneans, the lovely building erected originally for Mariamne's great-grandmother. Prochorus told his betrothed good-by—until they met tomorrow for religious worship—in the shadows outside the gate of the palace, while Simon Peter waited not far away.

"The followers of Jesus owe you much for bringing James ben

Zebedee back to the fold," said Peter when he came back to where the solid figure of the fisherman stood. "As long as one of the twelve still clung to the movement of rebellion, we were constantly in danger of being considered rebels against Rome. Now that James has severed his ties with Manahem and Barabbas we can go forward as a congregation with no question of our allegiance. Shalom, son of Chuza. May you soon be one of us."

Walking northward through the now largely sleeping city, past the remains of the earliest northern wall of Jerusalem and almost in sight of the walls surrounding the sanctuary area, Prochorus pondered upon what Peter had said. Deep in thought, he paid little attention to his surroundings—until the furtive sound of a footfall behind him in the darkness suddenly brought him up short.

He had accepted with gratitude Peter's offer to accompany him and Mariamne to the palace, but it had not occurred to him that he might be in danger himself during the brief walk from the Palace of the Hasmoneans to the Antonia. Reacting instinctively to the sound, he pressed himself against the wall of a building in the darkness and listened.

The tapping of footsteps behind him upon the paving stones came momentarily to his ear, then stopped, meaning, Prochorus was sure now, that whoever was following him had realized his presence was known. He had never experienced the sensation of being hunted and found it a distinctly unpleasant one. Standing there pressed closely against the wall of a darkened house, he made a quick survey of his surroundings, but could find nothing about the situation to reassure him.

He could see a torch burning over one of the gates of the Antonia, not far ahead at the end of the street, and knew it represented a haven of safety—if he could reach it. But the distance was still considerable and, if the pursuer was at all agile, he doubted his ability to reach the fortress before being caught. The only other choice was to wait in the shadows and hope for a chance to grapple with the assailant but, unarmed as he was, this appeared to be the height of foolhardiness.

Stooping so as to present the smallest possible target, in case the pursuer was armed with one of the deadly slings favored by shepherds and the brigands of the upland plateaus, or a swiftly thrown knife, Prochorus darted from the protection of the building and raced up the street toward the distant gates of the Antonia. A sudden clatter of footsteps behind him told him whoever had been stalking him in the darkness was now in full pursuit, but he was so busy watching his own footing on the slippery cobblestones of the street, already damp from the moisture that settled upon them with the chill of night at this altitude, that he had no time to look back.

The houses on either side of the street were dark, their windows shuttered for the night. Nothing was to be gained by trying to get help from that source, he knew, for long before he could rouse the occupants, the pursuer could be upon him. His only hope therefore was to try and gain the circle of brightness cast by the torch above the gate of the Antonia, where Roman soldiers would be on guard night and day and he would be safe.

His pounding heart threatened to burst from his throat as he raced on with a final spurt of energy produced by the knowledge that his life might depend upon it. He might have made it, too, for he was now no more than a hundred paces from the gate, had his foot not slipped on a dew-slick paving stone. Falling even as he tried to regain his footing, he struck the stones and rolled over several times; then his assailant was upon him.

So close was he to his goal that in the faint light cast by the torches over the gate of the Antonia he was able to recognize the swarthy features of Harith, the brother of Judas of Kerioth. He could even see the glint of the blade of the curved *sicarius* as Harith raised it above his head. Then in rapid succession he felt a heavy blow against his temple and, as his senses started to fade, a searing pain in his left side before blackness engulfed him.

Book Three

BABYLON

Prochorus awoke on a low couch in the small room he had been occupying in the Antonia. The sun shining through a window at the end of the room told him it was daylight, but he had no memory of anything that had transpired after he saw the face of Harith bending over him, as he lay upon the slippery flagstones of the street outside the Antonia on the night of the Passover. His throbbing head, however, plus the sharp pain in his left side when he moved, told him he had not escaped unscathed.

His movement brought a man who had been nodding in the corner to his side and he recognized Jonas, the balding Greek physician who, as a member of the household of Vitellius, had accompanied them to Jerusalem.

"How long have I been without my senses?" Prochorus asked.

"Three days," said Jonas. "If the stupor had continued much longer, I would have been forced to consider trephining the skull."

"Three days of unconsciousness? How could that be?"

"The thief who felled you was an expert. He knew just where to strike in order to render you insensible."

"He's an expert as both thief—and assassin. This time, I think he was playing the latter role."

"Why would anyone want to assassinate you in Jerusalem among your own people?"

"I think I know why. How did he happen to fail?"

"The guard at the gate recognized your voice when you cried for help and threw his spear at your assailant, forcing him to flee before he could finish his task. He stabbed you once but the point of the dagger struck a rib and saved you from death. I sutured the wound in your side and dressed it. If the humors don't form a flux and cause a fever you should be well in a week or more."

"Is the Tetrarch of Galilee still in Jerusalem?"

"I believe he and his party left for Tiberias the afternoon following your injury."

"Did anyone from his household come to ask about me?"

"I know of no one."

Mariamne would have insisted on seeing him if she had known of his injury, he was sure. Which meant that she had been taken away before she could learn of it—or suspect the reason behind it.

"No doubt I owe my life to you, Jonas," he said. "I wonder if I could ask a favor?"

"Of course."

"I have a friend in the Lower City named Mark. Would you send a message asking him to come here to see me as soon as he can?"

"I shall attend to it at once," the physician promised and listened carefully to the directions Prochorus gave him. "Now you should rest."

By the time Mark was ushered into the room where Prochorus lay, his headache was considerably better and, although the pain was still severe when he moved, he was able to be propped up on the couch. The young scribe was obviously somewhat apprehensive about being summoned to the Antonia, but when he saw Prochorus, a quick concern showed in his eyes.

"What happened to you?" he asked.

"The brother of Judas of Kerioth tried to assassinate me after I parted company with Simon Peter the other night."

"The Passover is our holiest season." Mark's eyes showed his horror. "No Jew would harm another at such a time."

"Apparently Harith is more thief than Jew. This time, though, I think he was sent to kill me."

"Why?"

"That's what I want you to find out."

"But how?"

"Didn't James ben Zebedee take refuge with Manahem and Barabbas, when he fled from Jerusalem during the persecution by Saul of Tarsus?"

"Yes. But he broke with them after you persuaded him to accept the amnesty proposed by the Legate."

"I don't want him to go back to the brigands," said Prochorus. "Only to use his connections to find out why Harith attacked me."

"I will ask him," Mark promised. "Peter has convinced James that he should remain in Jerusalem, at least for a while. Both John and he are related to the family of Jesus, and Peter thinks James ben Zebedee may become closer to James ben Joseph than he has been able to be."

"Is there a break between Peter and the *mebaqqer?*"

"It's more a question of doctrine. Peter preaches that Jesus died for our sins and that through believing in him we can be ready when he returns. John once told me he's convinced that Jesus is really the Word of God made flesh among us, so he and Peter are not far apart."

"What about James ben Joseph?"

"He and a few others who control the church here want it to remain a strictly Jewish sect under the law, like the Essenes. They're afraid for the congregation to grow much, or to preach actively, lest the Temple authorities start another persecution." Mark got to his feet. "But I am wearying you by talking too much. I will see both Peter and James ben Zebedee tonight. As soon as we learn anything about why you were attacked, I will bring you word of it."

ii

Prochorus' headache cleared up quickly and in a few days he was able to resume some of his duties. Vitellius was leaving Jerusalem shortly for Antioch in preparation for the mission to negotiate terms of peace with King Artaban of Parthia. Antipas, Prochorus learned, had offered to accompany the Legate and the offer had already been accepted. Angry though he was with the Tetrarch of Galilee for his treatment at the reception, Prochorus could not see any reason to oppose the move for the negotiations would have to be conducted in the Aramaic tongue, which was spoken widely in the East. And though capable translators—such as Prochorus himself—were at the Legate's command, it would be a decided advantage to have a negotiator of royal rank speaking the same language as the Parthian king.

Toward the end of the third day, a visitor was brought to the room where Prochorus was dictating some of the letters Vitellius wished to send out before leaving for Antioch. To his surprise, it was not Mark but Simon Peter.

"Mark came to me with your request," said the man Jesus had affectionately called The Rock. "It took a little time to get the real answer."

"Did you learn why Harith attacked me?"

"Yes, but Harith is dead. Manahem executed him."

"Why?"

"It's a rather long story but I thought you should have it, so I came instead of Mark. You see, Manahem is something more than just a brigand."

"I recognized that the first time I saw him."

"People like Manahem are hard to understand. They are part scoundrel, part hero, and part god—at least as far as many Jews are concerned. To exist under a ruler of our own selected by God has always been our greatest ambition, so in the past we have followed false Messiahs—like Manahem's father, Judas the Gaulonite. But now that the Son of God has been sent to earth and will soon return to rule over us and bring to Israel the glory God intended for it to have, all of that has been changed."

"I thought you didn't regard Jesus as an earthly ruler."

"We don't," said Peter. "But now that he has come as a spiritual Messiah, there will be no need for a political one."

"Mark tried to explain it all to me once, but I must admit that I don't yet understand."

"You will in time—when the Lord wills it."

"Why me?"

"Who can tell what the Lord has in mind for you?" said Peter. "If you had asked me two years ago when Saul of Tarsus was hounding our people and sending them to prison—or when I watched Stephen bleeding and torn from stones cast by witnesses whose cloaks Saul himself held as an agent of the Sanhedrin—I

would never have said God would call him to preach the Way. Yet
He has done so."

"Are you saying that God has a purpose for Manahem—besides
being a robber?"

"Manahem, at least, is convinced of it. More important, he realizes how valuable it is to have someone like you—a Jew—in a position of trust and honor with the Legate of Syria. It would be the
rankest folly for any Jew to destroy you."

"Then why did Harith—"

"He was paid by Herod Antipas to assassinate you."

"I suspected that," said Prochorus. "But I still don't understand
why he was executed."

"Manahem and the rest of the Zealot party want to see the
Romans out of Judaea, but not by putting the son of Herod the
Great in the place of a procurator. Because Harith took a commission from Antipas to kill you he was tried by a court of his own
fellow rebels—and executed."

"I still don't understand why Antipas would want to kill me. I
can't marry Mariamne unless the Legate approves, and he would
hardly do that without consulting Antipas."

"The princess is not the real reason why the Tetrarch wanted you
killed," said Peter. "Vitellius is an experienced statesman but he
knows little about internal political affairs in this part of the world,
while you know them intimately. Antipas probably thinks you will
advise Vitellius against turning over the tetrarchy of his brother
Philip to him."

"How could I do anything else, when King Aretas would have to
go to war then to protect his treaty rights with Damascus and the
other cities of the Decapolis?"

"That is what makes you particularly dangerous to Antipas,"
Peter pointed out. "You recognized at once that, as ruler of Ituraea,
he would have armies on two sides of the Nabateans, with every
chance of winning a quick war with Aretas. But knowing little about
the internal affairs of the province, Vitellius might not realize it
until the damage was done and the whole area embroiled in a war,
with the Parthians almost certainly siding with King Aretas."

Prochorus moved to the window and stood there, looking out

across the city toward the hills that lay to the northeast. They constituted a physical barrier between him and Mariamne, who was in Galilee by now, but no more so than the political one that also lay between them.

"I'm sorry to be the bearer of bad news." Peter came over to put his arm across the younger man's shoulder in one of the warm gestures of companionship that were so characteristic of him. "I wanted you to understand the whole picture, so I came to tell you."

"At some risk to yourself, I know," said Prochorus gratefully.

"With Caiaphas no longer High Priest and a new Procurator in Jerusalem—both of which are your doing—I think we Nazarenes will be allowed to worship in peace, particularly with James ben Joseph at the head of the church. But what of you, my son?"

"I must be where I can watch Herod Antipas—which means I must go on the expedition to Parthia with Vitellius."

"Talk to John while you are in Babylon and tell him it is safe now to return. And be sure that the Son of God will protect you on the way."

"Why—when I don't even accept him as you do?"

"We are all part of God's purpose, carrying out our allotted tasks. When the time comes for you to know your role in the Way of Jesus, it will be revealed to you, as it was to Saul of Tarsus."

iii

When Peter left, Prochorus went immediately to the Legate's chamber. He found Vitellius reading some dispatches which had arrived that afternoon by courier.

"I have a request to make, sir," he said.

"If it is for a sick leave at Jericho," said Vitellius with a smile, "your request is approved."

"I would like to accompany you to Parthia for the conference."

Vitellius frowned. "We leave day after tomorrow and will be riding hard for Antioch, where a legion is being made ready. With your wound that might be painful—even dangerous."

"If I fall by the wayside, I can always take ship from Caesarea."

"I should like very much to have you with me, but there may be a better way for both of us." Vitellius' voice became brisk. "The meeting to negotiate the new treaty with Parthia will take place on a bridge that spans the Euphrates near Babylon. I shall not take an army but we must make a show of force with troops from this area, to convince Artaban that he has no hope of weaning away part of Syria from Roman rule. Herod Antipas is raising a contingent of auxiliaries from Galilee and Peraea, and I would also like to have at least a cohort from the former territory of Philip, but I have no intention of placing them under the command of the Tetrarch of Galilee. Have you ever had any military training?"

"A little—in Tiberias and in Antioch. Decurion Cassius Longinus and I often exercised together."

"I know Longinus well. His father and I are in the Senate—not that the senatorship amounts to much since Augustus. What I have in mind is appointing you to the temporary rank of tribune and giving you the task of raising the cohort from Ituraea. You can meet us on the way to Parthia, probably at Palmyra."

"I know nothing of soldiering, sir."

"That isn't necessary since your real duty is to be my representative. But provincials are accustomed to obeying the orders of Romans in uniform, so you will need a rank commensurate with the size of your cohort. I will arrange for Centurion Sextus Latimus to be your aide; you can safely leave all military questions to him."

"When shall I leave, sir?"

"Take Sextus with you and spend a week at Jericho; the rest will do you good and you will be that much farther on your way to Ituraea. We shall meet two months hence at Palmyra and journey to the Euphrates and Babylon together."

iv

A week less than two months had passed when Prochorus, wearing the uniform of a military tribune and accompanied by Centurion Sextus Latimus, brought the column of soldiers behind them to a halt at the caravansary, or public camping ground, located on the outskirts of the desert metropolis of Palmyra. A natural caravan stopping point on the ancient route between Babylon and the West, the oasis of Palmyra had been called Tadmor in the time of Abraham when, accompanied by his family, his flocks and his herds, the Hebrew patriarch had journeyed along what was even then called the Fertile Crescent, the classic route to Canaan and Egypt or, by turning northward, to Asia Minor.

Orders elevating Prochorus to the temporary rank of tribune commanding a cohort—which existed then only in the imagination—had been prepared immediately after his conversation with Vitellius. The following day, he and Sextus Latimus, a grizzled veteran of many campaigns, had left for Jericho. Restless to be doing something, Prochorus had remained at the lovely city of the palms only a week, however, while his wound finished healing. Then he and Sextus had journeyed up the east bank of the Jordan to the Sea of Galilee where they had crossed over and gone on to Magdala to spend a day at his father's home before circling the northern end of the lake and entering the former domain of the Tetrarch Philip, where the cohort Vitellius had assigned to his command would be raised.

Wanting no clash with Antipas before he had solidified his position and justified the confidence of Vitellius in giving him the task of raising and commanding a cohort, Prochorus had made no attempt to see Mariamne at nearby Tiberias. Leaving Magdala the following day, he and Sextus had ridden eastward along the Way of the Sea and crossed the Jordan at the Jisr Benat Yakub—the Bridge of Jacob's Daughters. There the water ran swift and cold from its several sources at the foot of Mount Hermon, before plunging into the lovely blue Sea of Galilee visible far below the road they were traveling northeastward toward Caesarea Philippi.

The Parthians had more than once raided the eastern part of the province, so Prochorus had little difficulty in raising the six hundred auxiliary troops Vitellius had assigned to him. On the march eastward by way of Damascus to Palmyra, Sextus had been able to whip them into a fairly capable military organization, although auxiliaries were not expected to display the unquestioning courage and obedience to orders that had made the Roman legionary the finest and most highly skilled fighting machine the world had ever seen. In the process, Prochorus, too, had learned much about military discipline and practice.

In the warm sunshine of Palmyra the cohort went about the task of setting up camp with considerable enthusiasm, knowing they could expect to rest there for a few days while waiting for the arrival of Vitellius and the remainder of the party. It was not necessary to surround the camp with trenches and palisades, as was customarily done by Roman military forces in enemy territory. This was to be a mission of peace to establish a definite boundary with the Parthians, a boundary which, hopefully, would not be constantly violated, as had been the case since the unfortunate expedition of Crassus in the time of Julius Caesar, when an entire Roman army had been destroyed in the desert wastes between the Orontes and the Euphrates.

The city of Palmyra, centered around a fertile oasis with two gushing springs, had first become prominent during the eastward march of Alexander the Great centuries earlier when he had made it a major military base. The Romans had further fortified and enlarged it into a frontier post located almost at the edge of the vast Tigris-Euphrates Valley, one of the three major cradles of civilization. In the constant seesaw struggle for power between the Parthians—as the Romans called the Persians—and the Roman Empire, Palmyra enjoyed the priceless advantage of an adequate water supply. In addition, its isolated position had enabled the city and the surrounding area to remain largely independent, whether it was ruled by the Seleucid emperors, whose dynasty had succeeded that of Alexander the Great, or the more recently arrived Romans.

Like Antioch, the center of Palmyra was a wide thoroughfare lined with shaded porticoes supported on stone columns quarried from the jagged cliffs of the Anti-Lebanon range lying somewhat to the north and west. At the four main crossing streets, magnificent arches had been erected, giving it a façade rivaling any city in the empire, except perhaps Rome itself.

While Sextus was drilling the cohort the morning after their arrival, Prochorus went into Palmyra, eager for a chance to see this fabled oasis of which he had heard so much, but anxious also to determine, if he could, what was the temper of the Parthians with whom they would shortly be engaged in negotiations.

The most striking feature of the oasis city, he saw at once, was the magnificent Temple of the Sun. Completed a few years earlier, its stone columns were still unmarred by the biting sands of the desert storms that so often whipped this entire area. Dedicated to a trinity of gods made up of Malak-Bel, the God of Earth; Yarhibol, the Sun; and Aglibol, the Moon—the latter being Assyrian gods handed down from the days of Sennacherib—the temple boasted the largest open court in the entire Roman Empire, with a colonnade of Corinthian columns in rows of four almost fifteen hundred paces in length. As he stood before the great temple, gazing up at the tall columns and the elaborate carvings capping them, Prochorus felt a hand pull at his sleeve and looked down to see a dirty, bright-eyed urchin standing there.

"Noble Roman," the boy said, "would you like to witness a sacrifice to the god Malak-Bel?"

"I am a Jew. Why should I witness the rites of Baal?" Prochorus had recognized the similiarity of names to those of Moloch, or Marduk, and Baal, ancient Semitic pagan gods against which the Torah of the Jews constantly inveighed.

"My ancestors, the Assyrians, conquered your ancestors long ago and placed them in captivity," said the youngster impudently. "You might be able to see why our god is superior to yours."

"I still have no wish to witness your rites." Prochorus couldn't help grinning at the boy's brash assurance.

"Would your honor like to visit the bazaars then? There is much to be bought and I can see that you are not cheated."

"Very well," Prochorus agreed, knowing a commission for the boy would be tacked on everything he bought. He was surprised by the diversity of goods offered for sale in the bazaars that lined both the main thoroughfare and the crossing streets on either side of it. Like the shops found in the Street Called Straight of Damascus —along which he had marched with his cohort when they passed through that ancient city—the establishments in the shopping area of

Palmyra formed a small composite world set down here on the desert oasis almost halfway between Antioch and Babylon.

Silk from China, gorgeous in color and unbelievably filmy in texture, reminded him of Mariamne and he bought enough for a headcloth to cover her golden hair. Jewels from India and the craggy hills of Armenia to the north; magnificent robes, tunics and other articles of dress from Persian looms; incense and spices from Arabia to the south; purple-dyed cloth from Tyre to the west; fine glassware and bottles from the Phoenician cities of the Mediterranean coast; even some of the parchment sheets from Byblos which were now beginning to replace the rolled-up scrolls of older times; fine wines from Syria and the grape arbors of the Orontes Valley— the whole bazaar area teemed with people buying and selling. He could see, too, why this region with its vast revenues in trade and taxes was so important both to Rome and to Parthia. For peace here could only result in benefit to all concerned, with the increase in trade, once it could flow freely in both directions.

He returned to the camp late that afternoon to find Sextus Latimus taking his ease in the shelter of one of the many leafy arbors the caravansary provided. From a dish on the table at the older man's elbow came the savory aroma of roast meat; beside it was a basket with chunks of bread and a skin of wine.

"Drink this and have some food." The Roman officer reached for a cup and poured Prochorus some wine. "I had our orderly buy a kid and roast it over the coals this afternoon, so we could have fresh meat for dinner."

Prochorus drank the wine and tore off a chunk of bread, dipping it into the juices in the bottom of the dish before cutting off a slab of the meat for himself with a dagger he wore.

"What were you doing all day?" Sextus asked. "Ogling temple maidens?"

"I'm a Jew. Our religion forbids us to take part in pagan ceremonies."

"Most religious ceremonies are without meaning because so few people are religious," said Sextus. "I've seen the Pontifex Maximus in Rome slay eight oxen at once on the altar in the Temple of Jupiter Capitolinus. It was supposed to be a very special occasion, thanking the god for a great victory, but all I saw was a lot of blood and thrashing and bawling. The *victimarii* could hardly even hold the bulls while the blood drained away, so I decided that only a stupid god would get any pleasure out of that ceremony."

"I never thought of it that way."

"Perhaps it's just as well. If you did, you might decide that even your god couldn't be pleased very much by the smoke and the stink of burning entrails and hides that rises above your Temple." Sextus leaned over to spear a chunk of meat with his dagger and carry it to his mouth, then hacked off another piece of bread and sopped up the rest of the juices in the dish.

"When I was stationed in Galilee a few years ago," he continued, "I heard and saw the Nazarene they called Jesus. He had a faculty for stirring men's souls and demanding allegiance, even though reason told you an obscure carpenter couldn't possibly be starting a new religion."

"Great crowds followed him in the beginning, I remember seeing them in Capernaum."

"After it was rumored that Jesus had fed five thousand with only a few fish and a loaf or two of bread, some of the Galileans even got excited and wanted to name him king. But he refused to let them do it and after that his following began to drift away."

"When I was in Jerusalem several years ago, the followers of the Nazarene were preaching there. More than five thousand people had joined with them." For some reason, which he could not have explained at the moment, Prochorus felt impelled to defend Jesus.

"I remember reading some dispatches from Jerusalem about it in Antioch. That must have been the reason Pontius Pilate let the High Priest have a free hand in dealing with them."

"Caiaphas almost succeeded. My friends among the Nazarenes tell me the congregation has almost stopped growing."

"It couldn't have amounted to much, in any event," said Sextus. "A purely Jewish religion would have little appeal in cities like Antioch, Alexandria or Rome. Too many cults are there already and too much money is spent on temples and fat priests who live without working." He got to his feet and stretched himself.

"Give me a few more days and I will almost make soldiers out
of these recruits of yours. Meanwhile I shall go into the city and
see what I can learn in the drinking houses. Sometimes you find
more truth there than in official dispatches."

v

Vitellius arrived at Palmyra three days later and immediately re-
viewed the cohort of auxiliaries raised by Prochorus and Sextus
Latimus.

"You have done well," he told them. "If Antipas doesn't delay
us, we can get on with our journey to Babylon. The word from
Rome is that Emperor Tiberius may not last much longer. I would
like to get the treaty with Artaban signed before the Parthians
learn how near he is to death, or they may dally, hoping for better
terms from the new Emperor."

"Who will that be, sir?" Prochorus asked.

"Caligula—unless the Praetorian Guard decides to become king-
makers—but he's a poor choice. It's a pity Augustus had no heirs
though. Rome knew her greatest glory during his reign; Tiberius has
been a mere housekeeper."

Prochorus debated speaking to Vitellius about Mariamne but decided against it, knowing that, if he accused Antipas of trying to
have him killed in Jerusalem, only his word would be set against
that of the Tetrarch of Galilee, since he would not involve James
ben Zebedee by revealing James's former connection with Manahem.
He spoke about it instead to Sextus and received the promise of
the centurion to inquire among the officers of Antipas' contingent
of Roman troops when they arrived and seek to learn what he
could about her from that source.

Vitellius had traveled light from Antioch, with only a cohort of
household troops and several secretaries. Even with Prochorus' cohort
the number of troops was brought to no more than a thousand men.

When Antipas arrived several days later, it was with all the splendor of an oriental monarch, but his troops were few, less than half

the number Prochorus had raised. His baggage train was strung out for more than a mile, however, and the tent he had erected for himself was luxurious enough for the entertainment of a king.

"The Fox is playing a clever game as usual," Sextus observed to Prochorus as they watched the arrival of the Tetrarch of Galilee and his company. "He knows how much the Parthians dote on splendor and hopes to make Artaban think he is more important than he really is."

"How important is he? I've never been able to decide."

"In my opinion he's a liability. When Antipas put away Aretas' daughter for Herodias, he made an enemy who will one day strike a dagger into his back and provoke a civil war we will almost surely have to settle with a legion or so of Roman soldiers."

"On which side?"

"Both—eventually. When Rome starts letting subject kings battle among themselves without punishment, the empire will be dissolving already, so both rulers will probably be replaced. Antipas got away with letting the brigands in Lower Galilee go unpunished so they could foment trouble for Pontius Pilate, because Pilate was a drunkard and a fool. But he's very much mistaken if he thinks Vitellius can be duped that easily."

Vitellius wasted no time in starting for the Euphrates and the meeting with King Artaban. He did not hide his displeasure at Antipas for bringing so much baggage and so few soldiers, but his coldness seemed to have no effect whatsoever upon the Tetrarch of Galilee. At the end of the first day's march, Sextus, who had ridden for a while with the officers of the small detail of Roman troops assigned to the Tetrarch's household, reported to Prochorus.

"Your lady love is shut up in that castle of Herod's east of the Salt Sea," he said.

"Machaerus?"

"Yes."

"Why?"

"My guess is that he's holding her as a prize, to be given where it will do him the most good."

"With King Aretas?"

"Where else? Antipas obviously expects to gain considerable prestige during the negotiations with Artaban of Parthia. He brought all that baggage to make it appear that he's a real power and the rest of us merely part of his train."

"Surely King Artaban wouldn't be fooled by that."

"The Parthians have felt Roman swords too many times not to recognize where the real power lies," Sextus assured him. "The people Antipas really hopes to fool are the Nabateans. By now he knows Vitellius will not recommend to the Emperor that he be made ruler of Philip's tetrarchy or even Judaea, as long as Aretas is waiting to sting his backside at the first opportunity." He hesitated, then went on. "Did you know that Antipas has been trying to arrange a marriage between Princess Mariamne and Aretas' son?"

"Yes. She told me about it in Jerusalem."

"No doubt he figures that, by claiming to have negotiated the treaty with the Parthians once we have completed it, he can impress Aretas and tie the Nabateans to him by marriage again."

"It might work."

"I'll wager a month's pay against it," Sextus said cheerfully. "If you'd ever traded with Arabs you'd know they can take the hide off you before you even realize you're being skinned. My guess is that Aretas is holding Antipas on the line like a hooked fish, waiting to land him."

The baggage brought by the Tetrarch of Galilee kept the column moving slowly, so it was nearly a week before they saw the broad muddy flood of the Euphrates at Dura-Europos, a major crossing point on the caravan trail to the East. At this point the column turned south, following the course of the river through the fertile basin extending for some distance on either side of it. Days before they reached Babylon itself, they could see striking evidence that the great river was a most important trade route, a startling sight for Prochorus, who had never seen a really navigable river before, the Orontes at Antioch being too shallow for major shipping.

By means of an elaborate network of canals, the entire lower Tigris-Euphrates basin had been turned into a maze of trade routes, as well as a source of water for the irrigation that made the whole area a veritable garden. A steady stream of water-borne traffic moved on the river in small shallow-draft boats that were usually rowed, or poled wherever the water was shallow enough. Larger vessels were sometimes propelled by sails but more often drawn by animals plodding along towpaths.

Upstream from the Persian Gulf came ivory and precious jewels from the eastern coast of Africa, as well as exotic imports from India. Phoenician ships had been trading with that far-off land since before the days of Solomon, their vessels driven by the monsoon winds that blew steadily from one direction for half the year, then reversed themselves for another six months. Goods from Syria and Asia Minor, brought by caravan to the river far upstream, were floated down to Babylon and other cities of the Tigris-Euphrates delta. And caravans of camels, following the desert routes where a star was often the only guide, also brought goods from Egypt by way of the King's Highway that paralleled the east bank of the Jordan past Petra, Philadelphia and Gerasa before heading eastward across the desert wastes. There the Nabateans and other Arabic people were perfectly at home but other travelers shortly found themselves wandering in circles before thirst and death claimed them.

As they approached Babylon, the country became more and more heavily populated and the band of fertile soil reclaimed by irrigation along the riverbank wider.

"You can see now why the Parthians could hold out against Roman rule for so long," Sextus said to Prochorus as they rode along at the head of their cohort, a smart military-looking group compared to the rather motley train of Antipas, whose soldiers and baggage animals made up the tail of the column. "From the Euphrates eastward almost to the valley of the Indus the area is thickly settled."

"Why would they make peace now?"

"Military leaders obtain territory and a large following through glory gained in battle—if they win," said the Roman officer. "But they hold them only by filling empty bellies after the fighting is done and the booty has been spent on wine, women and useless geegaws that women love. To keep a people happy and contented, trade is required. Julius Caesar knew that, so he built roads wherever he went and let traders follow him."

"Perhaps that was the greater part of his genius."

"I'm sure it was," Sextus agreed. "Having built the roads, he could then move troops rapidly in case of an insurrection. Lately Rome has grown fat and rich and lazy under Tiberius, so demand has been created for the luxuries that come out of Persia. With Syria well governed under legates like Flaccus and Vitellius and cities like Antioch and Alexandria growing larger all the time, King Artaban can see the advantages of a stable frontier. Besides, in a hundred years his people have had time to forget the great victory they won over Crassus that sent Parthian cavalrymen almost to the walls of Antioch."

"I never could understand why a Roman general would strike out across the desert, knowing he would have to fight the Parthians without any means of supplying his troops."

"Crassus was more politician than general," Sextus explained. "Caesar was making great conquests in the West at the time and he felt that he had to equal Caesar's feats in the East, but all he managed to do was to die before Caesar did."

"It seems that the fate of nations is determined by the men who lead them. When one is wrong all must suffer."

"It's not quite as simple as that," said Sextus. "Consider your own country. The empire of Herod the Great, even at its highest point, was small compared to that of Parthia and Rome. Yet the fate of that empire still affects them both materially and will for many, many years."

"In what way?"

"If there is ever peace among the warring factions of the Jews, we Romans will not have to occupy ourselves crucifying your people to maintain a stable frontier in this region, so Rome and Parthia will be in balance. King Artaban knows this and has now agreed to sign the treaty. But if the Jews start killing each other again Artaban will tear up his treaty and try to see what he can gain by moving westward. In the end, everybody will lose. The Jews cannot possibly hope to gain freedom and meanwhile many will die in the conflict between Parthia and Rome."

"The Zealots believe they can set up a kingdom of Jews alone, with a king of their own ruling them, as in the days of Judas Maccabeus years ago."

"They are only deluding themselves. If the Jews stage another rebellion we Romans will turn your traditional enemies, the Samaritans and the Nabateans, loose upon you and Jerusalem may well be destroyed, as the Nazarene predicted. In any event the Jews alone couldn't possibly win a major victory where Antony and Cleopatra tried to build an eastern empire for themselves and failed. Actually Herod the Great may have been the only one who profited by that particular venture; he did it by playing them off against Octavian and making the best bargain he could." Sextus looked back to where Antipas was being borne in an elaborately decorated litter.

"Yonder potgut's father was an important man and a capable ruler, no matter how cruel he may have been, but he had no luck when it came to fathering a son who could follow in his footsteps. Antipas is certainly not the man for the task and neither, I suspect, is Agrippa—though from what I've seen of him, he certainly stands far above Antipas."

"Do you think Agrippa will ever rule in Judaea?"

"He may—but I doubt it. Agrippa's mistake was in growing up in Rome at the court of Caesar—not that he had much choice about it since he was held almost as a hostage for the good behavior of the Jews. The trouble is that one who lives at court—particularly in Rome—sees so much deviousness and grows so devious himself in promoting his own fortunes that he loses the ability to plot a straight course and follow it." He gave Prochorus a probing look. "Have you decided where your own loyalties will lie when the next controversy arises amongst the Jews?"

"I hadn't thought about it. Why do you ask?"

"In times of rebellion, Rome badly needs men she can trust. You are enough of a Jew to be accepted by Jews, but enough of a Greek to let logic rule your actions instead of blind emotions. And you are something very rare anywhere, an honest and intelligent man of high principles." The centurion grinned. "In fact that's probably your only weakness."

"Would you have me change it?"

"I don't really know. In less than a decade you have risen from a student scribe to the rank of tribune—"

"Temporary only," Prochorus reminded him.

"The rank could become permanent—and considerably higher, too, if the dice fall right for you. Originally the task of a tribune was to represent the mass of the people against their rulers and see that they were given justice. You might still accomplish just that in Judaea, if you decide well in advance where your true loyalties shall lie."

"What difference would it make, since Jerusalem must fall anyway?"

"Why do you say that?" Sextus asked.

"You warned just now that it could happen, but Jesus of Nazareth went even further. The main reason why the Sanhedrin condemned him on the charge of blasphemy was his prediction that Jerusalem and the Temple will be destroyed."

"That was the excuse—not the reason," Sextus corrected him. "I studied the account of the Nazarene's trial, in Pontius Pilate's records. His prophecy that Jerusalem and the Temple would be destroyed formed the charge on which he was convicted of blasphemy by the Jewish court, so the death penalty could be demanded by the Caiaphas faction that controlled it."

"Why wasn't he stoned then—as any other Jew convicted of blasphemy would have been treated?"

"The case of Jesus of Nazareth involved far more than simply a breach of Mosaic law. His immense popularity with the people made him a threat to Caiaphas' group of Sadducees because they were afraid his denunciations would make them lose control of the Temple revenues. To the Romans, Jesus was a potential rebel leader because so many people listened to him; if we hadn't crucified him then, it would have had to be done later. Whether he intended to do it or not—and I don't think he did—he was drawing rebel elements around him like flies to a honey pot. And don't forget that he named himself the Messiah."

"But in a different sense from what the word means to the radical element."

"What Jesus meant was of little importance," said Sextus. "What *did* matter was what people thought he meant."

Prochorus gave Sextus a startled look, for the centurion was saying almost word for word what Manahem had told him that afternoon long ago on the road above Tiberias about the plot even then being hatched in Jerusalem to make Jesus of Nazareth announce himself as the Messiah.

"Judas the Gaulonite also claimed to be the Messiah and look what he accomplished," Sextus continued. "I was only a legionary in that campaign but I shall never forget it."

"Surely you don't think the land might be torn again as it was then."

"Only one son of Herod the Great is still alive and he plots every day to gain control of his father's old empire. Agrippa is only a grandson but he also seeks to have Rome make him ruler there. The Zealots long to see a theocracy with themselves in control of the treasury and you tell me the Nazarenes expect their leader to return as king. With so many forces pulling and tugging for control, how can it end in anything except another blood bath?"

vi

When the column finally approached Babylon, Prochorus was startled by the size and magnificence of the Parthian capital. He knew it to be one of the oldest population centers in the world but though its greatest period of magnificence had long since passed, even in its waning, Babylon was still magnificent, spread over the countryside as it was, with a network of canals connecting the city with the broad expanse of the Euphrates. Shipping had increased in volume as they followed the great river downstream, and near Babylon itself the waterways were almost choked with boats of all sorts.

Vitellius was an experienced diplomat and had gracefully acceded to the suggestion of King Artaban that the conference he held at the center of a long bridge spanning the Euphrates somewhat upstream from the heart of the city. In this way, Roman troops would not actually enter Babylon, with the implication of subjection, and negotiations could be carried on between two sovereign nations with no offense to the pride of the Parthian army, whose ability to hold its own against the proud legions of Rome had been demonstrated more than once.

Here the strategy of Antipas in bringing quantities of baggage was revealed. From the pack animals in his part of the train—comprising fully half of it—now appeared a magnificent tent or pavilion which was erected over the center of the bridge to shelter the negotiators. Cushions in profusion were produced for their comfort, silver goblets and plate for the nightly banquets, and a considerable quantity of Syrian wine and such preserved dainties as salted fish of the lake region, all of which were very much liked by the Parthians.

Since Antipas himself insisted upon translating the Greek spoken by Vitellius into the Aramaic tongue spoken by the Parthians, Prochorus' participation was limited to making certain that the Tetrarch of Galilee did not add promises or conditions favorable to him which might interfere with the smooth flow of the conference. The Jewish sabbath fell during the middle of the parley and, in deference to the faith to which Antipas gave at least lip service, negotiations were suspended on that day. Prochorus asked and received permission to go into Babylon to attend services at one of the several synagogues, hoping to find John ben Zebedee, whose address had been given him in Jerusalem by Mark before his departure.

Since Nebuchadnezzar had conquered Judah and Jerusalem more than five hundred years earlier and carried off much of its population to his capital, the Jewish colony in Babylon had grown steadily to become one of the largest and most influential in the entire Diaspora, second only, perhaps, to that in Alexandria. Jewish money-lenders in the Parthian capital exchanged letters of credit and interest with bankers in Jerusalem, Alexandria, Antioch, Tarsus, Ephesus and even Rome. In fact, much of the trading between these centers was carried out by the bankers, and caravans owned by Jewish mercantile interests also plied the dusty routes of the desert in competition with those of the Nabateans and others.

For his visit to Babylon, Prochorus did not wear the uniform of a Roman tribune but put on instead a robe and sandals like any other traveler. John was not at home at the address he had been given, but he had no trouble finding the synagogue where he was told John was preaching.

He had not been surprised to learn from Mark that John had received a warm welcome in Babylon. The farther one went from Jerusalem and the "Rabbis of the Porch," the more liberal the Jews became in departing from the rigid tenets of Mosaic law. For this reason those of the Diaspora had so far been generally more receptive to the teachings of Jesus of Nazareth than those in Jerusalem, since his doctrine contained many overtones of Greek philosophy and even some tenets of the mystery faiths, one of which—the worship of Ahura Mazda, the so-called Light of the World—had actually had its beginning in Parthia.

As he walked along the broad central thoroughfare of Babylon, almost as wide as the great Via Caesarea of Antioch, Prochorus could not help being impressed by the evidence of past magnificence all around him. In the hills overlooking the Sea of Galilee he had occasionally come upon remains of cities long since crumbled to dust, bits of masonry or a shard from a jar or clay tablet upon which was impressed the strange picture writing used by the Egyptians long before Abraham had come into Canaan. Here in Babylon, however, he could see in one sweeping glance a record of the decline of a great city over many thousands of years. A decline which could only remind one of a philosophical bent that eternal verities like truth and reverence for God—who had seen all this magnificence come and go and would see the same process taking place again and again through countless millennia of the future— were the only really imperishable facts of creation.

Prochorus had no difficulty in finding the synagogue to which he had been directed. And since Babylon was still a junction point between the west and the teeming distant cities of India and China, the presence of a strange man did not cause any stir. Like all Jewish places of worship, the synagogue faced toward Jerusalem and the Temple. In deference to the warmth of the climate the windows were open, and as he approached, he could hear the stirring phrases of the Shema being recited, indicating that the worship service had just begun.

As he stepped into the back of the building and took a seat on one of the benches there, the elder who was conducting the service for that day took a scroll of the law from the Ark where it was kept and handed it to the chazan, who read the passage of the day in Hebrew. Immediately afterward, he translated the reading into Aramaic before returning the scroll to the elder to be replaced in the Ark. Had this been a largely Greek city, such as Alexandria or Tarsus, the passage would have been translated into Greek, for many of the Jews of the Diaspora, particularly the young who had been born there, had little knowledge of Hebrew. But the universal language here was Aramaic, just as it was in Galilee; and hearing the translation, Prochorus felt immediately at home.

A passage from the Prophets was read next. When Prochorus heard the familiar prediction of Isaiah concerning the coming of the Messiah, he was certain who the teacher of the day would be, although he had not yet been able to recognize the back of John's head in the row of men occupying the front benches next to the elevated platform called the *bima*, upon which sat the elders of the congregation and where stood the desk from which the chazan was now reading.

In synagogues outside Jerusalem and Galilee, as well as in more distant parts of the Diaspora, congregations were not always able to support a teacher of their own. As a result, rabbis from Jerusalem and a few other large cities traveled on a regular circuit, speaking from a different pulpit each sabbath and being paid by the offerings of the congregation. Sometimes, when a teacher proved very popular —as John apparently had become here in Babylon—he would remain in one of the Diaspora synagogues for some time, teaching until the elders decided he had used up his welcome.

A prayer followed the reading from the Prophets and finally the elder called for any who might wish to address the congregation to do so. It was then that a slender man who had been sitting in the front row rose to his feet and ascended the few steps to the *bima*.

Prochorus' first sight of John after several years told him why he had not been able to recognize his friend among those on the front row. John's hair had grown distinctly gray, a product, he suspected, of the persecution by Saul of Tarsus which had forced many of those who had been closest to Jesus to flee for their lives from the Holy City.

"Men and brethren." John's voice had deepened and attained more force, more confidence, since Prochorus had last talked to him. "Let me speak to you once again of what was said by the Prophet Joel:

> "In the days to come—it is the Lord who speaks—
> I will pour out my spirit on all mankind.
> Their sons and daughters shall prophesy,
> your young men shall see visions,
> your old men shall dream dreams.
> Even on my slaves, men and women,
> in those days, I will pour out my spirit.
> I will display portents in heaven above
> and signs on earth below.
> The sun will be turned into darkness
> and the moon into blood
> before the Great Day of the Lord dawns.
> And all who call on the name of the Lord will be saved."

The opening sentences of John's sermon were familiar to Prochorus for the words were almost the same ones Mark had used in describing the sermon Peter had delivered in Jerusalem at Pentecost. Mark had been inclined to favor Peter, whose secretary he had become. But he had admitted that the formulation of the early appeals, which had resulted in so many people flocking to join the Nazarene congregation, had been largely John's. It had been John, too, who persuaded Peter to go with him to the Porch of Solomon in the Temple and there hurl the challenge of Jesus into the very teeth—as it were—of the chief priests and the Sanhedrin, whose inner circle had condemned the Nazarene to death.

To Prochorus' ears, as John continued, the words seemed to flow with much the same rhythm as the songs of David, the sweet singer of Israel. Yet with them went a subtle change, not only in the speaker but in the tenor of his discourse. In Galilee, John had always stood in shadow, first of Jesus and later of Simon Peter, whose broad shoulders and stocky form had towered over the slender body of the son of Zebedee. Now, however, he was the master of his audience, a speaker of great power whose words held them enthralled.

Caught up in the beauty of John's phrases, Prochorus found himself watching Jesus of Nazareth walking the shore of the beautiful lake, illustrating his simple teachings of sin and repentance with earthy stories—parables which even a child could not fail to understand. He followed the crowd into Jerusalem as Jesus rode upon a colt—fulfilling again the ancient prophecy. And he felt the agony of the condemned man when he was scourged by the Roman soldiers until his flesh hung in shreds upon his body, and was forced to carry the crossbeam to which he would shortly be nailed.

The description of the events of those last tragic hours, as given by the speaker, was extraordinarily vivid. It confirmed what Prochorus had been told, namely that John, at great peril to himself, had remained with Jesus after the arrest in the Garden of Gethsemane that night and had followed the man he served all the way to the cross erected upon the Place of the Skull called Golgotha.

For the first time Prochorus heard the story of the agony suffered by Jesus there and, painted by John's stirring words, saw the heartbreaking picture of the broken body being lowered into the tomb just before sunset—lest it hang upon the cross and be defiled by vultures during the sacred season of the Passover. John's voice took on a new note of triumph as he spoke of finding the stone rolled away on the morning of the third day and of how Jesus had appeared to him and some others at the Place of the Seven Springs in Galilee, sending them back to Jerusalem to continue the work there.

As he ended his address, John told in a voice ringing with pride how Jesus himself had singled him out with the promise— and who could doubt it listening to the confidence in the voice of the speaker?—that he would live to see the return of the Messiah to earth in his full glory.

Even before he finished speaking, people began to leave the benches and move forward to fall on their knees around the *bima*. And filled suddenly with a conviction that washed away all doubt, a feeling of kinship with the Nazarene and with all men—yes, even with God himself—that gave him a never-before-experienced sensation of power, Prochorus found himself with the others kneeling before the rostrum. When John's hands touched his bowed head, a sudden glory blinded him for a moment while he experienced a sense of communication with a divine source of life like nothing he had ever known before.

Filled with this new feeling of power, certain that what had come upon him was what he had heard described by others among the followers of Jesus as the Holy Spirit, Prochorus knelt there with his heart fairly bursting and uttered an unspoken prayer of thanksgiving to God for this gift of something greater even than life itself. Afterward—how long he didn't know or even care—he heard John's voice cry, "Prochorus," and raised his eyes to look into the face of his friend.

"There were so many today, I didn't realize it was you." John put his hand beneath Prochorus' elbow and lifted him to his feet to embrace him.

"The sense of power that came over me now." Prochorus spoke with wonder still in his voice. "That feeling of communion with God. What is it?"

"You have received the gift of the Holy Spirit!" John's eyes shone with joy. "God be praised for making you one of us! And for granting me the boon of leading you to see the Way."

vii

Over bread, cheese and goat's milk in John's quarters a short distance from the synagogue, Prochorus heard the story of his friend's escape to Babylon with a caravan he had joined in Peraea, after his flight from Jerusalem to escape persecution by Saul of Tarsus. Because the House of Zebedee had for a long time exported dried fish to a Jewish merchant in the Parthian capital, John had been welcomed there and had become a member of the Jewish community. Invited to speak in the synagogue on the first sabbath after his arrival, he had found a warm reception for his teachings by many of the Jews in Babylon. And in spite of opposition by a few who clung stubbornly to the old ways and the strict Pharisaic interpretation of the law, he had already gained a considerable following for the Way of Jesus.

"But enough of myself!" John spoke with his old exuberance. "What brings you here?"

"I am an adviser to the Legate Vitellius—with the temporary rank of tribune."

"You have come a long way since that day on our pier when you had decided to become a fisherman."

"I owe everything to you—even what I am today."

"No," John corrected him. "I knew that day you could never really be a fisherman. Your mind is much too good for that."

"As yours was."

"Is—not was. When Jesus called me on the shore of the lake, I was made over in an instant from a mere fisherman into what he wanted me to be, just as I hope you were molded this day according to God's purpose. But tell me more about yourself."

Prochorus gave his friend a running account of the period since he had last seen John in Jerusalem. When he came to his most recent visit to the Holy City and his meeting with James on the Mount of Olives, John's eyes shone with gratitude.

"The one thing I hated most about being forced to flee from Jerusalem was leaving James behind with Barabbas and Manahem," he said. "But I know now that even then the Lord had a purpose in sending me here."

"The amnesty granted by Vitellius has removed all danger for both of you," Prochorus assured him.

"Are you saying I should return to Jerusalem—when all goes so well here?"

"You need not fear Saul of Tarsus any more. He is one of you—"

"How could that be?"

"I heard it from Simon Peter himself." John listened closely to the story of Saul's conversion on the road to Damascus, and when it was finished, shook his head in wonder.

"God does indeed move in mysterious ways," he said. "That Saul should turn about and become one of us is even more remarkable than that I should preach the gospel of Jesus here in Babylon."

"Or that I should come to know the Nazarene and receive the Holy Spirit at your hands."

"Jesus alone can bestow that gift," said John. "You received it because you deserved it."

"I think you are needed in Jerusalem," Prochorus told him. "The congregation is shrinking under the new leader, James ben Joseph."

"That, too, may be the Lord's purpose."

"How?"

"Jews of the Diaspora are more broadly educated and not so tightly bound to the strict interpretations of the law put upon us by the Rabbis of the Porch. The real opportunity for spreading the Way may eventually lie in places like Babylon, Alexandria and even in Rome."

"But if the Way as you call it dies in Jerusalem, many will say it was because Jesus died there—and did not live again."

"Peter is still there and others of the disciples."

"They lack the driving force I heard in your voice here today," said Prochorus. "Mark says Peter yields to James ben Joseph when it comes to the affairs of the congregation because James is a near kinman to Jesus. Peter has been spending more and more of his time preaching in other cities, too. He told me himself that he hopes to go to Rome."

"Some of those driven away by Saul of Tarsus did go to Rome, as I came to Babylon." John's tone was thoughtful. "They will need the support of an apostle, too, if we are to expand the work westward."

"If you were in Jerusalem, Peter could go to Rome," Prochorus insisted and John smiled.

"You are very persuasive, but I must still think about it. Tell me, how does it go between you and the lovely Mariamne?"

"Not very well, I'm afraid." Prochorus told of his experience in Jerusalem and what Sextus Latimus had learned.

"The Fox is always plotting to gain more territory and more power," John agreed. "But the Parthians are in close contact with the Nabateans through the caravans that cross the desert between here and Petra. You can be sure they will support Aretas, if Antipas seeks to close them in or gain control of Damascus."

"What he really wants to control is Jerusalem."

"Yes. But for that he needs peace with Aretas."

"To be sealed with a marriage," Prochorus said glumly. "That's why he shut Mariamne up in the fortress of Machaerus."

"Artaban is no fool; I'm sure he will see through the Fox's little scheme. But with Antipas weaving another of his webs, this is no time for the congregation in Jerusalem to speak with an uncertain voice. When do you start back to Antioch?"

"The conference still has two days to run. At the end Antipas plans a great banquet in the pavilion he has erected on the bridge."

"I shall certainly not be invited to the banquet." John grinned. "Suppose I join you on the following day."

"I'm sure the Legate wouldn't object."

"Then it's settled. And be sure the Lord has some great purpose for you in letting you see the Way here and giving you the gift of the Holy Spirit. I count myself favored by God that it has come to you through my hands."

viii

The feast given by the Tetrarch of Galilee and Peraea to celebrate the signing of the new treaty establishing the boundary between Rome and Parthia and pledging the two countries to eternal peace and friendship was lavish even for Babylon. Much of the requirements for it, the plate, the silver and even some of the more costly viands, had been brought in Antipas' long baggage train. The rest he purchased in Babylon, drawing upon letters of credit he had brought with him from bankers in Galilee and Jerusalem. The affair was held in the lavish pavilion he had erected at the center of the bridge over the Euphrates and, as they were walking back to their quarters on the west bank of the river after the feast, Prochorus and Sextus discussed the evening.

"I have no love for the Tetrarch of Galilee," said the centurion. "But I can laud his choice of wine and food."

"I was too worried about Mariamne to notice," Prochorus admitted.

"Look at this thing logically," Sextus advised. "Artaban has as much to gain from peace on this frontier as Rome does, so I doubt very much that he will take a hand in the quarrel between Aretas and Antipas—especially when he knows Vitellius would not approve."

"I hope you're right," Prochorus said fervently. "By the way, a friend of mine will be going back with us as far as Damascus. His name is John ben Zebedee."

"Wasn't he one of the disciples of Jesus of Nazareth?"

"Yes."

"Are you sure it's wise to identify yourself so openly with the Nazarenes? After all, their leader was crucified for treason—even if in error."

"I have become one of them."

"I noticed the change since your visit to Babylon." Sextus showed no evidence of surprise. "But take my advice and don't speak openly about the return of the Nazarene that his followers are so sure will come about—at least not yet."

"Why?"

"You have reached a high place in a very short time, but I'm convinced that you can go even higher. If the Nazarenes are as innocent of sedition as they appear to be, they can use a friend in high places. If they are not, you are too loyal to want any part of them."

"But—"

"To Rome a man's religion is his own affair, so long as it doesn't affect his loyalty. The teachings of the Nazarene appeal strongly to many people and I suspect that before long many prominent men will be numbered among the 'Christians,' as they are called in Antioch. But if the faith is to survive, it must have influence in government too—for its own protection."

"Why do you say that?"

"When a political faction in Rome wants to increase its power, the quickest way to do it is by starting stories about the Jews. Many people owe Jews money and are easily persuaded to listen in the hope of getting out of their debts."

"We Nazarenes aren't concerned with such things."

"Most Christians are Jews, so they will be classed in people's minds as Jews. High priests come and go in Jerusalem and you can never tell when one of them may start another persecution or stir up the Jews in other cities against you. Think about that and be careful. And tell your friend to stay out of Antipas' sight. You never know just what the Fox might do."

The day after the reception celebrating the treaty, Antipas announced that he must return at once to Galilee on affairs of state. Such was his haste, in fact, that he sold his pack mules and bought camels, the ungainly animals sometimes referred to as "ships of the desert." By now, however, Vitellius and his party were so thoroughly tired of Antipas and his pretentiousness that no one made any objection to his decision.

The Roman column made a more leisurely departure the following day. John ben Zebedee joined them early that morning, riding a horse he had purchased on the advice of Sextus. Although in a Roman column the troops marched, the pace of trained soldiers was considerably faster than that of ordinary travelers by foot, and all except the soldiers themselves rode.

"Shall I stay out of sight?" John asked Prochorus.

"I told Vitellius you are a friend from Galilee who would like to return with us. He made no objection."

"I learned something that might interest you yesterday from the dealer in camels and horses who sold me my mount," said John. "Did you know that Antipas hired an Arab to guide him across the desert to Philadelphia by way of the oasis of Canatha?"

"No, but I heard him say several times that he was afraid Aretas might attack while he was away, so it was a sensible thing to do."

"He also hired a special driver to ride the swiftest camel he could buy to Damascus and from there to Tyre. The man left yesterday."

"Why would he do that?"

"The seller of animals asked that question too. He was told that special dispatches were being sent to Rome by way of Tyre."

"Are you sure about this?"

"The man who sold Antipas the camels is a member of my synagogue. He saw the packet of scrolls with the seal of the Tetrarch on them being delivered to the camel driver by Antipas' personal scribe."

Prochorus had no need to ponder over the information John had given him; its implications were all too clear.

"Stay here with Sextus while I ride ahead and consult the Legate," he told John. "If he requires your presence I shall send back for you."

ix

Vitellius listened in silence while Prochorus repeated what John had told him. But the rise of color in the Legate's cheeks betrayed his anger.

"Obviously Antipas intends for his report to reach Rome before my own is sent from Antioch," he said. "But what can I do?"

"You might forestall him by sending a special courier to Antioch by way of Emesa with your own account, hoping it will get to Rome before the Tetrarch's letter does."

"Do you advise that?"

Prochorus shook his head. "A Roman army was once lost following that route so you might be sending the courier to his death. Besides, you would have no way of being certain whether or not he had arrived there, until you get to Antioch yourself."

"Is there an alternative?"

"I think so," said Prochorus. "The Emperor trusts you, sir, else he would not have placed the peace of the eastern frontier in your hands. He will probably resent the Tetrarch's going behind your back, and besides, Prince Agrippa is in prison at Rome for plotting against the Emperor—"

"Then you believe Tiberius is not likely to look with favor upon any descendant of Herod the Great?"

"My guess is that the Emperor will recognize the purpose behind this move by the Tetrarch Antipas and will wait for your report, sir."

"If I am ever emperor you shall be to me what the great Marcus Vipsanius Agrippa—and a plague on his jackal namesake—was to Augustus," the Legate assured him, then his face brightened. "Besides, who knows? Antipas is traveling across the desert by a hazardous route, with an Arab for his guide. He might end up in Petra, a prisoner of Aretas—or a corpse. Whichever it is, I shall be glad to see the last of the Tetrarch of Galilee and Peraea for a while." Vitellius smiled. "A better thought—I may even make you ruler there in his place."

Discreet inquiries in Damascus, when they reached there some two weeks after the departure from Babylon, confirmed the fact that a courier said to be bearing official dispatches for Rome had indeed passed through there by camel, heading for Tyre on the seacoast. But this news was quickly overshadowed by an ominous report that King Aretas of Nabatea, taking advantage of Antipas' absence in Babylon, had launched a swift attack through lower Peraea, seizing the fortress of Machaerus that formed the major anchor of Antipas' defenses in that region, as well as most of the surrounding territory.

For a while, according to the reports, Aretas had even threatened to cross the Jordan and pillage Jericho. But Marcellus, the new Procurator of Judaea, had promptly moved troops to the Jordan crossing to protect Jericho and Aretas had decided not to cross the river.

The Nabatean king still held Machaerus, however, and it was reported that, when Antipas had arrived in Galilee a full week earlier by way of the desert caravan trails, he had made the mistake of launching a hasty attack against Aretas. Having only limited forces, he had been thrown back with staggering losses and for a while it appeared that he might even lose the thriving lake region to the swift-striking cavalrymen of the Nabatean king.

To Prochorus the worst news of all was that Mariamne had been captured by Aretas and was being held as a hostage along with the Roman detail attached to the garrison of Machaerus. He was certain, too, that Antipas could not be relied upon to pay the necessary ransom, since Mariamne's only real value to him had been as a possible prize with which to cement an alliance with Aretas—now obviously out of the question.

The news of the Nabatean attack was of sufficient gravity to force Vitellius to pause at Damascus for a council of state. It was attended by the governor of Damascus who, since the Nabateans now enjoyed special trading rights there amounting almost to actual hegemony over the prosperous city, naturally favored Aretas; Sextus Latimus; Prochorus; a tribune named Cestus Gallus who commanded Vitellius' personal guard; and, of course, Vitellius himself.

"We have no way of knowing the exact situation of the Tetrarch Antipas," Vitellius said in opening the meeting. "Since most of you are more familiar with this part of the world than I am, your advice and counsel are badly needed."

"I say let the Fox fend for himself," said Sextus Latimus. "After all, he put away Aretas' daughter of his own will and caused all this trouble."

"We cannot punish Aretas without an army at our backs," said Cestus, evaluating the military situation. "Which means we must go to Antioch and raise new levies of auxiliary troops."

"If I go against the Nabateans with anything less than an army so powerful that they cannot stand against us, Rome is liable to suffer defeat," Vitellius agreed. "And I don't have to remind any of you that, if this occurs, the treaty we have just made with Parthia will not be worth the ink used to write it." He turned to Prochorus, who had not yet spoken. "You are more personally concerned in this affair than any of us, since I understand that your betrothed is a prisoner at Machaerus. What do you say?"

"My personal involvement must have nothing to do with any decision you make, sir." Prochorus spoke slowly, for his thoughts were just beginning to fall into a definite pattern. "As you say, the whole question of peace on the eastern frontier for another hundred years hangs in the balance, so a defeat to Roman forces at the hands of King Aretas would be a disaster."

"Yet we cannot let subject rulers make war with each other at will, else the whole structure of the empire will begin to disintegrate," said Vitellius.

"Peace has just been established on the eastern boundary after more than a hundred years of intermittent conflict," said Prochorus. "When King Aretas is reminded that he has already avenged the insult to his daughter by defeating the Tetrarch and that to keep on with this venture means facing the might of a Roman army, I think he will see the wisdom of withdrawing from the territory he has conquered in Peraea."

"Are you saying the Legate should beg Aretas to make peace?" Cestus Gallus demanded incredulously.

"No," said Prochorus. "But a letter *ordering* Aretas to withdraw to the boundaries of his own realm and free all hostages, on pain of imperial displeasure, should do the same."

Sextus Latimus whistled softly. "It's a bold move."

"And a sensible one," said Vitellius. "Are we all in agreement that it shall be done?"

"Who is going to deliver this ultimatum?" asked Cestus. "I've seen some of the tortures these desert people inflict on captives before death. They're enough to make even a strong man retch."

"I request permission to bear the letter to King Aretas, sir," said Prochorus.

"With how many men?" Cestus asked.

"One—myself."

"Two," said Sextus Latimus, and Prochorus gave him a look of gratitude. "I have had some experience in dealing with these desert people, sir. If the two of us cannot accomplish the mission, nothing less than an army will do it."

"You two will ride south tomorrow," said Vitellius. "This afternoon Prochorus and I will compose the letter to Aretas. It must be in words that will not make him angry but leave no doubt of the consequences if he does not withdraw his forces."

"The voice of the turtle but the tongue of the serpent," Sextus said to Prochorus with a grin as they were leaving the room. "You will need all of Solomon's wisdom to compose that letter, my friend."

Vitellius and his staff were quartered in the palace of the governor of Damascus. When Prochorus came back to his room after completing the draft of the directive to King Aretas, he found John ben Zebedee waiting for him. The long journey from Babylon seemed not to have troubled the slender Galilean at all, even though he was neither a soldier nor an experienced traveler. His face was tanned from the days on horseback and his eyes glowed with their usual confidence and assurance.

"Sextus tells me you're going to Machaerus, with an ultimatum to King Aretas," he said.

"Yes. The Legate and I just finished writing the order."

"Do you think he will obey?"

"I'm wagering my life on it—and the release of Mariamne."

"*If you get to Machaerus*"—John put special emphasis on the words—"you may be able to reason with him."

"Why do you say 'if' I get to Machaerus?"

"I have been listening in the market place and along the Street Called Straight. Aretas is said to hold all of southern Peraea, and roving bands of Nabatean tribesmen are no doubt pillaging there. If you fall into their hands, you will probably not reach Machaerus at all."

"Have you a better plan?"

"Before the Lord called me, I was one of the disciples of John the Essene—most people called him the Baptizer. I even lived for a while in one of the Essene communities on the shore of the Salt Sea, thinking I would become a teacher or a scribe. My dedication wasn't strong enough for that sort of life, so I came back to Galilee, but I did learn a lot about the country. If we follow the Jordan southward from Jericho, keeping to the paths that connect the Essene communities together, we could probably avoid contact with any pillaging bands of Nabateans and be safe."

"Sextus and I are Roman citizens. Aretas would hesitate to kill us, but you are a Galilean and a subject of Antipas, so you would be tortured and killed if we are taken."

"I could pose as an Essene. The Baptizer condemned Antipas publicly for putting away Aretas' daughter and marrying Herodias. It cost him his life but since then the Essenes have had nothing to fear from the desert people."

"Couldn't you draw me a map of the paths near the Salt Sea?"

"When they travel from community to community, the Brothers of the Light guide themselves by secret landmarks known only to them and to some of the other sects that have retreated there," John explained. "Even those who know the way sometimes have trouble getting through. As for danger to me, Jesus watches over me even when I sleep and whatever he wills for me will come to pass."

"Does he expect you to take the risks that can be avoided?"

John smiled. "The Master told me I shall live to see him come again, so I will be in no danger. But if you refuse to take me, you may never see Princess Mariamne and will probably lose your head into the bargain."

"You shall ride with us," Prochorus agreed. "If we are captured, I shall swear that you are an Essene guide we hired to lead us to the fortress."

x

The wisdom of following John's advice became apparent even before the three travelers reached the agricultural colony of Betharamtha on the east side of the Jordan, a half day's journey north of where the main road westward from Jerusalem crossed the river near Jericho. There they began to meet straggling bands of refugees moving northward toward Galilee. Mostly these were composed of women and children, the Nabateans having either killed the men or seized them for sale in the slave markets of Petra.

Rather than risk the entrapment John had warned against, they crossed the river at Adama, some distance upstream from Jericho. There the Jordan made a steep bend and the swift current constantly undermined the sandy cliffs on the western bank, causing them occasionally to tumble into the stream and dam it completely. Whenever this happened, the river bed southward was left dry for several days—as in the time of Joshua—until the pressure building up behind the earth dam upstream eroded through and the river once again cut a new channel for itself.

South of the road to Jericho and Jerusalem they followed the course of the river through a wild rocky area of hot springs and boiling geysers where the deep inner fires of the earth broke through, as they had broken through, nearly two thousand years earlier, at the south end of the Salt Sea to destroy the cities of Sodom and Gomorrah. Here they were forced to lead the horses much of the way, lest a sudden burst of steam from the earth beside the rocky path—or sometimes in the road itself—terrify the animals and make them throw the riders.

It was the wildest and most desolate region Prochorus had ever seen and the thought of Mariamne being shut up in a castle in the very midst of it made his heart contract with concern and longing. John led them well, however, and shortly before nightfall on the day following their departure from Adama they came to an Essene community in the hills behind the Springs of Callirhoe, almost halfway down the eastern side of the Salt Sea.

It was the first time Prochorus had seen one of the Essene settlements. Everything was spotlessly clean, but with a sterile ascetic quality that somehow had a coldness about it he hadn't expected. John spoke of this as they were bathing shortly after their arrival in a pool fed by a warm spring whose water was so highly mineralized that it caused their skins to tingle.

"Are you surprised at what you see here?" John asked.

"I had always thought of the Essenes as being like those who take the Nazirite vows, men with matted beards and rough clothing, living in tents among the rocks."

"Some do, but where they gather into communities like this, cleanliness becomes almost as important as godliness."

"What do these people do besides wash themselves?"

"Sextus said we must rest our horses tomorrow; to have them go lame in this country would be a disaster. I will take you to the scriptorium in the morning and you can see for yourself."

Anxious though he was to free Mariamne, Prochorus had not argued against the centurion's decision that their mounts needed a day of rest before going on to Machaerus. After the morning ablutions and a rather limited meal of dates and goat's milk with chunks of bread, he and John went to the scriptorium. A large room in the center of the cloister, it was built of stone and plaster like the other buildings, with a roof of palm trunks upon which rushes had been placed and covered with wet clay. In this climate the clay soon baked to the hardness of pottery in the hot sun and became almost indestructible, even though buffeted almost constantly by howling winds that swept through the gorges forming much of the shore line.

In the center of the scriptorium was a large writing table built of masonry blocks with benches on both sides. Unlike most buildings in this settlement, the scriptorium had many windows and was well lighted and the benches were filled with scribes. Some were diligently copying documents on sheets of leather so thin that they could be sewn together to form a continuous roll. Others worked with the conventional type of papyrus and also the more recently popular parchment, while two men laboriously etched letters upon thin copper sheets which were then rolled up to form tubes.

Some of the documents being copied appeared to be the ordinary writings of the Torah and the Prophets, such as were read in synagogues all over the world at the sabbath services. Others, John told Prochorus, were the scriptures of the Essenes themselves, the most important a "Manual of Discipline" by which members of the sect were governed, a set of rules written down long ago in even more detail than the written law of Moses so beloved by the Pharisees.

A philosophical document also formed an important part of Essene literature, a covenant of steadfast love which appeared to be an essential characteristic of all their communities, no matter where they were located. From a brief perusal of the latter, Prochorus saw that it contained a considerable discussion of the two natures of man, the good and the bad, and the constant battle that went on within each man's heart between forces of light and darkness. Still other writings appeared to be psalms similar to those of David found in the Jewish scriptures.

From what John told Prochorus about his own brief stay in an Essene community, plus what he was able to read in snatches from the Essene scriptures, looking over the shoulders of the copyists, it was obvious that, while the Jews believed themselves to be the chosen people of God, the Essenes considered themselves to be the elect among the Jews. For this reason, they expected to be favored with a high place in the kingdom to be established by the Anointed One, whom they called the Teacher of Righteousness, and were, in fact, devoting their lives to preparing themselves for his coming.

At another time he might have been struck by the many analogies between the teachings of the Essenes and those of Jesus of Nazareth; in the beginning, John told him, many of the Nazarene's followers had actually been Essenes. At the moment, however, he was too concerned with the problem of freeing Mariamne to think about anything else, and the next morning they pushed on southward along the hidden paths by which the Essenes traveled, moving always toward the fortress of Machaerus still some distance to the south.

xi

Ten days after the conference in Damascus, Prochorus, Sextus and John ben Zebedee drew rein one afternoon and looked across a wild forbidding valley to the top of yet another mountain, as they had done on dozens of occasions during the last several days. This time, however, they could see the castle of Machaerus crowning the highest peak in the immediate area, a grim reminder that even in such a desolate region man had felt the need to erect a citadel for his protection.

Since leaving the Essene community at Callirhoe, they had ridden through a jumble of cliffs and arid valleys where at night the winds howled like the wails of professional mourners and the sun threatened to broil them by day. Now and then they glimpsed the strange sea into which the Jordan poured; its water was leaden in color when seen from the heights at midday but changed to a lovely blue in the early morning and later afternoon. Prochorus had visited the Salt Sea once before, when he accompanied his father on a trip searching for new markets for the fisheries Herod Antipas had established on the Lake of Galilee. Then he had waded into the briny flood and found it so buoyant that he had been lifted from his feet.

From time to time as they approached Machaerus, they had glimpsed horsemen, silent sentries on the heights, but as yet they had not been troubled, confirming Prochorus' belief that the area in the immediate vicinity of Machaerus was probably policed by the more disciplined soldiers of the Nabatean army. They made no attempt at concealment now and, seeing a road leading up the slope toward the fortress itself, rode in that direction.

In a closer view the forbidding palace-citadel of Herod the Great was massive, turreted and surrounded by earthworks, obviously to prevent scaling attacks. It was a formidable guardian of a barren frontier, and its easy submission to the Nabateans—according to the reports received in Damascus—could only mean that among those who had garrisoned it, many had been quite willing to exchange the rule of Herod Antipas for a king more of their own blood.

Looked at now from the midst of the wilderness, there seemed little reason why King Aretas would covet the southern tip of Peraea, until one remembered that not far to the west lay the King's Highway. One of the two or three oldest roads, or rather caravan trails, in the world, this route was the shortest and most direct road between Damascus and the opulence of Egypt. And, as long as it passed through Peraea, with the frowning strength of Machaerus overlooking it, Arab caravans could never be sure the ruler of the district might not decide to demand tribute for crossing his territory.

The refusal of the King of Edom more than a thousand years earlier to let the Children of Israel pass along this same road had caused untold suffering when they were forced to detour around Edom. Should this happen again, Petra could be cut off from the rich markets of the Decapolis cities at Philadelphia, Gerasa, Damascus and even Babylon, dealing a blow to the largely pastoral economy of the Arab state.

To the south, an opening in the hills marked the course of the river Arnon which, dry most of the year, became a rushing torrent during the few weeks when rain descended upon the upland plateaus. There, John said, the Nabateans had built water-storage reservoirs and turned a section of this wilderness into a garden, as the inhabitants of Peraea had done somewhat farther to the north at the agricultural colony of Betharamtha.

"That's quite a bastion for three men to attack," said Sextus as they paused to study the fortress. "Where shall we begin?"

"At the main gate, of course," said Prochorus. "We represent the Emperor of Rome, so they must not think we doubt our welcome."

"You can see why the whole district fell, once Machaerus was taken," said Sextus.

"Especially when there was treachery within the walls," John added.

"The Fox is hardly one to inspire loyalty in his subjects," Sextus agreed. "With petty rulers like Antipas gobbling up everything they can, it's a wonder Rome doesn't lose more provinces than it does." He grinned. "Shall be begin our assault on the castle?"

Prochorus nodded and urged his mount forward. Both he and Sextus were in full uniform, but John wore the rough homespun tunic of an Essene, with a Nabatean-style headcloth to protect his head from the sun. While they waited at the top of the hill for the horses to get their breath, both Sextus and Prochorus had dusted themselves off and removed the desert-style headcloths they had been wearing, substituting the plumed helmets of Roman officers which they had carried in the packs strapped behind their saddles.

"I'm glad the sun's going down," Sextus said with a grimace as they started down the trail to the valley from which they would make the last ascent to their destination. "With these metal pots over our skulls, a few hours of this sort of sun would bake our brains."

Sensing grass and fresh water ahead, the horses quickened their paces and the valley was quickly traversed. Halfway up the hill, however, they suddenly found themselves surrounded by a detail of Nabateans, dark-faced men in flowing robes commanded by an officer who wore the curved sword favored by Parthian cavalrymen.

"By what right do you enter the territory of King Aretas of Nabatea?" he demanded haughtily.

"It is also the territory of the Emperor Tiberius." Prochorus didn't give ground. "We bear a letter from the Legate Vitellius of Syria to your King."

When the officer hesitated, obviously taken somewhat aback by his air of assurance and authority, Prochorus added, "I am Tribune Prochorus and my companion is Centurion Sextus Latimus of the Roman army."

"Who is he?" The officer nodded toward John.

"An Essene who serves as our guide."

"From whence do you come?"

"Damascus. The Legate learned there of your King's attack upon the territory of the Tetrarch Antipas."

"We have captured the lair of the Fox," the officer boasted. "Take that message back to Antipas and tell him if he seeks to retake it we will tie him to a tree for the vultures to feed upon."

"I represent Legate Vitellius and the Emperor," Prochorus said curtly. "Not the Tetrarch of Galilee."

"Give me your letter, then," said the officer. "I will see that it is handed to the King."

The words told Prochorus that Aretas was at the fortress, which meant that Mariamne was almost certainly there too. What was more, Aretas' presence meant that he would be able to negotiate directly with the Nabatean ruler for the release of the hostages without dealing through intermediaries, with the consequent loss of time.

"I was instructed by the Legate to deliver the letter I am carrying directly to King Aretas," he told the officer. "Take me to him!"

The Nabatean stiffened and for an instant Prochorus thought he was going to order their arrest. So far Sextus had remained silent as befitted an officer of lesser rank; now he spoke.

"Unless you are willing to commit your King to fight the legions, I would think twice before harming two Roman officers and their guide on an official mission," he warned the Nabatean officer. "You can be sure Roman troops will not run away like jackals, as the troops of Herod Antipas did."

"Come with me," the officer said abruptly. "The King himself shall decide what to do with you."

xii

Aretas IV was in every sense an aristocrat of his race, the swift-riding men of the tableland plateaus west of the Jordan and the desert oases between the Jordan Valley and that of the Tigris and Euphrates far to the east. Dark-skinned, hawk-faced men like this had pastured their flocks and herds and driven their caravans in this land long before the coming of Abraham to Canaan. A proud people who troubled others little when they were left in their chosen habitat, their allegiance to Rome was actually voluntary, brought on by their having shrewdly sensed that the power in the West could afford them a valuable market for the wool from their flocks and the products of their herds.

Aretas occupied a throne chair in what had been the banqueting chamber of the palace, with the chief officers of his army and his advisers flanking him on either side. Prochorus and Sextus Latimus marched smartly down the length of the chamber and came to attention before the throne chair. John had been kept waiting outside.

"Tribune Prochorus and Centurion Sextus Latimus from the staff of the Legate Vitellius," Prochorus announced. "We bear a letter from the Legate to King Aretas."

"I am Aretas. Welcome to Machaerus, Tribune." The tall man in the throne chair appeared to be about forty. A sprinkling of gray showed at his temples and in his well-trimmed beard. His skin was dark like most Nabateans' but his eyes were a startling shade of blue and their gaze was direct and intelligent. An honest man and a proud one, Prochorus thought—which meant that he must speak carefully and consider his words. But if he presented his arguments logically, he could be hopeful of success.

Aretas clapped his hands and a servant appeared with a tray bearing goblets of wine, part of the treasure, Prochorus suspected, that Antipas was said to have stored away in the several palaces he maintained.

"You must be thirsty after your journey," said the Nabatean King. "Make yourselves comfortable while my chamberlain translates the letter for me."

Prochorus and Sextus seated themselves on a cushioned bench and sipped the wine while Aretas' chamberlain—a Greek, judging by the lightness of his skin compared to the others and by his features—translated the letter into Aramaic.

"Are you familiar with the contents of the letter, Tribune Prochorus?" Aretas asked when the translation was finished.

"Yes, Your Majesty. I helped compose it."

"I thought your name sounded familiar. You are the confidential adviser to the Legate for whom everyone has such great respect."

"I do have the honor to be his adviser, sir."

Aretas turned and spoke for the benefit of his court: "The Legate Vitellius requests that I withdraw my troops from the territory claimed by the Tetrarch of Galilee and give up the Roman hostages I am holding."

"Including, I believe," Prochorus dared to add, "a princess who is the ward of the Emperor Tiberius."

A rumble of anger from the military officers ceased abruptly when Aretas made a sharp chopping gesture with his hand. The ruler of the Nabateans obviously allowed no insubordination among those who served him.

"Since you had something to do with the composition of the letter, Tribune Prochorus," he said, "you should be prepared to defend your request before me. I contend that I have only retaken land that is rightfully a part of my people's heritage."

It was a thorny question, for a wrong answer might mean failure of the mission and perhaps death for all. Nevertheless he had to counter Aretas' claim or see his mission fail almost before it had begun.

"The Legate of Syria cannot alter the boundaries of the territories that make up the Roman Empire; only the Emperor has that power," he reminded the Nabatean ruler. "If you wish to press your claim to the section of Peraea lying south of the Jericho Road, I shall be glad to lay your request before the Legate for transmission to Rome with his recommendations."

"Your reputation for skill and diplomacy is well deserved," said Aretas, and Prochorus realized with a rising sense of elation that half the battle had been won. The King of the Nabateans was no fool; having accomplished the humbling of his former son-in-law, he was no doubt searching for an excuse to withdraw that would satisfy his passionately nationalistic people. To preserve face, however, he must still make some show of objecting.

"Nevertheless my honor has been besmirched by the jackal who sits in Tiberias," Aretas continued. "How does Rome propose to pay me for the loss?"

"Any affront to your honor has been more than avenged already by your great victory here," Prochorus assured him. "The taking of this fortress is a remarkable military feat—to say nothing of the booty you have already sent to Petra."

Aretas' chuckle told him he had guessed correctly. What was more, both of them knew Antipas couldn't very well claim reimbursement without revealing the extent of his own hoarding, much of it no doubt gained by hoodwinking the Procurator Fiscal of Syria, who was concerned with the collection of taxes but could hardly keep a close watch upon such details from Antioch.

"Your arguments are brilliant, Tribune Prochorus," said Aretas. "But you are a single soldier—two if we include Centurion Sextus. If I give the order, both of you will die before you draw another breath. Do you expect me to yield to two men?"

"Both Centurion Sextus and I wear the eagles of Rome," Prochorus reminded him. "For that reason we represent the dragon's teeth that can destroy you and your people."

Aretas frowned. "The teeth of the dragon?"

"The tribune refers to an ancient tale among my people," the Greek chamberlain interjected. "It tells of a dragon that was killed and its teeth drawn and sown. Wherever they fell, armed men sprang up immediately to form an irresistible army."

"Are you threatening me?" Aretas inquired but there was no bluster in his tone.

"Only reminding Your Majesty that you could hardly wish to see thousands of your people crucified before your stronghold of Petra, as happened at Sepphoris years ago during the War of Varus, when the Jews rebelled against Rome. Besides, I have recently returned from Babylon where a treaty was signed between Rome and Parthia, binding both countries to eternal peace and friendship."

"Treaties are written on papyrus." Aretas snapped his fingers. "It burns easily."

"Having concluded the treaty, King Artaban will hardly be pleased at being forced to choose between Rome and Nabatea. Recently you realized your ambition for commercial rights in Damascus, but if the Legate were to recommend that these be withdrawn, I am sure the Emperor would follow his advice. I need not tell you what effect that would have both upon you and upon Parthia."

He had been saving the most effective argument to the last. When he saw a thoughtful look come into Aretas' eyes, he knew the thrust had gone home.

"Your arguments are eloquent, Tribune Prochorus," the Nabatean King conceded. "I will consider them and confer with my advisers. You shall have my decision in the morning."

"One more thing, Your Majesty."

"What now?"

"The matter of hostages. May Centurion Sextus see them?"

Aretas waved his hand in a gesture indicating that they were of no particular value.

"They are Romans," said Prochorus. "Besides, the Legate was informed that Princess Mariamne of the Hasmonean line is also a prisoner."

"The Tetrarch of Galilee offered the princess in marriage to my son. How could she be a prisoner?"

"The princess is not his to give in marriage to anyone," Prochorus said bluntly. "She grew up in the household of Emperor Tiberius and I doubt that he will look with favor upon anyone's holding her against her will."

This was the nearest to a naked threat he had made but bold measures were necessary if he were to save Mariamne.

"What if she elects to remain here?"

"We must be assured of that from her own lips."

Watching the play of expression upon the mobile features of the Nabatean ruler, Prochorus could surmise the thoughts behind them.

In the end, as he had hoped, greed got the better of other emotions. Losing control of Damascus could be a bitter blow to Nabatean trade, as well as destroying any hope that the city Aretas now largely controlled through a commercial treaty might eventually be his altogether. With such high stakes it was not likely that he would let a mere girl become a stumbling block.

"The centurion may see the hostages and Princess Mariamne," Aretas conceded at last. "I will give you my final decision on withdrawing in the morning."

Prochorus was fairly sure he had won the battle but one precaution remained. Mariamne needed to be warned not to show any sign that his relationship to her was other than that of a Roman officer sent to free her from captivity. For if their betrothal were to be revealed, Aretas might decide he had been outsmarted, with the result that the entire affair would collapse and his and Sextus' lives be lost into the bargain—to say nothing of John ben Zebedee. Fortunately, as Sextus was leaving for another part of the palace under the guidance of one of the Nabatean officers, Prochorus had a chance to shake his head quickly and hoped the grizzled centurion would realize his meaning.

"Your beloved is unharmed," Sextus reported when he returned about a half hour later to the chamber assigned to him and Prochorus. "She sends you her love but, when you see her next, she will be as unresponsive as the Sphinx of Egypt."

"And the other hostages?"

"They have been well cared for, but some have minor wounds, so we shall have to move slowly on the way out of here. It might be better to request an escort from Aretas so we can take the King's Highway in safety."

"I shall insist upon it."

"Are you that certain of his decision?"

"He has everything to gain and something very important to lose —his hold upon Damascus."

"Reminding him of it was a master stroke," Sextus agreed.

"Did you see John?"

"He is quartered with Aretas' servants and should be safe as long as they think he's an Essene." Sextus clapped Prochorus on the shoulder in an affectionate gesture. "You handled this well, my young friend."

"I'll be glad when it's finished."

"It was finished when you warned Aretas that he might lose control of Damascus. If Rome had more diplomats like you representing us in these foreign territories, the legions could stay in the barracks most of the time drinking wine."

"And growing fat so your enemies could easily catch you unawares—as happened to Antipas."

"By the way," said Sextus, "Princess Mariamne doesn't want to go back to Galilee. She's afraid of her uncle."

"So am I. But what can we do?"

"Hide her somewhere. Tiberius can't last much longer and Caligula knows nothing about this part of the world—or anything else much except carousing with his cronies in Rome. With Vitellius backing you, Caligula might approve your marriage to the princess after he becomes Emperor." He grinned. "If you can stand having Antipas for a relative."

xiii

The following morning Prochorus, John and Sextus were routed out of bed and escorted to the main gate of the fortress. There they found Mariamne and the hostages, a rather bedraggled-looking group of soldiers under a decurion with his arm in a sling. Mariamne was a little thinner than when Prochorus had last seen her in Jerusalem and there were dark shadows under her eyes. But she was as lovely as ever and the warm light in her eyes told him what he wanted most to know—even though she kept her face impassive. King Aretas had provided her with a horse, a beautiful young mare whose spirit was in keeping with Mariamne's own. Aretas himself rode with the detail of troops that escorted them out of the fortress.

"My petition to the Legate and the Emperor for the lands I have taken is written here," he told Prochorus, handing him two small scrolls.

"I shall see that they are delivered. And I shall tell the Legate that you are evacuating Machaerus."

Where the road leading to Machaerus joined the King's Highway a short distance east of the castle, Aretas turned south toward Petra. Prochorus and his party took the road northward and that night found them in Jericho. He took as his headquarters a small but lovely palace which Pontius Pilate had often occupied there in winter, when the climate of Caesarea farther to the north on the coast was often raw and cold. There, at last, he and Mariamne were alone and she came into his arms.

"When they told me two Roman officers had arrived, I hardly dared hope it would be you," she said. "I was afraid Aretas might trick you as he did the troops of Uncle Antipas in the fortress."

"How did he manage to take Machaerus so easily?"

"Traitors inside the walls let the Nabateans in during the night. We awoke to find the castle in their hands."

"But you weren't molested."

"Not if you don't count being followed around by that idiot son of King Aretas' called Aboud."

Prochorus grinned. "Don't you know by now that all men lose their senses before your beauty?"

"All except you." She made a face at him. "When you saw me this morning, you were as cold as ice."

"That was the diplomat—not the lover. I'm as bad as the rest, else why would I risk my life and Sextus' to rescue you?"

She leaned over to kiss him. "Tell me the truth. Wouldn't you have come to Machaerus, even if I hadn't been a prisoner there?"

"Yes."

"Why?"

"Because I love a princess and, to deserve her, I must make myself a prince." Prochorus put his arm about her waist and drew her close. "Why else?"

"I think there was much more to it than that."

"Your uncle asked the Legate for help."

"But not to have two men retake Machaerus after he had been defeated before he even got near it. Uncle Antipas will be furious when he hears what you have done."

'And even angrier when I tell him you will not return to Tiberias."

"How are you going to arrange that?"

"I can remind him that he endangered the life of a ward of Tiberius when he shut you up in Machaerus. If that doesn't impress him, I shall warn him that Vitellius will not be pleased when I tell him Antipas hired Harith to kill me in Jerusalem."

"How do you know that?"

"Do you remember James?"

"He came back from the Mount of Olives with us on the afternoon of the Passover, didn't he?"

"Yes. James learned from Manahem that Antipas hired Harith to kill me. Manahem executed Harith for taking your uncle's bribe."

"Will there ever be an end to treachery and violence?" Mariamne shivered and moved closer to him.

"Not so long as men are ambitious to gain power and control over others. Or until Jesus returns to set up the Kingdom of God on earth."

She gave him a startled look. "When did you become a follower of the Nazarene?"

"In Babylon—about a month ago. John was preaching there and, as I listened to him, it was as if the hand of God reached down to touch me and fill me with his spirit and his power."

"You really dared to come to Machaerus because you felt it was your duty to try to prevent war and save lives that would be lost because of it, didn't you?"

"Those lives—and yours."

"But you said you would have come if I hadn't been there— risking your life to save people you didn't even know."

"Jesus gave his life for all. Those called by him can do no less."

"Help me to understand," she begged. "Then perhaps I, too, can be changed as you have been."

"Is the difference that obvious?"

"I noticed it the first time I saw you at Machaerus this morning and I remember seeing the same thing in the eyes of the Nazarene that day, when Uncle Antipas and the others were tormenting him by putting a crown of thorns upon his head and a purple robe about his shoulders. They called him the King of the Jews and mocked him then, but I could see that he was far more of a king than any of them could ever hope to be."

"If you recognized that, you are halfway to becoming a Nazarene yourself."

There in the garden at Jericho, with the stars shining overhead and the rush of water from the Fountain of Elisha filling the night air, he told Mariamne everything he had learned from John and Peter and Mark about the man who had died on the cross and had broken the bonds of death to rise from the tomb.

"When the time comes, the Lord will touch you with his hand as he did me," he assured her. "At the moment, John and I think it will be better for you to remain with some friends of his outside Jerusalem."

"Where?"

"In an Essene community John knows about on the west side of the Salt Sea, about halfway to Engedi. It's called Ir Hamelakh—a Hebrew name that means Salt City."

"But the Essenes allow no women in their settlements."

"This one does. Besides, it's close to Jerusalem and when I go back to Antioch, Marcellus, the new Procurator there, can watch over you—in case Herod Antipas should try to spirit you out of the province."

"Why do you have to go back to Antioch?"

"After I tell Herod Antipas what has taken place, I must report to the Legate. He is raising an army in Antioch and will be happy to know the need for fighting has ended."

"What about us afterward?"

"Emperor Tiberius is dying, and after Caligula is crowned Emperor, I shall ask Vitellius to approve our marriage. Sextus thinks there's a good chance that Rome will not object."

"Uncle Agrippa is in Rome, he might help us."

"Isn't he a prisoner?"

"He and Caligula are very close, so when Caligula becomes Emperor the prison doors will probably be opened for him. I will write him about what you have been able to do and I'm sure he will help persuade the Emperor to approve our marriage."

xiv

A short distance west of Jericho a side road led southward along the cliffs overlooking the Salt Sea to the thriving oasis of Engedi and beyond it to Masada, another of the fortress cities built by Herod the Great. From the tall cliffs on the western corner, so to speak, of the lake, near where the Jordan entered it, the view was breath-taking as Prochorus and Mariamne reined in their horses early next morning.

The air was clear, and southward along the western shore they could see almost to Engedi halfway down the lake. Nearer at hand a line of tall reeds marked the profile of the narrow plain at the foot of the cliffs where the water lapped against them. The land here was like a piece of parchment crumpled up by a giant hand into ridges and valleys, with no discernible pattern save that the whole landscape ended abruptly at the water's edge. Farther to the south, a long peninsula known as the Lisano jutted out like a tongue into the water, dwarfing many lesser fingers that broke the even contour of the shore line.

Prochorus had ridden a short distance southward with John and Mariamne that morning along the road leading to the lakeside community of Ir Hamelakh where she was to seek refuge. The way was rough and lumps of black bitumen could be seen jutting from the chalky cliffs beside it, while in places pools of the black, sticky material boiled with a pungent sulphurous odor, warning that the fires of the earth lay here just beneath the surface of the land.

When John discreetly fell back and was hidden by a turn of the road, Prochorus pulled his horse close to Mariamne's and leaned over to kiss her good-by. She clung to him for a moment, until the movement of the horses, made nervous by the strong smell of brimstone in the air, separated them and they drew apart.

"Take me with you, darling," she begged. "I don't want us ever to be separated again."

"I must go to Tiberias and report to Herod Antipas," he reminded her. "I am only a tribune and if your uncle ordered me to leave you there, neither of us would have any choice except to obey."

"I'm still afraid."

"John will see that you are comfortably situated with his Essene friends at Ir Hamelakh before he goes to Jerusalem to tell Marcellus where you are. Both of them are my friends, so you will be given any message I send them."

"How long will it be before we can be married?"

"Only a few months—if our plans work out."

"Would you be willing to help Uncle Agrippa in return for his helping us?"

"I talked to Sextus about that last night, and we both think this area might be quieter with a ruler who is at least part Jew. I'll admit that I wasn't particularly impressed with Agrippa when I knew him in Tiberias, but the circumstances weren't in his favor then. In any event he could hardly be worse than Antipas."

"Shall I write him?"

"Write him—but promise nothing. My first loyalty is to Vitellius."

"Be sure God will watch over you and keep you safe, darling," Prochorus said when John came into view riding slowly. "You can trust John ben Zebedee with your life.

"Guard her well, old friend," he said to John in farewell. "She is more precious to me than life itself."

John smiled. "The writer of proverbs spoke well when he said:

> A perfect wife—who can find her?
> She is far beyond the price of pearls.

I suspect that you are the richest of men, my friend. Go with God."

Prochorus watched them ride southward until a turn of the road and a jutting cliff shut them from view. As he rode back to join Sextus, his heart was heavy, for he was far from certain that Agrippa would be able to help them—or that he could trust Agrippa any more than he could Antipas. For both men were possessed by the same inordinate ambition to rule over all that had been the realm of Herod the Great.

XV

By the time Prochorus finished telling the Tetrarch of Galilee and
Peraea that two men—he didn't mention the presence of John
ben Zebedee—had accomplished the withdrawal of the Nabatean
invaders from the southern part of Antipas' territory and the return
of the fortress of Machaerus to his rule, the normally unhealthy
color of the Galilean ruler was almost purple and he was breathing
heavily with anger.

"You exceeded your authority in allowing him to withdraw without
punishment!" he snapped.

"The letter I bore from the Legate instructed King Aretas to
withdraw to his own territory," Prochorus corrected him coldly. "I
delivered the letter and he obeyed its instructions."

"Aretas cannot be allowed to pillage at will," Antipas spluttered.

"I am going to Antioch to report to the Legate. Do you wish to lay
a formal complaint before him?"

"Vitellius is obviously afraid to anger the Parthians, who are in
league with Aretas. The Emperor himself shall hear of this."

Prochorus made no comment, for what Antipas said was very
nearly true. Peace on the vast frontier of the East was far more
important to Rome than a quarrel between two petty kings.

"What about the hostages?" Antipas demanded. "Did you let
Aretas keep them?"

"I left them at Jericho. By now they should have reported to the
Procurator Marcellus at Jerusalem."

"And Mariamne?"

"She chose to stay in Judaea."

"At your suggestion, no doubt."

"I did suggest it."

"By what right?"

"She is a ward of the Emperor and, if she had not been practically
a prisoner at Machaerus, she wouldn't have been captured by the

Nabateans. She will be quite safe under the protection of Procurator Marcellus until she decides what she wishes to do."

"We shall see about that," said Antipas. "You may go now, Tribune."

"I shall tell the Legate of your gratitude for the return of your territory." Prochorus turned on his heel in what he hoped was a crisp military maneuver and left the room. Outside he called for Sextus and their horses.

"We will stop at my home in Magdala for the night and then go on to Ptolemais to take ship for Antioch," he told the centurion.

"So the Fox didn't like our giving his castle back to him," Sextus said with a grin. "It did make him look like a fool for two men to succeed where his forces were defeated."

"He's not such a fool as to let Aretas go unpunished if he can manage it. Before we get to Antioch, you can be sure a letter will be on the way to Rome, protesting directly to the Emperor."

"It was ever a fox's way to double back on its tracks and try to turn the tables on its pursuers," said Sextus. "And coming so soon after Antipas' letter from Babylon telling how he accomplished the Parthian treaty singlehanded, the Emperor may well be inclined to listen to his complaint. We may have to invade Petra yet; I only hope I'm not selected for the job."

"Why?"

"I've been told that it's a veritable fortress, accessible only by way of a narrow passage where not more than three or four men can fight abreast. A dozen could hold it against an army—and Aretas has considerably more than that to draw upon."

At Magdala, Chuza, who had visited Petra, confirmed what Sextus had said about the strength of the Nabatean stronghold and its inaccessibility, as well as the dire consequences that could be expected if Antipas succeeded in persuading the ailing Tiberias to order an army sent against the Nabatean capital.

"Why would Antipas risk his own tetrarchy when he knows any army Rome sends against Petra will almost certainly be defeated?" Prochorus protested.

"I told you once before that your only real weakness may be that, being honest, you can't think like those who aren't," said Sextus. "If the Legate is ordered to send a Roman army against Petra, it will be Rome that is defeated, not Antipas. Then Vitellius would have to answer to the Emperor, probably with his post as Legate, and nothing could please Antipas more than that."

"But Antipas would then be at the mercy of the Nabateans," said Prochorus.

"Petra lies far to the south and even in a retreat no Roman commander would leave the fortress of Machaerus without a garrison. In Roman hands it would keep Aretas from taking any more of Antipas' territory, leaving the Tetrarch of Galilee free to see what he can connive in the way of a new kingdom out of a less knowledgeable Legate than Vitellius."

"So he wins even when he loses?"

Sextus shrugged. "That's the way of a fox until you trap him."

"Or he traps himself."

"There you go again, thinking like an honest man," Sextus warned with a grin. "But I hope you're right."

xvi

Four months later a peremptory dispatch arrived in Antioch from Emperor Tiberius, ordering Vitellius to raise an army and punish the King of the Nabateans for attacking territory ruled by the Tetrarch of Galilee and Peraea. Vitellius was further directed, as proof that the order had been carried out, to send to Rome either Aretas himself or his head, if he fell in battle.

However unwilling he might be, Vitellius had no choice except to obey and moved southward to Caesarea with two legions. At the provincial capital for Judaea and Samaria, he divided his troops, sending one force through Lower Galilee to cross the Jordan east of Scythopolis, while he went on to Jerusalem. It was the season of the Passover again and Vitellius was planning to collect as many soldiers as Marcellus could spare him, once the need for guarding the city during the religious holiday was over.

Having given up his temporary military rank—for which he had no ambition—in favor of his old position as trusted adviser to Vitellius, Prochorus accompanied the Legate and took up residence with him in the Palace of Herod on the western side of the city. Antipas was in Jerusalem too, flushed with success at having maneuvered the Legate he hated into a position from which only he could profit. Feeling between Vitellius and Antipas was tense until, on the day after the Passover, startling news arrived.

Prochorus first heard of it when Vitellius and Marcellus came into the room in the Palace of Herod where he was working with several scribes, preparing the necessary requisitions and orders for acquiring at Jericho the food and transportation needed to move an army southward along the King's Highway to Petra and begin a siege of the Nabatean stronghold. Both men looked pleased.

"You can stop what you're doing," Vitellius told Prochorus happily. "A military galley arrived at Joppa yesterday afternoon. Emperor Tiberius died a few weeks ago at Baiae. There will be no war with the Nabateans—at least not until I receive instructions from the new Emperor."

"Is it Caligula?"

"Yes—worse luck for the empire. I fear we are in for troubled times."

"I for one will be glad of a change—even so," said Marcellus. "I much prefer soldiering to governing."

"Will a new Procurator be appointed?" Prochorus asked.

"Marullus a member of the Equestrian Order, already has been," said Vitellius. "He is without imagination, but with you to advise him here, he should serve well in Judaea and Samaria."

"Is that to be my assignment, sir?"

"As long as I am Legate, though I cannot tell how long that will be. A new Emperor usually likes to appoint new governors and this one seems to be no exception. He has already made Agrippa king of the Tetrarch Philip's old domain."

"King!" Prochorus exclaimed. "That gives him a higher rank than Antipas."

"I'm on my way to tell the Tetrarch of Galilee the news now," said Vitellius. "Would you like to accompany us?"

Prochorus shook his head. "I hold no grudge against him, sir."

"Even though he tried to have you killed?" Marcellus asked.

"What's this?" Vitellius demanded.

"You may remember that I was attacked here in Jerusalem once, sir," said Prochorus. "The man who tried to kill me was a brigand named Harith, hired by the Tetrarch."

"Why wasn't I informed of this?"

"You left Jerusalem before I received proof, sir. The negotiations with King Artaban were about to take place then and it would have done no good to create ill feeling between you and the Tetrarch Antipas."

"As it turned out, we might all have been better off if you had," said Vitellius. "I would have sent him back to Galilee from Damascus and he wouldn't have been able to undermine me with the Emperor by sending his own report of the negotiations at Babylon. Still, the knowledge that Agrippa now holds a higher rank than he does will be enough of a punishment for Antipas. What I don't understand is why he wanted to have you killed?"

"Princess Mariamne and I are betrothed, sir. The Tetrarch hoped to marry her to the son of King Aretas—until the attack on Machaerus." An idea suddenly came into Prochorus' mind. "I intended to ask your approval of our marriage when an opportune time arose. This may be it."

"Why do you say that?"

"The princess was a ward of Emperor Tiberius. Now that he is dead it might be considered that his approval is no longer necessary."

"I can see some grounds for that assumption," Vitellius agreed. "And since I shall probably be Legate only a few months longer, one of my last official acts can at least be to reward you properly for the service you have given me."

"I ask no reward, sir. But if you would approve our marriage, both of us would be very grateful."

"I shall do more than that—if you agree to one stipulation."

"I am under your command, sir."

"With Antipas plotting in Galilee and Agrippa in Ituraea, Judaea could easily become one of the most troubled spots in the empire. Marullus is a good man but it will take him some time to learn the things he will need to know to govern effectively in Judaea and

Samaria. Meanwhile Rome will need a skilled diplomat here, one with experience and understanding of the problems peculiar to this part of the world. I am going to appoint you Deputy Governor of the province to remain here in Jerusalem."

"I don't deserve such an honor."

"You deserve anything I can give you," Vitellius assured him. "After all, you saved Rome from war with Nabatea once by persuading King Aretas to withdraw from Machaerus. I suspect that the death of Tiberius has saved us from it once again, but I can see troubled times ahead for this region and the immediate future of your own people may well be determined by what you do here. Where is Princess Mariamne?"

"At a community on the shore of the Salt Sea."

"How long will it take you to bring her to Jerusalem?"

"It is only about a two hours' ride each way. We should be back before sunset."

"I shall marry you myself tomorrow morning in my capacity as Governor," Vitellius promised him. "It's the least I can do in return for all the help you have been to me."

xvii

"I almost wish we could both stay here forever," Mariamne said as she pulled her mare to a stop at the crest of a ridge of chalk cliffs overlooking the Salt Sea and turned back to look at the white buildings of Ir Hamelakh where she had spent the past six months. "You cannot believe how peaceful it is compared to life in Tiberias or Jerusalem."

Spread out along the side of a ravine just below a series of caves that turned the slope almost into a honeycomb, the white masonry buildings with their brown roofs of palm trunks and baked clay were large enough to house the several hundred scholars and recluses who had chosen to live there apart from the world outside, copying and preserving the ancient Jewish scriptures and the teachings of the Essene sect. The scriptorium which, as usual, formed the center of the cluster of buildings was at least twice as large as the one John had shown Prochorus at Callirhoe. Equally large in proportion were the pools for bathing which formed an integral part of all Essene communities.

The water supply was more than ample, coming from a large spring that burst from the earth well above the village itself. Tumbling over a low cliff in the form of a waterfall—a strange sight indeed in this arid region—the waters of the spring were gathered into a rock-lined pool. From this reservoir part of it was piped to the village. The rest was used to irrigate the lush gardens growing nearer to the water's edge.

"Some people leave the world to find peace," Prochorus said as they resumed their journey along the road that wound up and down across the cliffs and valleys in an almost due-west direction toward Jerusalem. "But I suspect the greatest peace of all comes to those who can find it amidst the cares and tribulations of life from day to day."

"I'll never be afraid as long as I'm with you." She turned in the saddle to face him and what he saw in her eyes filled him with a happiness as great as he had ever known.

As they neared the city, her mood of momentary depression began to lift and she talked happily of tomorrow—her wedding day. Prochorus, too, was caught up by the anticipation of what they had been waiting for so long since she had so calmly informed him—on the way to Magdala one afternoon—that she had chosen him for herself the first day she saw him in the palace of Antipas at Tiberias.

About a third of the way to Jerusalem, where the road climbed to a high point, a squat forbidding structure came into view, silhouetted in the afternoon sunlight. Recognizing the Herodium— the palace-tomb where Herod the Great was buried—Prochorus urged their mounts forward, hoping Mariamne wouldn't see it.

The brief glimpse of Herod's tomb reminded him once again that the spirit of the despot—who had killed his own wife and strangled his own son lest they endanger his rule of the empire he had carved out for himself through every sort of betrayal and treachery—still stalked this unhappy land, this time in the forms of Herod's son Antipas and his grandson Agrippa. These two were almost certain to be at each other's throats soon and he could only pray that, in their struggle for power, the lovely girl riding by his side—who also bore the blood of Herod the Great in her veins—would not once again become a pawn in the desperate game being played for control of an empire.

Book Four

ROME

Tax monies had been accumulating in the tetrarchy of Herod Philip—now a kingdom under Agrippa—since the death of its former ruler. With ample funds, something he had lacked most of his life, plus the favor of the Emperor Caligula, Aprippa was in no hurry, however, to take up residence in his new domain. He delayed going there from month to month but, since the kingdom was ably governed by Roman administrators under the direction of the Legate Vitellius, his absence made no real difference in its status.

Two reasons finally led to Agrippa's return to his native land; one was the change in legates when Petronius succeeded Vitellius in Antioch; the other was the mounting evidence that Caligula, although Emperor of Rome, was indeed a madman.

Agrippa was much too clever and too well acquainted with Roman government not to realize that the real rulers of the empire were the bureaucracy of freedmen, who had gradually assumed political control during the period when Tiberius had been in retreat at Capri, plus the Praetorian Guard, the dominant military power in the city of Rome itself. He could understand therefore the advantage of not being closely allied with Caligula, when the flagrant excesses of the Emperor finally came to shock even sophisticated Romans, and decided to visit his kingdom in his grandfather's old domain. His journey there was not, however, without incident.

The right to exist practically as a separate people, granted to the Jews in the time of the Ptolemies several hundred years earlier, had been a cause of constant friction between the Greek element of Alexandria, Egypt's largest city, and its large Jewish population. The ostentatiousness that accompanied King Agrippa's progress through the Egyptian capital was therefore like a spark set to tinder; riots in which Greeks attacked Jews raged through the city for almost a week and continued even after Agrippa's departure for his own kingdom, a portent of what was to come in other cities of the empire, where Jews controlled much of the wealth.

In Jerusalem, life had been very pleasant for Prochorus and Mariamne. Marullus, the new Procurator of Judaea and Samaria, was a rather indolent man who had been given the governorship of the province because of his friendship with Caligula. He was quite content to leave the administration of the often turbulent city to the priestly authorities and to Prochorus as Deputy Governor. And since Prochorus was a Jew and understood the conditions peculiar to Jerusalem and Judaea, there had been a period of relative peace.

The new position Prochorus now occupied did not allow him to be of much help to the Synagogue of the Nazarenes, however. Under the leadership of James ben Joseph, the kinsman of Jesus who had become the *mebaqqer* of the congregation following the persecution by Saul of Tarsus, the Nazarenes had been careful to follow the rituals customary with all Jews: daily prayer in the Temple, observance of the regular feast days and sacrifices, and strict obedience to Mosaic law, as interpreted by the Rabbis of the Porch and other Pharisees. But whereas in the days following Peter's stirring sermon on Pentecost the whole congregation had been charged with an air of excitement and fervor, the atmosphere now was almost one of complacency. John, who had once more become a part of the congregation upon his return from Babylon, gave Prochorus an explanation.

"They are waiting for the *parousia*—the coming of the Lord," he said.

"But you told me Jesus instructed the disciples to go out into all the world and preach."

"Peter and Philip, one of the seven deacons, have done that," said John. "But James ben Joseph and other leaders of the congregation in Jerusalem believe Jesus meant that the teachings of the Lord should be carried only to the Jews, and even then only where we are invited."

"How can you carry on Jesus' work if all of you stay here in Jerusalem and wait for his coming without doing anything else?"

"Not all of us agree with James," John admitted. "In Caesarea, Peter baptized the Centurion Cornelius of the Italian Band and his family, all of them gentiles. And the Lord himself revealed to Peter in a vision at Joppa that the law concerning unclean foods no longer holds true. But James fears that, if we publicly advocate relaxing the provisions of the law of Moses, we may earn the enmity of the Temple authorities—as when Peter and I were arrested and brought before the Sanhedrin."

"You were freed to do as your heart guided you then—by no less an authority than the Rabban Gamaliel."

"True," said John. "I often speak outside Jerusalem now, even making converts of gentiles, but James ben Joseph considers them only proselytes and not really Jews."

"I think he is misguided," said Prochorus. "Unless the leaders are filled with a new spirit, the Way—as you call it—will soon disappear."

"Peter and I agree that our future growth lies outside Jerusalem, but as long as we daily expect the coming of the Lord, we must keep alive here the foundation on which he will build the kingdom of the Messiah."

"Suppose Jesus doesn't come soon?"

"We have his promise. And I have an especially personal one for myself alone—that I shall live to see his return."

"Where is Saul of Tarsus?"

"In the desert, I believe. Probably somewhere near Damascus."

"Saul changed once. What if he should return again as a persecutor?"

"If that is God's will, I shall not hold it against Saul."

"Where is your part in all this?"

"My place is here; we are all agreed upon that—at least for the time being."

"And Peter?"

"The world outside is calling him. He told me a few days ago that he is thinking of going to Rome."

"Why so far away?"

"There are already some Nazarenes in Rome. Under Caligula many who are uncertain seek a way of life that gives them some source of purpose, so the teachings of Jesus should fall upon fertile ground there, as they did at first here in Jerusalem."

But remembering the way Jesus had moved thousands with his preaching when he was alive, Prochorus found it hard to reconcile the waiting attitude of the Jerusalem congregation with the dynamic fervor that had characterized the man they served.

ii

Prochorus' first knowledge that Agrippa was actually in his kingdom came in the form of a letter requesting that he meet with the new monarch at his mountain capital of Caesarea Philippi. Being very fond of her aunt Kypros and the children, Mariamne was excited at the prospect, but Prochorus did not answer the request until he had sent dispatches northward to Marullus in Caesarea and to the new Legate, Petronius, in Antioch, requesting their advice and permission.

A letter of approval came from Marullus a few days later. The dispatch from Petronius was an order for him to come to Antioch for a conference before going on to Caesarea Philippi. He and Mariamne therefore took ship at Joppa and several days later were in the Syrian capital.

Petronius proved to be of a different cut from Procurator Marullus. A spare man with the nose of a Roman patriarch, his warm brown eyes lit up when he saw Mariamne.

"How lovely you are, my dear," he said. "No wonder your husband has kept you shut up in Jerusalem."

"She was captured from me once, my Lord Governor," said Prochorus. "I am making certain that it never happens again."

"I remember hearing the story from my old friend Sextus Latimus," said Petronius. "It's a very romantic one."

That evening was an informal affair with Petronius and his wife, Domitia. When the meal was finished, Domitia took Mariamne away for a discussion of purely womanly subjects, leaving Prochorus alone with the Legate.

"I asked you to come here before going to Caesarea Philippi," said Petronius, "so we could discuss the turn events may take, now that King Agrippa has decided to live in his kingdom."

"Is he likely to return to Rome?" asked Prochorus.

"Not while Caligula is Emperor. Agrippa is indebted to Caligula for freeing him from prison and making him King of Ituraea. But he is much too clever to ally himself with a madman."

"Then what we hear is true?"

"Probably worse. Vitellius assured me that you are one of the few men in Roman service out here who can be trusted without question, so I am following his advice and being perfectly frank with you."

"There is one thing I should tell you," said Prochorus. "I have become a follower of Jesus of Nazareth—a Nazarene, as we are called in Jerusalem."

"The sect that are called Christians here in Antioch?"

"Yes, sir. Some of my best friends are leaders among them."

"The head of one of the Jewish synagogues here wrote me a letter just after I arrived, complaining against the group," said Petronius. "But I have discovered nothing to their discredit either here or elsewhere in the province."

"Rome has nothing to fear from the Nazarenes," Prochorus assured him. "Jesus of Nazareth was crucified, it is true, but only when the chief priests conspired against him because he spoke out freely and exposed their failure to live up to their vows."

"Socrates was forced to drink the hemlock for somewhat the same reason. Any man who dares to think differently from the common herd—even though his actions are above reproach—is usually attacked by others."

"I could never understand why."

"The answer lies in the realm of philosophy, but I am not well enough versed there to give you the answer. My guess would be that early in life most people develop a fixed set of ideas about the world and the place of mankind in it—particularly themselves. They wear this like a comfortable toga or robe ever afterward and resent anything that might tear or destroy it."

"Have they no desire to learn anything new?"

"A few do—like you. But most are afraid of new ideas, lest they see themselves naked and realize that others also know how small and insignificant they really are."

"Jesus of Nazareth taught that all who believe in him are thereby akin to God and need no longer feel themselves small and insignificant," said Prochorus.

"It is an interesting philosophy—and an attractive one. You must tell me more about it sometime, but now I want to hear your opinion of King Agrippa."

"I'm sure he would like to rule over all of what was his grandfather's kingdom."

"That is certainly a natural ambition," said Petronius. "How did he and Tetrarch Antipas get along when Agrippa was living here before?"

"Like dogs ready to attack each other. The Tetrarch lost no opportunity to humble Prince—King—Agrippa."

"Agrippa could do little about it either, since he was practically Antipas' prisoner," said Petronius thoughtfully. "Yet now that his rank is higher than Antipas', he has every right to lord it over the Tetrarch of Galilee and hasn't done so. I wonder why?"

"Perhaps being King is enough."

"I doubt that," said Petronius. "Agrippa grew up in Rome as one of the young princes in the household of the Emperor. Ambition to outdo the others is the strongest emotion among them. Besides, there's the story of the owl."

"I'm afraid I don't understand, sir."

"It's a strange tale; I never knew how much is true and how much somebody's imaginings. According to the version I heard, when Agrippa was put in prison after he returned to Rome following his quarrel with Antipas, an owl settled on a limb of a tree just over his head, while he was standing in chains in the prison courtyard. Another prisoner, a German tribal chief, saw the bird and told Agrippa the appearance of the owl was an omen meaning that he would soon be released and raised to a high position."

"That has already come true, at least."

"According to the story, the German chief also said that, when Agrippa next sees an owl, he will have only five days to live."

"It's a strange story."

"And probably not any truer than a lot of such fables," said Petronius. "Have you thought about what you are going to say to Agrippa in Caesarea Philippi?"

"I don't know, sir. His letter gave no inkling of why he wanted to see me."

"I think he would like you to smooth the way for him to assume the governorship of Judaea and Samaria, if he can flatter Caligula into giving it to him. If his rule is to be peaceful—and profitable— he must please the priestly hierarchy, as you have done, which means assuring them that things will not be changed in Jerusalem."

"Shall I help him convince the priests, sir?"

"If you think it would be best for the province."

"I'm not at all certain just what would be best for the province," Prochorus admitted. "Things have gone fairly smoothly in recent months—"

"Mainly because you have been a leavening influence and a buffer between Antipas and Agrippa," Petronius assured him. "Did you know that Antipas has been petitioning the Emperor behind my back to have Judaea and Samaria added to his tetrarchy, with the rank of king?"

"I'm not surprised. He tried a direct appeal to the Emperor once before."

"And would have succeeded if Tiberius hadn't died before an attack could be launched against the Nabateans."

"Do you think he will succeed now, sir?"

"Who can tell?" Petronius shrugged. "The disturbances at Alexandria, when Agrippa landed there on his way to Caesarea Philippi, certainly indicate that many Jews admire him greatly, probably considerably more than they do Antipas."

"Perhaps that's why the Tetrarch Antipas made his appeal to the Emperor."

"Perhaps, but the time to have made the appeal would have been when Caligula first came to the throne. Things are always in a spirit of turmoil then and Antipas' request might have been approved without anyone in Rome looking very carefully into the real situation. Now he's a little late."

"I think the Tetrarch Antipas would be content to leave things as they are," said Prochorus, "but not his wife. Mariamne hears occasionally from her aunt in Tiberias. Mostly the letters are full of complaints because Agrippa was raised to the rank of king but occasionally she mentions that her husband has been ill. When I was a member of his household, he suffered much with a painful inflammation of his foot."

" 'Tetrarch's toe,' they call it in Rome." Petronius grinned. "Sometimes legates get it, too, but rarely here in Syria; we stay too busy." Then he sobered. "Perhaps it isn't fair to ask, but I know you will tell me what you believe is true. If it should come to a decision between Antipas and Agrippa as ruler of Judaea and Samaria, which would you choose?"

"King Agrippa," Prochorus said without hesitation.

"Why?"

"King Aretas and the Tetrarch Antipas still hate each other as much as ever. If the Tetrarch ruled Judaea and Samaria, he might feel strong enough to attack Nabatea."

"What if the provinces were given to Agrippa?"

"He already has a boundary with Nabatea along the southern part of Auranitis and the King's Highway to Damascus passes through his kingdom," Prochorus pointed out. "Agrippa would have every reason not to cause trouble with Aretas, especially when he seeks to unseat the Tetrarch Antipas and gain the whole of his grandfather's empire."

Petronius nodded thoughtfully. "Herod the Great was greedy for power, like all despots, and it seems that his descendants have inherited his greed, if not his ability. I am counting on you to discover the truth for me, while you are in Caesarea Philippi."

iii

An ancient road led from Tyre—the Phoenician seaport city whose glory had vanished abruptly when Alexander the Great conquered it by building a mole across open water to the rock-girt island upon which it stood—to Caesarea in the foothills of Mount Hermon near the source of the Jordan. The way traversed what Prochorus was sure was some of the loveliest country in the world, the rolling hills of Upper Galilee and the district sometimes known as Syro-Phoenicia, so he and Mariamne did not hurry but enjoyed to the full the succeeding vistas of beauty that opened out before them as they journeyed eastward, after debarking from Petronius' own galley at Tyre.

Shortly after his accession to the throne, the Tetrarch Philip had taken the ancient city of Paneas and transformed it into a luxurious new capital which he called Caesarea Philippi. Agrippa had been in residence only briefly but there was evidence that he was already busy. The city was bustling and prosperous and buildings were going up everywhere: new baths fed by the springs that burst from the rocks all through this area, a new forum where Ituraea's king— he had chosen to be named from the northernmost extension of his rule—could judge between his subjects when complaints were brought before his elevated judgment seat, and many other structures were rising in all parts of the city.

Mariamne and Prochorus were warmly received by her aunt, Queen Kypros. Agrippa was away but was expected to return the next day; meanwhile, they were given an apartment in the palace and were introduced to the personal *secretarius* of the King, a freedman named Fortunatus who had come with Agrippa from Rome. Prochorus found Fortunatus agreeable enough but Mariamne's reaction, as they were dressing for the usual leisurely Roman dinner that evening, was different.

"Did you see the way Fortunatus was looking at me?" she asked.

"A woman as beautiful as you are should expect admiration."

"His eyes make me uncomfortable. I wouldn't trust him."

"King Agrippa obviously does," said Prochorus. "He seems to have given Fortunatus much of the responsibility for the day-to-day governing of the kingdom."

"Do you think it's being governed well?"

"I can tell you more about that after I spend tomorrow morning in the forum and the market place talking to the people, particularly the merchants."

"Aunt Kypros seems to be happy."

"She's entitled to that much. Her husband has certainly caused enough trouble for her in the past."

"The girls are beautiful, too, Drusilla more than Berenice. They will be real charmers when they grow up."

Prochorus laughed as he drew her close. "The feminine descendants of Herod the Great are always beautiful, even to the third generation. I still have to pinch myself to realize that one of them belongs to me."

"Young Agrippa will be a handsome young man," said Mariamne. "He must be about eleven now, so it will soon be time for him to go to Rome."

"Why would he be sent there?"

"Petty kings are almost always required to send their sons to Rome. The excuse the Emperor gives is that they need to be educated so they will know how to rule when their turn comes, but actually they're hostages—as Uncle Agrippa was for a long time."

"Perhaps knowing Roman politics will be as good for the son as it was for the father."

"It isn't just Roman politics they learn," she said. "The princes vie to outdo each other in gaining the favor of the Emperor and the freedmen who run the government. After they deal in intrigue awhile, it becomes part of their character and they are no longer capable of anything else."

"Did I ever tell you that you're a very intelligent young woman?"

She looked up quickly and, seeing that he was entirely serious, said, "Why do you say that?"

"Sextus said almost exactly the same thing once, when we were discussing your uncle Agrippa. If your theory is correct, he's already busy conspiring to overthrow Antipas and have Marullus replaced as Procurator of Judaea and Samaria—by himself."

"Can he do it?"

"Replacing Marullus shouldn't be difficult. He has little talent as a governor—"

"And has only succeeded as well as he has because you have kept Jerusalem quiet."

"Spoken like a loyal wife."

"Because it's true. Aunt Kypros told me that Uncle Agrippa says the same thing."

"I do my best, but the Legate and I both agree that Judaea and Samaria might be better off governed by a descendant of Herod the Great who is at least part Jew and preferably a Hasmonean. If Agrippa has decided to give up intrigue and rule well—as he seems to be doing here in Caesarea Philippi—I shall be the first to recommend that he become King of Judaea and Samaria."

"Even though it means you will be out of a job?"

"Out of one and into another. I spoke to Manaen before we left Antioch. The Christians there are growing rapidly and Mark's cousin Barnabas—he was one of the seventy that were next in importance to the disciples themselves among the immediate followers of Jesus—has come from Jerusalem to supervise their work. The Antioch church is thinking of sending out men to tell about Jesus in the cities of the Diaspora and Manaen thinks a Jew who is half Greek—like myself—may be the answer."

"Did you commit yourself to go?"

"I wouldn't do that without consulting you; besides, everyone agrees that I am needed where I am now. But if Agrippa takes control of Jerusalem, he would hardly want a former deputy governor in his retinue—especially a relative by marriage."

"A long time ago you said you wanted to study philosophy in Alexandria," she reminded him. "Have you given that up?"

"No—merely postponed it in the face of more urgent matters."

When she shivered and drew closer to him, he asked, "What's wrong, darling?"

"I can't help feeling that what you call urgent matters are a threat to us, like the owl that perched over Uncle Agrippa's head in the story you told me about him."

"That was only a fable, probably thought up by the German chieftain to gain favor with Agrippa."

"By predicting his death?"

"Don't forget that he predicted his release first—and a return of good fortune."

"Which has already come true."

"But not necessarily because of the prediction. Tiberius was dying and Caligula was Agrippa's friend, so the German chief was merely predicting what everyone already knew would happen. He probably added that part about the owl appearing again to call attention to himself and the story."

"Do you think Uncle Agrippa can really unseat Uncle Antipas?"

"Not unless your aunt Herodias envies Queen Kypros so much that she makes Antipas do something foolish. After all, the only real fault Rome has ever found with Antipas was his divorcing Aretas' daughter. And that was settled a long time ago."

"I wonder if it really was," said Mariamne. "Aunt Kypros asked me last night whether I knew anything about a store of weapons Uncles Antipas is supposed to have at Sepphoris."

"Sepphoris is a fortress like Machaerus. He would certainly keep some armament there."

"Enough to equip seventy thousand men?"

Prochorus gave her a startled look. "Did she name that figure?"

"Yes. And when I told her I knew nothing about it, she asked whether I thought you did."

"Which means that Agrippa isn't entirely certain whether or not the rumor is true."

"I thought of that; you see, I didn't grow up in Rome for nothing. But why would he keep that many weapons in Sepphoris?"

"Perhaps to equip brigands like Manahem that he has always protected in Lower Galilee, in case Agrippa should try to unseat him, as Aretas almost did. Or Antipas might even dream of another rebellion that would place him on the throne at Jerusalem. Barabbas and Manahem are still in the hill country and, with a weak procurator ruling in Caesarea, they may even be stronger than ever. With enough men, Antipas could strike eastward to take Caesarea Philippi and southward through Samaria to seize Jerusalem at the same time."

"When?"

"Perhaps when Caligula is removed from the throne and Rome itself is torn apart fighting over who shall be his successor, as happened after Julius Caesar was killed. The empire can hardly stand being governed by a madman much longer; someone will try to unseat Caligula and there will be civil war."

She shivered again although the room was warm. "What can we do?"

"Nothing but enjoy ourselves until King Agrippa reveals his intentions. I don't think he asked us here merely to see his beautiful great-niece and her commoner husband once again."

iv

A day spent in the market place and the forum of Caesarea Philippi, listening and occasionally asking an unobtrusive question, gained no information that Prochorus didn't already have—or suspect. New buildings were going up everywhere, paid for out of the vast revenues that had been accumulating in the province since the death of Philip, and with thousands of people on Agrippa's payroll, the new King was easily the most popular man in the province. That he had also carefully cultivated a good relationship with the Nabateans, who now largely controlled Damascus through a commercial treaty, was obvious from the free passage of Nabatean caravans through the city and the presence of their merchants in the market place.

Since the former province of the Tetrarch Philip had always been made up of a polyglot population, composed as much of Syrians, Persians, Phoenicians and Greeks from the Diaspora as Jews, Agrippa had wisely allowed all religions to be practiced freely there, although adhering strictly to the Jewish faith himself. In fact, Prochorus learned, Agrippa had become so pious—either sincerely or because he could see that it was good for him—that on the sabbath he often read the sections of the law and the Prophets from the *bima* of the largest synagogue there.

In the matter of the weapons Antipas was supposed to have stored at Sepphoris, Prochorus got nowhere. The few to whom he casually mentioned the subject cut him off shortly or looked away quickly, by which he judged that the rumors probably had real substance. When he came back to the palace at the end of the afternoon, he found Mariamne ready to scold him for being late.

"Uncle Agrippa got here just after the noonday meal," she reported. "He asked for you at once."

"What did you tell him?"

"That you had never been in Caesarea Philippi and wanted to see the new buildings he's putting up. Now get your bath and dress quickly; I had the servants bring up a tub of water for you since there's no time for you to go to the baths.

"I laid out your best robe and the golden chain Vitellius gave you before he went back to Rome," Mariamne called through the door of the adjoining chamber while Prochorus was splashing in a large tub filled with warm water. "We are dining with the King and Queen and young Agrippa."

The others had already gathered in the large triclinium when Prochorus and Mariamne arrived. They were to dine Roman fashion, with couches for reclining arranged around a centerpiece of magnificent flowers. At their entrance, Agrippa rose at once and came forward to greet Prochorus cordially. Fortunatus too was there, apparently a frequent occurrence, since he seemed to be entirely at ease.

"Welcome to my capital, kinsman," Agrippa said heartily. "While I was busy in Rome, you managed to steal my favorite niece."

"I count myself the most fortunate of men, Your Majesty," said Prochorus as he took the couch beside Agrippa, the place of honor to which the King directed him. Mariamne was next to Fortunatus which, he was sure, did not particularly please her but he could not have told it from her manner.

Agrippa looked in much better health than when Prochorus had last seen him at Caesarea a long time ago and at Tiberias, where he had served briefly as the *agoranomus* in charge of the markets. The months of imprisonment in Rome had removed considerable weight which the King of Ituraea had not yet regained, though from the way he ate and drank during the feast that followed, Prochorus suspected that he would shortly be as portly as ever. The main change, however, was in Agrippa's manner, which was now self-assured and even jovial, where before it had been petulant and complaining.

"You have come a long way from the day you visited me in Tiberias, Prochorus," Agrippa said in the midst of the meal. "A long way."

"So have you, Your Majesty," Prochorus said, and Agrippa roared with laughter.

"I see that my niece has not married a dullard. But then she was always clever, even as a little girl. Tell me, how did you ever get out from under the thumb of my brother-in-law Antipas?"

"The Legate Flaccus was having trouble with his scribe. He took me on the recommendation of Cassius Longinus."

"I remember young Cassius well," said Queen Kypros. "A very handsome and capable young man."

Stately rather than beautiful, Kypros was in every way queenly, yet gracious with it all. She had been a pillar of strength to Agrippa in his most troubled days, Prochorus knew, saving him more than once from follies that might have cost him his head.

"Young Cassius' father is one of the most eminent jurists in Rome," said Agrippa. "If I am ever called to account for my sins before the imperial courts I could wish no fairer judge than Cassius Longinus the elder."

The meal proceeded leisurely; when the sweets were finished, young Agrippa, a handsome but rather slight boy, left the triclinium. The wine was flowing freely by then but Prochorus drank sparingly, sensing that the real reason for his invitation to Caesarea Philippi would shortly be revealed and wanting all his faculties about him when it was.

"I suppose you've been wondering why I invited you and Mariamne here," Agrippa said at last. "I can assure you that it is on a matter of great importance."

"I am only a civil servant, Your Majesty. And couldn't possibly be of much importance to you."

"That's where you're wrong." Only a slight slurring of Agrippa's words betrayed the effect of the wine. "You are known to be dependable, faithful and honest, all of them stellar virtues. A long time ago in Tiberias, I offered to sponsor you for a career in the administration of Roman government."

"I remember very well," said Prochorus. "You wished me to spy on the Tetrarch Antipas."

Agrippa guffawed and reached over to slap his secretary on the shoulder. "What did I tell you, Fortunatus? This is an honest young man—with principles. Someone we can depend upon."

"I'm sure of it, Your Majesty," said Fortunatus and winked at Prochorus—or Mariamne.

"What is it you wish Prochorus to do, Uncle Agrippa?" Mariamne asked.

"I want him—and you too, my dear—to go to Rome."

"Rome!" Prochorus was so startled that he spoke louder than he intended. "I know nothing of Rome, sir."

"That's not important," Agrippa assured him. "What's important is that Rome knows nothing about you, yet you are intelligent enough to see things as they are and honest enough to send word to me of what is happening."

"Surely others more familiar with the government than I could serve you much better," Prochorus protested.

"Fortunatus knows who is stealing from whom all the way to the throne. He is also known to be my man and would be immediately suspect—but not you."

"What would I be expected to do?" The idea was beginning to take hold of Prochorus' imagination and, when he saw the look of excitement in Mariamne's eyes, his reservations began to melt away.

"The Emperor Caligula is my friend, but for good reasons it is best that my presence not be associated with his rule. Your task is to watch and listen. You read and speak Latin, don't you?"

"Yes."

"So much the better. Romans don't expect visitors from the provinces to understand Latin, so they often say things before them they might not otherwise say. When you hear something I should know, you are to write me by the imperial post. The fact that you will write the letters yourself removes still another possible leak."

"I can do better than that," said Prochorus. "If I write them in Hebrew, few between here and Rome would be able to understand."

"A perfect solution!" Agrippa cried and lifted his wine goblet. "To a perfect spy!"

Prochorus felt a moment of doubt at the word and Fortunatus saw it in his face. "What's wrong?" he asked.

"That word 'spy'—among Jews it has an evil meaning. And I must tell the Legate Petronius why I'm going to Rome."

"I shall tell him myself in a letter you will carry, when you sail from Caesarea," said Agrippa. "Petronius and I agree on how my grandfather's kingdom can best be governed—after all, I didn't grow up in Rome for nothing. But we will need some excuse for your going there just now."

"Why not to have his marriage to Princess Mariamne approved by the Emperor?" said Fortunatus.

When he saw Mariamne grow pale, Prochorus knew that she, too, realized the significance of the statement, as well as the naked threat it represented, although Fortunatus had spoken the words very casually. Suddenly he felt a chill of apprehension about the possible consequences of a step which he had now practically taken, but there was no going back.

"Wasn't your marriage ever approved by the Emperor, my dear?" Agrippa asked Mariamne and she shook her head numbly.

"It was at the time of Emperor Tiberius' death," Prochorus explained. "Imperial affairs were in considerable confusion, especially here. Legate Vitellius married us himself."

"This gives a perfect reason for your being in Rome then," said Agrippa. "I shall send a letter to my dear friend and companion, Caligula, telling him of the oversight and asking his blessing. It will be only a formality and afterward you can stay on in Rome—to observe."

The matter was left there but that night Mariamne clung to Prochorus like a desperately scared child until she fell asleep. Just before dawn, she awoke screaming in the throes of a nightmare whose details she would not reveal. She lay in his arms and finally went back to sleep but he was sleepless until dawn, searching for a way out of the dilemma in which the ambitions of Agrippa had placed him. He found none, however, nor could he very well refuse Agrippa's offer. The Legate Petronius had admitted to being favorably inclined toward Agrippa and the new King's own behavior had been extremely circumspect, so to offend Agrippa by refusing would necessarily mean incurring the displeasure of Petronius.

It would be better to go on to Rome, he decided finally, hoping the capricious temper of Caligula would be so allayed by receiving a letter from his dear friend Agrippa that he would give imperial approval to the marriage.

v

Watching their ship being warped to its berth at the quay of Ostia, the seaport city located a short distance west of Rome, Prochorus found some of his apprehension melting with the excitement of reaching the center of the Roman Empire at last. Mariamne stood beside him upon the raised afterdeck of the vessel; when he reached out his hand to cover hers, she smiled, although a little uncertainly.

"Cheer up," he told her. "This could be the most important journey of our lives. With the letter from Petronius and particularly the one Agrippa is sending, we have no reason to believe the Emperor will not approve our marriage."

"It's just that there's so much evil here and you are so good," she said. "I'm afraid of what they may do to both of us, but particularly to you."

On the quay a crowd had gathered: merchants, visitors, government officials, port authorities, all waiting for the final act of docking. As he watched, Prochorus thought of his last conversation with the Legate of Syria in Antioch before he and Mariamne had taken a carriage for Seleucia where they had boarded ship.

"You will find Rome different from Antioch and far different from Jerusalem," Petronius had warned him while they were waiting for the package of official dispatches Prochorus was to take with him to be wrapped in oiled parchment to protect them from dampness on shipboard.

"That troubles me a little," Prochorus admitted. "After all, I know nothing about the city."

"Your wife grew up in Rome so she can guide you there. Just remember that you have coped successfully with Herod Antipas and Agrippa, two of the wiliest plotters I know, and you once faced a king and made him give up a castle."

"Aretas was only looking for a way to give it back without losing face to Herod Antipas. My arrival gave him the excuse he needed."

"You still saved us from war and I am counting on the same sort of natural ingenuity to stand you in good stead in Rome. I think the Jews are going to need an eloquent voice there, if they are to forestall the insane idea Caligula seems to be getting that he is a god."

"Surely he will not go through with it, sir."

"A madman can be convinced of almost anything, and people looking for ways to advance themselves are always willing to prey upon that weakness. Did you know that Herennius Capito is already talking of setting up an altar in Jamnia where people can worship the Emperor?"

Prochorus shook his head, his face grave. An estate lying south of Joppa in the *shephelah*, the fertile coastal plain stretching southward from Mount Carmel, Jamnia was a crown colony, so to speak. Neither Petronius as Legate nor Prochorus as Deputy Governor of Jerusalem had any jurisdiction over it, and its steward, Herennius Capito, reported directly to Rome, paying the taxes he collected into the Emperor's private treasury.

"The Jews in Jamnia will never countenance anything like that," said Prochorus. "Violence will break out the moment he attempts it."

"Violence which could spread to the whole province," Petronius agreed. "And all because one man seeks to toady himself into imperial favor. That's why both Agrippa and I need an intelligent observer in Rome."

"I shall do my best, sir."

"We both know that or we would not have sent you. Unfortunately I have no way of knowing what sort of reports the Tetrarch Antipas has been sending directly to the Emperor, but he knows I prefer Agrippa, so you can be certain they aren't complimentary to either one of us. And certainly Herodias will not let Antipas rest until she equals or exceeds Queen Kypros in rank."

"It's a foolish reason to wreck the peace of a land that has never known it very long anyway."

"The fate of empires often turns upon the most foolish of reasons," said Petronius. "Look where Cleopatra led Mark Antony. Nobody profited from her ambition either, except perhaps Herod the Great—and he only by knowing when to switch sides."

"Perhaps Antipas has inherited some of his father's cunning," Prochorus suggested, but Petronius shook his head.

"The Tetrarch of Galilee is a dolt. Herodias has the cleverness there but she is so blinded by envy of Queen Kypros that she doesn't see clearly any more. I think we're in for serious trouble before the question of which one of them is to outdo the other is settled. I only hope we can avoid another war."

Watching the bustling activity of the port of Ostia now while the gangplank was being lowered, Prochorus felt some of the problems which had seemed so acute in the former empire of Herod the Great recede into the background.

"It's Tribune Cassius!" Mariamne cried, pointing to the dock where a handsome young man in a carefully pleated toga was striding through the crowd.

"I received your letter and came to meet you," Cassius called to them as they were coming down the gangplank to the quay. He embraced Prochorus and took Mariamne's hands in order to admire her.

"I told Prochorus once you would be a beautiful woman, Princess," he said warmly. "But I used mere words when I should have used superlatives."

"A woman who knows she's loved is always beautiful." Mariamne blushed with pleasure at the compliment. "I'm happy to see you again, Tribune Cassius."

"Not tribune any longer." Cassius had gained weight, Prochorus saw, and with it a great deal of confidence. "Father persuaded me to become a lawyer."

They made their way to the carriage in which Cassius had driven from Rome. It was a *cisium*, a very light vehicle capable of considerable speed. Traffic was heavy as they drove along the stone-paved road to the imperial city. A stream of carts and conveyances of all kinds transported the cargoes of ships which docked at Ostia to the markets of Rome, while another flowed westward toward the port city to load other ships for trade with the far-flung population centers of the empire. Cassius handled the horses expertly and kept up a steady flow of comment as they approached the city.

"I thought you were going to be an administrator," Prochorus said as the swift vehicle fairly flew over the paved road.

"I shall—later," said Cassius. "But Father feels a knowledge of law will help me, when I am assigned as a provincial governor. Besides, no quicker way of making a name for yourself exists than through the law."

"How can that be when a lawyer is supposed to defend his clients free?" Mariamne asked. "Or has the rule been changed since I left Rome?"

"The rule is still the same." Cassius grinned. "But no law says a client cannot be grateful. The real ladder to fame, though, is through prosecuting lawbreakers, mainly political officials of the faction you oppose. If I can win a few such cases, I can hope to be elected *praetor* and one day perhaps even *praetor peregrinus*."

The office of *praetor*, Prochorus knew, comprised some sixteen magistrates whose duty it was to act as judges in interpreting Roman law for the jury trial which was the privilege of every Roman citizen. That of *praetor peregrinus* was concerned with cases in which one or both parties did not possess the highly valued Roman citizenship. Set down in written form for the first time over five hundred years earlier in the Twelve Tablets containing the essence of Rome's judicial system, Roman law was modified from time to time through interpretations and decisions by the various praetors, who were elected to office annually. Thus it was a living, not a static, body of regulations.

"The office of *praetor peregrinus* deals mainly in cases arising outside of Rome and Father says my experience in Syria will be of great value to me there," Cassius explained. "After I have spent a year or two in that office, I can expect to be appointed a provincial governor."

"We need a procurator in Judaea and Samaria now," said Prochorus. "Marullus is a weakling."

"All that will be settled soon," Cassius assured him. "Caligula loves Agrippa like a brother."

"What about Antipas?"

"He and Herodias are here."

"In Rome?"

"Yes. They arrived nearly a week ago."

"Petronius knew nothing of this when I left Antioch."

"He may not know it yet; the Fox has a habit of hiding his actions from the legates. But Antipas will have his work cut out for him if he seeks to outbid Agrippa for Judaea and Samaria."

"Has it come to that already?" Mariamne asked.

"Perhaps you were too young to know much about politics when you lived here, Princess. Gold can buy almost anything in Rome today, with Caligula spending fortunes on his favorites."

"Is he really mad?" she asked.

"Who can say? Or rather who dares to say?"

"Would the senators let him rule if he's mad?" Prochorus asked.

"In Rome almost everybody does what seems best for his own fortunes; loyalty has very little to do with it. At first Caligula was very popular, largely because he gave corn to the masses to gain their favor and was careful to behave circumspectly. But his venture to conquer Britain was a failure; the armies marched to the shores of the Fretum Gallicum so he could look across the channel and see Britain, then turned and marched back again."

"Surely his generals gave him better advice than that," said Prochorus.

"Caligula lacks the advantage Flaccus and Vitellius had, and Petronius has now, of having someone like you with the courage to advise him, even if the advice was contrary to his desires. A general can lose his head like anyone else if he crosses an emperor like Caligula."

"I'm beginning to wonder if we were wise even to come to Rome," said Prochorus.

"You were wise, if you wish to go any higher with your career."

Cassius gave him a keen look. "Aren't you here to plead Agrippa's case?"

"Our main purpose is to obtain the approval of the Emperor for our marriage. But I am also acting as an observer for both King Agrippa and the Legate Petronius."

"Watching Antipas, I suppose?"

"And whatever else concerns Syria. Has Antipas made any representations to the Emperor yet?"

"He only arrived here a week ago and much of that time has been spent trying to find an advocate to present his case before the Emperor. He tried my father first but I advised him to have no part in pleading a lost cause. Caligula is too fond of Agrippa for Antipas to have any chance to gain Jerusalem—and a crown for Herodias."

"Then Antipas hasn't seen the Emperor?"

"At the moment Caligula is at Baiae sulking over the failure of his campaign in Gaul," said Cassius. "Rome hasn't seen him for several weeks."

"When do you think we should present the petition for approval of our marriage?" Mariamne asked.

"Any time but now. My advice is to stay in Rome and enjoy yourself on Agrippa's money. I can introduce you to some very interesting people and, when Caligula returns in a better mood, you can make your petition to him. Besides, it will be to your benefit, Prochorus, to know some of the people who will be in authority one day."

"When will that be?"

"When the time comes you will know," Cassius said cryptically. "The less you know before that, the better off you will be."

"I must do one thing," said Prochorus. "Petronius in Antioch and Agrippa in Caesarea Philippi need to know as quickly as possible that Antipas is here."

"You will have no trouble there," Cassius assured him. "A military galley leaves Ostia once a week bound for the East. As Deputy Governor of Jerusalem you can request that your letters be carried on it and be sure they will reach Antioch at least twice as quickly as they would by way of the imperial post."

vi

Augustus had claimed that he found Rome built of brick upon his ascension to the throne and left it built of marble upon his death. Which wasn't entirely true of anything except the central part of the city, for outside the heart much of Rome was composed of two-, three- and five-story buildings, all of them of wood and many in an advanced state of disrepair. The central part of the city, however, was impressive enough, as Prochorus observed while he, Cassius and Mariamne were walking from the stable where they left the carriage—wheeled vehicles being forbidden on the streets by day because of the congestion—to Cassius' home.

The imperial palace stood on the Palatine, one of the seven hills of Rome, where both Augustus and Tiberius had built magnificent structures. South of the Palatine, located between it and the Aventine, was the great Circus Maximus, scene of many gladiatorial contests and capable of seating a hundred thousand spectators. The Roman Forum lay between the Palatine and Capitol hills, with many famous buildings surrounding it: such structures as the Basilica Julia, the House of the Pontifex Maximus—the High Priest of Jupiter—where Caesar's pyre had been set into flame, the House of the Vestal Virgins, the Basilica Aemelia and others. Surrounding this area were temples of various gods worshiped by the Romans, such as Saturn, Apollo, Castor and Pollux and even Julius Caesar.

Cassius' father's home was located on a typically narrow street easily accessible to the central part of the city; to reach it they had to pass through an area which he identified as the Subura. Here the houses were in startling contrast to the magnificent structures in the neighborhood of the Forum, although the distance between was very short. The streets were narrow and jammed with people, while the buildings towered upward sometimes as much as seven stories above ground, the lowermost levels usually devoted to shops while the uppermost were used for living quarters.

Not even in Antioch had Prochorus seen such a polyglot population, with people from all corners of the vast Roman Empire constantly going and coming. Beggars and riffraff which Cassius contemptuously dismissed as the masses of Rome were everywhere too. Impudent and lazy, they subsisted mainly, according to Cassius, upon the corn given them by the emperors to hold their allegiance and thus prevent the senators, who were supposed to be the real governing body of Rome, from wielding too much power.

At Cassius' home they were introduced to his father, the famed jurist, and the rest of the family. Cassius' sisters entertained Mariamne while Prochorus wrote letters to Petronius in Antioch and Agrippa in Caesarea Philippi, telling them about the presence of Herod Antipas in Rome and the fact that the Tetrarch of Galilee and Peraea had apparently not yet been able to see the Emperor. Cassius then took him to Roman military headquarters at the barracks of the Praetorian Guard where arrangements were made for the dispatches to be sent immediately by way of one of the swift military galleys that sped important communications to all parts of the empire accessible by water, and thence overland by mounted couriers.

Even by the time of Julius Caesar a hundred years earlier, Rome's walls were already stifling its growth. In a move to relieve some of the congestion, Caesar had extended the official limits a mile outward in all directions. Augustus, in turn, had divided it into fourteen regions, thirteen of these on the left bank of the Tiber, while the fourteenth, called the Regio Transtiberina, was located across the river. Yet the city grew steadily and, with it, the congestion.

Wherever they settled throughout the empire, Jews of the Diaspora tended to live together, the better to observe their own religious customs and rights and also as a matter of self-protection. In Rome, by far the greater number, variously estimated as high as thirty thousand, made their homes in the district across the Tiber from the main part of the city. There they were protected by the Roman Law of Associations which allowed any established religious group to register with the authorities and thus be left to practice their religion undisturbed without being required to subscribe to the official religion of Rome, the worship of Jupiter Capitolinus.

Jews were also legally free to establish their own synagogues where they worshiped very much as did those living in Jerusalem. The usual feasts were observed, the Mosaic law was obeyed, except that, as in all cities of the Diaspora, its provisions were not so rigidly followed as they were among the stricter Pharisees in Jerusalem itself. Jews were involved in many important activities in Rome, too, Prochorus learned. Some were artisans, but more were merchants, importers, and moneylenders, operating great banking establishments with branches throughout the empire, where drafts were honored, saving travelers the necessity of carrying considerable amounts of money on their persons, an open invitation to robbers.

Since it might well be weeks or months before Caligula returned to Rome and they would be able to petition for approval of their marriage, Prochorus decided to rent a small section of a house in the Regio Transtiberina, where he and Mariamne would be among their own people. His purpose in doing so was twofold. First, he suspected that he would learn more of what he needed to know there and, second, he had no desire to bring any more attention than was necessary to the fact that a princess of the Herodian house was in the city. He particularly wanted also to avoid coming in direct contact with Herod Antipas and Herodias.

A few discreet inquiries revealed that one of the synagogues of Rome was largely populated by followers of Jesus of Nazareth and there he and Mariamne went for the sabbath service following their arrival in the Imperial City. The building proved to be a modest one and the people who filled it appeared to belong to the less wealthy elements of the city. This in itself did not surprise Prochorus because the teachings of Jesus had always appealed more to the poor and the downtrodden than to the rich, who usually belonged either to the Pharisee or the Sadducee class.

Having worshiped many times in the Synagogue of the Nazarenes at Jerusalem, Prochorus and Mariamne were familiar with the simple prayer Jesus himself had taught his followers. The service opened as usual, with this prayer, then a broad-shouldered man with iron-gray hair and warm intelligent eyes ascended to the *bima* and began to read from a small scroll. The scroll was not kept in the cabinet called the Ark, as was customary in synagogues with the scrolls of the law and the prophets, but was carried to the pulpit by the reader.

As soon as he started to read Prochorus recognized the words of a sermon Jesus had delivered to a great mass of people from the heights called the Horns of Hattin overlooking Capernaum and Magdala, for Mark had read portions of it to him in Jerusalem and had explained that Peter had dictated the words. It was called the Sermon on the Mountain but Mark had explained that it was part of a much longer document upon which he was working, containing the sayings of Jesus as they had been remembered by Peter and John. The scroll in the speaker's hands Prochorus judged to be a copy of the one upon which Mark had been working.

When the service was finished, the speaker left the *bima* and came down the steps to greet Prochorus and Mariamne.

"I am Aquila," he told them. "We are pleased that you joined us for the sabbath.

"Friends in Jerusalem have written me about you," Aquila said when Prochorus gave their names. "We are indeed indebted to you for the kindly treatment our fellow Nazarenes have been receiving there recently."

"I was brought to the Way by the Apostle John," Prochorus explained. "My wife is awaiting the call of the Holy Spirit."

"Two excellent reasons for rejoicing." Aquila beckoned to his wife, a rather plump woman who was talking to some others in the congregation on the other side of the room. "Come over here, Priscilla," he called. "These are fellow Nazarenes from Jerusalem."

"We are just going home for the noonday meal," the woman said after greeting them warmly. "You must join us."

"If we would not be intruding," said Prochorus.

"It is an honor to entertain the Deputy Governor of Jerusalem and his lovely wife, Princess Mariamne," Priscilla assured them. "We live only a little distance away."

The home proved to be like many in the Transtiberina, three floors above a shop, the latter containing rooms for weaving and also benches for sewing.

"I am a tentmaker and weaver," Aquila explained as they were eating. "We make tents for officers in the Roman army as well as sails for ships."

"How did you become a Christian?" Prochorus asked.

"Christian? The word is not familiar."

"The name was given to the Nazarenes in Antioch," Prochorus explained. "Originally it was meant to be a term of reproach but Manaen and Barnabas and some others have chosen to regard it as a banner of honor."

"Christian," Aquila repeated the word. "It does have an arresting ring to it."

"Here in Rome we are known as the followers of Chrestus," Priscilla volunteered. "Many of our own brother Jews would make that a term of derision, too, but we ignore them."

"Are there many of you in Rome?" Mariamne asked.

"Perhaps a thousand altogether," said Aquila. "We are careful to meet in small groups and worship as our people always have, so we cannot be accused of leaving the Jewish religion and thus lose our protection under the Law of Associations."

"How did the first Nazarenes get to Rome?" Prochorus asked.

"Travelers who visited Jerusalem for the religious feasts heard Jesus teach there before he was crucified and came back to tell of him. Others came here after being driven out during the persecutions of Saul."

"The scroll you read from this morning—"

"The Sayings of Jesus?"

"Yes. I was wondering how it came into your hands."

"The Sayings were sent to us not long ago by Peter. They were brought here by a centurion named Cornelius who was converted with his family in Caesarea."

"It must be the same one Mark was working on," said Mariamne.

"A copy, I think," said Priscilla. "Do you know Peter and John well?"

"Peter heard our betrothal vow."

"And John has been a close friend since I was a boy," Prochorus added.

Aquila's eyes lit up. "It must be a glorious experience to work with that group in Jerusalem and see the congregation grow, as the words of the Master are spread abroad."

"It isn't growing any more," said Prochorus.

"With Peter and John teaching from the Porch of Solomon, surely the people realize that the Messiah has come and that he died so all might live."

Prochorus gave a quick résumé of what had happened in Jerusalem since the persecutions, the shrinking of the Nazarene congregation, and the turning of Peter and many of those who had been closest to Jesus to other fields.

"That must be why Peter sent us the Sayings," said Priscilla.

"And why he is coming to Rome himself," Aquila agreed.

"Are you sure?" Prochorus asked. "There was only talk of it when I was last in Jerusalem."

"Peter sent word by Cornelius that he would soon be with us," said Aquila. "We have been passing the Sayings about from one group to another so they can be read each sabbath and in our homes during the week. But some think the Master meant one thing and some another, so divisions have already arisen among us. When Peter comes, he can settle all our questions; after all, he heard the Master speak the very words we read from the scroll."

Prochorus found himself wishing it were John who was coming. He was sure that, with his almost mystical understanding of Jesus and his purpose, John could interpret the Master's words for the sophisticated residents of Rome far better than Peter. For although it was true that Jesus had designated Peter to be the rock upon which the church would be built, the broad-shouldered fisherman had still been content to let James ben Joseph shackle the congregation of Jerusalem in the toils of the same law against which Jesus himself had inveighed so strongly that the priestly authorities had finally conspired to have him convicted of treason and executed, lest he burst asunder the whole fabric of custom and tradition under which they held the people enslaved.

vii

Prochorus and Mariamne spent the first week of their residence in Rome exploring the city. With her as his guide, he began to appreciate the source of Rome's greatness, as well as its weaknesses.

The single fact that all roads in the sprawling empire led to the golden milestone, the Milliarium Aureum at its center, he decided, was in itself a great cohesive factor. Plus the fact that, except for the inevitable taxes required for defense and for day-to-day operations in government, Rome placed few restrictions upon its subjects, even in far-off lands.

Governed generally by their own rulers, except where turbulent conditions such as those in Jerusalem required the presence of a Roman procurator, the subjects of the empire enjoyed the benefits of a system of justice which, in spite of the usual amount of bribes and corruption in any government, managed to be reasonably fair. And certainly the ending of the seemingly endless internecine wars which had plagued so much of the world before the Pax Romana had been instituted by force of arms was in itself a benefit of incalculable magnitude to the citizens.

Prochorus was not one to be content long with idleness. Watching Herod Antipas was his immediate concern but that required little effort, for the Tetrarch of Galilee followed a predictable routine. Each morning at the small palace he had rented, complete with a staff of servants, Antipas dressed himself in an elaborately pleated toga of rich material and was carried in a sedan chair to the Forum. There he listened to the discussions of the Senate, when it was in session. Under the emperors, however, that body had became little more than a debating society incapable of carrying out its decisions, unless they coincided with the will of the Emperor, so this was a fruitless occupation. Afterward, Antipas was busy talking to various senators and other officials, as well as discreetly bribing, it was rumored, the freedmen who really governed the empire.

Antipas' activities continued even into the night, and almost every evening saw a procession of palanquins, sedan chairs and other magnificent equipages depositing guests at the door of his rented palace, to be fed on choice viands and made drunk on fine wine in the hope that they could influence Caligula to decide in his favor the question of what to do with Judaea and Samaria. And knowing the frailty of human virtue, plus its susceptibility to bribes, Prochorus inevitably became concerned lest Antipas was getting somewhere with this method of pleading his cause.

"Don't trouble yourself," Cassius assured him when he voiced his fears. "The people who eat the Fox's food and drink his wine are only small fry. Those who are well informed wouldn't risk the Emperor's anger by endorsing Antipas—though they will no doubt take his money." He grinned. "In fact he offered me some of it a few days ago to serve as his advocate."

"He can pay you far more than I have the authority to pay."

"I wouldn't have taken the case anyway. Many people come to me because my father is one of the leading judges in Rome. What they don't know is that I could no more influence him in making a decision than I could dry up the waters of the Tiber."

"Suppose Antipas is able to bribe the freedmen in power?"

"He has already bribed Janus, the one closest to Caligula; but that doesn't mean his money will do him any good. I reminded Janus of the great friendship between Caligula and Agrippa, so you may be sure he will advise Caligula in your favor. By the way," he added, "have you noticed that the Emperor is having his palace joined to the Temple of Jupiter?"

"I saw some work going on there but didn't know what it meant."

"He has decided that Rome's twin gods should dwell in twin buildings connected to each other."

"Twin gods?"

"Jupiter and Caligula."

It was chilling news and Prochorus did not underestimate its gravity. "What shall I do?" he asked.

"Nothing—until Antipas makes the first move. Or until Caligula actually proclaims himself a deity."

"When will that be?"

"For Antipas, I think the time is growing short. Herodias grew up

in Rome, so she must realize by now that they are not influencing
people who can really help his cause. Eventually he must go to the
Emperor at Baiae. When he does, we shall go too."

"Shouldn't we present the request for the approval of our marriage then?" said Mariamne, who had come into the room while
they were talking.

"Let's get this business about Agrippa and Antipas settled first,"
Cassius advised. "If Prochorus is successful in keeping Antipas from
becoming King of Judaea and Samaria, Agrippa will owe him a
considerable debt. Then if Agrippa has requested the Emperor to
approve your marriage as you say he promised to do, it will be as
good as done."

Knowing Antipas, Prochorus was sure the Fox had not simply
been lulled into security because people who might influence Caligula were willing to take his money. Nor did he underestimate the
shrewdness of Herodias and the fires of her ambition to outshine
Kypros. His suspicions were verified several weeks after his conversation with Cassius, when the advocate hurriedly appeared at
the house they had rented in the Transtiberina.

"We must go to Baiae at once," he said. "Antipas has learned
that you are in Rome and surmises your purpose here. He left
last night after dark and will surely try to reach the ear of Caligula
before us."

viii

The imperial playground of Baiae with its magnificent view of
the cerulean Gulf of Puteoli occupied a small strip of coast a little
north of Neapolis. One of the most beautiful spots in the world,
not only did the curving arc of land encompass the small protected
body of water but low cliffs and rocks rising directly from the sea
offshore broke the long rollers from the west, letting only a gentle
surf wash the sandy beaches where highborn Romans frolicked in
gay abandon.

Back from the water, the land rose in an even slope and the lush green foliage of vineyards and olive groves almost hid the ornate villas of the wealthy who came there to enjoy the water, the sun, the warm climate and, particularly, to insure their positions in imperial favor. Rising in a series of terraces from the sandy shore, the land was fertile and gardens bright with flowers surrounded the villas. On one side of the bay was the mountain called by the Greeks Pausilypon—"Freer from Cares"—but here the only care was for what insanity, what indecency, the demented mind of Caligula could produce next.

Lucius Licinius Lucullus, general, financier, art lover and master gardener—he had introduced the cherry tree into Italy from Pontus on the shores of the Black Sea a hundred years earlier—had built a magnificent palace on the headland overlooking the sea at Baiae. There Tiberius had come in his last days, a lonely, dying old man, to look across the bay to the Isle of Capri, where he had spent so many years governing the empire *in absentia* through the freedmen he had trusted more than he did the aristocrats of Rome who made up the Senate.

Cassius' family had a small villa at Baiae and there Prochorus and Marianne came with him just as dusk was falling and the moon was rising over a headland, making a path of silver across the tranquil water of the small bay. Prochorus would have been entranced by the beauty of the surroundings, the lush perfume of the flowers blooming everywhere, and the song of the night birds, had he not been much concerned lest Herod Antipas might have stolen a march on him by bringing his petition directly to Caligula, a move that could seriously affect the peace of the province of Syria and particularly the always simmering subprovince of Judaea and Samaria, the heartland of the Jews. In addition, there was the matter of obtaining the approval of Caligula for his marriage to Marianne, for although they had been married by Vitellius and were living together as man and wife, if the Emperor should withhold approval, the bonds would no longer be in force legally. He did not voice his concern to Marianne but, remembering that Antipas was not called the Fox for nothing, he was sorry now that he had allowed Cassius to lull him into waiting in Rome instead of coming here and approaching Caligula directly.

Cassius' family villa was located on a jutting promontory of rock thrust out into the sea. The advocate left for the Emperor's palace as soon as they were settled there and, since they had not been expected by the couple who looked after the villa when the family was not in residence, Prochorus and Mariamne had only some cold meat and wine for supper on the terrace in front of the villa.

"Don't be disturbed, darling," she said. "If Caligula doesn't approve our marriage, we will run away together."

"Where? Rome covers the world."

"You spoke once of going out to tell of Jesus. There must be places where no one would ever hear of us, if we change our names and don't make our presence widely known—places like Britain or Egypt."

"What sort of a life would that be for you—a princess in one of the most important royal families of the empire?"

"I gave all that up willingly to marry you."

"But where has it gotten you?"

"In your arms—where I would rather be than anywhere else in the world. After all, I could have had a palace and a crown long ago—in Nabatea or elsewhere—but I chose to go with you because I love you."

"Will you forgive me?" He came over to the wall around the terrace to sweep her into his arms. "With you—and the assurance Jesus gives us of eternal life—I am the richest man in the world. How could I be such a fool as to doubt myself?"

"Rome does that to men, and Baiae is even worse, in spite of its beauty. As soon as your task here is finished, we will go home where we belong."

"In Rome no one seems to do anything because of the good he can accomplish or because it will help someone else." Prochorus shook his head in bafflement, like a bull at bay. "Each thinks of nothing but himself and how to get ahead of his fellows."

"That's why I'm glad I'm not a princess any longer—or a queen. Now the Emperor will not require my children to grow up in Rome as hostages, as young Agrippa will have to do."

They saw a light coming up the road to the villa and presently Cassius appeared, carrying a lantern in his hand. Both rushed down to meet him as he entered the villa and extinguished the lantern. His face was somewhat flushed and the smell of wine was on his breath.

"That chamberlain of Caligula's, Helicon, has a massive capacity for wine like all Egyptians," said Cassius wearily. "I had to get him drunk before I could get any information out of him."

"What did you learn?" Prochorus asked.

"Antipas has requested an audience and it has been granted. He took the precaution of sending a gold chain with his letter of application, knowing Caligula loves gifts as a child loves sweets."

"Then Uncle Agrippa has no chance," said Mariamne. "He gave us no money for bribes."

"You may not need it," said Cassius. "I talked Helicon into giving us an audience at the same time as Antipas. It will take a powerful argument to outweigh that golden chain but perhaps we can think of something between now and tomorrow morning."

"Surely the Emperor will see that Prochorus wants only what is best for Judaea and Samaria," Mariamne protested.

"When it comes to recognizing an honest man, there's a mote in Caligula's eye," said Cassius. "You can hardly blame him, either; all his life he's been surrounded constantly by liars, sycophants and flatterers. Helicon told me something else, though. When he returns to Rome, Caligula intends to proclaim himself a god officially and require everyone in the empire to worship him."

"It will make little difference who rules in Judaea then," said Prochorus soberly. "The whole country will be aflame."

ix

Caligula's villa was the largest of the many ornate structures erected at Baiae in testimony to the wealth and importance of their owners. As Prochorus, Mariamne and Cassius were ushered by a servant to the banqueting hall—scene, according to popular gossip, of some of the wildest and most depraved orgies imaginable—Prochorus found himself wishing he was better prepared for the audience that was to follow. But since he had not the slightest idea what direction events might take, it was obviously futile to anticipate anything.

He had considered leaving Mariamne at Cassius' villa, fearing that her beauty might incite the imperial lust. Cassius, however, had assured him that at the moment Caligula had eyes only for his latest favorite, an actor called Apella of Ascalon. And besides, he was quite conscious of how much the presence of the great-grand-daughter of Herod the Great beside him would increase the respect with which most men regarded him.

Caligula had not yet arrived, but the chamber was half filled with courtiers, government officials and those hoping for favors. Herod Antipas and Queen Herodias stood at one side of the throne chair where Caligula would sit. When Prochorus, Mariamne and Cassius were ushered to places on the other side, the Tetrarch's beefy face flushed with anger.

"So you have become Agrippa's lackey?" Antipas greeted Prochorus. "How much is he paying you?"

"I represent the Legate Petronius. I believe you know my advocate, Cassius Longinus."

"I know he is getting rich by peddling his father's justice for gold," said Antipas, and it was Cassius' turn to flush. Just then a trumpet announced the coming of the Emperor and any answer the young advocate might have made was cut off.

Although it was early in the morning, Caligula's tunic was already stained with wine. In his late twenties, he was quite tall and prematurely bald, the golden wreath sitting upon his head as a crown looking odd against the almost bluish skin of his scalp. This, along with sunken eyes, dark-shadowed from dissipation, hollow temples and a sallow skin, gave him an almost cadaverous look but there was nothing of death in his eyes. They glowed with wine and with something else which Prochorus suspected to be the spirit of evil that had already shown itself as Caligula's dominant characteristic.

"We must be very careful what we say," Cassius murmured beside Prochorus. "He can be a very devil when he looks as he does now."

Caligula took his seat upon the throne chair and a dark-skinned man, whom Cassius identified in a whisper as Helicon, the Egyptian chamberlain, stepped forward. Holding in his hand a tablet handed him by a scribe sitting at a table in front of and to one side of the rostrum upon which the throne chair sat, he announced: "The Tetrarch Antipas of Galilee and Peraea has a request to put before Your Majesty."

"Welcome to Baiae, Antipas," Caligula said, agreeably enough. "I was but a boy when I saw you last."

"Most noble Caesar." Herod Antipas bowed as low as he could with his rather large paunch. "May I present Queen Herodias?"

Herodias was overdressed for the occasion; her fingers glittered with jewels and a necklace of precious stones hung around her neck. Mariamne, on the other hand, had chosen to wear a silken tunic and over it a stola of the same material, without any jewelry. Compared to Herodias, she was a picture of quiet beauty and composure.

"Were you not once at Rome, Queen Herodias?" Caligula asked.

"Only for a little while, sire."

"I believe you are the sister of my dear friend Agrippa."

"Y-yes." When the color drained from Herodias' cheeks, Prochorus realized that Caligula knew perfectly well what had brought Antipas and his wife to Rome and was playing with them, as a fisherman might play with a hooked fish for his own perverse enjoyment.

"Please give your brother my highest felicitations when you return to your tetrarchy," Caligula said easily and the moment of tension passed—but not before Antipas had put his hand to his throat and opened the collar of his robe, as if he were choking.

"Cassius Longinus!" Caligula cried with what appeared to be genuine pleasure, when he saw the young lawyer. "What brings you to Baiae?"

"I am serving today as an advocate, Your Majesty."

"For whom?"

"For my friend Prochorus, Deputy Governor of Jerusalem and envoy of the Legate Petronius. May I present him and his wife, Princess Mariamne of the Hasmonean house."

"You are neglectful in not giving the princess her full title,

Cassius," said Caligula. "She is also a descendant of Herod the Great and therefore doubly royal in our sight."

As Mariamne acknowledged the compliment with a curtsy, Caligula spoke to Prochorus: "How is my dear friend Petronius?"

"He was well when I left Antioch, sire."

"And Jerusalem?"

"Quiet."

"A credit to your governorship, no doubt," said Caligula with an odd smile that sent a cold chill through Prochorus. "Thank you for bringing such a lovely addition to our court in the person of Princess Mariamne." He turned to his chamberlain. "Proceed, please, Helicon."

"The Tetrarch of Galilee and Peraea petitions Your Majesty to place the provinces of Judaea and Samaria under his rule," Helicon read from the tablet in his hand. "He affirms that there has been peace in the territory of the Jews for many years and that the inhabitants will be less liable to break the peace if they are governed by one of their own faith. He further states that such a move is logical, since the territory was once part of the area ruled by his father Herod, the son of Antipater."

"I shall hear arguments supporting the Tetrarch's claim," said Caligula, and a tall man who had been standing back of Antipas stepped forward.

"Albion!" Caligula greeted him with evident pleasure. "Are you the Tetrarch's advocate?"

"I have that honor, Caesar," said the lawyer.

"Albion is the most expensive advocate in Rome—and the most unscrupulous," Cassius whispered to Prochorus. "Antipas must have hired him after I refused to represent him."

"Proceed, please," said Caligula to the advocate.

"The Tetrarch Antipas respectfully calls Your Majesty's attention to the fact that he has ruled in Galilee and Peraea for some many years," said the lawyer. "During this time the taxes have been honestly collected and paid to the Procurator Fiscal of Syria in Antioch. Herod Antipas was also largely instrumental in negotiating the treaty of peace with Parthia and he has protected the eastern frontier of his territory against depredations by robber bands and others. He affirms that he has the confidence of the chief priests in Jerusalem and the respect and affection of the people in the city."

"A truly impressive list of qualifications," said Caligula and, at the sardonic note in his voice, a murmur of amusement ran through the room. Albion, however, appeared undisturbed.

"During the procuratorship of the unfortunate Pontius Pilate, whom you banished yourself to Vien in Gaul because of his intemperate acts," he continued, "the Tetrarch Antipas worked to keep down rebellion and to maintain peace. All of these efforts he feels indicates that he is qualified to govern the province of Judaea and Samaria in addition to Galilee and Peraea."

"With what rank?" Caligula inquired casually.

"That, of course, is for Your Majesty to decide." Albion's tone was unctuous. "But I would point out that, although he rules a much smaller territory, King Agrippa already holds the title and rank of king."

"So he does," Caligula said on the same sardonic note. "So he does."

"With your permission, Caesar." Cassius Longinus stepped before the throne chair to stand beside Albion. "Certain facts should be brought to your attention, before you give a decision in this matter."

"By whom?"

"By me—on behalf of my client, Deputy Governor Prochorus of Jerusalem."

"It seems to me that, in asking to rule Judaea, the Tetrarch of Galilee has impugned the ability of your client," said Caligula, leaning back in his chair and making a small tent of his fingers, which were long and the nails dirty and jagged. "Under these circumstances the Deputy Governor should wish to speak in his own defense."

Cassius' jaw dropped and Prochorus realized that Caligula had deliberately trapped them. Like a gladiatorial contest between an unarmed man and a beast, he was pitting Prochorus against the wiliest advocate in Rome, for the perverse enjoyment he and his court could gain from the contest. When Cassius cast an imploring glance at Prochorus, he knew he had no choice and stepped forward to face the throne and the mocking eyes of Caligula.

"I feel no need to defend my governorship, sire," he said quietly. "The Tetrarch Antipas states in his petition that there has been peace in the province. However, I have no argument against his request."

"Not when it means that you will no longer be Governor of Jerusalem?" Caligula asked.

"I wish only what is best for the city and the province. But I would put a question to the Tetrarch Antipas, if I may?"

"He is here. Ask him."

"I wish to know what the Legate Petronius recommends in this case."

When Antipas frowned, Prochorus was sure he realized the trap into which he had been led. If Antipas claimed approval by Petronius, Prochorus could deny it as representative of the Legate. And if he admitted that he had not consulted Petronius, Caligula might be prejudiced against his claim.

"Syria has had many legates during the time my client has governed his province, O Divine One." Albion had been in hurried consultation with his client and now spoke quickly. "It is a long way from Jerusalem to Antioch and the Legate Petronius has not visited the area since assuming his post, so the Tetrarch felt that Your Majesty would understand the situation better than the Legate."

Cassius started to object but Prochorus shook his head as Caligula turned once again to him.

"Do you represent the Legate officially?" Caligula asked.

"I am his designated envoy, sire."

"Then you are empowered to recommend approval or disapproval of the Tetrarch's request that he govern Judaea and Samaria." The mocking eyes of Caligula told Prochorus he was deliberately being baited by having pressure applied to him in a situation where he had everything to lose and nothing to gain, no matter what his recommendation actually was. If he approved the claim of Antipas, it would mean the end of his own position as Deputy Governor of Jerusalem; if he did not, he could be accused of being selfish and prejudiced.

"I was given no such authority," he temporized, then, on a sudden inspiration, added, "Of course, it never occurred to the Legate Petronius that such a request would come to Caesar without his knowledge."

Albion started to protest, but Caligula forestalled him: "Your advocate, Cassius Longinus, tells my chamberlain that you are very highly respected in the government of Syria and have been a valuable adviser to three legates. Is this true?"

"I have served Legates Flaccus, Vitellius and Petronius," Prochorus admitted.

"Then you should be highly qualified to advise me, as you advised the legates, should you not?"

"In that case, sire," said Prochorus, "I must say that—"

"O Divine One!" It was the Egyptian chamberlain.

"What is it, Helicon?" Caligula asked.

"I have just been informed that an envoy has arrived from King Agrippa bearing a letter for you."

"Agrippa?" Caligula's face brightened. "By all means let us hear the letter from my dear friend and companion."

A man who had been hidden from Prochorus' view by the press of people on the other side of the dais where the throne chair sat now stepped from among them.

It was Fortunatus, Agrippa's freedman secretary and close adviser!

x

Mariamne gasped with surprise at the dramatic appearance of Fortunatus; nor was Prochorus any less startled by the freedman's presence at Baiae.

"Fortunatus!" Caligula greeted him warmly. "How goes it with your master and his family?"

"All are well, sire." Fortunatus was fully composed as he stepped into the open space before Caligula's throne and bowed low. "King Agrippa would have come himself but he is occupied with affairs of state and did not know until a few weeks ago that the Tetrarch

Antipas sought to lay claim falsely to the province of Judaea and Samaria."

"This is an outrage." Albion started to protest but Caligula shut him off with a peremptory wave of his hand.

"Quiet, Albion," he said. "Your turn will come later."

"When it came to my master's ears that the Tetrarch Antipas sought to undermine his just claim to a portion of his grandfather Herod's estate," Fortunatus continued, "King Agrippa decided to write a letter to Your Majesty setting down the true facts."

"You said 'just claim,'" Caligula interrupted. "Why is Agrippa's claim any more just than that of the Tetrarch Antipas?"

"King Agrippa, sire, is not only descended from the great Herod but is also a grandson of Queen Mariamne of the Jewish royal house, the Hasmonean dynasty that wrested the territory from Antiochus Epiphanes and later entrusted it to Roman rule."

"True," said Caligula. "I had forgotten that."

"As such," Fortunatus continued, "he carries in his blood not only his Roman heritage through the great Herod, his grandfather, whose loyalty to Rome was above reproach, but also the purest of Jewish heritages through the Hasmonean line. Therefore, only he, of all the descendants of the great Herod, is fit to rule Judaea and Jerusalem in his grandfather's stead."

"You make a convincing advocate as always, Fortunatus," said Caligula. "I wish your master were here to listen as you plead his cause."

"If I may speak, sire." Albion at last managed to gain a word but the wily Fortunatus forestalled him.

"My lord, King Agrippa, was most anxious that you read the letter I bear, sir." He held up a scroll and moved toward the table where the scribes were sitting.

"Read it yourself—aloud," said Caligula and grinned. "You wrote it, didn't you?"

"Yes, sire."

"Then let us judge the quality of your authorship."

"There are some serious charges in the letter, sire—"

"More the reason why we should hear them at once—and in public. Read it, please."

The look Fortunatus shot Herod Antipas as he started to unroll the small scroll was one of pure triumph. The Tetrarch of Galilee, however, looked as if he were going to faint as the reading began:

"Herod Agrippa, Rex, to Gaius Caesar Germanicus, Imperator of Rome. May you have long life—"

"That is more than many here today would wish me." Caligula laughed shrilly. "Proceed, please."

"Concerning the disposition of the province of Judaea and Samaria, about which we have spoken many times, I would disclaim any wish to rule over it, esteeming the governorship of the procurators appointed by Caesar to be just and fair."

Fortunatus paused so the significance of what he had said would not be lost upon Caligula.

"That Agrippa is a schemer," Cassius whispered to Prochorus with a note of admiration in his voice. "He wants Jerusalem even more than Antipas but by disclaiming any wish to rule there, he throws Antipas into a bad light."

"I would wager that part is Fortunatus' doing," said Prochorus. "Agrippa isn't clever enough to think of it."

Fortunatus began his reading once again:

"I do, however, feel that certain things should be brought to Your Majesty's attention, since they seriously affect the peace in all of Syria, and even the border with Parthia."

Several of Caligula's ministers had been standing among the group beside the dais; now they moved forward a little, the better to hear what was being read. Caligula, too, was listening intently and, watching him, Prochorus began to wonder if he really was as mad as people thought him to be—or simply evil.

"It has come to my attention that the Tetrarch of Galilee and Peraea has recently sent confidential envoys to Babylon, seeking to promote the help of King Artaban of Persia in removing the southern part of Syria from Roman rule and creating an independent kingdom stretching from the Great Sea to the Euphrates, with himself as emperor."

"It's a lie," Antipas cried in choked tones.

Fortunatus ignored the interruption but, watching his face, Prochorus saw a smile flicker across it for a moment and realized just how much pleasure the man who only a few years ago had been a slave was getting out of the destruction of the rich and hitherto powerful Antipas.

"One of these envoys was captured recently and was persuaded to confess both his and his master's perfidy."

"Where is the man now?" Caligula's full lower lip, usually wet because of his tendency to slobber, trembled with anger. "Why was he not brought before me for questioning under a lash?"

"Unfortunately the man died while being questioned in Caesarea Philippi," said Fortunatus.

"Under torture?" Caligula licked his lips. "What method was used?"

"He was scourged, sire, but when they heard the extent of his crimes as an agent of the Tetrarch Antipas, the soldiers may have laid on the lash somewhat more heavily than usual."

"I wish I could have seen it." Caligula turned to glare at Antipas. "So must die all who would defend our rule by treachery."

"Your Majesty." Antipas was almost beyond speaking. "This man lies."

"Go on, Fortunatus." Caligula ignored the interruption.

"King Agrippa, has discovered evidence that the Tetrarch of Galilee and Peraea has also been conspiring with two brigands named Manahem and Barabbas to foment an uprising in which he would seize my master's kingdom, as well as Judaea and Samaria. It was all part of the same plot."

"What say you to this?" Caligula demanded of Antipas, but the Tetrarch choked when he tried to speak and a slave had to be dispatched for a cup of wine. In the interim, Albion finally managed to speak.

"O Divine One," he said, "this letter is a pack of lies, concocted by one who, but for the generosity of the Tetrarch Antipas in making him *agoranomus* in Tiberias, would have starved when the Emperor Tiberius drove him from Rome because of his debts and his recklessness in all things. The Tetrarch Antipas has served Rome well and befriended King Agrippa when no one else would take him in. Yet now he is repaid with a tissue of lies and charges which can have no basis in fact."

"Are you accusing my dear friend of lying, Albion?" Caligula's tone was frosty.

"Not of lying, sire, but of listening to false advisers." Albion saw his error in time. "Perhaps this very freedman Fortunatus, who appears before us."

"Why would Fortunatus seek to destroy the Tetrarch Antipas?"

"Why else but to obtain an even higher place in King Agrippa's favor?"

"My Lord Emperor." It was Fortunatus.

"Yes?"

"Accusations of this sort are what you would expect from an advocate, since it is a lawyer's duty to lie in order to promote his client's case. But one is here who is quite familiar with conditions in the area, having served there in the capacity of Deputy Governor of Jerusalem. Let him testify to what he knows."

"An excellent suggestion," said Caligula. "Where is Pro—what is his name?"

"Prochorus, sire," said Fortunatus. "He is standing over there beside the dais—with his betrothed, Princess Mariamne."

"Betrothed?" Caligula exclaimed. "Wasn't she presented to us just now as his wife?"

"Princess Mariamne is of royal blood in both the line of Herod the Great and the Hasmonean house—even as is my Lord King Agrippa," Fortunatus explained. "She cannot be given in marriage except with imperial approval and such approval was never obtained."

"What is this?" Caligula's face reddened with anger as Prochorus stepped forward in the space before the dais. "Is my will being subverted?"

"No, sire." Prochorus was not surprised to find Mariamne standing beside him. "Princess Mariamne and I were betrothed some years ago in Jerusalem according to an old Jewish rite. We were married by the Legate Vitellius and we came to Rome recently to present a petition to Your Majesty that our marriage be approved by you. King Agrippa assured me that he would write you requesting that approval."

"Nevertheless you were married without my approval," said Caligula.

"Or that of King Agrippa, her guardian," Fortunatus volunteered.

"Only because he was in prison," said Prochorus.

"I remember now," said Caligula. "Agrippa was in prison—for supporting me."

"I was living in the household of my uncle Antipas at the time," Mariamne interposed but Prochorus could have wished that she had remained silent. He could hardly expect support from Antipas when the Tetrarch of Galilee expected him to verify Agrippa's charges of treason.

"Did the Tetrarch of Galilee give his approval?" Caligula demanded.

"Ask him, sire," said Mariamne quickly before Prochorus could speak, but when all eyes turned to Antipas he knew her suggestion had been a mistake.

"I was neither asked nor did I give my approval," Antipas said hoarsely. "And I deny—"

"We shall consider later what shall be done with you," Caligula told Prochorus sternly. "At the moment I would know what you have to say concerning the charges that have been made against the Tetrarch of Galilee and Peraea."

"I know nothing that would impugn the loyalty of the Tetrarch to Rome," Prochorus said firmly and there was a murmur of surprise from the audience. In a world where intrigue and counterintrigue were the order of the day, Roman politicians could hardly expect to hear a man who had just been maligned by another testify in the latter's favor.

"Are you saying you don't believe the charges are true?" Caligula demanded.

"I seriously doubt that the Tetrarch Antipas has any desire to rebel against Rome," said Prochorus. "As his advocate has pointed out, he has ruled his district faithfully since the death of his father, who was one of Rome's strongest supporters."

"What of the charge that he is in league with Parthia?"

"That can be nothing but a fabrication."

"Why do you say that?"

"Parthia is far stronger than any empire the Tetrarch would be able to build in the East. Even if he tried, he would inevitably be swallowed up, for the Parthians are known to be in league with the Nabateans, the bitter enemies of all Jews and Herod Antipas in particular. Only a fool would wish to exchange a Roman master for a Parthian one."

"Your argument is eloquent," Caligula conceded. "Proceed."

"The Tetrarch Antipas was one of those who negotiated the treaty of peace with King Artaban of Parthia, when the noble Vitellius was Legate of Syria. I was present myself during those negotiations."

"With only Centurion Sextus Latimus as his aide, Prochorus also persuaded King Aretas of Nabatea to give the fortress of Machaerus and the southern territory of Peraea back to Uncle Antipas, after King Aretas captured it and held me prisoner," Mariamne volunteered.

"A romantic story," Caligula admitted.

"It is a matter of record, sire," said Prochorus. "You need only to read the reports from Antioch for that year to see for yourself."

"Is it true that with only one aide this man persuaded a Nabatean king to give up a fortress and considerable territory taken from you?" Caligula demanded of Antipas.

"He was acting as the agent of the Legate," Antipas admitted grudgingly. "Aretas already knew Vitellius was raising an army to drive him from my territory."

"The Tetrarch neglects to explain that King Aretas only attacked him because of an insult, when Herod Antipas divorced the daughter of Aretas," said Fortunatus.

"I remember the incident now," said Caligula. "It was just before my uncle Tiberius died, but that doesn't excuse the failure to gain approval for the marriage of a royal princess who was a ward of the Emperor. Or the attempt to flout my will."

"This happened before your elevation to the throne, sire," said

Prochorus. "The Legate Vitellius appreciated so much my preventing a war with Nabatea that he gave his blessing to our marriage."

"Which he had no right to do," Caligula insisted stubbornly.

"If I may ask the Deputy Governor of Jerusalem a question, Your Majesty, it may help bring out the truth," said Fortunatus.

"By all means," said Caligula, and Prochorus braced himself for another attack.

"Did the Tetrarch of Galilee once try to have you assassinated?"

"Yes."

"Why?"

"Probably because he had learned of my betrothal to Princess Mariamne."

"A secret betrothal?"

"Yes."

"Why then have you spoken in the Tetrarch's behalf?" Caligula demanded. "It seems to me that you have every reason to hate him."

"I only wish to see justice done," Prochorus insisted.

"In the name of Jupiter!" Caligula burst out. "Does he deserve anything except death for seeking the death of another?"

Prochorus hesitated before making the only possible explanation —the true explanation but one which he sensed might send him to prison. Fortunatus obviously knew a great deal about him already, however, and unless he volunteered to answer with the truth, he had little doubt that the freedman would extract it from him.

"I belong to a religious group among the Jews called the Nazarenes, Your Majesty," he said. "We are taught to love our enemies and do good to those that hate us."

"Love your enemies?" Caligula looked at him incredulously. "What sort of a religion is that?"

"He is a follower of Jesus of Nazareth," said Fortunatus before Prochorus could speak. "Known in Rome as Chrestus."

"I never heard of him either," Caligula admitted.

"The man is dead—crucified by Roman authority on a charge of treason after being condemned by the Jewish high court, the Sanhedrin."

Caligula looked at Prochorus for a moment and, even depressed as he was, he could not help thinking there was pity in the Emperor's eyes, perhaps the last emotion he would have expected to see there.

"Do you deny that you are the follower of a traitor?" Caligula asked.

Beside him Prochorus heard Mariamne catch her breath in a sob. Even that, however, could not make him deny the truth that had come to him that day in Babylon.

"I am a follower of Jesus of Nazareth," he said, and now his words rang with pride. "He was wrongly executed for treason. Pontius Pilate, the Procurator of Judaea and Samaria at the time, admitted himself that he could find no wrong in him."

"Yet he was crucified. Why?"

"To please the chief priests and the mob in Jerusalem." Suddenly inspired, Prochorus added: "Pilate was later exiled by you to Gaul for murdering Samaritans who wished only to worship in their own way on Mount Gerizim, a right granted to all by the Law of Associations."

"You, Cassius, and you, Albion," said Caligula. "Come before me."

As the lawyers moved closer to the dais Prochorus reached out to take Mariamne's hand to reassure her. Strangely enough, he felt no sense of depression; like John and Peter at the Porch of Solomon in Jerusalem, he had publicly announced his loyalty to the Son of God to the loftiest level in the empire and what happened henceforth would be in the Master's hands.

"Is what this man claims concerning the law in this matter true?" Caligula asked the lawyers.

"It is," said Cassius promptly.

"I would expect that answer from you, since your client is before us," said Caligula. "What say you, Albion?"

"The Law of Associations does protect all religious sects that register themselves as such," said the lawyer. "Still, other things must be considered."

Albion, Prochorus recognized, was deliberately clouding the issue, hoping to turn Caligula's attention away from the accusations made against his client in the letter from Agrippa. And with Caligula already prejudiced against him, the move could have a powerful effect.

"What things?" the Emperor demanded.

"First it should be determined whether or not this man Jesus was indeed a traitor. If so, the members of the sect he began while he was alive would be guilty of treason."

Prochorus started to protest but Caligula forestalled him.

"What about you, Princess Mariamne?" he asked. "Are you also a follower of Chrestus?"

"My wife has never espoused the Nazarene faith, sire." Prochorus spoke quickly before Mariamne could answer. "She has not even been baptized."

"Baptized?" Caligula looked blank. "What is that?"

"A rite or sacrament—whereby those who would follow Jesus of Nazareth are accepted as members of the group."

"It's something like the rite of the *taurobolium* in the worship of Mithras, sire," Fortunatus volunteered.

"All that blood?" Caligula recoiled, blanching at the thought.

"We use only water," Prochorus hurried to explain but the damage was already done, for in Caligula's mind henceforth anything connected with Jesus of Nazareth would be identified with the rite of *taurobolium*. Part of the Mithraic mystery cult, it included having the initiate descend naked into a pit covered by a grate, after which a young bull was slaughtered upon the grate and its blood allowed to pour down upon the skin of the would-be disciple, cleansing him, it was claimed, of past sins and allowing him to be born anew.

"The imperial records and those of three legates in Antioch will show that I have served faithfully ever since the Tetrarch Antipas made me his chief scribe years ago, Your Majesty," Prochorus continued, although he knew in his mind that any defense he made was probably useless now. "I prevented at least one rebellion in Jerusalem and Judaea when the Roman standards would have been brought there uncovered. And I forestalled a war between the Tetrarch Antipas and King Aretas of Nabatea. Only a few weeks ago I was a guest in the palace of King Agrippa at Caesarea Philippi. He suggested that I come to seek your approval for our marriage and promised to send a letter requesting it. I am at a loss to understand why Fortunatus, the agent of King Agrippa, now insists upon injecting the question of my marriage into this hearing—"

"Your Majesty," Fortunatus tried to interrupt but Caligula shut him off with a peremptory movement of the hand.

"The only explanation I can give," Prochorus continued, "is that Fortunatus knew he had no case against the Tetrarch Antipas and that I would support him."

"Even though he tried to have you killed?"

"My only concern is for the good of the Jewish people and for peace under Roman rule. Whatever the Tetrarch Antipas' faults may be, he has ruled his tetrarchy well and no rebellion has occurred there since the days of Judas the Gaulonite, soon after the death of Herod the Great. Surely he can be forgiven for wishing to rule more of his father's kingdom and for desiring to be a king, especially since the man he gave refuge to when he was starving has recently been made a king."

"You could take lessons from this man, Albion," Caligula said admiringly, his fickle emotions momentarily swayed—as Prochorus had hoped they would be—by the arguments. "He is doing a better job defending your client than you did."

Albion remained silent as Prochorus continued: "Peace in Judaea and Samaria means peace on the entire eastern frontier. But let the balance be upset, as Fortunatus accuses the Tetrarch Antipas of trying to do, and Parthia will dare to attack once again, as will the Nabateans, who covet the rich territory around Jericho and along the east bank of the Jordan River. Herod Antipas would therefore be a fool to foment a rebellion in the hope of ruling Judaea and Samaria."

"This traitor you served—Chrestus?" said Caligula. "Did he want Judaea and Samaria?"

"Jesus of Nazareth is the Son of God," Prochorus said quietly. "He was sent to earth to show all men that God's mercy can give them eternal life and he has no wish to rule except in the hearts and souls of men."

"You speak as if he were still alive but Fortunatus claims he was executed by Pontius Pilate. What is the truth?"

"Jesus of Nazareth rose from the dead—"

"Like the young god in the Eleusinian mystery?"

"I know nothing of that, sire. Only that Jesus rose—"

"It is claimed by the Nazarene's followers that he will return to rule over the entire world." Seeing his case being demolished, Fortunatus sought to arouse the anger of the madman in Caligula—and succeeded.

"Greater than Jupiter?" Caligula's voice was shrill. "Or myself?"

Prochorus said nothing; the damage had been done. Caligula, however, was not content.

"Are this God you worship and His son greater than Jupiter Capitolinus?" he demanded again and Prochorus could give but one answer:

"The Most High gave a law to His people, the Jews, more than a thousand years ago, sire, long before there was a Rome—"

"And that law?"

"'You shall have no other gods except me.'"

xi

For a moment there was a dead silence in the chamber, then two sounds shattered it. One was a sob from Mariamne, the other a shrill command from Caligula.

"Guard! Arrest that man! For treason!"

No one spoke in Prochorus' defense and, knowing that it was hopeless, neither did he. A tribune of the Praetorian Guard who had been standing beside the dais, alert for any sign of danger to Caligula, reached him in two swift strides and took his arm. As he was being led away, Prochorus turned quickly to Mariamne, who moved beside him.

"Go with Cassius," he told her. "I will send you word later what to do."

She nodded and moved from the space before the dais to stand beside Cassius Longinus, who had resumed his position among the group there.

"Tribune Cherea!" Caligula ordered. "Hold that man here, we may need further testimony from him."

Prochorus was kept at the other side of the dais from where Mariamne was standing, not far from Herod Antipas and Herodias.

"Are there any further matters to be brought before me?" Caligula inquired, obviously with the purpose of terminating the audience, but Fortunatus had not yet finished his lethal work.

"Sire!" he cried and Caligula turned toward him, shaking his head like a child disgusted with an elder.

"I have already heard you—"

"But not the last paragraph of King Agrippa's letter."

"Read it then, but hurry."

Fortunatus unrolled the scroll again and began to read:

"*I deplore treachery in any form, but I must not fail to bring to Caesar's attention the fact that the Tetrarch of Galilee and Peraea has an arsenal of weapons in his palace at Sepphoris in Upper Galilee, sufficient to equip seventy thousand men.*"

"Seventy thousand!" Caligula exclaimed. "Can this be true?"

"King Agrippa has proof of it," said Fortunatus. "I would suggest that you ask Tetrarch Antipas whether he denies it."

"Albion!" Caligula snapped. "Bring out your client."

Antipas was past speaking as he staggered from the crowd into the open space before Caligula. He made several ineffectual attempts but only uttered a harsh croak and, even if he were not guilty, his obvious terror testified strongly against him.

"Give him wine," Caligula ordered contemptuously. "Perhaps then he can tell us the truth."

"Your Majesty." Albion tried to speak in his client's behalf but Caligula would have none of it.

"I want to hear his own explanation—if he has one. Seventy thousand weapons! It's unbelievable!"

Antipas gulped the wine a servant gave him and finally managed to find his voice, although it was still little more than a croak.

"The weapons were for defense against brigands," he stammered and Caligula gave a snort of disbelief, while a wave of laughter came from the audience.

"Try again," he commanded. "Surely you can do better than that."

"The Nabateans hate me. I must be ready at all times to equip troops to move against them."

"Seventy thousand well-armed men could conquer Judaea and Samaria and the territory of King Agrippa," said Caligula. "Besides, we have just heard that two men were once able to subdue the Nabateans. You must do better than that, Tetrarch."

"The weapons are there for no other reason."

"No other reason except for use in the revolt you planned in order to create an empire for yourself in the East," Caligula accused.

"No, no, sire!" Antipas appeared on the point of fainting.

"You weary me with your treachery." Caligula waved him away with a summary gesture and looked down at the scribe's table. "Record my decision that Herod Antipas is removed from his position as Tetrarch of Galilee and—what is the name of the other district?"

"Peraea, sire," Fortunatus volunteered.

"Of Galilee and Peraea and is banished to Gaul—"

A choked sob came from Herodias and Caligula looked around to see what had caused the interruption.

"I seem to remember that you are related to my friend Agrippa," he said to her.

"I am his sister, sire."

"Then I shall be merciful to you as a token of gratitude to your brother for exposing this plot against him and against me. The sentence of exile does not affect you, so you are free to remain in Rome."

"I choose to follow my husband." Herodias' voice was firm and Caligula shrugged.

"You are both exiled to Lugdunum Converarum in Gaul. Your tetrarchy and your estates and everything you own shall become the property of King Agrippa."

Caligula left the dais, ending the audience. Across the chamber, Prochorus saw Fortunatus approach Mariamne but she turned her head sharply and moved away with Cassius Longinus, ignoring the freedman contemptuously. Fortunatus only shrugged, however, and turned to look at Prochorus with a mocking light of triumph in his eyes.

As Prochorus was ushered from the room by the tribune who had arrested him, he had a final glimpse of Mariamne, her shoulders straight, her head proudly erect as befitted a princess but with tears streaming down her cheeks. Nor could he do anything to reassure her, for he could not be at all certain that, before many dawns, he would not lose his own head, a form of execution to which, as a Roman citizen, he was entitled, instead of the painful and degrading crucifixion reserved for escaped slaves and traitors.

xii

The central prison of Rome, where those accused of capital crimes were held, was a large building which also served as barracks for the Praetorian Guard. From Baiae, Prochorus was taken to a cell there the day after his denunciation by Caligula. He had been given no opportunity to communicate with Mariamne since his arrest, other than his instructions to her just before the tribune took him away. Nor did he make any attempt to see her, knowing that the sight of his present condition could only make things worse for her.

Although Prochorus had no way of knowing it, the cell to which he was confined was actually one of the more comfortable ones in the lower level of the prison. He learned the reason the following day, when a centurion in full uniform came into the room and extended his right arm in the Roman grip of friendship and greeting.

"I am Cornelius," he said.

For a moment the name meant nothing to Prochorus; then he recognized on the officer's sleeve the insignium of the Italian Band, one of the most elite groups in the Roman army, and remembered where he had heard the name before.

"You are a Chris—"

"Keep your voice low," Cornelius warned. "Prisons are full of those who gain for themselves through informing on their fellows. Yes, I am the centurion converted in Caesarea by Simon Peter."

"Aquila told me you brought the scroll with the Sayings of Jesus to Rome."

"I was transferred here from Caesarea about six months ago," said Cornelius. "The strength of the Praetorians is being built up by the generals, in case Caligula becomes mad enough to do something more foolish than building a bridge of boats from Baiae to Puteoli."

"Why would he do that?"

"He does have a reason—at least to a mind like his. Years ago he consulted an oracle to determine whether he could ever become Emperor and was told that he was as likely to ride a horse over water from Baiae to Puteoli. So he is building a bridge to ride a horse across it and prove the oracle wrong."

"Then he is indeed a madman."

"Worse than that. Since the hearing at Baiae, he has finally proclaimed himself a god, and those who would gain favor with him are now busy worshiping him publicly."

"I'm afraid I precipitated that," said Prochorus but Cornelius shook his head.

"He has been thinking about it—and talking about it—ever since he came to the throne. What I don't understand is why Fortunatus tried to destroy you, when Agrippa had sent you here to be his observer."

"How did you know Agrippa sent me here?"

Cornelius smiled. "The army has its own system of spies; after all, a detail from the legions is stationed in the capital of every petty king worth talking about. Our information travels even faster than official dispatches."

"Fortunatus covets my wife," Prochorus explained.

"A freedman—and a princess?"

"He has higher ambitions. And Agrippa is heavily obligated to him now, so no one knows how high he will go."

"Agrippa wouldn't be such a fool as to give him a princess of both the Herodian and Hasmonean houses in marriage."

"Has Antipas really been sent to Gaul?"

"He and Herodias left almost at once. He's a fool but he deserved better from Caligula than what he was given."

"Then you don't believe the story about the seventy thousand weapons?"

"Roman officers in Galilee and Caesarea have known about them for years. They were part of an arsenal placed at Sepphoris following the War of Varus, when Judas the Gaulonite tried to seize the area long ago, but most are rusted and of no value. Agrippa probably heard about them when he was *agoranomus* at Tiberias but kept the information to himself, until he could hurt Antipas most by making it known. He could count on Caligula to be so angry and so suspicious that he wouldn't allow the real explanation to be brought out in court."

"Could it be if Caligula allowed it? Antipas might still be saved if it were."

"No trial will be held. There is no appeal from a decision by the Emperor."

"Then I am lost."

"Caligula didn't sentence you. He only ordered your arrest on a charge of treason."

"Is there any hope at all then?"

"Jesus conquered the tomb itself. There is always hope for those who trust him."

"I trusted him when I confessed him before Caligula."

"Forgive me," said Cornelius. "I did not mean to imply that your faith had wavered."

"I'm not sure it wouldn't, especially when I think of what may happen to Mariamne."

"Apparently Agrippa didn't trust Fortunatus completely; we have just received word that he is coming to Rome. Now that he rules two thirds of his grandfather's kingdom, Agrippa's next move will probably be directed toward gaining control of Judaea and Samaria."

"What will happen to Mariamne?"

"I'm sure she will be safe. Legally Caligula dissolved your marriage to her and made her a ward of Agrippa. But you are still married to her, as I understand it, according to Mosaic law."

"Fortunatus managed to get our marriage dissolved under Roman law with Agrippa's help; Agrippa may be able to have it declared invalid by the Sanhedrin."

"I doubt that he will go that far," said Cornelius. "Your friend Sextus Latimus told me what happened in the Nabatean question. My guess is that Agrippa is not likely to forget that Antipas was almost able to use Princess Mariamne once as a prize to cement an alliance with Aretas. Ever since Agrippa helped to settle a boundary dispute between Tyre and Damascus, in favor of the Damascenes, Tyre distrusts him. It is quite possible that, by arranging a marriage between Princess Mariamne and the king of one of the Syro-Phoenician petty states, he may hope to improve his relations with Tyre, as well as his chances of adding Judaea and Samaria to his kingdom. But all of that will take time, so Agrippa isn't likely to give Princess Mariamne to someone like Fortunatus, when she is so much more valuable to him. Meanwhile we may be able to do something about your situation."

"What?"

"I don't know yet. You have powerful friends in young Cassius and his father and we Nazarenes are not entirely without influence."

"If Agrippa makes an alliance with Syro-Phoenicia, he will be as powerful as his grandfather ever was."

"Not as powerful, even though he might have more territory. Augustus was heavily indebted to Herod the Great for coming over to his side after the trouble with Antony and Cleopatra, but Agrippa has served neither Tiberius nor Caligula that well. If Caligula ever realizes that Agrippa actually left Rome to avoid being closely identified with him, the situation could change as quickly as did that of Saul of Tarsus from being persecutor to proclaimer of our Lord's way."

"But Jesus apparently had a positive purpose for Saul—while I have nothing to look forward to."

"Neither does Saul yet, except in Tarsus. When I saw him there about a year ago, he was beginning to wonder whether he had been called only to return to his home city. I stayed in Tarsus long enough for him to copy the Sayings but, after reading them, he was confident that the Lord's purpose for him would shortly be revealed. I have discovered for myself that everything a man needs for the nourishment of his soul is contained in the words of the Lord."

"Could you bring me a scroll of the Sayings?" Prochorus asked. "I heard Aquila read from it the first sabbath I was in Rome but I have never seen the entire scroll itself."

"We have only a few copies of Mark's account in Rome, but I will try to bring you one for a few days at least. Meantime take heart."

"Will it be possible for my wife to visit me?"

"Not for a while; the rules are very strict about prisoners accused of treason. But I can take a message to her."

"Tell her I love her and that I will send word to her of what she is to do as soon as I can decide what is best. And don't forget the Sayings."

xiii

Cornelius brought Prochorus a small scroll the following day; it was in Aramaic, the language Jesus himself had spoken. Reading it, he experienced once again the warm feeling of a new power and assurance flooding through him, as it had on that day in Babylon when he heard John tell the story of Jesus. For the Master himself had said, only a few days before his own trial and death:

> *When they lead you away to hand you over, do not worry before-hand about what to say; no, say whatever is given to you when the time comes, because it is not you who will be speaking: it will be the Holy Spirit.*

Reading the scroll a second time, Prochorus was not at all surprised to discover in the opening paragraphs an answer to the problem of how to keep the woman he loved safe until his own fate should be decided. It had been there all the time in the passage Mark had written as an introduction to the account of Jesus' own words, but he had been so disturbed when he read it the first time that he had not realized how it applied to him and to Mariamne.

Mark had written of John the Baptizer, when the Essene prophet first announced the coming of the Messiah:

So it was that John the Baptist appeared in the wilderness, proclaiming a baptism of repentance for the forgiveness of sins. All Judaea and all the people of Jerusalem made their way to him, and as they were baptised by him in the river Jordan they confessed their sins. John wore a garment of camel-skin, and he lived on locusts and wild honey.

There was a place where Mariamne could be safe until his fate was decided, a place where the people wore rough garments and lived simply. And even if he did not return to her, he knew she could find peace there, for he remembered her words when they had paused on the hilltop overlooking Ir Hamelakh on the shore of the Salt Sea between Jericho and Engedi.

"I almost wish we could stay here forever," she had said then. "You cannot believe how peaceful it is compared to life in Tiberias or Jerusalem."

The immediate problem was how to get her started on the way to Judaea before Agrippa arrived in Rome but, now that his soul was at peace concerning his own fate, he thought he saw a way. At his request, Cornelius arranged for Aquila to visit him the next day.

"We have been praying for you daily," the sailmaker told him as they embraced in greeting. "Have they tortured you?"

Torture for the purpose of obtaining evidence was accepted as a matter of course in Roman courts, except where Roman citizens were concerned. Only his being a citizen with the right of appeal to the imperial courts had protected Prochorus so far, but if Caligula remembered him and personally ordered an examination by torture, that protection, too, would be lost.

"Cornelius has made it as easy for me as he can," Prochorus told Aquila. "But you can do something for me, if you will."

"You need only to ask."

"It is important that my wife leave Italy before King Agrippa arrives—and with as little notice as possible. Can it be arranged?"

"She would almost certainly be seen if she leaves from either Ostia or Puteoli, the port of Neapolis," said Aquila. "But I am to deliver a new set of sails to a shipmaster at Brundisium at the end of the week. That might be the answer."

Located on the eastern—or Adriatic—shore of Italy some distance to the south, Brundisium was the beginning of the famed Appian Way that led to Rome and a terminus on the shores of Italy for travelers who preferred the overland route westward through Greece rather than sailing all the way around the toe of the Italian boot to Ostia. The distance across the southern portion of the Adriatic Sea from Brundisium on the Italian shore to Dyrrhachium on the coast of Greece was very short and there was a regular ferry service across the mouth of the Adriatic for travelers who chose this route. As Aquila had said, too, Mariamne's departure from that port would be much less liable to be observed than if she took ship from Puteoli or Ostia.

"Would you be willing to arrange passage for her?" Prochorus asked Aquila.

"Of course."

"You will find her at the house we rented in the Transtiberina or at the home of Cassius Longinus. Tell her to take ship under another name and debark at Joppa for Jerusalem. There she is to seek out John ben Zebedee and ask him to take her to a place of refuge she has used before."

"She will want to know about you."

"Tell her I am well and that I will join her as soon as I can."

"What if she refuses to go?"

"Tell her she can help me most by letting me have the assurance that she is safe."

Two days later Cassius Longinus came to Prochorus' cell, accompanied by a plump man with a fringe of gray hair around an otherwise bald pate. His eyes were bright with intelligence, warmth and understanding and Prochorus found himself liking him from the start.

"This is Stratopedarch Vibius L. Marsus, one of the imperial magistrates," said Cassius. "He is a friend of my father's and myself. I have asked him to advise me in handling your defense."

"Your case is a very interesting one." The magistrate took a seat on the bench that served as both seat and bed and folded his hands over his small paunch. "We have not had a test of the Law of Associations recently. With so many new organizations and religions in Rome, it should be very rewarding."

"Will I be tried before you, sir?"

"Your case has not yet been arraigned for trial. The Emperor is still at Baiae—building his bridge of ships." A brief smile crossed the magistrate's face. "We have no way of knowing how long that will take, or the outcome."

"The longer the better," said Cassius. "Until Caligula files charges against you, nothing will be done."

"Except that I must remain in prison."

"That regrettably cannot be remedied," Marsus admitted. "But at least it is better than the scourge the emperor often orders in cases where treason is involved."

"I am not guilty of treason," Prochorus protested.

"After reading the account of the trial of Jesus of Nazareth, as reported by Pontius Pilate, I am inclined to agree with you," said Marsus. "I would rather class the Nazarene as a—prophet is the word I believe you Jews would use. The Legate Flaccus made a report of the incident, too, and strongly reprimanded Pilate for yielding to a mob. Such actions by a Roman governor can only diminish the respect of our allies for Roman justice."

"The problem," said Cassius, "is how to keep Caligula from bringing a charge against you until he forgets what happened."

"That could take years," Prochorus protested.

"The Emperor's memory is not quite that long," said Marsus dryly. "Sometimes he forgets things from one day to another."

"We're hoping this may be true in your case," said Cassius. "Can nothing else be done?"

"Two courses of action are possible," said Marsus. "If another Nazarene would swear in the imperial court that all of you belong to the Jewish faith and are therefore protected by the Law of Associations, the record of Pontius Pilate might be introduced to prove that Jesus of Nazareth did not plot treason against Rome."

"Are you asking whether I know of anyone who would swear to this?" Prochorus asked.

"That is roughly what it amounts to."

"What if the ruling goes against me?"

"Naturally your witness and all who call themselves Nazarenes would then be subject to a charge of treason."

"We are worshipers of the same God and we pay our taxes to the Temple like all Jews," said Prochorus. "But I couldn't ask any Nazarene to risk his life to save mine."

"I told Marsus you would say that," said Cassius resignedly. "But I must warn you that it may cost you your life."

"Jesus once said: '*A man can have no greater love than to lay down his life for his friends.*' All Nazarenes are my friends so you can see that I have no choice."

"An admirable thought," said Marsus. "But I wonder how many people are willing to follow it."

"All those who truly serve Jesus of Nazareth are."

"Fortunately there is another alternative," said the magistrate. "If Cassius here requests a report from the Legate Petronius at Antioch concerning you, an investigation of your case can be initiated by the court. Such reports take time and time is what you need. Do you think Petronius would give you a good report?"

"I'm sure he would. He already knows I am a Nazarene and that they seek no trouble for Rome."

"As your advocate, I shall ask that it be obtained," Cassius promised. "And I will see that the request goes to Antioch by the slowest means of transportation."

"Thank you both for your efforts," said Prochorus. "I wish there was some way I could repay you."

Marsus smiled. "It is enough to have the privilege of knowing a man of honesty and courage. I must read more about this Nazarene who did so much to mold the hearts of the men who follow him."

The days passed slowly, the only bright spot being a report from Aquila that Mariamne had sailed from Brundisium. Once she was safely away from Italy, Prochorus' worries concerning her were considerably lighter, for he knew she would be safe in the Essene community on the western shore of the Salt Sea. Then, almost six months after his imprisonment, he was taken one day under guard to a room in the prison where another man waited.

It was Agrippa.

xiv

The King of Galilee, Peraea and Ituraea had gained some weight since Prochorus visited him in Caesarea Philippi but otherwise appeared unchanged. Seeing him again, Prochorus felt a surge of anger that, weakened as he was from the long months in prison, made him momentarily dizzy. When he swayed on unsteady feet, Agrippa quickly came around the table to steady him and guide him to a bench.

"It is nothing," Prochorus protested. "Only a momentary vertigo."

"You can't tell me anything about prisons," said Agrippa. "I spent many months in this very one before Emperor Tiberius died. How is Mariamne?"

"I don't know," said Prochorus, truthfully enough. "I had her leave in order to escape from that treacherous freedman you sent to destroy me."

"You may find this hard to believe but Fortunatus had no instructions from me to attack you."

"What about the letter you were to send asking the Emperor to approve our marriage?"

"Fortunatus carried it but must have destroyed it for reasons of his own. He has been dismissed from my service, even though he claimed he had no choice except to destroy you, when you came to Antipas' defense. Tell me, why would you speak for Antipas after he once tried to kill you?"

"Truth is more important to me than revenge."

Agrippa studied him for a moment as if he were something he had never seen before—and still couldn't understand. "A man of integrity can be both a thorn in the side and a bulwark," he admitted, "but unfortunately you can never be certain exactly when he will be which. I don't know why I should value your opinion of me, Prochorus. If Caligula happens to remember you, your head could fall at any moment and I may even have risked his disfavor by coming to see you."

"What could you possibly want from me?"

"Your good opinion for one thing."

"Could you expect to win that—after this?" His gesture took in the prison cell.

"Believe me, I had no ambition to injure either Antipas or you," Agrippa assured him. "Judaea and Samaria are what I really want; they're the heartland of my grandfather's empire. If I had gained them, I would have been perfectly willing for Antipas to have the title of king in Galilee and Peraea, but Herodias couldn't stand Kypros being a queen when she was only the wife of a tetrarch. When your letter came warning me that Antipas intended to lay claim to Judaea and Samaria by a direct appeal to the Emperor, I had no choice except to forestall him in any way I could. As it happened I was in the midst of concluding a treaty with Aretas settling the matter of trade with Damascus, so I had to send Fortunatus. But how could I know of his passion for Mariamne? Or that he would try to destroy you because of it?"

The explanation was both plausible and facile and Prochorus was tempted to believe it. Or as much of it as could be believed when dealing with such a skilled deceiver.

"Besides," Agrippa added, "the very idea of a freedman like Fortunatus aspiring to marry the great-granddaughter of Herod the Great is an insult."

"Yet she married me."

"I was incensed about that, too, until I looked into your ancestry. In Jewish eyes the line of David is more noble than either the Hasmonean or the Herodian lines that are in my heritage, so I could hardly object to you as a kinsman by marriage. You served me well by notifying me that Antipas was already in Rome, so I am deeply grateful to you, but both Cassius and I agree that, with Caligula in his present state of mind, it's best not to remind him of you. The result could be an order for your head without a trial."

"When did you see Cassius?"

"When I passed through Antioch, Petronius told me you had been arrested and asked me to do what I could to help you. I went to Cassius as soon as I arrived and also talked to Marsus. He is an old friend and will probably be the next Legate of Syria, if I still have any influence with Caligula. Marsus also agreed that your case should not be brought to the attention of the Emperor now."

"Then I am to remain in prison?"

"Actually you may be better off here. You cannot imagine what it is like to see an empire being destroyed by a madman. Caligula seizes women whenever he wants them. If they are married he pronounces them divorced, marries them for a night or a week, then divorces them. The royal treasury was almost bankrupted to build that bridge of ships across the bay at Baiae, so he could ride a horse over it."

"Did he succeed? I hear little news here in the prison."

"A storm took care of that. The only pity is that Caligula was not one of the hundreds who were drowned when the boats were overturned."

"Aren't you afraid to speak such thoughts aloud?"

"I know you will not repeat them and the Praetorian barracks are the only place in Rome where they could be spoken with impunity." Later, Prochorus was to remember Agrippa's cryptic statement and realize its significance, but at the moment he was too concerned for himself and for Mariamne to pay close attention.

"You still haven't told me what you wish from me," he said.

"Perhaps forgiveness."

"I never condemned you."

"That I find hard to believe, when you thought I had failed to request approval of your marriage by Caligula."

"My faith teaches love even for one's enemies."

"I could never do that." Agrippa changed to a brisk tone. "To be entirely honest, what I need most now is your advice. You are more Jew than I, so you know my people better than I do. You have served in Jerusalem and are familiar with the political ambitions of the priesthood and the Pharisees. Too, your Greek blood gives you logic and ability to weigh all sides of a question before making a decision. Petronius tells me that's why you have been so valuable to the last three legates of Syria."

"At least they trusted me," Prochorus said pointedly, but Agrippa ignored the barb.

"Caligula has finally convinced himself—not that it was very

difficult—that he's a god and has finished joining his palace to the
Temple of Jupiter Capitolinus. That was all right for Rome but a
fool named Herennius Capito in Jamnia erected an altar there even
before Caligula announced his divinity and tried to make the Jews
in Jamnia bow down to it."

"Only a fool would do that."

"He's an ambitious fool—which is even worse. The Jews in
Jamnia destroyed the altar and, if Herennius Capito had let it go
at that, nothing else would have happened. Instead he wrote to the
Emperor describing the incident and demanding that the Jews be
punished. I hurried to Rome as soon as I heard about it but the
damage has already been done. Caligula has ordered a golden
statue of himself placed in the Holy of Holies in the Temple at
Jerusalem."

"He might as well set fire to the Temple and the city. The whole
country will be aflame before the statue can be placed there."

"Petronius asked me for advice but what could I say? Caligula
cannot be reasoned with and the order has already gone to Syria to
have the statue made."

"How long ago?" At his tone, Agrippa's shoulders, which had
drooped, straightened a little.

"It had just arrived when I left Antioch."

"Was a time limit set for putting it in the Temple?"

"I know of none. Why?"

"A statue of the Emperor should be fashioned only by the finest
sculptors in the area, which means the Phoenicians," Prochorus
said pointedly. "Then it must be overlaid with gold, a very tedious
process."

Agrippa was all attention now. "How long should this preparation take?"

"Six months at least. Then the decision must be made as to just
when it should be placed in the Temple so as to impress the largest
number of Jews with the importance of the Emperor."

"The Passover, of course." Agrippa picked up his cue. "The city
is jammed with people then."

"And it's almost a year away."

"I will have a confidential letter written to Petronius at once," said Agrippa. "Who knows what will happen in a year?"

"You might also take another measure, if you really want to keep the peace. But it entails some risk on your part."

"All my life, my main ambition has been to rule in Jerusalem as my grandfather did. But, if Judaea rebels against Rome, I shall never realize it. What is your plan?"

"One similar to what Herodias did when she wanted to destroy John the Baptizer, after he named her an adulteress for divorcing her husband to marry the Tetrarch Antipas."

"I was in Rome at the time," said Agrippa. "My memory of the story isn't very good."

"Herodias got Antipas drunk during a feast and had her daughter Salome dance before him," Prochorus explained. "When Antipas made Salome a drunken promise of anything she wished, Herodias told her to ask for the head of John the Baptizer upon a platter. Actually, Antipas had no wish to destroy John; after all, he was considered to be a prophet and they are usually sacred in Israel. But he had made the promise before a large number of people and felt that he had no choice except to give Salome the gift she asked."

Agrippa stroked his chin thoughtfully. "When Caligula is pleased with some attention or some honor, he frequently offers the one who pleased him any gift he desires."

"He spoke several times of his affection for you during the hearing at Baiae. I'm sure you could trade upon it—if you are willing to take the risk."

"Any risk is not too great, that saves Judaea from destruction," said Agrippa. "If I give a great feast and get Caligula drunk enough, he might make a public promise to give me whatever I wish."

"Would you dare ask him to rescind the order placing the statue in the Temple?"

"If it comes to that, yes. But first we shall see what the delay you suggest can accomplish."

"With almost a year to go, that is probably wise," Prochorus agreed.

"By the way," Agrippa said as he was leaving the cell, "I cannot get you out of prison but I have managed to have you moved to more comfortable quarters, Kypros will be glad to give Mariamne refuge, too, if she should need it."

"She is safe and as happy as she can be with me in prison." The implication that Prochorus still didn't trust Agrippa was there but he took no offense, for each understood the other now. They were co-conspirators at the moment and so must trust each other, but only because they shared a common purpose, that of saving Judaea from the flames of a bloody rebellion.

xv

Agrippa was true to his word and the condition of Prochorus' imprisonment improved immediately. Instead of being held in one of the cold damp cells in the lower level of the prison, he now occupied a fairly comfortable room above ground. Bars still covered the windows, it was true, and the door was always kept locked. But the new cell contained a couch, a table and a chair, and his jailor, an affable legionary who had served through campaigns in all parts of the world before losing a leg, kept him informed of the news outside.

Thus he learned that, as he had suggested to Agrippa, the Legate Petronius had ordered a statue of Caligula sculptured by the finest craftsmen in stone in the Phoenician city of Sidon, a compliment which was said to please the Emperor very much indeed. After the statue was finished, several additional months were required to cover it with gold leaf and wagers were soon being taken among the more sophisticated observers of the Roman scene on just how long Agrippa and Petronius would be able to delay the final act that would see the statue installed in the Holy of Holies.

When more than six months had passed and it was rumored that Caligula was becoming impatient to have himself recognized as a god in Jerusalem, Prochorus knew the placing of the statue could not be delayed much longer. And when Petronius was reported to be massing, at Caesarea and other points throughout Judaea and Samaria, the troops that would be needed to impose the will of

Caesar upon the rebellious Jewish people, whose religion not only forbade the worship of graven images but of any gods other than their own, it was obvious that a crisis was rapidly developing.

Prochorus had not seen Agrippa for a month, but he was not at all surprised to learn that the King of Ituraea was about to give a great feast in the Emperor's honor. The night of the feast, he was unable to sleep, so perturbed was he over what was certain to happen in Judaea, if Agrippa failed in the stratagem they had worked out months before. But with the morning meal came news that the order for the image to be placed in the Temple had been rescinded, though he had to wait until Cassius Longinus came that afternoon to discover just how it had been accomplished.

"You should have seen Caligula's face when he realized he was trapped," said Cassius gleefully. "Agrippa risked his head to save Judaea."

"But he did save it?"

"For the time being, at least—until Caligula thinks up more mischief. Actually Caligula had to rescind the order because not to do it would have made him lose face before the people he loves most, the toadies and sycophants who surround him."

"How did Agrippa manage it?"

"Mainly by getting Caligula drunk, which is no small feat. And by flattering him all evening, which is a lot easier. The feast must have cost Agrippa a fortune—everybody of any importance in Rome was there—but nothing less would have flattered Caligula into offering to grant Agrippa's fondest wish. It was a clever plan and it's too bad an innocent man has to be the victim."

"What do you mean?" Prochorus asked quickly.

"Caligula has ordered Petronius to kill himself."

"Why?"

"He was looking for a scapegoat and finally decided that Petronius' delay in having the statue made frustrated him from carrying out his original plan. Someone had to be the target for his anger and it couldn't be his beloved Agrippa, so Petronius was the logical choice."

"It should be I, not Petronius."

"Why?"

"I persuaded Agrippa to put the plan in motion long ago."

"The delay in making the statue—or the feast?"

"Both."

"You deserve to be a statesman. Such plotting could win you a high place in Rome today."

"If I confess my part in it to the Emperor, perhaps he will let me die instead of Petronius."

"Volunteer your life for another to a fiend like Caligula?" Cassius stared at him in shocked disbelief. "You would only end up by destroying Petronius and yourself."

"At least the burden of guilt would be lifted from my soul."

"Don't talk foolishness," the lawyer said harshly. "You acted from the very highest of motives to save your people from destroying themselves. They have been saved and you should be content with that."

"I still feel guilty for Petronius' death."

"It is better that one should die than a whole nation."

"If the argument is valid—yes."

"Why do you say that?"

"When the High Priest Caiaphas sought to destroy Jesus of Nazareth secretly, he used that same argument before the Sanhedrin. With it he gained the support of some who thought Jesus a prophet and therefore entitled to speak out as he wished."

"It's still a good argument."

"Only if it represents truth—not just an excuse to remove someone who stands in the way of your ambitions."

"Surely you don't deny that many would have died if the statue had actually been placed in the Temple."

"No," Prochorus admitted. "Agrippa told me that, while the statue was being made in Sidon, a delegation of Jews from Jerusalem actually went to Petronius and told him it would be carried into the Temple only over their dead bodies."

"So you have no argument," Cassius said triumphantly. "Besides, if you go to Caligula now and confess the stratagem you devised for thwarting him you would be sentencing Agrippa to death too."

"I hadn't thought of that."

"Didn't you once tell me you are convinced that Agrippa has a better chance of bringing peace to Jerusalem and Judaea than anyone else?"

"Better than anyone I can see at the moment—yes."

"Then, if Petronius must die, it is at the whim of a madman, not because of the act of a statesman," said Cassius, and although Prochorus wasn't entirely convinced, he could see a great deal of logic in what Cassius said.

"Is there any chance that my case may come to trial soon?" he asked, but the lawyer shook his head.

"We were hoping Caligula would travel abroad again, as he did when he crossed Gaul to the Fretum Gallicum. Then we could bring you before one of the Praetorian prefects, where your case would be judged only according to the law. But I think Caligula is afraid to leave Rome, lest he find himself without a throne."

"What about the cost of all this? I have nothing."

Cassius Longinus looked at him in surprise. "Didn't you know that Agrippa is paying for everything?"

"No."

"He bribed the chief jailor to let you have this cell instead of the dungeon you were in. He even pays for the food you eat."

"Then he may not be as bad as I thought."

"Agrippa is no better and no worse than any other man who aspires to rule an empire. The fact that it's his grandfather's former empire only makes his ambition more understandable."

"But why would he defend me?"

"Possibly because Fortunatus was responsible for your being here, though I don't think that has much to do with it. What Agrippa wants to preserve is your mind. Obviously he thinks he's going to need it when he comes to rule in Judaea and Samaria."

"There are moments when I doubt whether I even possess a mind any more."

"The scheme that kept Caligula's statue out of the Temple proves you still do," Cassius assured him. "A Jew is rarely able to think of his people, his homeland or his god without his thoughts being strongly colored by emotion; even Agrippa realizes that his overwhelming ambition to rule his father's old empire influences his thinking. A Greek or a Roman, on the other hand, couldn't pos-

sibly think like a Jew but, since you are both, plus being intelligent
and levelheaded, you are invaluable to both Jew and Roman alike,
as you have proved many times."

"What has it earned me? A prison cell."

Cassius went to the door of the room and looked out through
the small barred opening that gave access to the hall outside before
coming back to stand close beside Prochorus.

"Death is only a heartbeat away, even for an emperor." He spoke
in a whisper. "You may be out of here much sooner than you even
dreamed."

Any encouragement Prochorus had felt at Cassius' parting words
slowly ebbed as months passed and his condition did not change,
except that now he was allowed to have a few visitors from outside
the prison in addition to Cassius and Agrippa. The latter had not
come again since the dinner when he had tricked Caligula, but
Prochorus could understand that it might be risky for him to be
seen with one who had formerly been the Deputy Governor of
Jerusalem, possibly starting a rumor that the scheme whereby he
had saved the city had not been entirely of his own doing.

Aquila came regularly but could report only that conditions in
Rome were worsening steadily under Caligula's rule. The treasury
was already bankrupt and new taxes were being levied to cover the
Emperor's growing excesses. When these reached the provinces,
Prochorus knew, there would be riots and uprisings and more
difficulties for the already troubled empire. Then one day the door
of his prison opened and a broad-shouldered man entered. At the
sight of him, Prochorus leaped to his feet to embrace him.

It was Simon Peter.

xvi

"Thank God you are safe," said Peter. "When we heard in
Jerusalem that you had been arrested on a charge of treason, we
feared for your life."

"I almost lost my head—and still may. Can you tell me anything
about Mariamne?"

"Before I left, I asked John to visit the Essene community and see her. She is well and sends you her love."

"How does it go in Jerusalem?"

"There has been no more persecution."

"Is the congregation still shrinking?"

"It doesn't grow," Peter admitted. "But we are making progress in other fields. Barnabas brought Saul to Antioch from Tarsus a few months ago. They plan to carry the words of the Master to other cities."

"While the church at Jerusalem is slowly dying?"

"Not dying," Peter corrected him. "It must always be kept alive against the time when the Lord comes again. In going outside, we are only obeying his instructions to go into all the world and preach. Jesus himself gave me that task, when he sent me to baptize Cornelius and his family at Caesarea."

"Then there are to be two leaders of those who follow Jesus? James ben Joseph in Jerusalem and you in the lands outside?"

"Jesus alone is the leader of us all; in his kingdom no man is greater than another. How could any of us claim precedence, when he gave his life for us all?" Peter changed the subject. "What about you?"

"I must stay in prison until my case is brought to trial."

"What if I should swear to the Emperor that we Nazarenes are only a sect among the Jews?"

"Would it be the truth—when you are already carrying the Way to gentiles and even to Rome?"

"The Jewish faith has always found converts among gentiles. There are proselytes in every synagogue of the Diaspora and we Nazarenes are no different."

"I still couldn't let you take the risk."

"Why not, when it's true?"

"Truth is dead in Caligula's Rome."

"Truth is never dead," Peter corrected him gently. "Men only fail to see it—like Pontius Pilate asking Jesus 'What is truth?' when it was there before him."

"Herod Antipas was blind to it too. Do you think what happened to him and Pilate was a punishment for what they did to Jesus?"

"The Master's death was the fulfillment of prophecy going back even to the time of Moses," said Peter. "Jesus told me that one night when we were camped in the mountains near Caesarea Philippi, but I couldn't understand it then. Besides, he wouldn't let us publish it abroad."

"Things might have been much simpler if he had."

"The truth that Jesus is the Son of God could not have become evident without his resurrection. I even doubted it in my heart until we found the open tomb. You knew I denied him at the palace of the High Priest just before he was crucified, didn't you?"

Prochorus nodded. "I couldn't understand how you could at first, but after these months in prison, I can now. There are times when any man's faith can waver."

"Even the Master's did once."

"When was that?"

"Just before he was arrested in the Garden of Gethsemane, he asked the Father to let the bitter cup of death pass from him. But his weakness was only for a moment; then he placed himself in God's hands as we all must do, if we are to find peace."

"Could what happened to me be part of God's purpose?"

"I'm sure it is—though the pattern may not be visible to you for some time to come."

"What about Pontius Pilate? And Herod Antipas?"

"Pilate was an agent of prophecy, as I told you. Herod's fate was a fulfillment of the curse upon his father."

"For the murder of Mariamne's grandmother?"

"That, too, but particularly because he slew the children of Bethlehem at the time of the Lord's birth."

"I never heard that story," Prochorus admitted.

"It was in the time of Augustus," said Peter, "when Quirinius was governor of Syria. . . ."

Listening to the beautiful story of the birth of Jesus of Nazareth— the coming of the shepherds to worship him as he lay in the manger of the crowded inn at Bethlehem; the bright star that had guided the seers from far-off Yemen; the terrible crime committed by Herod the Great in seeking to destroy the babe the visiting wise men had named the King of the Jews, by murdering all children in Bethlehem under the age of two; and the miraculous escape of Joseph, Mary and the child when they were warned in a dream to flee into Egypt—Prochorus found the faith which had sometimes wavered during his long months of imprisonment begin to be strong once again.

"God has said that the sins of the fathers will be visited upon the sons, the grandsons, and the great-grandsons," Peter said as he ended the story. "You can see why I think these things have happened to the descendants of Herod the Great."

"If you carry it to the grandsons, that would mean Agrippa."

"And the great-grandson, young Agrippa."

"But King Agrippa persuaded Caligula to give up putting his statue in the Temple and saved Judaea from rebellion. That alone would seem to earn his freedom from the curse."

"God uses both the just and the unjust in carrying out His purpose," said Peter. "He rewards them according to His will."

"Perhaps that accounts for the story of the owl."

"What do you mean?" Peter asked and Prochorus recounted again the story of the prophecy that, when next an owl perched above Agrippa's head, he would die in five days.

"It might be part of the curse," Peter admitted. "I don't know."

"Can he never escape it? There must be some good, even in Agrippa."

"Jesus forgave Saul of Tarsus, though he persecuted our people and stood by when Stephen was stoned. If King Agrippa repents of his sins and asks forgiveness, it shall be given him.

"I may be here only a few weeks," Peter said in parting. "Can I take a message to the princess when I return?"

"Could I write it and send it to you tomorrow by Cornelius?"

"Of course."

That afternoon Prochorus sat down to write the letter Peter was to take to Mariamne. For a while the words he sought would not come, as one part of his mind still fought against crystallizing the decision he had resolutely sought to avoid but which, in the light of what Simon Peter had told him of how Jesus, though influenced momentarily by doubt, had finally gone on to face his fate, he could not put off any longer.

When the words finally came, he sat down and began to write:

My darling,
Simon Peter is in Rome and visited me yesterday. He tells me you are well, for which I give thanks daily in my prayers. Each day, I awaken longing to see you again and each night I lie awake, knowing it may be years—if then—before I shall. Knowing this, I can no longer be selfish and hold you in prison too.
I have my faith in Jesus to sustain me, but the Holy Spirit has not yet come upon you, so alone you have nothing. The Emperor has dissolved our marriage and only the vows we made that night in Jerusalem at the Passover bind you to me now. Realizing that I have no right to hold you to them because of my own selfishness, I absolve you from them and I pray that God will bless you and bring you the happiness I hoped to give you, but which it is no longer in my power to give, for I have no hope any more except to live from day to day.
Whatever you do, know that my love goes with you.

Always,
Prochorus.

As the last words were being written, he turned his head quickly, lest she see the stain of tears upon the scroll.

xvii

Two days after the visit of Peter, Cornelius came into Prochorus' cell early in the morning as the guard details were being changed. The centurion's face was lined with fatigue, his eyes were red from lack of sleep and, when he spoke, his voice was hoarse, as if he had been shouting.

"The Italian Band is one of the noblest units in the Roman army," he said in a tone of disgust. "We can boast of service from the river Thamesis in Britain to the Euphrates, yet here I am doing police duty in Rome."

"I thought citizens were supposed to stay off the streets at night."

"They are, except when bound to and from banquets and entertainments or with the wagons that haul food and supplies to the markets. It's not those who make duty in Rome dangerous, or even the occasional robbers, but bands of the wellborn, roistering and fighting the police for their own pleasure."

"Isn't this something new?"

"It began with Caligula. He and his cronies often put on masks at night and go pillaging through the city for the fun of it, haling honest citizens out of their beds and raping young girls."

"When the Romans wanted to put down an uprising in Jerusalem, they cut down the leaders on the spot and it was soon over," Prochorus reminded him.

"That would quickly solve the problem here, too, if we were free to act. But let one of Caligula's favorites feel the sword and whoever commands the guards that night will earn the headsman's ax. Meanwhile my men are being slashed because they dare not thrust a blade through those who attack them for fear that one of the Emperor's favorites may be behind the cloth hiding their faces."

"Or Caligula himself?"

"That would be the solution of all our problems." Cornelius didn't bother to lower his voice. "But I'm a soldier, not a murderer. Enough of my own problems, though. Peter said you wanted to see me."

"I have a letter for you to give him. Did he tell you he's leaving Rome soon?"

"Yes. He has taken passage on a ship from Brundisium bound for Pontus. From there he will make his way southward through Cappadocia to Antioch and Jerusalem."

"That's the long way around. Is he in danger?"

"No. Queen Tryphaena from that area is in Rome visiting relatives. She is related to the Emperor's uncle, Claudius, and has shown an interest in hearing more about the teachings of Jesus. Peter is going to Pontus with her party. He hopes to gain a foothold for the Way on the shores of the Pontus Euxinus by preaching there."

The thought of the fabled lands along the shores of the largely landlocked body of water popularly called the Black Sea from the dark color of its waters pushed Prochorus' concern for himself and Mariamne momentarily into the back of his mind. How he would like to be sailing with Peter to the fabled cities of Trapezus and Chersonesus, where caravans of silk, spices and other precious goods from India and even China far to the east transferred their cargoes to ships for transport to Rome and other cities of the empire. There, he would be safe from the plottings of Agrippa and, through John and the Legate Petronius, it would probably be possible to arrange passage for Mariamne to join him.

"You sent for me," Cornelius nudged him gently from his reverie.

"I was going to send a letter to Mariamne by Peter, but I have changed my mind." Prochorus took the small scroll from beneath the pillow on his couch. The materials for writing had been furnished by his jailor, at some ten times what it would cost outside, and he had spent most of a day writing and rewriting the letter. Unrolling the parchment from the wooden center, he tore it into pieces.

"What changed your mind?" Cornelius asked.

"What you said about Peter—and Pontus. If the Master is sowing the seeds of his Way that far afield, he may still have some use for me."

"I never doubted that he would," said Cornelius as he stood up to leave. "Besides, a letter can always fall into the wrong hands."

"Agrippa's?"

"Yes."

"But he doesn't seem to be active."

"One thing Agrippa learned in prison was to bide his time," said Cornelius. "At the moment he in some disfavor with Caligula but, even though the Emperor believes himself a god, I doubt that he's immortal. With Caligula out of the way—"

"Is that liable to happen?" Prochorus asked quickly but Cornelius only shrugged.

"He cannot live forever, and when a change of rulers occurs, Agrippa may well find himself King of Judaea and Samaria, what he has been working toward for so long. If I know him though, he'll not be content with that, and being able to give the great-granddaughter of Herod the Great to one of the kings of the surrounding territory would be a strong talking point in negotiating a treaty of support."

"I don't think he can find Mariamne, and I shall not take the risk of writing to her again," Prochorus promised. "Is the Legate Petronius dead?"

"I don't think so. The order for his suicide was deliberately sent by the slowest route. The winter storms are already beginning and the vessel it was on might even be shipwrecked."

"As well expect the sun to stand still."

"Your scriptures say Joshua did just that—and God answered."

"Joshua had an army behind him and an enemy he could fight," said Prochorus. "While I—I have no hope."

"Here is your hope." Cornelius dropped to one knee and scooped up a handful of parchment fragments from the letter Prochorus had torn up. "The princess obeyed without question, when you sent her away to wait for you. If you give up now, you will betray her faith in you—and her love."

xviii

Traditionally the time of the winter solstice, when the sun was at its greatest distance away, was an occasion for great abandon in Rome in connection with the celebration of *sol invictus*, the Unconquerable Sun. Like Apollo—next to Jupiter Capitolinus the favorite god of the Romans—Mithras too, was considered to have taken his origin from the sun, as were the Persian Ahura Mazda, the Nabatean Dusares and many others.

Generally, the two weeks following the winter solstice were a time of celebration and wanton behavior, as merrymakers feasted, drank and gave themselves over to debauchery of all sorts. Since the period was considered one of worship for all the many gods of Rome, everybody had an excuse for participating. Besides, in Caligula's Rome license was always rampant and what few vestiges of decent conduct remained were easily cast off.

The Christians and Jews of Rome took no part in such pagan

ceremonials. Instead they celebrated the Feast of Lights, a lovely ceremony in which each member of a family lit a candle in every room until the whole house was ablaze with light. The windows were left open, too, so all might see.

For the prisoners, neither ceremony had any meaning, save that the shouts of the merrymakers outside intruded upon their sleep and the cells in the stone-walled prison were cold from the winter winds that swept down from the mountains to the north. As for Prochorus, it was a time of deep despondency, since the evidence outside his prison window of just how eagerly the inhabitants entered into the sort of debauchery characteristic of Caligula's rule promised little for him in the way of the future. Then, oddly enough—as if in reaction to the abandon of the solstice celebrations —rumors began to fill the prison. The jailor brought the first to Prochorus with his breakfast one morning in the new year.

"They are saying in the barracks that the Praetorians and the senators are at last ready to make common cause against Jupiter's twin," the old legionary said.

Jupiter's twin could be none other than Caligula himself, since the Emperor had not only announced himself to be the twin brother of Rome's official god but had also placed his baby daughter—born a short time earlier—on the lap of the statue in the adjoining temple, naming Jupiter her father along with himself. The rumors of plottings against the Emperor that appeared in the prison from time to time had so far proved to be only words. But if the Senate, which traditionally disliked both the military and the Emperor, was now working with the soldiers, it could only mean that the elected body, long subordinated to the will of the despot, hoped to regain through the overthrow of Caligula the power it had possessed in the days before Augustus, when Rome had been a republic.

"Who among the Praetorians would have the courage to take part in such a conspiracy?" Prochorus asked.

"Cherea for one."

"The name means nothing to me."

"It will—and Sentius Saturninus, too."

For the first time Prochorus dared let himself hope the jailor's story was more than simply another baseless rumor. For Sentius

Saturninus was a senator of repute, one of the few who had dared to demand a return to senatorial power as in the days of the republic. And even though his protest had so far been as futile as all other opposition to the deranged Caligula, Saturninus could serve as a rallying point for those who longed for freedom in case Caligula were to meet with the accident that had befallen other Roman despots.

"Cherea is the tribune who stands beside the chair of the Emperor," the jailor rattled on, and Prochorus remembered the tall officer who had seized his arm on Caligula's orders at Baiae, it seemed now ages ago.

"What is the plan?" He tried to keep the excitement that was beginning to rise within him out of his voice. "Poison?"

"Poison is for women who would be rid of their husbands so they can take a lover." The old soldier spat contemptuously into the corner of the cell. "Would a tribune of the Praetorian Guard use anything except his sword?"

"It should be easy—with Cherea standing beside the Emperor at all times."

"If that were all it would be done already," said the jailor. "But the senators want to rule afterward, so they must talk and talk and talk."

"Isn't it possible that the Emperor may hear of the plot?"

"He probably knows of it already."

"Then how can—"

"Didn't you know that Caligula is a god?" The old man cackled. "Gods cannot die at the hands of mere men."

With anyone else except Caligula, none of it would have made sense, Prochorus thought; but then little the present Emperor of Rome did made sense anyway. The march to the channel separating Gaul from Britain; the bridge of boats from Baiae to Puteoli; the joining of his palace to the Temple of Jupiter and naming himself the twin of Rome's favorite god; the crimes he had committed—all were the acts of a madman and who could be censured for daring to hope the time had come for an end to the monster who was Jupiter's twin?

Then he reminded himself that, as a follower of Jesus of Nazareth, he could wish for no man's death. John—who alone

among the disciples had stood at the foot of the cross during Jesus'
last hours—had said that the Master forgave his tormentors but,
looking into his own heart now, Prochorus knew his faith was not
up to so great a test. He could not wish life for Caligula when it
would almost certainly eventually mean his own death; nor was his
faith equal to the task of freeing Mariamne from her vows.

Sitting there in the cold prison, able to do nothing to control his
own fate, and wondering whether he really had any right to call
himself a true follower of Jesus of Nazareth, he experienced the
deepest despair he had ever known. Nor could he comfort himself
any longer with the assurance of eternal life, when he lacked
confidence enough in the strength of his own faith to be certain he
deserved it.

Then, like a spark beginning to turn to flame deep inside him, he
felt the warming touch of Jesus' own spirit erase the doubt and the
pain from his soul. When the sun burst from behind the clouds that
had hidden it all day, and its rays shone through the barred window
of the prison to form a cross-shaped shadow upon the wall of his cell,
he felt peace and certainty once again begin to flood his soul, the
same peace and certainty to which John had first led him in
Babylon.

He could hope—and pray—that it was not God's purpose for him to
die in a Roman dungeon cell or under the headsman's ax. He could
hope also to see the land and the woman he loved once again. But
if this were not to be, he could still face whatever fate awaited him
proudly, as John had told him Stephen, the first martyr to lose his life
for the Way after Jesus himself, had done.

xix

When the event all Rome had been expecting finally happened, it
was rapid—and final. Being in prison, Prochorus could, of course,
take no active part in the events, which he would not have done
anyway. Their course, however, was faithfully reported to him almost
hourly by his jailor.

It began in the theater just about dinnertime, but events taking place outside the building quickly overshadowed the onstage miming. The drama itself was titled *Cinyras* and had as one of its climaxes the pretended crucifixion of a robber onstage, a happening attended with the shedding of much spurious blood, some of which spattered the spectators near the stage, particularly a nobleman named Asprenas, who became very indignant and stamped out of the theater to change his clothing.

Actually, the play was a portent in itself, for the action included the assassination of the heir to the throne of Macedonia. Confident of his own immortality as a god, however, Caligula saw no warning in the onstage action, in fact he became so bored with it that he left in the middle of the play for the baths and his dinner.

While Caligula was inside the theater, Tribune Cherea, described to Prochorus several days earlier by his jailor as being foremost in the rumored assassination plot against Caligula, had been at his usual post outside the door of the theater. Impatient finally with the tactics of the senators, who wished to be sure that no dictator would take Caligula's place, Cherea had been on the point of going inside to thrust the Emperor through with his sword, much as was happening onstage, when Caligula's decision to leave gave him an opportunity to take action out of sight of the crowd inside the theater, in one of the passageways leading to the baths. Cherea's first sword slash between the shoulder and the neck failed to kill Caligula, however, and left now with no choice, if they were to save their own lives, others of the conspiracy fell upon the Emperor in a body and hacked him to death. In the resulting melee, a detail of German soldiers from Gaul, loyal to the Emperor because he paid them well to serve as his personal bodyguard, started killing all who might have had any part in the attempted assassination, not knowing yet that Caligula was already dead. And the first to fall, ironically enough, was the wholly innocent, Asprenas.

Dramatic though it was and fraught with particular importance for Prochorus, the story of the assassination, as recounted by the jailor, quickly became a comedy of errors when the conspirators began to quarrel over who should take the credit—or the blame—for Caligula's death. Those who had known of the conspiracy from the beginning failed to acclaim Cherea for his act but, instead, waited to see whether sentiment would develop for a campaign of revenge among the soldiers Caligula had paid so well, the slaves he had encouraged to inform against their masters, and the rabble of Rome which he had courted with free grain and great spectacles in the arena for their entertainment.

In the period of indecision immediately following the Emperor's death, two figures were reported to stand out most clearly. One was a public crier named Euaristus Arruntius who, more by the loudness of his voice than by anything else, managed to persuade the Germans that Caligula was already dead and that they should leave off their indiscriminate slaying of all who were in the theater or in the area of the palace where the Emperor had been killed, lest they incur the displeasure of whoever might succeed him. The other figure, and the most prominent, was Agrippa.

Being a Jew and therefore ineligible to succeed Caligula himself, Agrippa was able to represent a middle ground, so to speak, in the negotiations to determine who should rule in Caligula's place. The senators wished a return to the republic but dissension among themselves defeated them. Agrippa, however, shrewdly backed Caligula's uncle, Tiberius Claudius Drusus Germanicus, knowing that many senators thought him a dimwit because he was a recluse who spent much time with books and scrolls.

When Agrippa first sought the middle-aged Claudius to persuade him that he should be a candidate for Emperor, he had found him hiding, still fearing the wrath of the German soldiers who had been Caligula's personal bodyguard. To the officers of the Praetorian Guard, anxious to hold the position and power they had seized with the assassination of Caligula, Agrippa described Claudius as a weak and pliant ruler. Before the Senate, unable to agree as to just how the empire should be governed and with several of its members quite willing to put themselves forward as candidates, the wily Agrippa argued that the selection of an Emperor who was of royal blood in the Claudian line, and known to be of a mild disposition, represented as much increase in power as they could hope to accomplish at the moment.

In the end both factions listened to Agrippa's arguments and finally agreed upon Claudius as the next ruler of Rome. Thus Agrippa, who had grown up as a prince in Rome and was on intimate terms with its major families and royalty, became a king-maker, earning with one stroke the gratitude of the newly crowned Claudius, improving his already excellent position even more and proving himself, in truth, the savior of the empire.

In a Rome celebrating the death of a despot and the accession of a new ruler, only one group had reason not to praise Agrippa to the skies. This was the Senate, whose members quickly discovered, to their considerable dismay, that Claudius was intelligent, forthright and imperious, qualities which had been hidden earlier by his retiring manner and his presence for solitude and reading.

Whether or not Agrippa had recognized these qualities, so admirable in a ruler, before choosing Claudius as a candidate was problematical, but either way it made little difference. The most powerful man in the world was now in debt to the King of Ituraea, an obligation he quickly began to pay off by naming Agrippa king throughout the whole expanse of his grandfather's former kingdom, including the shining city of Jerusalem, the prize for which Agrippa had been working so many years.

Still in prison after the crowning of Claudius, Prochorus dared to hope Agrippa might feel enough of an obligation to him to plead his cause before the new Emperor and thus bring about his release. But, knowing Agrippa, he could think of several reasons why this might not be the course the new King of the Jews would follow. One was the fact that, by bringing about his release, Agrippa would be acknowledging an obligation in the matter of the trick that had defeated Caligula's wish to have himself worshiped as a god in Jerusalem. The other was that, now that he was Mariamne's guardian and her marriage had been officially dissolved by imperial decree, leaving Prochorus in prison left Agrippa free to use her as a prize in making a treaty with one of the kings in the area surrounding his new territory—providing, of course, he was able to find her.

When no word came from Agrippa in the weeks that followed the coronation of Claudius, who had immediately announced his intention to conquer far-off Britain, Prochorus became more and more depressed and certain that he would spend the rest of his life

in prison, if he were lucky enough to escape beheading. And when
word came that Agrippa had departed in state for his new domain,
he could almost wish for the headsman's ax to bring an end to his
agony. Then one spring morning several weeks after Agrippa's departure, Cornelius came into his cell and pulled up a stool to the
table before which Prochorus had been sitting, trying to write an
account of the events of his own life, for no other reason than the
realization that, unless he found something with which to occupy
himself besides brooding, he would go mad.

"Vibius Marsus is going to Antioch as Legate in place of
Petronius," Cornelius announced. "He sails in a few days."

Even the news that one of his two lawyers was leaving Rome
couldn't make Prochorus feel any worse than he already felt. For
with his case seemingly frozen forever in the imperial courts and
no hope of a hearing, he had little need of an advocate.

"Marsus makes no attempt to hide his dislike of Agrippa for
deserting you," Cornelius continued. "So his appointment has considerable significance."

"I cannot see why."

"What else could it mean except that our little Claudius is smarter
than even Agrippa realized? He has correctly evaluated Agrippa's
ambition—"

"And satisfied it—with the empire of Herod the Great."

"Not entirely—if I know Agrippa. Ambition is a strange sort of
force. It feeds on itself and so must increase or eat itself up."

"I am in no mood for philosophy."

"Nor am I a philosopher." Cornelius grinned. "But I'm a good
judge of men and would give odds that right now Agrippa is plotting
how to enlarge his empire. You knew that he got his brother
Herod appointed Tetrarch of Chalcis, didn't you?"

Chalcis was a small province lying north of Caesarea Philippi in
the valley between the Lebanon and Anti-Lebanon mountain
ranges. Surrounded by what were often called the Syro-Phoenician
city-states which were ruled directly by the Legate of Syria in
Antioch, Chalcis was small and of no significance. Unless—and
here Prochorus, his attention seized, suddenly sat up straight—it

were to be used as a bastion in a thrust northward beyond the boundaries of Herod's old kingdom to gain more territory.

"I thought you would see why Chalcis has become so important," said Cornelius. "Agrippa offended the Phoenician states years ago in their negotiations with Damascus, so they have little reason to love him."

"All the more reason why they wouldn't give up their independence."

"There are other ways of acquiring territory," Cornelius reminded him. "Agrippa has given his daughter Berenice to Herod of Chalcis as his wife."

"To her uncle?"

"When has incest troubled a descendant of Herod the Great? This is her second husband; the first was Mark, the son of the Alabarch of Alexandria, in Egypt. But he died a few months ago."

"I thought the Alabarch was in prison."

"He was; Caligula ordered him held after those riots in Alexandria, when Agrippa first went out to become King of Ituraea. But Philo Judaeus has persuaded Claudius to release him and the other Jews who were imprisoned with him."

"Is Philo in Rome?"

"Yes. Do you know him?"

"Only by reputation. He is the greatest Jewish philosopher and lawyer of this day."

"And a fine advocate."

"What are you implying?" Prochorus studied his friend across the table, his despair forgotten in the rising beat of his pulse.

"Philo has earned the respect of Claudius and has also gained a new position for Jews in the empire. If he pleaded your cause—"

"I have no money. Agrippa was my only patron and he left me to rot here."

"I don't think Philo would be moved by money. But he might feel gratitude toward one who helped promote peace in Jerusalem for a long time. Shall I ask him to visit you?"

"Please do—if for no other reason than that I once hoped to study philosophy with him in Alexandria."

"I suspect you are well beyond needing to study under anyone."
Cornelius got to his feet. "Perhaps that's another reason why Philo
will come."

"You spoke just now of Marsus and Agrippa," said Prochorus.
"What did you mean about Claudius being smarter than people
think?"

"Agrippa has never been satisfied with what he had. He's always
clawing to gain more and Claudius grew up with him, so he knows
him well. My guess would be that he sent Marsus to Antioch to see
that Agrippa doesn't get too ambitious—perhaps to rule all of Syria
as king."

"If that's what he wants he will soon try to make alliances with
Tyre and Sidon and the other Phoenician states."

"He's already begun. Marsus told me so yesterday."

"And with no daughter old enough to use as bait, he will search
for Mariamne all the more."

"Is she safe?"

"I think so. She is—"

Cornelius raised his hand, stopping the words. "Don't tell me.
Then, if he seizes her, you cannot doubt me."

"How could I, when you are working to free me?"

"When the spirit is in despair, doubt is natural. Haven't you
even doubted Jesus sometimes since you have been here in prison?"

"More than once," Prochorus admitted. "And perhaps never
more than just before you came today."

"Yet now you have hope. But tell me one thing; it may help me
when I ask Philo to come here. You still consider yourself a Jew,
don't you? Even if you're also a Christian?"

"Of course. Jesus told his disciples to go first to the Jews with
news of the Way. He is first of all the Messiah of the Jews and
afterward the Savior of the world."

"Good. You will hear from me soon."

"What sort of a man is Claudius, Cornelius?"

"Thoughtful, like yourself—and honest, I think. If Philo can be
persuaded to plead your cause as eloquently as he did the cause of
the Alabarch, you are as good as out of prison already."

xx

Several days later a visitor was ushered into Prochorus' cell by the jailor. He was middle-aged and short, with a flowing white beard, eyes that were filled with compassion, and wrinkles at their corners revealing him to be a man of humor as well. Prochorus got to his feet at once and went forward to take the outstretched hand of Philo Judaeus, probably the most highly respected Jew in the entire world.

"It pains me to find one who has done so much for our people in such straits, my son." The visitor spoke in Greek.

"Noble Philo—"

"Not noble," Philo corrected him gently. "Only a Jew who loves God, even as you do."

"Did Cornelius tell you I am a Nazarene?"

"It makes no difference." The words lifted a burden of worry from Prochorus' shoulders. "We worship the same God and are His children; nothing else is important between us."

Prochorus gave his guest the chair and took a seat upon the bench. "All my life I have looked forward to the day when I could come to Alexandria and study with you. But now—" He broke off without finishing the sentence.

"Now may well be the time. You know why I came to Rome, don't you?"

"To plead for some of our people who were arrested in the disturbances when King Agrippa visited Alexandria?"

"Not only that. Many more were jailed when they rose against the edict that sought to put the image of the Emperor Caligula into the Holy of Holies. Is it true that you were the author of the device that forestalled him?"

"Did Cornelius tell you that—or King Agrippa?"

"Cornelius. I saw the King only briefly before he departed for Jerusalem."

"I suggested the course of action that was followed."

"It was a brilliant stratagem. But it is strange that Agrippa never mentioned it to me."

"Would you have—when you were being credited with being the savior of your people?"

Philo gave him a keen look. "It would seem that you know King Agrippa well."

"Very well—since the days when he was *agoranomus* in Tiberias under Herod Antipas."

"You have lived through most interesting times. And you have been ill served by Rome."

"By Rome—and by Agrippa."

"Perhaps," Philo conceded.

"Both King Agrippa and the Legate Petronius took great risks, when they carried out my plan and saved the Jews from destroying themselves on the spearpoints and crucifixion frames of the Romans," Prochorus reminded the Alexandrian. "After King Agrippa arranged for Claudius to be chosen Emperor, he could have asked half the world of him and received it. Yet he chose not to bring my case to the attention of the Emperor—for reasons of his own."

"What do you think they were?"

"I cannot look into another man's soul—"

"But you can watch his actions and, knowing his background and his personality as you do, come to your own conclusions."

"I believe King Agrippa would rather have me here, so the gratitude of the Jewish people for keeping Caligula's image out of the Temple might not be diluted. But most of all, I think he is embarking upon a program of expanding his kingdom and realizes that, because of my loyalty to Rome and my understanding of his own character, I might oppose it."

"Yet you didn't oppose his being named ruler of Judaea and Samaria."

"No, because both the Legate Petronius and I hoped that a descendant of Herod the Great who is at least part Jew might be more acceptable to the people of Judaea than a Roman procurator. Yet I have been given no thanks for what I did—except this." His angry gesture took in the prison cell.

"Your friend the centurion thinks I might be able to intervene in your behalf."

"Would you—even though you are a friend of Agrippa's?"

"I am a friend of our people, as you have been," Philo assured him. "And I am convinced that you deserve better thanks than you have received. Now tell me all about your case."

It didn't take long for Prochorus to describe his mission to Rome as observer for both Petronius and Agrippa, the hearing before Caligula, the trick whereby Fortunatus had managed to have him arrested, and the long months, more than two years now, of imprisonment.

"What about Princess Mariamne?" Philo asked when he finished the account. "Is she safe?"

"She was when I last heard from her through a friend. She is in a place we knew of where we felt the people could be trusted not to betray her presence, but I forbade her to write me, lest the letter be traced back and her refuge revealed." He hesitated, then went on: "Do you think you can do anything for me?"

"You certainly deserve to be free as much as the Jews of Alexandria I represented here," Philo admitted. "And I believe you will be, when I tell the Emperor about your case."

"I would not have you risk what you have already gained."

"There should be no risk. I found Emperor Claudius both intelligent and understanding, with far more knowledge about the empire and its peoples than I had been led to believe."

"By Agrippa?"

"Among others. I came here hoping to insure the right of the Jews of Alexandria to worship the Most High in peace, with no harassment from the Greeks. But I think I gained a new freedom for our people everywhere."

"How did it happen?"

"Through no particular effort on my part," Philo confessed. "King Agrippa and the Tetrarch of Chalcis had apparently spoken to the Emperor before on the same subject. Perhaps because I had just pleaded the cause of the Jews of Alexandria successfully the Emperor called his *secretarius ab epistulis* back and dictated another document." He reached into his robe and took out a small parchment roll.

"Read this and tell me what you think of it. Being both a scholar and an expert in political matters, you can tell me whether it says what I think it does."

The brief document bore the imperial seal of Rome, so there was no doubting its authenticity—or the signature of the Emperor of all the Romans scrawled at the bottom. Its wording, as Philo had said, was extremely interesting:

Tiberius Claudius Caesar Augustus Germanicus, High Priest, Tribune of the people, chosen consul the second time, ordains thus; Upon the petition of King Agrippa and King Herod, who are persons very dear to me, that I would grant that the same rights and privileges should be preserved to the Jews which are in all the Roman Empire, which I have granted to those of Alexandria, I very willingly comply therewith; and this grant I make not only for the sake of the petitioners, but as judging those Jews for whom I have been petitioned worthy of such favor, on account of their fidelity and friendship to the Romans. I think it also very just that no Grecian city should be deprived of such rights and privileges, since they were preserved to them under the great Augustus. It will therefore be fit to permit the Jews, who are all in the world under us, to keep their ancient customs without being hindered so to do. And I do charge them also to use this my kindness to them with moderation, and not to show a contempt of the superstitious observance of other nations, but to keep their own laws only. And I will that this decree of mine be engraven on tables by the magistrates of the cities, and colonies, and municipal places, both those within Italy and those without it, both kings and governors, by the means of the ambassadors, and to have them exposed to the public for full thirty days, in such a place whence it may plainly be read from the ground.

"This is a declaration of freedom for our people everywhere." Prochorus assured Philo as he handed him back the parchment. "It deserves a place among us almost equal to the tablets of the law given to Moses."

"As I understand it," said Philo, "you were thrown into jail by

Caligula because you refused to name him and Jupiter Capitolinus as greater than Yahweh."

"That was the charge."

"Then it would seem that this edict by Claudius guarantees your freedom as it does the freedom of worship to Jews everywhere."

"I can only hope the Emperor will be moved by your eloquence."

"Not by my eloquence," said Philo. "But I think he will be moved by logic—and by humanity."

"Can you be sure my being a Nazarene will not be held against me?"

Philo smiled. "Wherever two Jews come together, an argument soon begins, so it isn't surprising that our God is worshiped in many ways by many groups. The important thing that unites us all is that we were chosen long ago by Yahweh as His peculiar people, and that we were given the law through Moses to guide us. The Nazarenes I know obey the commandments of Moses, though they may differ with many pronouncements by the Rabbis of the Porch, even as I do. But tell me more about Jesus of Nazareth; I've never had a chance to talk with a really intelligent follower of his before."

Prochorus recounted what he knew or had been told by John, Peter and others about Jesus. When he came to the story of the empty tomb and the Nazarene's appearances afterward, Philo interrupted him to ask:

"Are those who saw Jesus alive after death certain he was in the flesh? Or could it have been as a spirit?"

"I've tried to determine that question myself with no satisfactory answer. My own conviction is that he appeared to them as a spirit."

"That would be in accord with what I have been teaching about our religion for years," said Philo. "Have you had an opportunity to study the writings of the Greek philosophers?"

"Not very much. My teacher at the University of Tiberias encouraged me to buy scrolls containing some of them but not many were available there."

"I have sought to show my students that the best elements of our own faith and the teachings of Greeks like Socrates, Plato and Aristotle, or Nestor and Athenodorus among the Stoics, are very similar in principle and that there is no reason why Jew, Greek and others may not live in the world in harmony."

"Jesus taught that too."

"I'm sure he did, and that it can be done, if this edict by Claudius is obeyed everywhere, as it should be. All religious men, whether Jew or gentile, believe in an essential spirit that is immortal and cannot be destroyed, as opposed to material things which exist for only a moment in the sight of God. Each is distinct from the other but from time to time, in my view, mediators form a bridge, so to speak, between them."

"Could Jesus have been such a mediator? I once heard John ben Zebedee speak of him as the Word made flesh—the Logos."

"I have long regarded the divine wisdom, or Logos, as one of the mediators between the eternal spirit of God and the earthly material nature of man," said Philo. "Whether or not that Logos could take on human form, I am not prepared to say."

"Jesus once said God loved the world so much that he sent His son into it so all who trusted him and believed in him could have eternal life."

"Our views are certainly very similar, except for the stumbling block of the Logos actually becoming flesh," Philo admitted. "Do the Nazarenes adhere to the law?"

"In all respects," said Prochorus, remembering James ben Joseph and the patches upon his robe where his knees had worn through the fabric from praying in the Temple. "The Master himself once said he did not come to destroy the law but to fulfill it."

"Prophecy speaks of the fulfillment of the law by a Messiah," Philo conceded. "I have always seen him as a spirit sent to mediate between man and God, but whether we belong to the *Yahad* like the Essenes or the Therapeutae living just outside Alexandria, the Pharisees and the Sadducees in Jerusalem, the Stoics, or even the Epicureans among the Greek philosophers—all of us are committed to the pursuit of virtue. And since this is the highest aim of the thinking men, it makes no difference whether or not we are motivated by the concept of the all-prevailing good of Plato, the moral aims of the Stoics, or the kinship with God we Jews believe to be our own right. I cannot deny any man the right to come to God, whatever name he gives Him.

"But enough of philosophy." Philo got to his feet. "We shall discuss it more at length, when you come to Alexandria. I must go now to request an audience with the Emperor so I can plead for your release."

"I shall owe you my life if you succeed."

"Thousands of Jews owe you their lives for what you have already done. I shall only be repaying a small part of that debt."

Prochorus did not have to wait long. Late that same afternoon Cornelius and Philo came to his cell and left the door unlocked behind them. One look at their faces told him he was free at last.

"The Emperor—" His voice failed him but Philo supplied the words he could not utter.

"The Emperor has ordered you set free. You may go where you will."

"I have the order here." Cornelius handed him a sheet of parchment.

"Was—was he difficult to convince?"

Philo shook his head. "As soon as I told him Caligula imprisoned you for refusing to have any other gods before our own, the matter was accomplished."

"Where will you go?" Cornelius asked.

"To find my wife."

"In Judaea?"

"Yes." Then Prochorus sobered. "But I have no money for my passage."

"You need not worry about that," said Cornelius. "Because of my former service in Syria, I have been ordered to accompany Vibius Marsus to Antioch as military commander, when he goes there in a few weeks as the new Legate. You can go with us as an adviser—your old position—if you wish."

"You are also welcome to accompany my own party to Alexandria," said Philo. "We will discuss philosophy to our heart's content on the voyage. And if you insist on going on, I can lend you money to buy passage with a caravan bound for Judaea or Damascus."

"I owe you both more than I can ever repay." Prochorus looked from one of his benefactors to the other. "For the time being, though, it is best that my presence in Judaea not become known. That could hardly be feasible, if I became an adviser to the Legate of Syria, so I shall go by way of Alexandria."

"Are you sure you realize what you're giving up?" Cornelius asked. "In Antioch you can quickly rise to a high position once again."

"I am sure. And I think Mariamne will understand."

"Until there is a change in the region, perhaps you are right," said Cornelius, as he gave Prochorus the Roman grip of fellowship. "I know the Son of God will protect you."

Neither had mentioned Agrippa but both knew the real reason for Prochorus' decision to give up the opportunity to return to public life was the fact that, in so doing, Mariamne might be placed under her uncle's power.

xxi

The shadows cast by the peaks in the wild mountain range at his back were already darkening the blue of the Salt Sea before him, when Prochorus paused on the heights above the Essene community of Ir Hamelakh. Across the landlocked lake, the mountains of Moab rose in a serried procession and, although he could not see it at the moment, he could easily visualize in his mind the peak among them on which stood the fortress of Machaerus, where he had faced King Aretas and effected the return of the captured fortress to the control of Herod Antipas.

All that had been a long time ago and the course of his whole life had changed again and again since. But the peacefulness of the glassy surface of the lake, a brilliant mirror in the afternoon sunlight, the grandeur and majesty of the mountain ranges forming the cup in which it lay, the cluster of white buildings that made up the community lying below him close to the water's edge, even the colors of the small rainbow cast by the spray from the waterfall that supplied the Essenes with water—all of it seemed not to have changed for centuries. And, watching it, he felt a sense of peace begin to descend upon his own soul.

The way had not been easy since he had left Alexandria. With the loan Philo had made him, he had chosen to take ship to the ancient Philistine city of Ascalon, largely because, although Agrippa's domain now extended from Beersheba in the south far beyond even the classic limits of Dan in the north, not far from Caesarea Philippi, Ascalon was still an autonomous city-state under the direct jurisdiction of the Emperor of Rome. There, Agrippa could not disturb him, if indeed the King of Judaea even thought about him any more. And besides, a caravan trail led from Ascalon to Hebron, the ancient city of Abraham south of Jerusalem near the crest of the central mountain range of Judaea.

Prochorus had made his way with other travelers there and continued on to Engedi, the fertile oasis overlooking the Salt Sea where a great spring burst from the hillside. Moving northward alone along the shore of the sea that knew no life, he had come finally to the path leading down from the crest of the mountain range to the Essene community. Now, as his steps began to increase in pace with the steep descent, his heart also began to beat more quickly. And where the path leveled out on a terrace leading to the great spring that furnished water for the community, and the guardians of the caves pocking the hillside where the Essene scribes stored their writings for safekeeping in vessels of fired clay, he broke into a run.

Seen at close range, the gardens of Ir Hamelakh were green and rich, fed by water from the spring. A woman was walking in one of them. Her slender figure and the aureole of golden hair crowning her head reminded him of Mariamne, except that she held the hand of a child who toddled along beside her.

Then as he drew closer his foot disturbed a small rock on the way, sending it bouncing down the hillside. The woman looked up and, with a sudden pain of joy in his heart, he saw Mariamne again for the first time in more than two years. She recognized him at the same moment, too, and, pausing only to sweep up the child into her arms, ran to meet him.

They met at the edge of the village, half blinded by the tears of joy streaming down their cheeks. Disturbed by the sight of a man covered with the dust of his long journey and by his mother's sobbing, the baby, too, began to cry, and their exclamations of joy at being reunited and the baby's wailing turned the air for a moment into a veritable bedlam of sound.

Finally Mariamne disengaged herself from Prochorus' embrace and calmed the baby by setting him upon his feet, where the task of maintaining his equilibrium immediately required all of his attention. Prochorus was sure he would never see anywhere a more beautiful sight than her eyes when she said proudly: "See how strong your son is, darling?"

"His name?" Prochorus found his voice at last.

"Being a Jew, he could not be named Prochorus, lest the Angel of Death be confused and take the wrong one. I have called him what I knew you would have named him, if you had been here."

"John," he said. "John ben Prochorus."

Hearing his name, the baby held out his arms to his father. And as he gathered his first-born into his embrace, Prochorus knew that no joy he would ever experience could possibly equal that which filled him now.

Book Five

CAESAREA

Prochorus had not realized that he was staring unseeingly out the window of the large, many-windowed scriptorium, until Hilkiah, *mebaqqer* of the Ir Hamelakh congregation, touched his shoulder and brought him back to the present with a start. Instinctively he reached for the pen that had dropped from his fingers, spattering ink on the sheet of parchment upon which he had been copying verses from the Wisdom of Jesus ben Sira, a favorite book with the "yahad" who had withdrawn from the world here beside the Dead Sea to spend their lives in meditation and scholarly pursuits. But the *mebaqqer* picked up the ink-spattered sheet before he could touch it with the pen and held it up to the sunlight streaming through the window.

"Your work is excellent, my son, as always."

"But ruined now by my own carelessness." Prochorus had become very fond of the stately Hilkiah during the period of almost three years since he had arrived at the Essene settlement to find Mariamne and his son. They had been quiet years and pleasant, too, made particularly so by Mariamne's joy in having him and the little boy close to her. Most of the time she went about singing in the small building at the edge of the settlement where they lived—he was not an Essene and had made no attempt to become one, though he knew that many who had followed Jesus of Nazareth in his days on earth had belonged to the desert sect—but sometimes he had seen a thoughtful expression on her face when he caught her studying him.

The community on the shore of the Dead Sea was only one of several gathering places of Essenes. Men who had taken the stern vows of the sect were a part of all walks of life in Israel, he had learned, next only in number and importance to the Pharisees in the religious and political activities of the Jews. But this was by far the largest of the communities and at the same time the farthest removed from the teeming life of Jerusalem, only a few hours' journey away in geography but a million years distant in its outlook upon life.

"Do you remember what you were writing when you put down the pen?" Hilkiah handed him the sheet, face downward.

Prochorus flushed guiltily. More than once during the past six months he had spoiled one of the sheets upon which the patient scribes worked, copying the Jewish scriptures and the sacred writings of the Essene sect for preservation in the caves lining the cliffs above the settlement. Each time it had been because his mind wandered.

"Has Brother Jared told you how many I have ruined?" he asked with a wry smile.

"He has mentioned it," said Hilkiah. "I came by today to ask what has been troubling you, but there is no need for me to ask any more."

"Why do you say that?"

"The Most High himself has spoken to you through your pen and through the wisdom of Jesus ben Sira. Read the last lines on the page."

Prochorus turned the ink-spattered parchment over and stared at the words he had been writing. At first they were only familiar lines; then, as their meaning came to him, he stiffened and would have put down the page, if Hilkiah had not reached out to steady his hand.

"Read," he insisted, and Prochorus began at the top of the sheet:

"*All men come from the ground,*
  Adam himself was formed out of the earth;
  in the fullness of his wisdom the Lord has
  made distinctions between them, and
  diversified their conditions.
Some he has blessed and made more important,
  some he has hallowed and set near him;
  others he has cursed and humiliated by
  degrading them from their positions.
Like clay in the hands of the potter
  to mould as it pleases him,
  so are men in the hands of their maker
  to reward as he judges right.

Opposite evil stands good,
  opposite death, life;
  so too opposite the devout man stands the sinner.
This is the way to view all the works of the Most High;
  they go, in pairs, by opposite.

I myself have been the last to keep watch,
  like a gleaner following the vintagers.
By the blessing of the Lord I have come in first,
  and, like a vintager, filled the wine press.
Observe that I have not toiled for myself only,
  but for all who seek instruction.
Listen to me, you princes of the people,
  leaders of the assembly, lend ear."

Prochorus put down the page slowly, reluctant to meet Hilkiah's eyes, because he knew he would find reflected in them the proddings of his own conscience.

"These words were written over two hundred years ago," he protested.

"At a time of great trouble for our people, and of great oppression," Hilkiah agreed. "When forces of paganism and lust were harrying the souls of Jews everywhere."

"But what do they mean to me now?"

"Rome is an enemy of the Most High, as the Greeks were in the time of Jesus ben Sira. Did not a Roman Emperor seek only a few years ago to place his own image in the Most Holy Place?"

"But he was thwarted—by King Agrippa."

"The hand was Agrippa's, the intelligence was your own." Hilkiah seated himself on the bench beside Prochorus. "When you came here three years ago, I gave you refuge, as I had given refuge to your wife once before when her life was in danger. Your presence here has meant much to me, my son, but I realize now that I have been selfish. God was speaking both to you and to me just now in the words of ben Sira, when you wrote:

> *Observe that I have not toiled for myself only,*
>   *but for all who seek instruction.*
> *Listen to me, you princes of the people,*
>   *leaders of the assembly, lend ear.*

"You have the power to move men, to influence them for good with your mind and your words," Hilkiah continued. "God would never be content for you to spend the rest of your life here, copying words to be hidden away in clay cylinders."

"Why do you hide them away when few people ever go near the caves and they may never be found?"

"The forces of light and darkness forever strive for the lives of men; sometimes one is in the ascendancy, sometimes the other. As the Book of Jesus ben Sira says, I am convinced that the legions of darkness are gaining strength and will soon overcome the forces of light."

"For how long?"

"Who can say? But however long it may be, men who love God will need strength when the battle is joined again to sustain their faith. And where else can they find it except in the words God has given them through the mouths of wise men and prophets and through the history of a people chosen by Him?"

"Then it would seem to be important that I keep on with my work as a scribe."

"The forces of darkness may be pushed back a year, a decade or even a century," said Hilkiah. "But only if those with special talents use them freely and wisely."

"There is a parable in the Sayings of Jesus about that," said Prochorus. "He was speaking of money but he could just as well have been speaking of a special ability. He said that those who were given a talent but chose to bury it, because they were afraid to take the risk of making it grow, would receive no reward when the time of accounting came."

"The Nazarene was a great prophet and not the first to lose his life because he spoke out," Hilkiah agreed.

"As I may lose mine if I go back into the world of political affairs. I have felt the headsman's breath upon my neck once and it isn't pleasant."

"Duty is rarely pleasant. But a man's soul can grow on no better food."

"What shall I do then?"

"The Most High has spoken to you in the book of wisdom, warning you to be ready. When it is time for you to return to the world outside, He will call upon you in a way you will recognize."

ii

Disturbed by his conversation with Hilkiah, Prochorus left the scriptorium and, remembering that Mariamne often took little John and some of the other children at this time of day to play in the shallows at the edge of the lake, made his way downhill to the shore. He had no trouble finding them; the high-pitched chatter of children's voices and Mariamne's laugh were a music he had come to love. She looked up and smiled in welcome, when his shadow fell upon her where she sat on the sandy shore.

"You're early," she said. "Is anything wrong?"

"I spattered ink on one of the parchment sheets and Hilkiah sent me home in punishment," he said with a grin as he stretched out on the sand beside her and put his arms behind his head.

The children were playing at the edge of the lake. Naked and happy, they would run out into the water, until the natural buoyancy of the heavy salt concentration lifted them off their feet. Then they would splash ashore, pretending to be afraid and throwing water upon each other. Mariamne turned to look into his eyes and the look of merriment was suddenly gone from her own.

"You have been preoccupied a great deal of the time lately," she said.

"I didn't realize it myself, until I dropped the pen without knowing it this afternoon and sat looking out through a window. Hilkiah came upon me unawares and gave me a lecture."

"Did he reprimand you?"

"He thinks the passage I was copying when I fell into the reverie is God's way of speaking to me."

"Do you remember what it was?" she asked quickly.

"A few lines from the Wisdom of Jesus ben Sira."

"Repeat them for me if you can," she said and he spoke the last verses of the passage:

"Observe that I have not toiled for myself only,
but for all who seek instruction.
Listen to me, you princes of the people,
leaders of the assembly, lend ear."

"No!" Mariamne caught her breath and seized his hand, clutching it against her breast. "You have already risked more than any man should be asked to risk."

"Hilkiah could be wrong." He tried to comfort her by putting his arm around her, but her body was rigid and her eyes were filled with terror.

A sudden cry of fear came from the lake and he saw that small John had run out so far into the water that, when he floated, he was not able to touch the bottom with his toes and was afraid of being swept out farther. Gently removing Mariamne's hand, Prochorus waded out into the lake and pulled the chubby little boy ashore until he could find a footing and scamper the rest of the way himself, amidst shouts of laughter from his companions. When he came back to Mariamne, he saw that she had gained a measure of control, but her eyes were still dark with apprehension.

"Hilkiah could be wrong, darling." He reached down to pull her to her feet so they could walk along the shore together. "I wasn't cut out to be a scribe, so my mind wanders occasionally. It could be nothing more than that."

"I've known for more than a year that you must one day go back to the world outside," she said. "You admitted just now that you aren't cut out for what you are doing here."

"I haven't minded," he assured her. "After that year of prison in Rome, I welcomed the chance to regain my health and sort things out in my mind."

"Isn't it enough to be happy here—with me and your son?" She shivered and drew close to him for support and reassurance.

"I hadn't even thought of political affairs, until Hilkiah took me unawares this afternoon," he protested, but she only shook her head.

"I have been deluding myself that this could all continue because

I was so happy here with little John and particularly since you came from Rome. These people are preparing for a day of doom and doing nothing to prevent it from coming, while you have worked ever since I first saw you in Uncle Antipas' palace at Tiberias to further the welfare of Jews everywhere and oppose people like that brigand we met in the hills above Tiberias that afternoon—what was his name?"

"Manahem, the son of Judas the Gaulonite."

She shivered again, as if from a nameless dread, and he could feel the rapid beat of her heart as she clung to him.

"And that other man?" she said. "The one who tried to kill you in Jerusalem?"

"Harith is dead."

"Evil men seem to spring up everywhere, like the dragon's teeth you told King Aretas about at Machaerus. But why do you have to fight them? Can't others do it?"

"Others are doing it," he said. "Peter and John and Manaen with those in Antioch. Even Philo in Alexandria is adapting the teachings of the Jewish faith into a religious philosophy that Greeks can understand and follow. Certainly the edicts of the Emperor Claudius in Rome granting religious freedom to people everywhere cannot be anything but a part of God's plan for the world."

"What will your part be this time?"

"That we shall learn—in time," he assured her. "Meanwhile, let us not look forward to the coming of doom, as the Essenes do, but enjoy our life together here."

"It's a good life." She was regaining her naturally high spirits once again. "We have the flowers, the lake, the beauty of the hills—"

"And the promise of God." He pointed across the lake to where one peak loomed above the others at the northeastern end of the Salt Sea.

"There is Mount Nebo, where the Lord took Moses to show him the land that would be given to his people. And if the air were perfectly clear, we could see the snow on the top of Mount Hermon, there in the north. How can any man doubt God's purpose when he can see all about him the beauty and grandeur of the land the Most High has given him?"

But even as they climbed the slope to the settlement and their home, with little John scampering ahead up the path, both of them knew he had only been trying to push away with words the pall that oppressed their spirits. And any doubt that Hilkiah had indeed been speaking prophetically in warning Prochorus to be ready for a new turn of his fortunes was dissipated when a slender, yet familiar, figure in a robe torn and stained with blood staggered across the threshold of their small home at the Essene settlement a few weeks later.

The visitor's face was gray with exhaustion and his beard was powdered with the dust of travel by foot. It was John ben Zebedee and his first words told Prochorus that his brief period of retirement from the world was now ended.

"My brother James is dead, beheaded by Agrippa," John gasped. "And Peter is in prison."

iii

While Prochorus led John to a comfortable seat in the shade, Mariamne brought water in a basin and, with soft cloths, bathed his face and the scratches where he had stumbled and fallen beside the path.

"Now tell me the whole story," Prochorus said when the visitor had regained his breath.

"I suppose it all started when Agrippa became King of Judaea," said John. "Simon Kantheros, the son of Boethus, was High Priest. He knew how pious James ben Joseph is, so he allowed us the same status as any other congregation."

"What has Jerusalem been like under Agrippa?" Prochorus asked.

"Very prosperous. The people welcomed him with open arms and he did everything he could to please them. Work on the Temple was almost finished and Herod the Great built so many palaces and other structures, there wasn't much Agrippa could build. So he started a new wall around the suburb of Bezetha on the north side of Jerusalem. The Emperor heard of it though and stopped him before it was finished."

"Why would he do that?" Mariamne asked.

"Claudius didn't trust Agrippa entirely from the start," Prochorus explained. "Cornelius told me that was why Vibius Marsus was sent out to Antioch as Legate."

"Marsus has watched Agrippa closely," John confirmed. "And with good reason."

"Why do you say that?"

"At first Agrippa was everything a King of the Jews should be. He forgave some of the taxes, took an active part in religious services, and was hailed by Jews everywhere almost like a Messiah. The building of the wall brought prosperity to Jerusalem, and he even made the Palace of the Hasmoneans his home."

"What about Caesarea?"

"He constructed new buildings there, too, and enlarged the amphitheater. His biggest project, except the wall, was transforming the bay and the harbor of Berytus—"

"But that's in Phoenicia."

"He has been courting the good will of the Phoenicians," John explained. "When he offered to build a palace and a magnificent theater at Berytus, who could oppose him? I think he plans to transform it into another Baiae."

Mariamne shivered. "That's the Roman in him."

"I think what he really wants to do is expand his kingdom to include the Phoenician city-states and others of the smaller territories in Syro-Phoenicia. In Jerusalem, he is the most pious of men, but with the heathen of Berytus he's a great benefactor who worships in pagan temples and even sets hundreds of convicted prisoners to fight to the death against each other in the arena."

"Didn't Marsus oppose him?" Prochorus asked.

"Agrippa has been pleasing both Jew and gentile," John explained. "With Claudius in Britain, I suppose Marsus has been afraid to oppose him very strongly."

"Marsus would have to be careful," Prochorus agreed. "He has no way of knowing just how much the Emperor will support him when he comes back from the campaign in the West."

"I think the Legate first realized exactly what King Agrippa was doing about a year ago in Tiberias," John continued. "It was just after the great fight in the arena at Berytus, when the prisoners were set upon each other. Agrippa and Herod of Chalcis had entertained the leaders of the small Phoenician states north of Mount Carmel at Berytus. Afterward they went to Tiberias, where five kings had been invited to a great feast."

"Five!" Prochorus exclaimed. "Who were they?"

"Herod of Chalcis was one of them, of course; he is involved in all of Agrippa's plans. Then there was Antiochus IV of Commagene, with Cotius, King of Lesser Armenia, and his brother Polemon, King of Pontus. Sampsigeramus of Emesa was there too. Peter was in Galilee at the time and saw some of the festivities; he said they were really impressive."

"Where was Vibius Marsus while all this was happening?"

"The Legate was invited but he was a day late in coming. When he arrived, he must have suspected what Agrippa was about—"

"Cornelius would have, if he hadn't."

"In any event, the story is that Marsus secretly sent messengers to each of the kings gathered at Tiberias, notifying them that he did not approve of their presence there."

"By then, they had probably begun to suspect what Agrippa's purpose was in inviting them—and were no doubt glad of an excuse to leave," said Prochorus. "Except, of course, Herod of Chalcis."

"Peter agrees with you," said John. "The story in Jerusalem is that Agrippa was furious at Marsus and has vowed to have him recalled."

"He might succeed if Claudius still feels in his debt. But surely Agrippa's scheme to gain a larger kingdom for himself didn't have anything to do with the arrest of James and Peter."

"That was the doing of the new High Priest, Matthias, the son of Annas," said John. "Annas and his family have hated all Nazarenes ever since Joseph Caiaphas was deposed following the crucifixion of our Lord. With the High Priest supporting him, Agrippa knew he could control Jerusalem, as well as most of the Jews of the Diaspora, so he seized James and Peter to please Matthias." John's voice broke and for a moment he could not go on.

"My brother had no connection with the rebel element since

you persuaded him to come back to Jerusalem after the persecution by Saul," he continued. "Any one of us could have told Agrippa that—but he wouldn't wait. The Priestly Council is once again controlled by Annas and his family, so James was condemned and executed before we could arouse the people against what was being done."

"Wasn't Peter condemned at the same time?"

"No. Peter is a greater prize by far than either my brother or me. Agrippa is waiting to bring him before the Sanhedrin itself on some great occasion when the greatest number of people will see him executed."

"The Feast of Pentecost!" Prochorus exclaimed. "It was then that Peter spoke the sermon that turned so many people to follow Jesus and began the Congregation of the Nazarenes in Jerusalem."

"Agrippa may have that in mind," John agreed.

"How did you escape?" Mariamne asked.

"James ben Joseph risked his life to hide me. Agrippa was afraid to seize him because James is seen in the Temple every day and is admired by all because of his great piety."

"Are you sure none of Agrippa's spies followed you here?"

"I left by night through the Water Gate, wearing a robe belonging to Mary, the mother of Mark. I'm sure no one suspected that I was other than what I appeared to be, a shiftless woman who had failed to fill the water pots in her home before darkness fell."

"You should be safe here, then," said Prochorus. "It is Peter we have to worry about now."

"You cannot help him. If it is the Lord's will that Peter shall die, he will die. If not, you will only be risking your life needlessly."

"Prochorus had decided before you came that the Lord does not intend for him to remain here," Mariamne explained to John. "I hate to see him go, but I feel a voice speaking in my heart, telling me his going is the will of God."

"It is the Holy Spirit!" Prochorus exclaimed, his voice filled with joy. "Now that I know it has come upon you at last, I can be sure the Lord will protect you and little John."

"But what can you do?" John ben Zebedee protested. "You no longer have any authority in Jerusalem."

"Ambition may not yet have destroyed the better part of Agrippa's nature, and he still owes me a considerable obligation for the advice I gave him in Rome. I shall appeal directly to him for Peter's life."

"Shall we go to Jerusalem, too?" Mariamne asked, but Prochorus shook his head.

"The three of you will be safe in Antioch, until I can join you there. Marsus and Cornelius will protect you."

"Agrippa's men are searching for me," John warned. "They will be watching the roads and the seaports."

"They would never look for you in Ascalon," Prochorus assured him. "It's outside Agrippa's jurisdiction and you can take ship there for Antioch with Mariamne and John. When you get to Antioch, tell Cornelius and Marsus that I have gone to Jerusalem to release Peter and try to foil Agrippa's plans to rule all of Syria."

"Surely his plans for Syria aren't your responsibility any longer," Mariamne protested.

"Peace in Judaea and Samaria was my responsibility even before I became a Nazarene," said Prochorus. "If Agrippa tries to rule all of Syria, there will be rebellion everywhere because the Greek element that makes up at least as much of the population as the Jews, outside of Jerusalem itself, will never agree to having a Jew rule over them. And, once the fires of rebellion are started, Jerusalem could be consumed too."

"We must keep Jerusalem safe at all costs for the *parousia* of the Lord," said John. "But Agrippa may even be serving God's purpose by forcing us to leave Judaea—as so many did during the persecutions by Saul—and tell the story of Jesus to the world."

iv

Accustomed though he was to great buildings and teeming cities, Prochorus was surprised by what Agrippa had been able to accomplish in Jerusalem during the brief period since he had been crowned king of his grandfather's former realm. Easily the most impressive structure, though unfinished by order of Claudius, was the so-called Third Wall.

The city had been growing rapidly even before Agrippa's tenure began, much of the expansion taking place in the district known as Bezetha north of the Sanctuary area, the only direction in which the rough terrain surrounding Jerusalem was suitable for growth. From the old gate outside which Stephen had been stoned to death, the wall ran almost directly north past an area of ancient tombs to a corner, turning thence across what was called "Solomon's Quarries," from which had come the stone foundations for the first Temple, to a corner overlooking the natural fortification formed by the upper part of the Tyropean Valley. Though incomplete, the wall was battlemented and turreted in an impressive fashion, adding considerably to the defenses of Jerusalem.

In the Lower City, Prochorus was welcomed by Mark and his mother, who were overjoyed to learn that John had reached the Essene settlement safely. They insisted that he spend the night with them and, since the day was now well along and he was not likely to gain an audience with King Agrippa that afternoon, he was happy to accept their hospitality. About Peter they could tell him only that he was still in prison, although trial before the captive Sanhedrin was said to be scheduled a few days hence. Agrippa, certain of the verdict of the court, had even announced that the execution of the Nazarene leader would be carried out at a time when the greatest number of people could witness it and be warned against having anything to do with the new sect. That this almost certainly meant the Feast of Pentecost—some forty days away, since the Passover season was just finished—both Mark and Mary agreed.

"Is James ben Joseph still safe?" Prochorus asked.

"Even the High Priest Matthias would hardly dare attack the most pious man in Jerusalem," said Mark. "James spends hours each day praying in the Temple. All who go there regularly know him well."

"I suppose the Synagogue of the Nazarenes still follows the old ways."

"More than any other in Jerusalem," Mark confirmed. "Jesus said that he came to fulfill the law and James always has followed that principle. When the Lord comes again, his place here will be ready."

"What about the church at Antioch? Is it still growing?"

"More than ever, from what Barnabas says in his letters. Saul is there now. He preaches new things and is not so strict in obeying the law."

"That should gain proselytes, at least."

"And offend those who cling to the old ways," said Mark. "I think one reason why the elders of the congregation in Antioch decided to send Saul out to preach in the Grecian cities was the turmoil he has caused in some of the Antioch congregations."

"Isn't your cousin going with him?"

"Yes. I think he is to act as somewhat of a counterbalance to keep Saul from swinging too far away from the law."

"Does Barnabas ever speak of the Centurion Cornelius?"

"He mentions a tribune by that name," said Mark.

"It would be the same man. He was the leader of the Italian Band, one of the finest units in the Roman army, and deserved a promotion."

"You will have to work fast if you intend to persuade King Agrippa to release Peter," said Mark. "I heard in the Street of the Silversmiths today that the King leaves soon for Caesarea."

"Why the silversmiths?"

"Agrippa has ordered a robe of the finest cloth covered with the thinnest scales of silver. They say he plans to wear it at the games in Caesarea a week from now when the representatives from Tyre and Sidon come there to capitulate to him."

"Capitulate? I heard of no war."

"This is a different kind of war." Mark was obviously proud of being able to teach the visitor something he didn't already know. "When the Phoenician states resisted King Agrippa's efforts to bind them into an alliance, he cut off shipments of grain and other food to Tyre and Sidon from Galilee and the territory of Auranitis."

Knowing the region intimately as he did, Prochorus could understand how the move, if carried out with the ruthlessness of which Agrippa was quite capable, would cripple the Phoenician cities. Even before the time of David and Solomon, residents of the narrow coastal strip, whose land area had never been sufficient to supply them with food, had traded the skill of their stonecutters, carpenters and other artisans for the bounteous produce of Galilee and the neighboring district of Auranitis east of the Sea of Galilee. By cutting off their major source of food Agrippa could bring the residents of the Phoenician cities to heel quickly without unsheathing a sword.

"How does the Legate of Syria look upon all this?" he asked.

"Marsus has not interfered, perhaps because King Agrippa claims the embargo was caused by the presence of rebels in the hills of Upper Galilee where the caravans of food had to pass."

"Is Manahem still active there?"

"Manahem and his brothers, from what we can learn."

"How about Barabbas?"

"I have heard nothing about him lately," said Mark. "People are saying that the Legate makes no attempt to drive the brigands out because they hamper Agrippa."

"This time they would appear to be playing into Agrippa's hands."

"Not if he can't control them, after he promises grain, vegetables and fruit to the people of Tyre and Sidon," said Mark.

"It looks as though Agrippa might be crucified on his own cross then." Prochorus' mind was working rapidly, for a plan of action was beginning to take form there, a plan that might furnish him with the key he needed to open the prison cell for Simon Peter. "Perhaps I can help carve a *patibulum* to fit him."

v

Remembering the night when he had raced along this same street with the footsteps of Harith, the brother of Judas of Kerioth, echoing close behind him like the pulse beat of doom, Prochorus approached the Palace of the Hasmoneans, now the home of King Agrippa in Jerusalem, early the next morning. To the guard at the gate, he gave his request for an audience with the King and shortly was taken to an anteroom where a chamberlain met him.

"What do you wish of the King?" The man's manner was frosty.

"I was Deputy Governor of Jerusalem before King Agrippa came to reign here," said Prochorus. "We were in Rome together and he knows me well."

"Wait here a moment. I will see if he will grant you an audience."

The chamberlain's manner did not offer much hope of success, but while Prochorus was waiting, Queen Kypros started across the room. Seeing him, she stopped and frowned, then a welcoming smile suddenly broke over her face.

"Prochorus!" she cried. "Why haven't we seen you and Mariamne lately?"

"I was in prison for some time after King Agrippa left Rome, Your Majesty."

"Oh yes. That madman Caligula."

"And Fortunatus." When Queen Kypros looked blank, he added, "It was he who influenced the Emperor against me."

"Fortunatus was like that, always causing trouble. I'm glad he was banished to Gaul."

"Is he still there?"

"As far as I know. Tell me, how is Mariamne?"

"Never lovelier. We have a son who is almost four years old."

"A son! You must bring them both to see us." Her eyes were suddenly sad. "Young Agrippa is in Rome; the Emperor insists on keeping him there." She put her hand on his arm in a pleading gesture. "My husband has always liked and respected you, Prochorus. Try to persuade him that his grandfather's old kingdom is enough for any man to rule."

"I shall do what I can," he promised as the chamberlain appeared in the doorway.

"I regret that King Agrippa will not be able to see—" the man started to say but Kypros cut him short.

"Of course the King will see Prochorus," she said indignantly. "We are all very much in his debt. I will take him there myself."

While the chamberlain followed, Kypros led the way through several rooms into a fairly large study. Agrippa was standing beside the window, dictating a letter to a scribe who sat at a table with his pens, ink board, parchment sheets and rolls before him.

"Look who I found in the anteroom!" Kypros cried. "Our kins-man, Prochorus."

For an instant a look of guilt—or embarrassment—showed in Agrippa's eyes, then he smiled warmly. "Prochorus, of course." He turned upon the chamberlain savagely. "Why can't you ever pro-nounce people's names right? You would have let me turn an old friend away without seeing him."

The chamberlain backed out of the room, but Prochorus was not at all fooled by Agrippa's lame attempt to hide the fact that he had not intended to see him at all.

"Prochorus and Mariamne have a son," said Kypros.

"A son!" Agrippa seemed genuinely pleased and once again Prochorus steeled himself against the other man's undeniable charm. "Where are they now?"

"At sea—on the way to Antioch."

"You should have brought your son here so I could give him my blessing." Only a faint edge in Agrippa's voice betrayed his dis-pleasure. "After all, he is a descendant of the Herodian house."

"As well as of the Hasmonean and also the line of David," Prochorus said pointedly.

"True." Agrippa laughed. "I shall have to watch him when he gets older. With such qualifications, he might even rule one day in my stead."

"Mariamne and I want no more of Judaea and political affairs," Prochorus assured him.

"So?" Now there was a definite edge to Agrippa's voice. "You would tread upon a larger stage, that of Syria perhaps?"

"I must go." Kypros cut off any answer Prochorus would have made immediately. "You must bring Mariamne and the baby to see me, Prochorus. She was always my favorite niece, far more than Salome." As the Queen left the room, Agrippa waved Prochorus to a chair and seated himself.

"You may go," he told the scribe. "But leave your writing ma-terials here. I shall need you again before the morning is over."

When the scribe had closed the door, Agrippa said: "Kypros in-terrupted your answer to my question about your purpose in going to Antioch. Or is it a secret?"

"No," said Prochorus. "From now on I expect to teach the Nazarene faith in other parts of the world."

"Why not here?"

"The field is too restricted. Besides, you seem determined to stamp it out."

"The High Priest Matthias tells me you Nazarenes have sworn to destroy Jerusalem and the Temple. That alone would be enough to convict any Nazarene of blasphemy and send him to the Place of Stoning."

"The High Priest lies, even as others have lied before him when they wished to destroy us. We are Jews like any other congregation. And," he added pointedly, "protected by the Roman Law of Associations."

"It would appear not to apply in this case," said Agrippa.

"On the contrary," said Prochorus. "I was freed from a Roman prison by the Emperor himself on that basis alone at the request of Philo of Alexandria. An edict sent out by the Emperor at that time gives Jews everywhere the right to practice their religion unhindered. Surely you have seen it."

"Of course, but Claudius is in Britain. As a self-proclaimed Nazarene, perhaps you should remember that."

"I am still a Roman citizen, with the right to appeal to Caesar," Prochorus said bluntly. "Are you going to try to take that from me?"

"Certainly not." Agrippa was suddenly affable and Prochorus was quite certain of the reason—the stumbling block of Roman citizenship which the King had apparently forgotten. "We were friends years ago and there's no reason why we can't be now, Prochorus. What brings you to Jerusalem?"

"I didn't come for that but just now Queen Kypros asked me to persuade you to curb your ambition."

"For what?" Agrippa's tone was suddenly guarded.

"To rule in all of Syria perhaps."

"Women don't understand politics." Agrippa changed the subject. "What did you say brought you to Jerusalem?"

"I am here in the capacity of an advocate, to plead for the release of a prisoner."

"His name?"

"Simon Peter."

"The fisherman who is one of the leaders of the new sect?"

"Yes."

"I have already had one of the Nazarene's disciples beheaded."

"With no justification under the law."

Agrippa's eyes suddenly blazed with anger, then just as quickly filmed over, as if a curtain had been drawn across them, hiding his thoughts.

"You seem intent on picking a quarrel with me," he said. "I wonder why?"

"Perhaps the memory of the months I spent in a Roman prison after the death of the Emperor Caligula has influenced my thinking. Or the fact that my wife, my son and I have been in hiding because we were not sure our lives were safe after you became King of Judaea."

"'You accuse me unjustly," Agrippa protested, and whether the hurt in his voice was real or feigned, Prochorus could not be sure. "Even after Caligula died, the charge of treason was still in effect against you. Emperor Claudius is a cautious man. If I had applied for your release at once, he might have seen it as an opening wedge in a campaign to have amnesty granted to all political prisoners and would have refused. Then your case would have come up for immediate trial and you might have been condemned and lost your head."

There was just enough logic in the glib explanation for it to be true, though Prochorus was fairly certain that it was not.

"After the Emperor embarked on the campaign in Britain, I made application to the Roman courts to have you released in my custody, planning to free you and give you a position of importance in my kingdom," Agrippa continued. "After all, you governed Jerusalem more successfully than anyone did before me. But you were gone then and no one knew where."

It would have been easy to believe him and Prochorus was too kindly by nature to shut his mind entirely to the other man's explanation. Nevertheless, he did not take it completely at face value.

"Where were you by the way?" Agrippa asked casually.

"I went with Philo Judaeus to Alexandria." It was no lie to tell a half-truth and, as he had hoped, Agrippa took it for the whole.

"A fine city, Alexandria, particularly for one with intelligence and philosophical inclinations like yourself. If I were of the same temperament as you, I could choose no better place to live. Did you know that my eldest daughter, Berenice, was married to Mark, the son of Alexander the Alabarch?"

Prochorus hesitated, for if he denied the knowledge, it could reveal that he had been elsewhere much of the time. Fortunately, Agrippa did not seem to expect an answer.

"It was a great tragedy when Mark died so young," he said. "But Berenice is married to my brother Herod of Chalcis now— and very happy."

"I remember her from Caesarea Philippi and Tiberias, she is very lovely."

"Not as much as my younger daughter Drusilla, or your Mariamne," said Agrippa. "Berenice is possessed of a strong spirit like me —and like Mariamne, as I remember her."

"I count myself very fortunate to be married to her," said Prochorus.

"And to have a son who will not be snatched away to Rome when you've hardly had a chance to know him." This time Prochorus was sure the tinge of sadness in Agrippa's voice was real.

"When will Prince Agrippa be returning to Jerusalem?"

"Whenever Claudius is convinced he can trust me unreservedly, I suppose. Wouldn't you think he would be sure of my loyalty, when it was I who convinced both the Senate and the Praetorian Guard that he was a logical choice as Emperor?"

"Did you expect him to be as strong as he has turned out to be?"

"No." Agrippa chuckled. "If you could have seen him when I came to take him to the Forum to be crowned; he was still hiding, afraid the Praetorians would assassinate him as they did poor Caligula. But enough of the past. What can I do for you?"

"You can free Simon Peter."

"That is impossible. That man I executed—what was his name?"

"James ben Zebedee."

"He was known to have associated with Manahem and other rebels—"

"That was a long time ago, when a group of the disciples of Jesus of Nazareth tried to make him King of Judaea. James had nothing to do with them for ten years."

"Perhaps, but I was told differently and treason is still treason. This Simon Peter goes about preaching that Annas and Joseph ben Caiaphas conspired to have the Nazarene crucified illegally."

"That fact is beyond question," Prochorus said bluntly. "The records left by Pontius Pilate show it and Pilate was reprimanded by the Legate Flaccus because of it. I was there at the time."

"We still can't have a man going about shouting that the family of the High Priest are murderers. Besides, the Nazarenes teach that a Messiah shall come and tear down the Temple."

"Not tear it down, only that it will fall. Don't forget that several other temples have been destroyed on the same site. And the prophets repeatedly foretold the destruction of the Temple."

"Nevertheless that is blasphemy."

"Peter was tried once before the full Sanhedrin on that charge—and freed."

The look of surprise on Agrippa's face told Prochorus the King of Judaea had not known this, which meant that in their plottings against the Nazarene congregation the family of Annas had not told him the whole truth.

"Are you sure?" Agrippa demanded.

"Rabban Gamaliel is still alive. He spoke in favor of Peter and John—"

"John ben Zebedee?"

"Yes."

"I signed an order for his arrest too."

"John is on his way to a safe place. He is no more guilty than Peter or James."

"I wonder why I don't order your arrest for helping an accused criminal escape," Agrippa said thoughtfully. "Perhap it's because I admire a character as strong as my own, a man who doesn't fear death."

"Peter is my friend and John ben Zebedee showed me the way to eternal life," said Prochorus. "I must save them both if I can."

"You mentioned Rabban Gamaliel just now," said Agrippa. "What did you mean?"

"When Peter and John were brought before the Sanhedrin—not the Priestly Council that was controlled for years by Annas and his sons—on the same charges, Gamaliel warned the court that, if what Peter and John said and did was the work of men, it would come to nought. But that if it were the will of God that they should speak out and perform miracles as they were doing, the court should not hamper them, lest it find itself going against the will of God."

"The argument is logical," Agrippa conceded.

"The same could apply to you. Even the King of the Jews cannot go against God; others have tried it in the past and were stricken down for their pains."

"You should have been a lawyer." Agrippa shook himself as if to throw off the burden of Prochorus' argument. "You can twist facts into any pattern you wish—and very convincingly, too. But it is still true that this man Peter denounced God's High Priest and for that alone he would deserve death according to Jewish law. I would have executed him along with the lesser fry, but he is important enough to be saved for a public occasion—probably the Feast of Pentecost."

"Would you release Peter if I took his place?"

"No—for two reasons. First, your mind is too valuable to Rome and, I hope someday when you have come to your senses again, to me. Second, you are guilty only of impertinence toward me, which I can forgive because you once did both me and the Jewish people a great service. And because, even stubborn as you are, I admire you."

He had failed, Prochorus saw, but knowing Agrippa as he did, he had not really expected any argument, except one that promised some tangible reward for Agrippa himself in return for Peter's life, to succeed. Without arguing further, he made his final move.

"I will make a bargain with you," he offered.

"What sort of a bargain?"

"Is it true that you are going to Caesarea in a few days to receive the capitulation of representatives from Tyre and Sidon, after the Phoenicians were forced to their knees by your embargo on grain and other foods from Galilee and Auranitis?"

"Yes. Everybody knows that."

"Yet you cannot resume the shipments."

"Why do you say that?" Agrippa's eyes were wary now.

"Manahem and the other sons of Judas the Gaulonite are in the hills between Galilee and the Phoenician cities with a large band of brigands. If you pay the tribute they will demand on whatever moves toward Phoenicia, you will make no profit from having Tyre and Sidon in your camp. If you don't, you will not be able to furnish the food you are going to promise the Phoenicians next week in Caesarea."

"By Jupiter!" The explosion betrayed the Roman side of Agrippa. "You presume much—even upon our friendship."

"Only because the life of a fellow man is dear to me."

"Are you telling me you can persuade the brigands to let the food shipments pass unhindered?"

"Far from it. But I know Manahem—"

"Is that where you were hiding?"

"I haven't been in Galilee in three years, but I first met Manahem there at the time Jesus was being crucified here in Jerusalem. He was in league then with the Tetrarch Antipas in order to put Pontius Pilate in a bad light so Antipas would be appointed governor of Judaea and Samaria instead of Pilate."

"I always suspected that, but I never was able to find any proof."

"It doesn't matter now that both Pilate and Antipas have been banished to Gaul."

"Pilate is dead, at Vien. And Antipas, too."

"But Manahem is very much alive and as strong as ever—perhaps stronger."

"Do you know how to reach him?"

"Yes."

"What do you propose to tell him if you do?"

"That you will take him and his men into your service, paying them well to guard the caravan route connecting Galilee and

Auranitis with the Phoenician coast. Then, when you go to Rome to convince the Emperor Claudius that you should rule all of Syria instead of a legate, a strong argument in your favor will be the fact that you have removed the threat of robbery from most of the country."

"You are clever," Agrippa said, half grudgingly, half admiringly. "I sometimes wonder whether you don't know me even better than I know myself. What reward do you wish, if you succeed in this endeavor?"

"The life of Simon Peter."

"Nothing for yourself?"

"When my task is finished I shall leave your jurisdiction—for Cappadocia or perhaps Pontus."

"I can place you in the service of the King of Pontus."

"I shall be preaching to the poor and the downtrodden. A recommendation to the King would only make them look on me with suspicion. What is your decision?"

"I accept." Agrippa had never been one to dally. "Bring Manahem to Caesarea so I can talk to him face to face and I will give you an order for your friend's release."

"I shall need a safe conduct. Manahem wouldn't believe even me without it."

"You shall have it as soon as I can call my scribe."

"I can write that myself," said Prochorus. "After I leave Caesarea I shall have to rely on my old occupation to provide food for myself and my family."

Pulling a sheet of parchment before him on the table, he dipped a quill in an ink cup and wrote:

The bearer, Prochorus ben Chuza, and those who accompany him, are in my service. They will not be interfered with in any way and all they meet are hereby ordered to give them every assistance in reaching me.

Glancing over the words swiftly, the King seized the pen and scrawled "Agrippa Rex" across the bottom of the sheet, upon which he then poured sand to dry the ink.

"What are you doing?" he asked as Prochorus reached for another parchment sheet.

"Writing the order for Simon Peter's release."

"The order shall be given, but only when Manahem comes to me in Caesarea."

"I still insist on its being written in my own words," said Prochorus, and for a moment the two men faced each other across the table, like gladiators in the arena. Then Agrippa shrugged.

"Write the order and I will sign it," he said. "But I shall keep it with me until you have fulfilled your share of the bargain."

"Agreed." Prochorus picked up the pen again, wrote the order for Peter's release, and handed Agrippa the quill.

"I don't think you trust me entirely—which is a pity." Agrippa signed the sheet, poured sand on it and dusted it off before rolling it up and tying it with a bit of string. "If I am to expand my kingdom, I shall need civil servants, fellow Jews I can trust. The trouble with subject rulers is that most of them aspire to displace those in authority over them. Even my brother Herod of Chalcis has ambitions, but Berenice is looking after my interest there. She adores my son and will not see his inheritance nibbled away."

"Why aren't you content with what your grandfather ruled? That would seem to be enough for any man."

"Claudius rules more, yet but for me he wouldn't rule at all." Agrippa's face hardened. "Vibius Marsus was once my friend, too, but now he has become a jackal who sits in Antioch, waiting only for every opportunity to jail me, in case I aspire to more than I have now."

"Which you are doing anyway."

"But legally, don't forget that. A week from now in Caesarea, I shall take a long step toward achieving my goals. Tyre will give me a fine seaport and at Berytus I already have the means of making Roman petty officials fancy they are living like kings. Before Marsus knows what is happening, I shall see that he is sent back to Rome and I am appointed in his place."

"As Legate?"

"As King. Claudius' Roman campaign has secured the western frontier. When I point out to him that I can keep the eastern frontier secure he is sure to see that having me as King in Antioch is to his advantage."

"Can you be sure Artaban of Parthia will accept that?"

"Aretas and I already see eye to eye as far as this part of the world is concerned. With us controlling the caravan routes leading both to Egypt and to the West, Artaban will have little choice except to follow along with us."

"It's a grandiose scheme. Between the three of you, practically the entire eastern half of the Roman world would be under your control."

"My control," Agrippa corrected him. "Neither Aretas in Nabatea nor Artaban in Persia knows anything about Roman politics. I shall be their spokesman to Claudius, which means that for all practical purposes I shall rule the area myself."

"I doubt that even your grandfather aspired to that much."

"My grandfather was the son of an Idumean chieftain. The world he grew up in was small, limited by what I already rule. I was reared in a much wider world—with no limits at all."

"And so your ambition has no limits?"

"None except what, as a practical individual, I realize they must be." Agrippa grinned. "Could you imagine even a one-quarter Jew ruling in Rome?"

"Hardly."

"Here in the East, though, large colonies of Jews are found in every important city, controlling the very lifeblood of the region through the flow of money and trade. Every Jew looks toward Jerusalem and the Temple and, since I control them both, he looks toward me, whether he realizes it or not. One day the Jews of the Diaspora will be the agents who will help me seize control wherever I wish."

Agrippa smiled and reached an arm across Prochorus' shoulder in a gesture of comradeship as he guided him toward the door. "You can play a great part in this plan, if you will join with me. After all, we are kinsmen by marriage, bound together by the common bond that our children carry in their veins the blood of my grandfather Herod.

"Make no decision now," he said when Prochorus started to

object. "Complete your work in Caesarea and free your friend—if you can. Then think about what I have said and decide where your future lies—yours, your wife's and your son's. After all, a great-granddaughter of Herod and a princess of the Hasmonean house should not be simply the wife of an itinerant preacher and scribe."

"Mariamne has been content so far."

"Has she? Or does she simply tell you so because she loves you? Make certain the time doesn't come when she looks on what she could have had and hates you because of it. I shall expect you a week from now in Caesarea," he added briskly. "And I shall be very happy to see your mission succeed, even if it means releasing your friend from prison."

vi

Leaving the Palace of the Hasmoneans, Prochorus crossed the Tyropean Valley on one of the several bridges allowing access to the Sanctuary area from that part of the city and turned northward toward the fortress of Antonia. Everywhere he could see evidence of Agrippa's determination to carry the construction of the entire Temple area to final completion; new stone paving was easily distinguishable from the old, as well as repairs to crumbling walls and the sluices that carried off the water, when the torrential spring rains descended upon the area.

On the way he passed a seller of thornwood plodding along ahead of his donkey, its pack frame piled high with the dry wood that burned with such a hot flame in the kilns of the potters, yet left almost no ash. He could visualize in his mind another scene in which the thorns had played a part, a picture of a gentle man upon whose brow a crown of the green burnet bush had been pressed, until the needle-sharp points lacerated his forehead and sent blood trickling down his face. And he uttered a silent prayer that he would be able to free Simon Peter so the big fisherman, who had risked his own safety to comfort him in the prison at Rome, would not suffer torture on one of the crosses whose stark upright posts, left in place between crucifixions, loomed against the noonday sky on a hill ahead. Or from the stones that had beaten the body of Stephen to a bloody pulp in a corner of the east wall just north of the Temple area.

At the gate of the Antonia, Prochorus asked for the centurion in charge and was shortly ushered into the presence of a rugged man with weather-beaten features and grizzled hair.

"My name is Prochorus," he said. "I am a friend of Cornelius of the Italian Band and of Sextus Latimus."

"I know them both well." The officer gave him the ritual grip of greeting. "My name is Lysimachus. Did you know that Cornelius has been raised to the rank of tribune by the Legate Marsus?"

"I heard of it; the honor is well deserved." Prochorus grinned. "Would you believe that I was once a tribune for a few weeks, when Vitellius was negotiating a treaty with King Artaban years ago?"

"You must be the one who retook the fortress of Machaerus."

"With the help of Sextus Latimus."

"However it was done, it was a remarkable accomplishment," said Lysimachus. "How can I serve you, sir?"

"I am only a scribe now. It is I who should call you sir."

"Then we shall call each other by our real names. Where did you know Cornelius?"

"In the prison at Rome. Caligula held me for treason because I am a Nazarene."

"We have one of your fellow Nazarenes in prison."

"He is my friend."

"Oddly enough," said Lysimachus, "there are many such among the troops of the garrison."

"How can that be?"

"This cohort served for a time in Cilicia. A number of them were converted there by a very eloquent tentmaker—"

"Saul of Tarsus!"

"Do you know him?"

"I know of his work—and friends of mine are friends of his."

"From what I hear, he has so stirred the men of Antioch with his preaching that the priests in the Temple of Diana have started to plot his death."

"Could I possibly see Simon Peter?" Prochorus asked, but Lysimachus shook his head.

"Your friend is chained in the deepest dungeon and I have strict orders that no one is to visit him."

"Could you give him a message for me?"

"Of course."

"Tell him to take courage. I may be able to bring about his release."

"You will have to work fast then," said Lysimachus. "His trial before the Jewish court is set for the day after tomorrow. As soon as they reach a verdict he will be sent to King Agrippa for sentencing."

"I thought Peter's execution was to take place during the Feast of Pentecost."

"That may be," said Lysimachus. "I think Agrippa wants to have the verdict of the Sanhedrin recorded before he leaves for Caesarea. Then if he decides not to return for Pentecost, he can always order it carried out here in his absence and thereby escape some of the anger of those who feel that Peter was unjustly condemned."

"That must be the answer," Prochorus agreed. He couldn't help wondering whether he could trust Agrippa to keep his side of the bargain, however, and so decided to go in search of Manahem and arrange the visit to Caesarea as soon as possible.

One further precaution needed to be taken immediately, however, and Prochorus turned his attention to it after he had bidden Lysimachus farewell. Leaving the Antonia, he crossed the Sanctuary area to the southwest corner and followed the descending course of the Tyropean Valley to the Lower City and the house of Mary and Mark.

The young scribe listened intently while he told of his audience with Agrippa, the bargain he had made for Simon Peter's life, and the discussion with Lysimachus afterward at the Antonia.

"Do you think there is a chance that Rabban Gamaliel will

speak up once again at Peter's trial?" Prochorus asked but Mark shook his head.

"Gamaliel has retired from active participation in both his school and the court. He no longer even goes to the Porch of Solomon."

"Perhaps I should stay and defend Peter before the court. Many of the members know me from the time when I was Deputy Governor and might listen."

"You can help Peter more by going on with your plan," said Mark. "Agrippa has much to gain from making a pact with the brigands and opening the trade routes to Phoenicia from Galilee and the grain fields in the Valley of Jezreel south of Mount Carmel. He may not keep his bargain after you bring Manahem to Caesarea, but I think he will until you do. And with the King in Caesarea, we shall have a chance to plan some other way of delivering Peter."

"I shall leave for Galilee tomorrow then," said Prochorus. "But first I have a task for you—in Antioch."

"Antioch!" Mark's dark brown eyes lit up with surprise and pleasure. "I've wanted to go there ever since Barnabas left; he promised that I can accompany him and Saul, when they cross over to Crete to tell of Jesus there." Then his face sobered. "But it's more than a week's journey overland and I would arrive too late to help with your mission to Caesarea."

"There is a shorter way—by sea from Joppa," Prochorus reminded him. "If a ship doesn't come by the day after you get there, you can hire a fishing boat."

"I don't have that much money."

"Nor I. But I shall write a letter to Cornelius and the Legate Vibius Marsus for you to take with you. They will gladly pay your passage, once they read it."

The letter Prochorus wrote to Cornelius and Vibius Marsus that night was a long one. In it he set down everything he had learned about Agrippa's ambition to rule in Antioch, including the words of the King of Judaea himself. When it was finished, he sealed it, impressing into the soft wax the imperial inscription from the heavy seal ring which, as a former Roman official, he had been allowed to use. That right was no longer officially his, but he was counting on the seal to impress the master of the fishing boat with whom Mark might have to deal, if it became necessary to charter passage for the usually no more than two days' sail to Antioch.

vii

The morning was bright and sunny, when Prochorus departed for Galilee—and Mark for Joppa. Mark walked, since Joppa was less than a day's journey away, but Prochorus had purchased a horse because the time at his disposal was growing shorter by the hour. For the same reason, he took the most direct route to Galilee.

Known as the Central Highway, the official road through central Judaea and Samaria was not stone-paved, as were Roman roads in many parts of the empire, but was nevertheless a fairly heavily traveled thoroughfare. Following the crest of the central mountain ranges of Samaria, Prochorus moved steadily northward past the old cities of Bethel, Shechem and Samaria—renamed Sebaste after its reconstruction by Herod the Great—to where the road he was following joined the Way of the Sea, the great caravan route between Egypt and the Tigris-Euphrates basin.

This was a region sacred to Israel's memory, the land where Abraham and the patriarchs had pastured their flocks nearly two thousand years before. On another occasion, Prochorus would have liked nothing better than to pause and explore it, particularly with Mariamne beside him and his son a little older, so he might tell small John the exciting tales of Israel's past and watch his bright-eyed wonder as the stirring procession of heroic figures passed in review. But there was no time to be lost now, and late on the second day he paused to rest his weary mount upon a peak from which he could look down on Nazareth, crowning the top of a hill some distance away to the north.

It was an impressive view by any standard of comparison. To the west, the towering peak of Mount Carmel jutted out into the Mediterranean, the Mare Nostrum of the Romans. To the south lay the broad Plain of Esdraelon, only a little less fertile than the teeming region around the Sea of Galilee, while eastward rose the heights of Mount Tabor. Far to the north, shining like a beacon as the late afternoon sunlight turned its snow-clad summit into a pinkish crown, stood Mount Hermon.

Dominating the immediate area from a point some four or five miles to the north was Sepphoris, whose arsenal of rusty weapons, cached there during the rebellion of Judas the Gaulonite decades before, had brought about the downfall of Herod Antipas. Along the roads leading into Sepphoris from the Valley of Esdraelon, Prochorus could see carts and wagons hauling produce from the fields for the markets of the city. Though no longer the capital of the area as it had been in the time of Herod the Great, Sepphoris was still an important population center, as well as the location of the largest Roman garrison in the area, stationed there to help keep open the roads, which Agrippa must be able to use for the shipment of grain and other products from the fertile fields of that region to his new Phoenician allies. It was because of this obligation that he had been obliged to come to terms with Manahem and his followers, for the country was wild and forbidding and Roman troops were not very effective in such territory.

At a spring bursting from the craggy hillside in the Valley of the Doves, Prochorus paused to water his mount. The myriads of birds that made their home here in a narrow defile, perhaps a mile in extent, set up a bedlam of protest at being disturbed so late in the afternoon, when most travelers had already found shelter for the night. Daily men from the surrounding villages went into the defile with nets to trap the beautiful white birds for shipment to the sellers of doves in the Temple at Jerusalem, where they were prized as inexpensive objects for sacrifice. In hundreds of nests among the trees, Prochorus could see mother doves warming their eggs, or busy feeding the newly hatched fledglings, while, perched on the highest limbs, sentinel males watched the hawks and other predators that always circled above the gorge ready to swoop down and rob the nests of the succulent newly hatched birds. At a warning cry from one of the sentinels, a veritable cloud of angry doves would rise from the gorge to drive the invader away by the sheer force of numbers.

Where the Way of the Sea—proceeding northeastward toward Capernaum and the northern end of the Lake of Tiberias—crossed the road leading from Magdala and Tiberias on the lake shore westward to Ptolemais and the Phoenician cities, as well as southwestward to Caesarea, Prochorus turned eastward and soon came to his old home at Magdala. It had been years since he had seen his parents and there was a joyous reunion that night in the house overlooking the lake. After the evening meal, the three of them sat outside in the cool twilight watching the bobbing lights of the fishing fleet making its nightly journey northward to where the clear cold stream of the Jordan, pouring into the warmer waters of the lake, caused the fish to school as they had done throughout the memory of anyone now living and, indeed, of any written record.

"The country seems to be prospering," Prochorus observed. "I saw more carts on the road than I ever remember seeing before."

"Agrippa has just lifted the embargo on the shipment of grain and produce to the Phoenician cities," Chuza explained. "The farmers are bringing their crops into the markets of Tiberias and Sepphoris but soon they will be glutted and things will be once again as they were a few months ago, when the embargo was in effect."

"Then the caravan trails are still blocked by the brigands?"

"Worse than ever before."

"But Agrippa is a Jewish king. In Jerusalem, he seems to be very popular."

"He favors Jerusalem, so the priests will support him," said Chuza. "But here in Galilee taxes are heavier than they have ever been and people are angry because Agrippa has poured so much money into Berytus, which isn't even a Jewish city. The thousand men slain during the games, so the blood lust of Agrippa's Roman and Greek friends could be satisfied, are a bloody stain on his record too."

"In Jerusalem they say it was fifteen hundred."

"The story varies," said Joanna. "But even one death would stain his hands with blood and render him unclean."

"Then Galilee was actually better off with Antipas?"

"Far better," said Chuza. "Then a merchant sending grain and produce to Phoenicia or Caesarea knew how much he would have to pay the robbers—"

"And that part of it would filter back into the coffers of Antipas?"

"Yes. But at least the money was spent here in Galilee and Peraea, not in some heathen city like Berytus."

"Why would Agrippa build there?"

"To court the favor of the Phoenician merchants, why else?" said Chuza. "In the time of Solomon, Phoenician ships sailed from Ezion Geber in the south to the eastern coast of African and even to India. Agrippa hopes to regain that trade too."

"But the Nabateans control the caravan routes southward to Egypt and the Red Sea by way of the Arabah."

"King Aretas hated Antipas, because of his daughter. But he and Agrippa are close friends and allies."

"Then it's true that Agrippa hopes to form an empire here in the East, with himself as King."

"Not just as King," said Chuza. "Emperor."

"Emperor?" Prochorus exclaimed. "The man must be mad."

"Perhaps," said Chuza. "But one has only to watch his acts since he became King of Ituraea after Philip died to see the pattern. Once he rules the entire East as King, Agrippa can break away from Rome and declare himself Emperor."

"Would Rome allow it?"

"The real question is, could Claudius prevent it? In any war, three fourths or more of the troops who fight it are raised in the area where the fighting occurs. With Agrippa Emperor of an Eastern empire that included not only Syria but also Nabatea, Parthia and probably part of Asia—at least as far as the Propontis and the Hellespont—how could even Rome stand against him?"

"Then it was no accident that men like Polemon of Pontus were invited to the feast at Tiberias last year?"

"Accident?" Chuza's snort was eloquent. "It was part of an elaborate plan to gain a foothold north of Antioch, as he has already gained one on the Phoenician coast. Don't forget either that Alexander, one of the sons of Herod the Great, married

Glaphyra, the daughter of Archelaus, who was the last King of Cappadocia. Or that the King of Armenia was Polemon's son. There are large Jewish colonies in all those territories, so Agrippa has eyes and ears everywhere."

"I heard that he was furious when Vibius Marsus privately advised the kings who had been invited to Tiberias to go home."

"He was angry, but not too angry to give up the scheme. The kings returned to their homes, but Agrippa immediately put the embargo on wheat and other shipments to Phoenicia." Chuza shook his head. "He is like that creature in the Greek stories you used to read when you were a boy, the one who had snakes for her hair."

"Medusa—one of the Gorgons."

"As I remember it, every time one of those snakes was cut off, another grew back in its place. That's Agrippa. Cut him down in one area and he immediately springs up in another."

"The gaze of the Gorgons was supposed to turn the viewer into stone," said Prochorus.

"Not Agrippa. He has the power to charm even his enemies."

"No one knows that better than I," Prochorus agreed. "Tell me more about these Jewish colonies in Cappadocia and Pontus."

"I know little, except that they exist."

"Didn't Simon Peter visit there when he left Rome, while I was in prison?"

"I have heard that, but not from Peter."

"Mary of Magdala told us about it," said Joanna.

"Mary!" Prochorus' face lit up at the name. "Is she back in Magdala?"

"Yes. She and her husband Joseph, the physician, fled to Petra during the persecution by Saul. But when Saul was stricken by a fever while fleeing for his life from Damascus, he sought refuge with them in Petra. Mary and Joseph came back and are living here in Magdala again.

"Now we Nazarenes are being persecuted once again—by Agrippa," said Joanna sadly. "There never seems to be any end to it."

"I expect to bring about Peter's release from prison and I don't believe Agrippa will resume the persecution after Peter is free."

Prochorus quickly explained the reason for his presence in Magdala but, long before he had finished, Chuza's expression was troubled.

"Manahem might agree to a conference of peace," he said. "After all, he grows older like all of us, and it isn't pleasant for an old man to live in caves and hide from the soldiers, particularly in winter. But can you trust Agrippa to keep his promise to you?"

"It's my only chance to free Peter. I shall have to take it."

"What if Agrippa arrests him again?"

"I hope to persuade Peter to go northward with me, probably into Cappadocia and Pontus. Mariamne and litttle John have gone on to Antioch by ship and, when my mission in Caesarea is finished, I hope to undertake the task of spreading news about the Way of Jesus in that region. Mark says Saul and Barnabas are ready to depart for Crete to carry the gospel there and possibly to Pamphylia and Galatia on the mainland of Asia."

"It is a worthy aim," said Joanna. "I could not wish for you to serve the Lord in a better way."

"Beware the plottings of Agrippa, my son," Chuza warned, "and look behind as often as you do before. His way is that of a knife in the back and he is never more dangerous than when he seems to be your friend."

viii

Walking toward Tiberias, whose white buildings gleamed in the morning sunlight—he had left his horse with his father at Magdala, for a mount was of no value in the sort of terrain where the brigands lived—Prochorus was swept back nearly a decade and a half to the time when he had followed this very road with Mariamne the day before he had set out on the journey to Jerusalem that had marked such a complete turning point in his life. Mariamne's hand had been in his then and she had chattered gaily beside him as they walked along, stumbling a little at times because of his mother's overlarge sandals and clinging to him for support. The memory brought an answering warmth in his heart and a prayer that they might be joined again before long—this time with little John beside them.

At the crest of the road across the cliff overlooking the lake, he recognized the great boulder upon which he had stood on another morning and watched the happy party of Galileans on the way to Jerusalem with Jesus of Nazareth to celebrate the Passover.

He almost expected Manahem to appear in the roadway, like an apparition materializing out of thin air, as he had that same morning after the Nazarene and his party passed. But the road was empty, save for himself, and he concentrated on trying to pick out the crevice in the rocks from which Manahem's sentry had appeared on the afternoon when Mariamne had been with him. Behind that crevice, he knew, lay the path that wound up along the rocky hillside to the cave where he had been taken to meet the brigand leader.

He had no way of knowing whether Manahem was still using the cave. But even if he weren't, it was still an excellent vantage point from which watchers could detect the movements of caravans along the roads leading westward toward Phoenicia and warn the main body of the brigands whenever a likely prey appeared.

The crevice was well hidden and he passed it once without seeing it. But when he retraced his steps more slowly, he was able to make it out, a narrow passageway through the boulders lining the road, barely wide enough for him to squeeze through. When he found a well-worn path just inside the crevice leading steadily upward, he knew he had taken the first step toward finding his quarry.

He saw no one until he reached the top of the hill and the whole vast panorama of the lake country was spread out before him, from Bethsaida Julias in the north to Taricheae and the beginning once again of the Jordan at the south end of the lake. Then, as he paused to rest upon a prominently placed boulder where he was sure he could be seen for some distance in any direction, he heard the sound of movement and looked down to see a fierce-looking man in a rough homespun tunic holding a spear so the point was only an arm's span or two from his body.

"Who are you?" Prochorus thought at first it was Manahem, but a second glance told him the other was considerably younger.

"Prochorus ben Chuza. I am a friend of Manahem."

"Prochorus ben Chuza died in a Roman prison."

"I was freed and I have been in hiding," Prochorus explained.

"Where?"

"With the Essenes on the shore of the Salt Sea north of Engedi." Now that Mariamne and little John were safely on the way to Antioch, there seemed to be no point in keeping their hiding place a secret any longer. "Who are you?"

"Simon, the brother of Manahem."

"That accounts for the resemblance. Will you take me to your brother?"

"Why?"

"I have a message for him—from King Agrippa."

The young brigand's surprise showed in his face. "Agrippa has issued an order for Manahem's arrest."

"Nevertheless I carry a safe conduct signed by King Agrippa for myself and anyone who accompanies me." Prochorus held up the parchment sheet. "Your brother will be interested in what I have to say."

"You must be blindfolded," said Simon.

"If you insist," Prochorus said resignedly. "But your brother will tell you I wouldn't betray you."

The blindfold, the girdle of Prochorus' own robe, was quickly tied and the journey began. Walking would have been extremely difficult if Simon had been more adept at tying blindfolds but the lower edge of the cloth was held outward by the bridge of Prochorus' nose. By turning his eyes downward as far as he could, he was able to watch a small section of the path just in front of his feet and thus escape stumbling over small objects. Nevertheless, by the time he was brought to a halt and the blindfold was removed, his head was aching and he was thoroughly irritated with his captor.

Blinking a little to accustom his eyes once again to the bright light of the morning sun, Prochorus found himself in a natural clearing before the mouth of a cave. A bed of coals smoldered at one side of the clearing; over it was a haunch of goat meat beside a blackened and sooty pot in which a mixture of what appeared to be lentils, chick-peas and onions bubbled with a savory aroma.

Manahem sat on a rock not far from the fire. At his first glance, Prochorus was shocked by the change in the bandit chieftain for the years and the rigorous winter climate of the Galilean uplands had not been kind to the eldest son of the man who had once set the whole country aflame. Manahem's beard was almost white now and much of his hair was gone. One of his hands was gnarled by rheumatism and the robe he wore was of heavy cloth, though it was spring and the weather was already warm. All this, plus the fact that Manahem sat closer to the coals than anyone else, told Prochorus the bandit leader was not in the best of health—as Chuza had intimated last night.

"Prochorus ben Chuza." There was no lessening of the fires of interest in Manahem's eyes or the vigor of his voice. "Or have you undergone a resurrection—as the Nazarene's followers claim for him?"

"I am the same," said Prochorus, but Manahem shook his head, a little sadly.

"None of us are the same—or ever will be again. We were told you died in Rome. How did you escape?"

"Philo of Alexandria pleaded my cause with Claudius—after King Agrippa deserted me."

"Because if you came to Judaea people would learn that it was you and not Agrippa who planned the scheme to keep the image of Caligula out of the Holy of Holies."

"How did you know?"

"We may dwell in caves and attack from ambush, but we have friends in high places, even in the palace of the Legate at Antioch. Vibius Marsus has not hesitated to give you credit publicly."

"For which we owe the son of Chuza no thanks," growled a heavy-set man of about thirty whom Prochorus hadn't noticed before.

"You must forgive our kinsman, Eleazar, his bad manners, friend Prochorus," said Manahem. "Nevertheless he is right. If Petronius had obeyed the Emperor's orders and placed the statue in the Holy of Holies, the whole land would have risen up."

"With you as leader?"

"Who has the better right?" Manahem's eyes blazed for a moment, then the fires as quickly faded. "But I have no secrets from you, do I, Prochorus? You were with Herod Antipas when I was robbing caravans in Judaea to reveal the weakness of Pontius Pilate."

"And planning to seize Jerusalem in the name of Jesus of Nazareth."

A muttered interjection came from Eleazar but Manahem hushed any words he might have uttered with an upraised hand.

"I told you we have no secrets from Prochorus," he said. "Nor do we have reason to fear him, either. He is something our nation has produced perhaps only once before—and *he* was crucified—a completely honest man. Obviously you sought me out." Manahem addressed Prochorus again. "What brings you back to Galilee after all these years?"

Prochorus took the parchment sheet upon which he had written the safe conduct and handed it to Manahem. "Read this," he said, "then ask me what you will." Manahem read the sheet carefully and handed it back without showing it to any of the others.

"Perhaps you would like to rest inside the cave until the food is ready," he said. "I have some excellent wine from the grapevines of the Gennesaret plain. It was intended for Agrippa's highborn Roman friends at Berytus."

As Prochorus followed Manahem into the cave, which was quite roomy, though cool after the warmth outside, he saw the other man shiver and draw his robe closer around his shoulders.

"I'm getting old, friend Prochorus," he said. "Too old to be living in dampness and cold. I need a home and a place in the sun where I can sit—"

"And talk with the old men?" Prochorus asked with a smile, to which Manahem grinned.

"I have not yet come to that, though my brothers Simon and James and that firebrand Eleazar out there seem to think so."

He poured wine into a beautifully fashioned silver cup and handed it to Prochorus, then filled another for himself and drank half of it, while Prochorus was tasting the exquisite bouquet of the wine, before asking: "Why would you risk your life to visit me with a safe conduct from Agrippa?"

"James ben Zebedee has been beheaded and Simon Peter is in prison."

"I heard that. Did John ben Zebedee escape?"

"Yes. He has gone to Antioch with my wife and my son."

"A son! How fortunate you are! I have taken three wives but none have born me a son. Perhaps it's a curse—"

"Like the curse of Herod the Great?"

"I don't understand."

"The Torah says the sins of the fathers shall be visited upon the sons, the grandsons and the great-grandsons."

"Herod committed many sins, enough for all his descendants."

"Peter thinks the killing of the innocent children of Bethlehem, when the Messiah was born, has put a curse on the family of Herod."

"If there is such a curse the present wearer of Herod's crown seems to be thriving on it," Manahem said dryly.

"Peter thinks his time will come too."

"So it will for all of us. Now get on with your story."

"Agrippa is anxious for the supplies of grain and produce to start moving through to Phoenicia after he lifts the embargo next week."

"Especially since he is going to assure the men of Tyre and Sidon a few days from now in Caesarea that they will move?"

"Yes."

"He could insure that by paying us a tribute. It would save everyone a lot of trouble."

"Agrippa is prepared to do just that. I suggested it to him as part of the solution to the whole problem."

"Only part of it?"

"I also suggested that he take you and your men into his service to guard the roads."

Manahem started to laugh, then suddenly stopped. "You really mean that, don't you?"

"Of course."

"Why?"

"My only concern is to set Simon Peter free and stop further persecution of the Nazarenes. Agrippa wants to keep the good will of the chief priests, so he had James ben Zebedee beheaded and arrested Peter, but he wants something else even more."

Manahem nodded slowly. "To rule in all of Syria and perhaps more widely. But to do that he must have a private army of skilled fighting men who are not under Roman authority."

"I thought you would understand," said Prochorus. "The safe conduct was given me so I may take you to Caesarea to discuss the matter with Agrippa and arrive at an arrangement."

"You have lost none of your cunning," Manahem said with a note of admiration in his voice, then added quickly, "No, cunning is not the word; it applies only to those who have something to gain for themselves. Wisdom is perhaps a better word—or cleverness."

"Call it whatever you will," said Prochorus. "If I bring you to Caesarea for a conference with King Agrippa, he will release Simon Peter."

"Do you think he will keep his word—to both of us?"

"He has much to gain."

"And I much to lose—my life."

"Barabbas could carry on your work, couldn't he?" Prochorus asked but Manahem shook his head.

"Barabbas went mad two winters ago and hurled himself over a cliff."

"I heard nothing of it in Jerusalem."

"We managed to keep it a secret. Ever since he was released by Pontius Pilate, Barabbas had been growing more and more moody."

"Do you think knowing he gained his life through the crucifixion of the Son of God was the cause?"

"Perhaps. He certainly brooded a great deal over the whole thing."

"Are you going to accept Agrippa's offer?"

"I don't know; it will have to be discussed among us first. I would like to see that arena Agrippa has built in Caesarea, though.

They say the games he plans to hold there celebrating his victory over Tyre and Sidon will be as bloody as the ones held in Berytus."

"He has certainly come a long way since the day the owl lit over his head in Rome," Prochorus observed.

"Owl? What do you mean?"

Once again Prochorus told the story of the strange prediction of the German chieftain that, when next an owl appeared in the proximity of Agrippa, it would be an omen of death.

"What a burden it must be to carry that knowledge around with you all the time," said Manahem. "Now I know why they say Agrippa never goes hunting and avoids passing through wooded areas whenever he can."

"It's only a superstition."

"Dwelling here in the hills surrounded by caves and the remnants of dead cities, you can easily grow to believe in omens and warnings —the things you call superstition. Just now I have the feeling that Agrippa will not keep his word."

"Then you will not go to Caesarea?"

"I must talk with the others and sleep on it before I decide. After all, I have much to gain, as you say, and nothing to lose but my life—which isn't worth very much if I shall have to continue hiding in caves the rest of my days, while my joints stiffen and my body is racked by the ague."

ix

Prochorus remained inside the cave during the rest of the day; it was cool there and he was tired, so he spent much of the time sleeping. Whenever he awoke, he could hear voices outside, sometimes raised to an angry shout, and knew that Manahem and his followers were debating the offer he had brought from Agrippa. Finally, just as darkness began to fall, Simon, the younger brother, came into the cave and invited him outside.

The haunch of roast meat and the pot of lentils were in the center of a circle of men, some of whom had not been there that morning when Simon brought him to the brigand's headquarters, by which he

judged that most of the band in the immediate area had been called
in for the conference. In addition to the meat and vegetables, there
were flat cakes of bread which had been baked on stones set near
the coals, and fresh honey still in the comb. When Simon handed
him a wooden bowl, Prochorus took from his girdle—no longer
serving as a blindfold—the knife without which no traveler would
dare to be. Slicing off a piece of meat, he took one of the cakes
and expertly ladled a portion of the lentils and peas into the bowl,
then found a comfortable place with his back to a rock where he
could sit and eat.

"I see that city life in Rome didn't spoil you." Manahem looked
tired and his movements were slow as he ate.

"Hardly. I was in prison most of the time."

"Did Caligula really build a bridge of boats from Baiae to
Puteoli?" one of the bandits asked.

"So I was told," said Prochorus. "The whole thing happened
while I was in prison, so I never saw it."

"You were present when Herod Antipas negotiated the treaty with
Parthia on a bridge across the Euphrates, weren't you?"

"I was there, but Antipas was only an interpreter and observer, as
I was. The treaty was actually negotiated by the Legate Vitellius
and King Artaban."

There was a moment of silence, then another man asked: "How
much truth is there to the story that you took the castle of Machaerus
from King Aretas singlehanded?"

"Aretas gave up the castle, but I had powerful help—a Roman
centurion named Sextus Latimus." When a roar of laughter came
from the ring of men, he was sure he could detect a lessening of the
suspicion with which the newcomers had regarded him when he first
emerged from the cave.

"You can understand now why this man has been so successful,"
Manahem told the circle. "He isn't always boasting about his ex-
ploits—even though he has much to boast about. And you see why
I have decided to place my life in his hands."

Prochorus' heart took a sudden leap, for Manahem's words could
only mean that he had decided to go to Caesarea for the conference
with Agrippa and that Simon Peter would be free.

"When do we leave?" he asked.

"In the morning. Simon and James"—he indicated a wiry man who sat across the circle from him—"will accompany us."

"I still think it's folly not to take more men," said Eleazar with a scowl.

"We have debated that all day," Manahem said wearily. "What chance would ten men—or a hundred—have against the garrison at Caesarea? I am relying on Agrippa's word to protect me, but mainly on something I know I can count on without question—the integrity of my friend Prochorus."

The matter was settled then and Manahem went into the cave early to sleep. Having slept much of the day, Prochorus was not drowsy at the moment so he went to the edge of the clearing where he could be alone to think, conscious that more than one pair of eyes among the men in the encampment were watching him at all times.

Below, in a small valley, he could distinguish lights and decided that a village must be there, probably made up of the families of shepherds who each morning guided their flocks into the hills, where the grass grew lush and green in small pockets. Galilee was a land of beauty, though rarely of peace, and even though the earth itself was hidden by darkness, he knew that no part of it was more beautiful than this region around the lake, lying just out of sight to the east beyond a low ridge.

A verse from a poem he had read in Rome came to his mind and, although the Roman poet had been singing the praises of his own warm and fruitful land, his verse could just as well apply to the fertile cup in which lay the Galilean lake:

> But fruitful vines and the fat olive's freight,
> And harvests heavy with their fruitful wake,
> Adorn our fields: and on the cheerful green,
> The grazing flocks and lowing herds are seen. . . .
> Perpetual spring our happy climate sees,
> Twice breed the cattle and twice bear the trees.

The only quarrel with the words of the poet Prochorus could think of at the moment was the fact that, by judicious planting, it was quite possible along the fertile shore of the Sea of Galilee to grow as much as three crops a year. So brightly did the sun shine down into the deep cup in which the lake lay, and so protected were the fields, vineyards and groves lying there, that only during the hot summer months, when as many of the inhabitants as possible went up into the hills to escape the heat, was it impossible to grow the grain and the food which formed such an important source of export to the Phoenician cities of the coast and to Caesarea, the manmade seaport a little south of Mount Carmel.

A wave of sadness and nostalgia came over him at the thought of leaving this beautiful land, but he resolutely put the thought from him. The safety of his wife and his son was almost as important as the call of the Holy Spirit leading him to new tasks and new opportunities in the north. And from what he had learned about the region around the Black Sea, particularly the lands of Bithynia and Pontus along its shore and the mountains of Cappadocia lying inland from them, they almost equaled in beauty the land spread out before him now in the darkness.

"I spoke against what you propose to do." The harsh voice of Eleazar close beside him startled Prochorus; in his reverie, he had not heard the other man approach. "I think you are selling Manahem to Agrippa in return for the freedom of your friend."

"If Agrippa doesn't keep his word concerning Manahem, he will hardly keep it concerning Peter." Prochorus turned to face the brigand. "I have as much to lose as Manahem does."

"Not quite," said Eleazar. "Your Roman citizenship protects you from Agrippa but nothing except the word of the King protects Manahem."

"Or Peter."

"If Simon Peter was able to heal cripples in the Temple and raise a dead woman at Joppa, why can't he deliver himself from prison?"

"I don't know," Prochorus admitted.

"I say let Peter use his own powers."

"Manahem isn't going to Caesarea to save Peter. He's going because he thinks an alliance with King Agrippa may be better for him and the rest of you than being hunted all your lives."

"It's his brothers he's concerned about. Without Manahem—or

me—to protect them, they would be caught by the Romans in a week and crucified like their father was."

"Are you the leader of the band after Manahem?"

"I am the strongest of them all," Eleazar boasted.

"Then you need not be concerned. If Agrippa does seize Manahem —you are next in line as leader."

The silence that greeted the word told him the other man was thinking—and that the process was slow and somewhat painful. Eleazar, he suspected, was like so many who took up the trade of arms, or banditry, quick to attack and probably skilled in close combat but largely incapable of the mental effort that went into planning a campaign and coping with the change in tactics which often became necessary in the course of a battle.

"I hadn't thought of that," Eleazar admitted finally.

"Wouldn't you like to guard the caravans instead of robbing them? Then you could live in a town like other men and not have to worry about being captured and executed."

"It might be pleasant." Eleazar chuckled suddenly. "And who is to say we couldn't still demand some tribute from the caravan owners for protecting them, just as we do now for not robbing them?"

It was an interesting question of ethics and Prochorus did not choose to argue it with Eleazar, knowing he could not possibly make the other man understand such a thing as a principle.

"I think I shall go to bed," he said. "We have a long journey to make in the next two days."

"And one that may be your last," said Eleazar. "Sleep on that thought—if you can."

x

Toward the latter part of the afternoon on the second day after he had discovered the lair of Manahem and his band in the hills above the Lake of Tiberias, Prochorus entered Caesarea with the bandit leader and made his way, as unobtrusively as possible, toward the home of Philip, leader of the Nazarenes in the city. One of the seven deacons appointed during the early period of growth that the congregation at Jerusalem had experienced before the persecution by Saul of Tarsus, Philip had been one of the first Nazarenes to leave the Holy City and carry the Way of Jesus to other communities. He dwelt now in Caesarea with his daughters, keeping the flame burning which Peter had ignited at Pentecost in the days following the crucifixion of the gentle teacher.

A few hours after Prochorus and Manahem left the cave in the hills the morning before, the two younger sons of Judas the Gaulonite, Simon and James, had appeared on the road behind them. Both carried packs of food and a change of clothing, as did Prochorus and Manahem, but they had remained several stone's throws behind all the way and had even made camp separately the night before. The reason, Manahem explained, was the policy of the bandits to keep their forces strung out at all times when they moved from place to place, preventing the whole body of men from being attacked at one time.

Prochorus did not ask the reason for the presence of the younger brothers, presuming that they would serve as messengers, if anything went wrong. His reasoning was confirmed when, as they neared Caesarea, Simon and James halted on the crest of the last ridge, not far from where the giant aqueduct that supplied much of Caesarea with water had its origin in several great springs in the hills. There the two made camp, at a spot where they could easily watch the major activities of the city and, as Prochorus and Manahem went on to seek the house of Philip inside the walls, they could see the younger men eagerly watching the last of the chariot races in the great amphitheater.

Travelers they met on the road had told them the chariot races marked the beginning of the three-day festival that would culminate in the public celebration of Agrippa's victory over the Phoenician cities of Tyre and Sidon—a victory accomplished without a single sword stroke, through the simple expedient of threatening to starve their populations—with the bloodiest gladiatorial combats and fights between unarmed condemned prisoners and wild animals ever seen in the arena at Caesarea.

No matter how often he visited Caesarea, Prochorus never ceased to marvel at the energy displayed by Herod the Great in creating an entirely new city and harbor where before there had been only an anchorage for the fishing fleet known as Strato's Tower. More Greek than Jewish, both in architecture and in spirit, the city was a fitting monument to the cruel genius of the Idumean who, though not a Jew at all except by the forcible adoption of his people after their conquest by the Hasmoneans, had ruled over a domain fully as large as that of Israel's greatest kings, David and Solomon.

Into the water offshore, giant blocks of stone had been lowered carefully to serve as the foundation upon which still others had been erected, until a great stone arc had emerged from the waves as a breakwater and mole. The harbor opening was to the north, where the great promontory of Mount Carmel broke the force of both rollers and wind to tame the surf beating upon the shore, and the stone breakwater formed a pleasant promenade for the people on summer evenings. Upon it, partially as ornaments, but mainly to help with its defense, Herod had built several towers, the tallest bearing the name of Drusus, stepson of the Emperor Augustus.

Magnificent statues guarded the entrance to the harbor and still others—pagan symbols in the eyes of the Jewish population and therefore objects of hatred—were placed here and there about the city. In addition, Agrippa had commissioned Phoenician sculptors to fashion statues of his children, but these were kept in the palace, where they would be less of an affront to pious Jews, who numbered considerably less than half the population.

Prochorus and Manahem were welcomed and made comfortable at the home of Philip, but the Nazarene leader was less than enthusiastic about the welcome that might await them at the hands of Agrippa.

"I still don't think you can trust him, even with the safe conduct," he insisted. "After all, he signed it, so he can revoke it at will."

Surrounded everywhere in Caesarea with the evidence of Agrippa's wealth and power, Prochorus, too, felt some misgivings. But having come this far, he couldn't go back.

"I promised to bring Manahem to Agrippa before the final day of the festival celebrating the new treaty with Tyre and Sidon," he said. "But you can do this for me—if we are arrested, send word to Cornelius and Marsus in Antioch as quickly as you can."

"I will do that," Philip promised. "But I pray that it will not be needed."

"Will you also notify my brothers at their camp near the springs where the aqueduct begins?" Manahem asked.

"Of course. What shall I tell them to do?"

"Just notify them of my capture. They will know what to do."

Prochorus spent a restless night, although the couch given him by Philip was far more comfortable than the bed of cut boughs on which he had slept the night before, rolled up in the heavy cloak all travelers carried against the cool nights in the hills. In the morning, however, evidence of spring was everywhere, as he and Manahem walked to the palace of the King through the teeming city: in lush fruit from the Plain of Gennesaret offered for sale at the stalls of sidewalk vendors, the flowers that bloomed everywhere, and the warm breeze from the sea. And feeling its caress upon his body, some of his sense of foreboding of the night before began to melt away.

"If this were my cave in the mountains, I would still be moving stiffly and aching in every joint," Manahem said jubilantly, as they threaded their way through the crowd. "Yet here I can already feel them loosening up. I shall not go back to Galilee to live, of that you can be certain."

"What if Agrippa doesn't employ you and your men?"

"Then I shall move to the region around the Dead Sea, perhaps to one of the Essene communities. It's always warm there and bathing every day in the salt water would help my joints."

"The Essenes are a peaceful people."

"We wouldn't trouble them. By making our home somewhere on the east side of the lake, perhaps near the Springs of Callirhoe, we could prey upon caravans moving along the King's Highway and easily swoop down into Judaea by way of Jericho, when the time comes."

"Then you're still determined to lead an uprising?"

"Could the Jews ever be delivered from the hand of Rome by a grandson, or even a great-grandson, of Herod the Great? The Messiah must come from the line of David."

"He has already come."

"The Nazarene?"

"Yes.

"He was only a prophet, like John the Baptizer—a good man but no more than that."

Prochorus didn't argue the point. He was concerned at the moment with searching the area of quiet water encompassed by the great stone breakwater of the harbor but saw no Roman galley such as should be there, if his message to Vibius Marsus had been delivered by Mark. Still troubled, as they left the harbor and moved toward the palace, he wished devoutly that he knew just what to do and would have given much to be as unconcerned as Manahem seemed to be about the outcome of this whole affair.

Actually, his concern was more for Manahem than for himself. Whatever Manahem was, he had come to Caesarea trusting in the safe conduct and had thus placed himself at Agrippa's mercy while, if the worst happened, Prochorus could always appeal as a Roman citizen to the imperial courts—unless, of course, Agrippa were sure enough of his strength in this part of the world to ignore Roman law altogether.

The palace of Herod the Great and his descendants in Caesarea was a magnificent structure erected near the landward base of the mole that formed the harbor. Like all Herod's palaces, it was both fortress and dwelling, the massive walls buttressed with turrets, battlements and towers from which the garrison could aim arrows and even pour burning pitch down upon the heads of any attackers. At the gate of the palace courtyard, Prochorus had only to show the safe conduct signed by Agrippa's own hand for him and Manahem to be admitted at once to the king's audience chamber, where he was receiving petitions from his subjects.

"Bring those two men before me!" Agrippa ordered as soon as they were ushered into the back of the long room with the throne chair raised upon a dais at the end. The angry note in the King's voice told Prochorus something serious had happened since he had last seen Agrippa in Jerusalem, something that, judging from Agrippa's manner, could only bode ill for both him and Manahem.

"You!" Agrippa choked with rage as they moved forward. He gulped wine from a flagon upon a small table beside him. "How dare you come here after betraying me?"

"How have I betrayed you, sire?" Prochorus asked.

"The Galilean, Simon Peter! You helped him escape before you left Jerusalem!"

xi

"Peter is free?" The joy in Prochorus' voice only angered Agrippa even more.

"He walked out of the prison at night—and no hand was raised to stop him."

"It was a miracle. The Lord opened the prison doors!" Even as he spoke, however, Prochorus found himself remembering his conversation with the Centurion Lysimachus at the Antonia less than a week before and the statement of the Roman officer that there were Nazarenes among the Roman garrison. However Peter's release had been effected, though, the important thing was that his friend was free.

"I know nothing of Peter's escape, Your Majesty," he said. "But I do know that I have fulfilled my promise to you in Jerusalem."

"You will speak when I permit it," Agrippa snapped. "Who is this man with you?"

"I am Manahem, son of Judas the Gaulonite, noble King," the brigand answered before Prochorus could speak. "Brought here at your request under a safe conduct given to Prochorus ben Chuza."

A murmur of interest ran through the crowd that almost filled the audience chamber. Some at the back pushed forward, the better to see the man who had successfully defied both procurators and kings. Agrippa's voice, however, halted them.

"Give me the document," he ordered and, when Prochorus handed him the safe conduct, deliberately tore it to pieces.

"Prochorus ben Chuza agreed to bring Manahem into my presence in return for the release of the Nazarene, Simon Peter," he announced. "But since Prochorus' fellow conspirators in Jerusalem released Peter from prison illegally, you are all my witnesses that any agreement I may have made with these men was broken by them."

"I knew nothing of Peter's release until you told me of it just now," Prochorus protested indignantly.

"But you did arrange it with your fellow Nazarenes in Jerusalem."

"I no longer have any authority in Jerusalem," Prochorus said wearily. "If the King does not intend to keep his pledged word—"

"Strike him!" Agrippa shouted.

One of the soldiers standing by raised his hand to strike Prochorus, but the sight of a sudden rush of blood into Agrippa's face stopped him, as the King half rose in his seat, then suddenly swayed and sat down abruptly again.

"Wine!" he gasped while his right hand was tearing at the fastenings of his robe, pulling them apart over his heart, as if he needed more room for it to beat. A servant hurriedly handed him the silver goblet and Agrippa drank the wine down in a great gulp. Prochorus had started forward instinctively, to help in what was obviously a severe attack, though of what he did not know, but a man, a Greek by appearance, appeared from behind the dais and hurriedly took a pinch of some powder from a small case he carried and dropped it into the small amount of wine remaining in the goblet. He gave it to Agrippa, who drank it down eagerly and, after a long moment, the unhealthy color in the King's face began to recede.

"Take them away," he commanded hoarsely. "Bind them and bring them to the theater tomorrow to be thrown to the beasts during the celebration."

Before Prochorus could protest that, as a Roman citizen, he had the right of appeal to the Emperor himself, he and Manahem were seized by soldiers, dragged from the room, and placed in separate cells, where they were chained by their wrists and ankles to rings set into the stone walls. The cells were inside the mole itself, close to its landward end, and it occurred to Prochorus, as he vainly sought

sleep during the night without being able to lie down, that Manahem's joints must be troubling him because of the dampness. But
he could do nothing to help the brigand or himself, except pray for
their deliverance.

xii

Early the next afternoon, guards came to take Prochorus and Manahem to the amphitheater where, they were informed, Agrippa
planned to have them thrown to wild animals for the entertainment
of the crowd. To Prochorus' demands that he be sent to the Emperor for judgment, Agrippa had made no answer, by which he was
convinced that the King of the Jews shortly expected his power
in this region to exceed that of Rome.

The ankle chains of the condemned pair were removed so they
would be able to walk, but their wrists were still manacled. To
Prochorus' surprise, however, they were not taken to the cells beneath the great structure where ordinary criminals awaited execution by the lions and bears that quickly tore them to pieces. They
were taken instead to a box at the front, perhaps twice a man's
height above the arena floor and with a low rail in front of it, not
far from the golden-draped throne upon which the King himself
would sit.

"*Morituri te salutamus.*" Manahem murmured the words of the
gladiator's salute as they were brought into the box and met for the
first time since the day before. Prochorus was surprised by the relatively cheerful mien of the bandit, considering their hopeless position; in fact, Manahem seemed more concerned with studying the
crowd near the box in which they were guarded by four soldiers than
in his own fate. Prochorus understood the reason when he saw the
brigand leader's brothers, Simon and James, occupying seats not far
away.

"I thought your brothers were going back into the hills," he said.
"Wasn't that the message you asked Philip to give them?"

"I asked him to tell them if I was captured," said Manahem.

"They have never seen anything like this and no doubt couldn't resist the temptation to watch the games before going back."

"Even your own death?"

"We live with death every day," Manahem said with a shrug. "At least they can report to the others that I died bravely. What about you?"

"I hope I can forgive those who throw me to the beasts, as Jesus did the soldiers who crucified him."

"Can you forgive Agrippa too?"

"I hope my faith will be that strong—but I'm not sure it will."

"Fortunately I can wish him dead without any qualms," said Manahem. "Judging by that attack he had yesterday in the audience chamber, the time may not be long."

"I noticed that the physician was waiting nearby."

"It will take a greater physician than any Greek leech to save the King of the Jews, I suspect," Manahem said cryptically. "Ah, here he comes now."

Agrippa was being ushered ceremoniously into the royal box with the throne draped in cloth of gold. Poles had been erected at the corners of the box and ropes of golden thread strung between them to support a canopy to protect the King from the sun after he had addressed the crowd.

From the silver crown upon his head to the shoes on his feet, Agrippa's clothing was covered with thin scales of silver, polished until they shone with a blinding brilliance in the bright afternoon sunlight. But in spite of the awesome effect of the costume, Prochorus saw that his face was still mottled by the same unhealthy pallor he had noted when the sick man was being ushered from the audience chamber by the physician and his attendants after ordering the arrest of himself and Manahem.

"I doubt if Agrippa slept much better last night than we did," Manahem observed. "From the look of his face, I would wager that the wing tips of the Angel of Death are brushing his cheeks right now."

The crowd had set up a mighty shouting at the appearance of their King and he stood silently, supporting himself with a hand upon the back of the throne, until it subsided. At a somewhat lower level two undraped chairs had been placed on either side of the throne and two men who had followed Agrippa into the box moved into position behind them. They were dark-skinned, with the high cheekbones and juttingly prominent noses characteristic of Phoenicians, and Prochorus judged them to be the envoys from Tyre and Sidon.

At a nod from Agrippa as the shouting began to subside, the two men sat down, leaving the King of the Jews standing alone, except for the brawny guards with drawn swords who stood at the back of the box. When he moved to the rail it seemed to Prochorus, standing only a few paces away in the box to which the guards had led him and Manahem, that the King leaned forward a little and rested his hands upon the rail as if he needed its support to remain erect.

"My beloved people!" Agrippa's voice rang out over the vast amphitheater but Prochorus could see that a considerable effort on his part was required to shout the words. "I bring you this great spectacle in honor of the safe return of the Emperor Claudius to Rome." A great shout of acclaim went up at the announcement and he waited for it to subside before continuing:

"And to celebrate the signing of treaties of peace and friendship with our neighboring states of Tyre and Sidon."

There was another roar and Agrippa spoke a few words in a low voice, which could not be heard by the rest of the crowd, to the envoys from the Phoenician states. They stood up for a moment, then seated themselves again, but the fact that at least one of the parties to the new treaty was not pleased with its terms was apparent from the looks upon their faces. Agrippa blandly ignored them, however, and turned back to the rail, waiting for the shouting to subside.

"In a moment, I shall order the beginning of the games by casting two criminals of great importance to the beasts," he announced. "But first I would give you, my people, a small token of the generosity of your King."

At his words, perhaps a hundred men placed strategically throughout the vast amphitheater began to toss freshly minted coins to the people! There was a mild scramble as the crowd reached for the coins or grappled for them upon the floor beneath their feet.

Then, somewhere high up in the amphitheater, a man whose voice was so loud that it could easily be heard even across the arena in the less desirable seats occupied by the poor shouted:

"It is a god speaking—not a man!"

Instantly, as if prearranged—which Prochorus did not doubt that it was—other men in different parts of the amphitheater took up the same cry. And, after a moment of hesitation, the crowd began to echo it too.

Stunned by this unexpected turn of events, Prochorus was barely conscious that Manahem had turned toward where his brothers were sitting and was shouting too. Only his words seemed to be "Now! Now!" rather than the cry of divinity for Agrippa shouted by the crowd.

Agrippa had raised his arms to acknowledge the plaudits of the people and signal them to stop their cheering, when a grayish-black bird suddenly appeared, seemingly from the ranks of the crowd a little above the royal box. Flapping its wings and apparently half blinded by the bright sunlight, as if it were a nocturnal creature rather than a denizen of the sunlight, the bird soared uncertainly for a moment over the crowd. Then it swooped to a perch upon one of the ropes of the frame which had been erected above Agrippa's box.

Stunned by the sudden appearance of the bird, Prochorus could only watch in silence—as did the suddenly still crowd—while it clung to its perch, fluttering its wings to maintain its balance. Then, realizing what had happened and its significance, though with yet only a glimmer of understanding as to how it had come about, he shouted with all his force:

"It is an owl! The omen of death is fulfilled!"

Even before the owl reached its perch, hardly an arm's reach above his head, Agrippa had turned to look at it. Watching the King even as he continued to shout the slogan again and again, Prochorus saw the blood suddenly drain from Agrippa's face, leaving only the pallor of death. Seemingly staggered by an unseen blow, he swayed and reached for the railing at the front of the box but his hands slid over it, as if all power had left them. And as he lurched forward, his body toppled over the rail, hanging there for a second during which no one sought to help him, for all had been stunned by the sudden appearance of the owl.

Then slowly, like a doll made of rags, the body in the shining silver robe slid over the rail and fell to the ground of the arena below.

xiii

It was said later that hundreds were trampled in the rush of the crowd to escape from the arena where the King of the Jews, at the moment of his greatest glory when the people were acclaiming him a god, had been struck down by the curse predicted years before by a German chieftain outside the prison at Rome. Prochorus had no way of knowing, for in the pandemonium that ensued the soldiers set to guard him and Manahem hustled them from the arena and back to prison.

On the fifth day after Agrippa's debacle in the amphitheater at Caesarea, Prochorus was taken from the prison to the palace by his guards. From fragmentary accounts drifting into the prison, he had learned that the King had survived both the fall into the arena and the attack which had caused it. But all reports agreed that Agrippa was dying and could not last much longer. As to Manahem, Prochorus had only been able to discover that he, too, was still in prison, the order for their death apparently being held in abeyance pending the outcome of the King's illness and the decision as to who would succeed him.

The condition of the small portion of the city through which they passed on the way to the palace confirmed other news that had come into the prison, stories of battles between Greek and Jew which the legionnaires, who usually had little use for Jews, had not particularly exerted themselves to control. Even the palace had been broken into at one point, it was said, and the statues of Agrippa's children seized and set up in front of a brothel, where they were subjected to all sorts of indignities.

As to what was happening in other parts of the country, Prochorus could not even guess, though he was sure there would be riots when word of Agrippa's fatal illness seeped out from Caesarea to the surrounding region. And that these riots would be accompanied by looting, as was already the case in Caesarea itself, was without question.

Agrippa lay in a bedroom of the palace, propped up on cushions, with the physician in close attendance, along with several courtiers. His color was not good and his breathing was labored; for a moment Prochorus thought he might be in coma, since his eyes were closed and he showed no recognition of his presence. Then they opened and, after some effort, focused on Prochorus.

"Strike off his shackles," the King ordered and the guards quickly removed both the leg and wrist irons.

"Come closer, Prochorus," Agrippa commanded. "There are things I must say to you before—" A spasm of pain cut off the words and he could not continue until the physician gave him more of the powder mixed with wine.

"You should not talk, sire," the physician protested but Agrippa waved his protest aside.

"Nothing can save me now, Cheon," he said. "The dried poppy eases some of the pain, but makes it difficult for me to see clearly. Leave me, all of you, except Cheon and Prochorus. I have things to discuss with the son of Chuza."

Agrippa closed his eyes while the courtiers filed out of the room but opened them when the sound of the closing door told him his order had been obeyed.

"You cannot imagine what it is like to feel yourself a god, if only for an instant, Prochorus," he said with a wry smile. "Now I know why poor mad Caligula hung onto the idea so long."

"Perhaps you shouldn't—"

"Nothing matters now, except tying up the loose ends of my life before it ends. I have done you many a disservice, my friend, and none greater than the last."

"I forgive you," Prochorus told him.

"I know that; it is the way of the Nazarene."

"Jesus himself will forgive you, too, if you repent and ask him."

"It's too late for that. I am suspicious of last-minute changes of heart, especially when one gains from them. And I suspect your Nazarene—if he is indeed the Son of God—would be too. I knew in my heart that you were innocent in the escape of the Galilean but I was angry and baffled, so I struck out at you. In penance, I have written the Emperor, asking him to give approval to your marriage to Mariamne and to give your son royal rank."

"We don't want that," Prochorus protested.

"It doesn't matter," Agrippa assured him. "My son will rule after me, I hope—if the kingdom can be kept together until he is sent out from Rome. I hope you will stand beside him to advise him until he can take the reins in his hands."

"Your Majesty, I—"

"I have no right to ask," said Agrippa. "And there is probably no need. Cassius Longinus the elder is being sent to Antioch as Legate to replace Marsus. He will hold a firm hand, if you will advise the military commanders until he arrives and keep them from being too bloody in putting down those who riot."

"I will do what I can," Prochorus promised. "But on one condition."

"What is that?"

"Manahem must be released."

"Is that wise? He could be the rallying point for a rebellion in Galilee."

"I think I can persuade him against it. But in any event he trusted me—and you—and came here of his own accord."

"I will dictate the order for his release, also one giving you civil authority until someone comes from Antioch to take over for the time being." Agrippa took the goblet containing the poppy mixture and drained it. "I should have known the Most High would strike me down if I let them call me a god—yet I had to know what it was like."

"He has said, 'You shall have no gods except me.'"

"I learned that in my childhood; perhaps I should have remembered it. But who would have thought God would send that owl as an omen to strike me down?"

Momentarily, Prochorus debated telling Agrippa the truth he had figured out during the five days since the owl had appeared so dramatically in the amphitheater at Caesarea—that it had been brought there by Manahem's brothers, Simon and James, in order that, should Manahem be arrested, they would be able to create a diversion during which he might be set free. Where they had found it he didn't yet know but Manahem could tell him.

Deciding against revealing the truth, Prochorus kept still, and Agrippa closed his eyes again, this time for so long a period that Prochorus thought he was asleep. When he opened them finally, the pupils were like pinpoints and his voice was slurred from the effects of the poppy when he said: "Call for a scribe and write the orders so I can sign them before my hands are unable to hold the quill."

Prochorus quickly obeyed and the matter was attended to. Leaving Agrippa asleep with the physician beside him, Prochorus went to the commander of the Caesarea garrison.

"The King is dying," he told the tribune when the officer finished reading the order naming Prochorus himself as temporary regent. "You are to take control of this area in the name of the Legate Marsus in Antioch and continue even after the King's death. Send a crier throughout the city warning that all rioting must cease at once, on pain of death."

"It shall be done." The tribune could recognize authority and experience when he saw it.

"Swift couriers must also be sent to Jerusalem, Sepphoris, Tiberias and Caesarea Philippi, proclaiming the authority of the Legate Marsus during the illness of King Agrippa and ordering the commanders of the garrisons in each city to take control, not only of the cities but the areas around them."

"The couriers will be ready to ride by the time the dispatches are written," the commander assured him. "Is there anything else?"

"Yes. The prisoner Manahem is to be released."

The commander hesitated, until Prochorus handed him the order from Agrippa. "That shall be done too," he said, but Prochorus shook his head.

"I will take care of it myself," he said, "but I shall need a guard to strike off the shackles."

"I seem to have spoken too soon." Manahem stretched himself with a groan of pain as the last of the shackles were removed. "In a place like this, my joints ache as much as they did in Galilee."

"You will soon be outside in the sunshine. King Agrippa has signed an order for your release."

"And you are in command?"

"Yes."

"That's almost as much of a miracle as the owl lighting on the frame over Agrippa's head," Manahem said with a grin.

"Agrippa still thinks it was an omen. I haven't told him otherwise."

"Why do it then? To a man who pictured himself as a god, it is at least some consolation that the Most High himself struck him down in punishment. Is Agrippa really dying?"

"Yes."

"And you are back in your old job?"

"I am only acting in the name of the Legate Marsus to maintain order during the King's illness."

"What about afterward?"

"Agrippa hopes his son will be made King, with a wise and experienced statesman to guide him until he is older."

"You?"

"He suggested it, but I refused."

"Why? You are the one man in the whole kingdom best fitted for the job."

"I am enrolled in the service of a larger and more important king, Jesus of Nazareth."

"You could serve him in Jerusalem, as you did before."

"Jerusalem is only the smallest part of the kingdom now," Prochorus explained. "The church there has almost ceased to grow, but Barnabas and Saul are going out to Galatia and Peter has made a small start in Pontus and Cappadocia. Others have gone to Rome and elsewhere."

"And you? Where does your field lie?"

"At the moment in Pontus, to enlarge the start Peter has

made there. Later—who knows? The whole world waits to hear the words of Jesus of Nazareth."

"And for that uncertain future, you would give up becoming the right hand of a king—perhaps an emperor?"

Prochorus smiled. "You haven't read the sayings of Jesus, else you would know the answer. He once said, 'For what is a man profited if he should gain the whole world and lose his own soul?'"

"There's no danger of you doing that."

"I am no more than human. Don't forget that Agrippa started out hoping to rule a province but lost his life because he sought to rule an empire."

Manahem gave him a probing look. "Are you preaching me a sermon perhaps?"

"Only giving you a word of advice as a friend."

"A friend?"

"Have we been other than friends since that first day on the hills above Galilee? You saved me when Mariamne and I were captured by your men and Harith would have killed me. And you executed Harith after he tried to kill me in Jerusalem. Call it faith or the Lord's purpose, but our lives have been intertwined ever since."

"Even as yours has been with Agrippa."

"Because you and I are friends, I must ask one promise of you," Prochorus told him.

"What is that?" Manahem's eyes were wary now.

"Don't start a rebellion while the change to the next ruler of Agrippa's kingdom is being made."

"And if I do?"

"I shall hunt you down to destroy you. Don't forget that I know your hiding places and can recognize many of your men by sight."

Manahem studied him for a moment, then shrugged. "You would do it, wouldn't you?"

"As surely as you start the flame."

"Don't trouble yourself about me or my men; the time is not yet ripe," said Manahem. "But when it is, I pray that we shall find ourselves on the same side."

"So do I. Shalom, friend." Prochorus embraced the graying bandit leader in parting. "I will see you through the city gates so there will be no trouble."

At the gate, Prochorus asked the final question: "How did you manage to find the owl?"

"It was simple," Manahem said with a grin. "The owl is a predatory bird and likes nothing better than freshly hatched doves. The men who trap birds with nets in the Valley of the Doves often catch them, so I had only to send Simon and James to the Valley of the Doves the morning we left to be sure of having a dagger with which to strike down Agrippa if he betrayed us."

Watching the sturdy figure of Manahem climb the low slope along the path beside the aqueduct, Prochorus felt a sense of sadness at losing a friend. For, whatever else he was, the bandit leader had never gone back on his word.

xiv

The sun was shining brightly as the Roman galley, with the slaves at the oars pulling in a steady rhythm beat out upon the drum by the pacemaker, threaded the last part of the Bosporus Thracius which, with the Sea of Marmora and the Hellespont, separated the province of Asia from the Greek provinces lying to the northwest of the waterway. For the greater part of the narrow channel, the shore had risen sharply, with only an occasional narrow beach at the base of the hills. Now, as the broad expanse of the Pontus Euxinus, its dark waters revealing why mariners had long since named it the Black Sea, opened out before the vessel's prow, the great squaresail amidships of the galley was raised upon its mast and secured. As it filled with the breeze, the galley slaves rested on their oars, leaning forward so the weight of their bodies, chained to the rower's benches, would keep the blades above the water, yet hold them in instant readiness, should the wind here close to the shore prove fickle.

It was early autumn and before long the winter storms would begin, sharply curtailing navigation even through this landlocked body of water. The months had been busy ones for Prochorus, since the death of Herod Agrippa at Caesarea and the arrival a few days later of Marsus and Cornelius—they had been away from Antioch when John, Mariamne and small John arrived, so it had been necessary to send couriers for them before they could return and troops could be marched aboard a swift military galley for the voyage to Caesarea.

The transfer of authority had not been difficult. Once Marsus had been convinced that Prochorus refused to play a part in the administration of the territory, the measures of control which he had already initiated were merely continued until such time as the Emperor Claudius in Rome could decide whether to turn over to young Agrippa his father's entire kingdom, or once more place it directly under Roman rule through the procurators, who had governed there much of the time since the empire of Herod the Great fell apart shortly after his death.

Prochorus had gone back to Antioch with Marsus, leaving Cornelius in command. There he had conferred with Simon Peter—no longer in hiding now—about the work Peter had begun on his brief visit to Pontus and Cappadocia during his return from Rome. Saul and Barnabas had already departed on their long-planned journey and Prochorus himself was anxious to reach Pontus too. But there were a number of delays, particularly while the letter Agrippa had sent to Claudius before his death, asking approval of their marriage so the question might never arise again to plague them in a land where they were not known, could reach Rome and a reply be sent back.

The imperial approval had finally arrived, and they had departed from Antioch a month earlier for Ephesus, accompanied by John, who was anxious to meet some Christians in that city and give their infant congregation the impetus of a visit by one of the apostles.

A letter from Marsus had enabled them to arrange transportation on Roman military ships wherever such was available. It was on one of these that they had finally threaded the waterway giving access to the Pontus Euxinus on the shores of which, Prochorus hoped, a new world was waiting to hear the message he would bring. Now, as the ship quickened speed and the sail tugged at the mast, he and small John found a place on the raised afterdeck where the little boy could watch the helmsmen handling the heavy steering oars that held the sleek vessel on its course while the wind pushed it steadily eastward.

To the south, the coast line was steadily falling away, for their course was toward the central expanse of the sea, while to the northeast the dark shadow of a peninsula jutted far down into the dark expanse. Little effort was required to steer the ship with the sails drawing so strongly, and small John, a sturdy lad now, quickly tired of watching the steersmen. When he came to sit in Prochorus' lap the two leaned against the afterhouse, basking in the warm sun.

"Tell me a story, Father," the boy begged and Prochorus held him close while he considered what new tale he might tell this small version of himself.

"Once upon a time a famous Greek hero sailed these very waters," he began. "His name was Jason and he was seeking a great treasure, a golden fleece."

"What is a golden fleece, Father?" The boy's dark eyes, so much like his mother's, looked eagerly into his.

"The wool of a lamb, son. This one was made of gold—and a very great treasure."

"Will we find a great treasure, Father?"

Prochorus looked toward the prow where Mariamne was standing above the cutwater, holding to a stay as she watched the prow knife through the dark water. The breeze molded her robe to a body that was as graceful as that of any Greek goddess and, as the sun enveloped her head in an aureole of purest gold, a tide of happiness rose within him, filling him with such joy that for a moment he could not speak.

"Let's find a treasure, Father," small John insisted and Prochorus found his voice at last.

"We already have, son. We already have."